VEILED WAR

VEILED GODS: BOOK 2

JENNIFER MAUGHAN

VEILED WAR

VEILED GODS: BOOK 2

Jennifer Maughan

All rights reserved. Printed in the United States of America. No part of this book may be used or reproduced, distributed, or transmitted in any form or by any means, including photocopying, recording, or other electronic or mechanical methods, without prior written permission of the author, except in the case of brief quotations embodied in critical review, articles, and certain other noncommercial use permitted by the copyright law.

This book is a work of fiction. Names, characters, businesses, organizations, places, events, and incidents are either the product of the author's imagination or are used fictitiously. Any resemblance to actual persons, living or dead, events, or locales is entirely coincidental.

To my family and friends
who encourage and love me as I am

PANTHUM
FAURST
FLOATING CITY
THE RAV
N
W
E
S

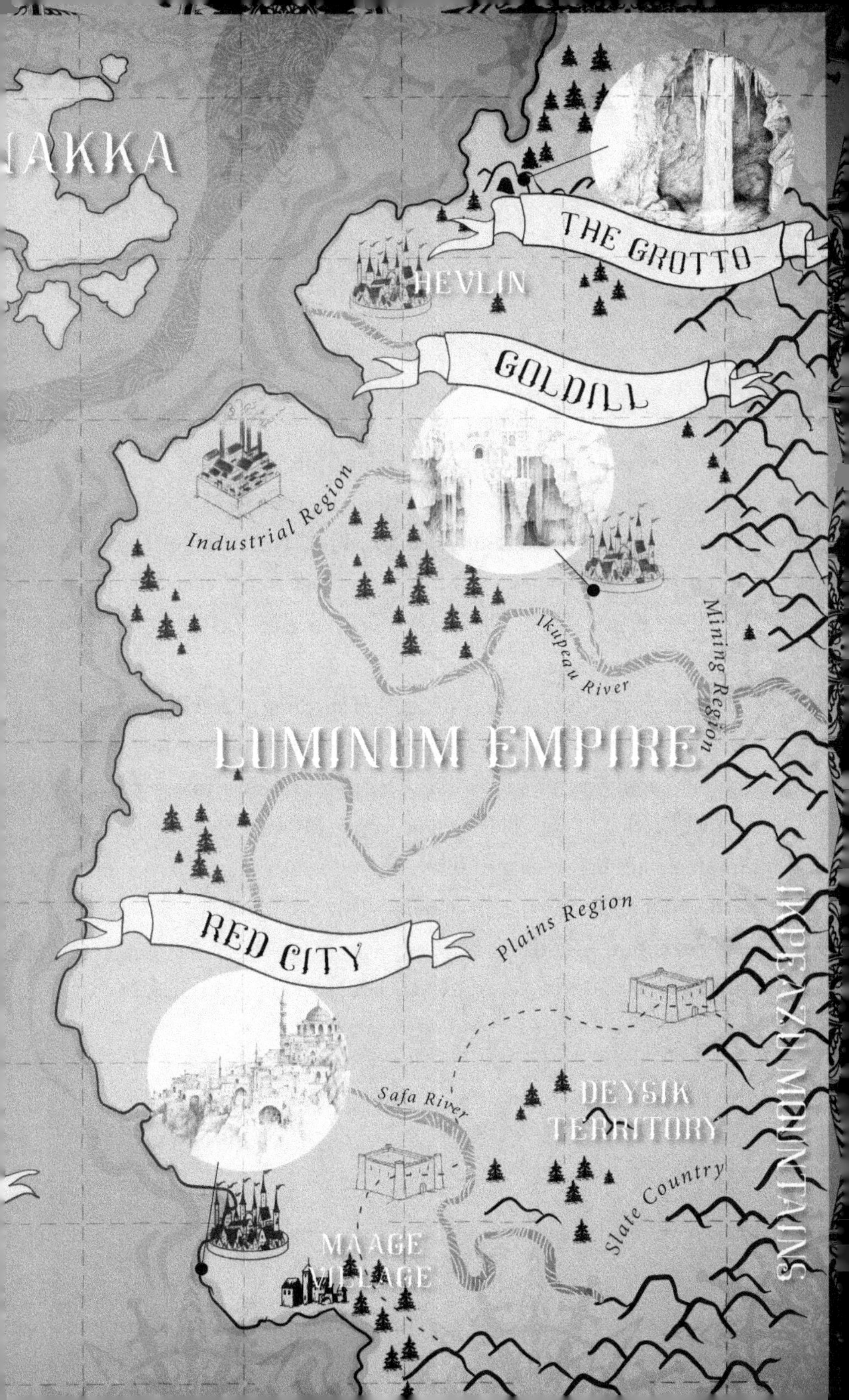

IAKKA
HEVLIN
THE GROTTO
GOLDILL
Industrial Region
Ikupeau River
Mining Region
LUMINUM EMPIRE
RED CITY
Plains Region
Safa River
DEYSIK TERRITORY
Slate Country
MAAGE VILLAGE
IMPEZA MOUNTAINS

Disclaimer

Hello my dear reader, thank you for taking this journey with me and I am so grateful you are here. Due to mature content, but nothing overly graphic, this book is intended for adults. There will be topics of conversation which include: (Briefly, men don't worry) menstruation, blood, abuse, gambling, child abuse. Due to current situations this may be triggering for some people.

I wrote this book over five years ago and anything resembling current situations is merely coincidental. I love politics and enjoy writing them into my books because such is life. There are two sides to every story. Neither fraction of culture is right or wrong. My main character, Alana introduces her upbringing to different land which causes friction and distrust. This is a natural in my mind.

My intention is for this to be an escape.

I hope you enjoy the ride, the end is a doozy! Don't skip ahead!

Contents

PROLOGUE

1,000 YEARS AGO

MOTHER

The runoff-slick cave walls are flecked with the precious blood of her Azure Warriors, who attempted entry before she called them off. It's pooling so thick in the moss and loam-covered dirt in some spots that it squishes under her boots as she follows the carnage while a gnawing numbness works on her eternal soul.

So much death.

So much *waste*.

The battle rages above, and with the loyalty of his Deysik, they would fight until the very last one if she didn't end him now. He needed to be dealt with, and she was the only one capable.

"I wondered when you would slither your way in here," a deep voice calls, bouncing off the rock, and ether, creating a disjointed echo that causes a shiver to run down her spine.

Her power builds in response to the sight of the dead men before her, slowly churning in desperate anticipation, but she needs to wait. She cannot act too quickly, or Ertune will gloat that she lost her edge. He always wanted to see what she was capable of—always pushing her to show her true powers, pushing her to explode with death to his gleeful delight. He wasn't the God of War for nothing. He earned that title as fairly as she earned hers in her old home, far from here.

God of Life.

How she hated it. Hated the title, the responsibility, the *caring* of fleeting mortals around her. She understood why they called her *Mother*, but she didn't approve of the campaign begat by a group of people, desperate for a savior to rescue their brethren across the sea on a continent she wished she would forget.

She didn't come with her armies because of the screams and cries of mortals being slaughtered, carrying across the air and through the stars, all originating in Luminum. Once a land of light, now cast into Ertune's shadow.

No.

Because of different whispers, ones of warning from dead Gods—ones Ertune slaughtered for over millennia—that called for her to stop him. She was the last one left.

The irony wasn't lost on her. They had once scorned her for being the weakest. Yet she is the last to remain after they fell.

"You were too arrogant to take the offering I gave when my armies arrived, Ertune," she replied, turning her head slowly. Torches burn intermittently throughout the collection of interconnected caverns, casting flickering shadows across the hollow space, her ancient eyes cutting through the dark. "Your men are spent, moving to the southeastern plains of Luminum."

The hem of her dress drags across the rock, a thin protection against the cold of the deep. She has no need of armor. No need for weapons on the battlefield. Especially not here.

Mortals cannot kill gods.

Only gods can kill each other.

And Ertune would not kill her.

He knew it, but it didn't stop him from sending his shapeshifting soldiers after her. They all died before they could come within ten yards of her.

They're why she's here now.

His Deysik. His soldiers.

His blights upon the world. She offered his Deysik a territory, hoping they'd see reason, but she wasn't surprised when they refused. If Ertune dies, they will die with him.

That's the way of all the Gods' gifts.

But Ertune found a way around the law of magic.

And so did she.

"Why would I take a proposition from a broken, forgotten slag? You abandoned *me!* You should be crawling on the floor begging for my forgiveness," the voice hisses, loathing and depthless. She shivers.

"Your insults are pathetic, Tunie," she says, smiling, knowing his feelings about her nickname for him. Ertune never liked anything informal or irreverent. It was why he never took that leap with her. "Try harder," she sings, "because we both know I'm neither broken nor a slag. Your lover, however... Where did you find her? A shallow trough? An algae-filled pond?"

His growl echoes over the rocks, through the stalagmites, and pools near her ears. A rock skitters somewhere in the cavern, but she knows it's a distraction. He's circling her position. He's faster than her, but she has traveled eons further than he ever thought her capable. She's no longer a weak god seeking protection from the others.

No. He eliminated them for her.

"I hear she has quite the set of lungs on her." Silence.

She comes to a gurgling spring, bubbling from an outcropping and cups her hand, gathering the water and bringing it to her mouth to drink. Their war beyond has been waging for nine months now, and her forces have pushed his Deysik back to the once great castle of the gods. It sits atop a hill, with the earth's spring-fed waterfalls cascading down to where she now stands at its roots.

"You're one to talk. You bestow powers on your armies of men and your favored acolytes. How many women did you gift? Ten?" His rich laugh, which once sent her heart racing with passion, now sours her stomach.

The sound of his voice shifts directions, the echo originating else-where in the cave. "My Deysik enjoyed lapping up their blood. They reported they could *taste* the explosive power you gave them. I fear it'll poison them, and they'll become weak. I may have to put them down like I should have done you."

"How many did it take to kill one of mine? A hundred? Four hun-dred?" she answers sharply, rage kindling in her veins over losing her friends. Only one of her acolytes remains, and she has her orders. "I have a sneaking suspicion that you're questioning your power in this war." Her eyes focus on the lines of rock, looking for a variable that doesn't belong. Turning slowly, she slips her hand in her pocket, feeling the object's heat.

Her voice shifts into a taunting croon, "Does she know how to ma-nipulate the energy in the minerals? Does she know how to draw power from the earth itself?"

She chuckles darkly, knowing that her words will be the proverbial knife between his ribs. "After all those years spent by your side, you never wondered why I asked so many questions. Read so many of your books? I heard you had them all burned, even executing the great librarians of Goldill after I left you for a better life. A life of laughter and *joy*. One that doesn't include a tempestuous bastard so predictable it's laughable."

"She's not my lover," his breath grazes the back of her skull, and before she could blink, he grasps her from behind, pinning her arms down with one of his as his other hand grips her throat in an ironlike embrace. His fingers refrain from digging into her flesh, but it was only to allow her to speak.

His nose grazes the smooth column of her neck, and his raspy voice sends her heart racing as ancient memories are forced to the front of her mind. "I burned the books because they reminded me of you. I couldn't bear to look at them and not see you carrying them around, pressing them against your body." She hears him grit his teeth. "I burned them all because you touched them and not *me*. I burned them because you chose *them* over me. I knew what you were doing and why you were reading them. I didn't care, Alana, because it was your way of attempting to be my equal. I couldn't reconcile what they caused. I slaughtered the librarians because you spoke of them fondly. They were your *friends*. Just like your acolytes."

His breathing turns ragged, and for a moment, she allows herself to briefly wonder about their once possible future before sense returns and, with it, hot fury. "If you were so enamored with me, why didn't you say anything? You were all I wanted. You chose to ignore *everything* except war with the others. I thought you'd be satiated now that you can contend with no one else. However, you surprised me by turning on the mortals. I was yours, and you didn't care until I disappeared. You speak of abandon, yet you deserted me first. Years I waited. Years I lingered. *Years—*"

Her breath comes out in sobs as her chest heaves against his arm, her throat bobbing with her swallows. How she wanted those rough fingertips to touch her with gentleness and love. But Ertune only understands one thing.

Violence.

She feels him shift his battle-hardened body behind her, seeping his hostile essence through her. His heightened emotion falls in waves, and she knows that if an observer were to look upon them, they'd see lovers embraced with glowing eyes—emerald green and azure blue. She fights against the waves of his power, attempting to drown her own.

Her breath comes out a sob, "Ertune, you must stop this. The mortals are crying out. The magic is being disrupted. It cannot go unanswered—"

"Did you not figure it out?" his voice cuts in sharp as a blade through a belly.

"Did you not realize *why* I slaughtered hundreds of thousands of mortals?" He jerks away from her, leaving her cold in more ways than just his words as he turns her around, eyes blazing, his skin tight with loathing, love, and obsession as he stares at her.

"You're experimenting with the power of the Gods, Ertune. It must stop. Now."

"How is it any different than what you've done? Then what you've twisted? It's unnatural—"

"What I've done is correct injustices. Your mission is destruction."

As his rough hands grip both sides of her neck, he speaks. "Where you learned to harness power from the earth, I've combined that knowledge with Roc's gift before I killed him. He may have been a recluse, always panting after you. I made sure to pluck off his scales and carve the webbing from his wings before I bled him dry."

Alana swallows, horror pouring over her like the waterfall above. "What did you do?"

Another pebble skitters across the stony floor of the cave. Awareness prickles the back of her neck. She's too late.

Ertune softens his voice like a lover. The same way she once imagined he would speak to her. Instead of sweet nothings, he cuts her with a threat, "I created my own Fire Jewel. Call off your forces, or I'll continue slaughtering every living soul on this continent before moving to your precious pets. Then we'll see the world burn together."

She moves her arm in a quick jerk, and his eyes widen. His dark hair falls into his face as he looks down at the object she stabbed into his heart.

He gazes up at her with a smirk. "Remember, I don't have a heart."

She returns it with one of her own, "I know. I stole it."

PART I

THE FORGE

Chapter 1
ALANA

Sunlight streams through a medium-sized window in a small bedroom, reminding me of the Pine Needle Inn. I watch as the world outside provides clues to this new continent I've arrived on. Golden brown, waist-high grass makes up the rolling terrain, with an occasional tree in the distance. The red dirt path cuts through the landscape like a scar, and wagons carrying supplies, weapons, and food rumble through the streets.

Azure Warriors, wearing their golden half masks under hoods, mingle with red leather-clad soldiers outside in clusters. The crimson clad soldiers outnumber the Blueys four to one, which leads me to believe we aren't in Luminum yet. I've only observed a handful of citizens, primarily people helping with the supplies, food, and laundry.

An hour ago, I woke in the slender bed dominating most of the space, using the tiny private bathroom to wash my body despite waking up with clean hair, skin, and nails… It would be slightly disturbing if not for the fact I remember a woman's voice caring for me while I fevered, bled, and vomited. It was both a dream and a nightmare. I heard Calix's voice. I listened to my brothers and Hagatha's.

I squeeze my eyes shut against the light as my memories plunge me back on the Ravager, with Canary dragging me over the deck away from Calix as a storm rages, his ship arriving too late.

I waver and catch myself on the window sill as grief nearly buckles my knees. I'm alone in a foreign country without Calix or *chaze* tea to comfort me. My mercenary contract has been sold to the Warlord, the Crown Prince of Luminum. Prince Dread.

My people's enemy.

How long have I been unconscious? I push away from the window sill and sink to the bed, twirling the silky softness of my belted robe through my fingers. Curiously, I open the garment and prod my new pink scar with my fingertips, finding it's only slightly tender—all healed.

The wound had been deep enough I needed stitches, but there's no sign of thread marks on my skin.

Light footsteps approach from beyond my room's door, and I tense, pulling my robe closed as the door opens. An exquisite dark-skinned, smiling woman with a work of art in braids for her hair holds clothing and a pile of supplies. She's wearing a shimmering light gray shirt and black pants with a leather bag draped over her shoulder. She looks to be mid-thirties with beautiful curves—the type I could never hope to gain.

"*Moskazi*! We were worried you'd never wake," she says in a soft, lyrical voice—like everyone on this continent—like Calix and my mother.

"Who are you?" I croak and cough. The woman rushes forward, tossing the clothes, hairbrush, and hair ties on the bed before pouring me a cup of spiced tea from the steaming carafe and pressing the mug into my hands. Her beautiful eyes track the cup as I slowly sip the hot, rich tea, holding a bite of honey and chamomile. I don't miss her glance towards the door before smiling warmly at me.

"I'm Diedra, the Royal Family's Surgeon. I've been taking care of you since last week and waiting for you to wake up," she says while rifling through her bag. I inhale slowly, extremely aware of my unconscious lapse of control.

Hagatha. The woman caring for me wasn't my friend after all. The realization sinks like a stone in my stomach.

It's silly to have the thought of home taken away. But all the same... It hurts.

"Your body reacted violently to the poison from the laceration you received while in the Red City pit. Because of this, you were delirious with a fever for seven days."

All blood drains from my face. I spoke of my family—of Fidir. Oh, Mother, help me. I look up at her in a panic, but she misreads it. Diedra's dark eyes soften. "Yes. The poison takes that long to work itself out of the body's system."

I nod and screw up my face in confusion, "What did you call me? Mos—"

Diedra smiles warmly, "*Moskazi*. It means Prince Dread belongs to you, and you belong to Prince Dread. It's all in the contract."

I nod, rubbing my forehead. I was out for a week. Diedra shifts, crossing her long legs. "If you don't mind terribly, I'd like to ask you a few questions to understand your health. As your contract states, the owner's responsible for caring for your person."

I swallow, not knowing what to do, but nod and sit back on my bed. I wonder if Canary is here somewhere. I pray to the Mother he is. I've never been asked questions by medical professionals. Deysik can usually detect if something is wrong in humans, but it rarely happens amongst our kind.

She pulls a chair at the table and turns it towards me. She pulls a pad of paper and a pen out of her bag, writing down a script I can't read as it's in Luminum.

"How old are you?"

"Twenty."

"So young and so skilled." Diedra gives me a look of respect I don't know what to do with. "How physically active are you? Training-wise... how old were you when you began your career?"

I fold my arms, looking out the window. "I didn't say mercenary work was my intended career, but I've been training since I was ten, more specialized in fighting for the last four. I train with body weight in calisthenics for two hours a day, with weapons for four to six depending."

Diedra shifts her head, her pen scratching across the paper, her brow furrowed. I shrug. "Depending on my opponent." I think back to Calix, how often we would train together, and how familiar we became. How I told him I loved him right before a wave ripped me from him.

I wipe my wet cheeks and clear my throat. "Where are we?"

Diedra pauses, writing and smiling softly, "We're in a outlying village just outside the Red City's borders." Her smile warms my chest. I'm grateful she's friendly.

I nod. She continues writing, talking as she does, "These next questions are going to be more personal, and I apologize if they offend you."

Again, I shrug. Diedra leans back in her chair, straightening her slender shoulders. "Have you been sexually active before?"

Heat explodes in my face, and I shake my head in a quick jerk. She nods, and the scraping of pen across paper fills the small room. "What medicinal herbs have you ingested regularly in your life? Is there anything we should know about or provide for you?"

"I haven't taken any herbs except my morning *chaze* tea," explaining the drink, which prevents menstrual cycles. All Rangers drink it.

Diedra's eyes and voice sharpen, her pen poised above her paper. "How long have you taken that?"

I swallow, feeling uncomfortable with the stillness radiating off of her body. "Since I was eight."

Diedra's face falls into one full of sympathy and compassion, and I don't understand it. "That tea is barbaric. It explains..." She pauses and breathes, "It explains why you were in your condition and pain this week."

I stared at her, my mind reeling. If I hadn't taken my tea... I try to wrap my brain around the memories of this week. I close my eyes and groan, putting my head in my hands, "It was you helping me, wasn't it."

I glance up at her, embarrassment rolling through me.

"Yes. There's nothing to be ashamed of. It just explains why you suffered the way you did." A pause, her voice is hesitant and soft. "Do you know the long-term effects of taking that tea at a young age? Is it common in Panthum?"

I shake my head, my long brown hair falling over my shoulders. "It's something everyone else takes after they turn eighteen. I don't know why I was given it so young."

Diedra nods her head and inhales a large breath. "The next question I have is about the scars on your abdomen and chest. How long have you had them?"

My voice comes out small, "Since I was eight."

Again, Diedra's sharp gaze flicks to me briefly, and her pen stops moving. It rakes against my nerves. "Is there a problem?"

"I'm thinking they might be linked. Did you start the tea after your injuries?"

I frown and think back to a time when I was in such pain I couldn't think. I don't remember taking it before. I nod.

"In countries without extensive knowledge or access to herbs, I imagine you were given the tea to ease the discomfort left behind by your scars—" she angles her head. "Deysik made?"

I frown as her full lips twist, and my stomach drops. This explains why Nash had the tea already in stock on his ship. Her voice is soft and gentle when she speaks, and her hand rests on top of mine, giving it a light squeeze.

"Under these circumstances, I'm compelled to inform you the side effect of taking the *chaze* tea so young is infertility. With the age it was given to you, you will not be able to bear any children. My knowledge is extensive, and I've not seen a single case of pregnancy under the age of fourteen. I'm so sorry, Alana."

I sit in stunned silence. No children. The inside of my nose stings with tears, and wet warmth slides down my cheeks. No children. It wasn't on my mind—of course not—but eventually, I wanted children. I don't know how to process this theft.

How can I feel robbed if I never had it? But I do. I nod, and Diedra stands, pulling me to my feet and swallowing me in a hug. I hadn't realized how much I need it. I sob into her shoulder and she holds me for a long while, rubbing my back, she soothes my broken heart. I'm desperately grateful for this woman and her kindness and compassion. I usually don't like strangers touching me, but after three months of no physical affection, I cling to her shoulders.

After a few minutes, I pull back, wiping my tears away. "Thank you, Diedra. What's next?" I want to move on from this painful topic. Although it is a blow, I decide it's probably for the best. The only person I remotely pictured in my future is dead.

"Get dressed and meet me downstairs for breakfast. We're going to leave soon. The Crown Prince is eager to return home for Currell."

"What is Currell?" I ask, focusing on the Uria Cloth she brought in for me. If I purchased someone for hundreds of thousands of gold marks, I'd want to protect my investment, especially after the scare of my poisoning... last week.

She pulls back. "Forgive me, Alana. There's much for you to learn about our country and customs. It's an imperial holiday of fighting, food, festivities, and the true reason behind it all... matchmaking!" she says with a thread of excitement in her soft voice. She knows my name—my actual name. I suppose it would have been on the contract. I nod, unsure what else to do. She smiles encouragingly, patting my shoulder before she gathers her things, her long, beautiful braids swinging as she does, and closes the door behind her.

I hear her footsteps depart, and I turn, staring down at my bed, deciding I can only control what I can control. I bend and neatly straighten the covers, nervous about everything. I reach for the clothing, feeling the Uria cloth—cloth from home, under my calloused fingers. It's a solid dark gray that seems to suck in the light and reflect it back in curves. Even my family couldn't afford the clothes impenetrable by steel, though we didn't need them.

Heavy tread comes from outside the door before it swings open, and a large male wearing a black leather vest and blue hood fills the small doorway. He's tall, broad, and powerful enough to snap my neck with his large hands. I freeze like a doe, sensing the presence of a hunter. His golden-masked face scans me from head to toe.

The Warlord.

I suck in a harsh breath, embarrassment and anger flushing through my body with a jolt. I snap, "Do you know how to knock, or do they not teach manners in your country?" My face burns as the Warlord jerks his head back and pauses momentarily, his thick, rough fingers still grasping the door handle. I can only imagine what he sees before him. A slender, wild-haired woman, glaring while holding clothes—his clothes—against her chest.

He ducks his head, his voice deep and distorted, "Forgive me." He steps out into the hall and closes the door with a snick. I nearly collapse to my knees with relief.

He reminds me so much of Calix I can't stand it. It's like digging further into a wound I want to keep hidden deep within my soul.

The pain reminds me it's real.

No Calix. No children.

Chapter 2

I walk down the rickety stairs of the Inn to the taproom doubling as a dining room. The scents of breakfast waft up, making my stomach growl, and I glance at the sideboard loaded with bacon, eggs, flapjacks, and fruit. The room's filled with Azure Warriors eating their breakfast.

It's hard not to seize at the site of the threat before I remind myself Calix was one of them. He was enough for me to fall in love with, it shouldn't be hard to find some sort of redeeming quality in these warriors. Their laws about protecting women, I wouldn't think would apply to me, being a mercenary.

What I do know is that their relationship with their neighboring Deysik is tense at best, and they bring in mercenaries to fight on their behalf. I'm not sure what Nash pandered to the Warlord when he purchased my indenture. I was too busy dying and being brought back to life.

At a lone table in the back corner of the room, Canary sits next to the Warlord and his pearl-masked companion. My friend's body is rigid, his face set in a tight mask of cold fury. I follow where his icy gray eyes are directed and find Diedra laughing with a group of men, her back to the reclaimed traitor. Everyone in the room is drawn to her like the center of gravity.

That is emotion on his face... jealousy!

It's clear from Nash's comments about Canary not being interested in women and how he's looking at the royal surgeon that he absolutely knows her and still holds an inferno of a flame for this woman.

The Warlord faces me. I swallow, dipping my head in awkward acknowledgment, and I sidle up to the sideboard, loading up a plate of food before turning to the room of tightly packed warriors to search for an empty chair. Diedra jumps up from her seat and approaches with a smile.

"Come join us, Alana. I'd love to know more about you." Her warmth and kindness radiate from her; I don't detect a flicker of deception in her expression. It softens a part inside of me. I hadn't realized I was concerned she would hold my history against me. I'm grateful she's sensitive enough to figure out I don't want to focus on the news she broke.

Carrying my plate, I follow her back to her table next to the Warlord and Canary's, and she settles me in a seat where, annoyingly, I'm facing the high-ranking royals.

My eyes travel over my new employer, taking in his powerful body, relaxed with an arm slung over Canary's chair, watching me with clear interest despite my lack of facial features to study. I gulp and spear some scrambled eggs. "What would you like to know?"

I eat my food carefully, knowing the Blueys are staring. My knee bounces with nerves in the presence of this dark-haired woman everyone respects. I want her to like me—not because she's essential with her position as the royal family's surgeon, but because I'd like to have a female friend. I'm starved for it. Baylor's daughters, Hagatha and I, were very close. I miss their humor, love, and support.

"Everything. Where were you born? Who are your parents? When did you start training to become a Ranger? What's it like in Panthum? What are your beliefs in the Mother? What brought you to Faurst and led to your being seajacked? Don't think I won't share in return." Her questions are sincere and curious, so much so that I don't suspect any ulterior motives. I realize she's repeating a question or two from her earlier medical history, and I know that's for the Blueys' benefit.

I ponder how to answer her probing questions as I finish my food.

"I was born on the Riband in Panthum, where my family lives." She frowns at my glossing over divulging details about my family. Instead, I expand, "It's a large swath of territory in the northwestern part of the country. We have a steep tradition of training to become Rangers—protectors of our kingdom. I began at a young age—everyone's encouraged to learn defensive techniques—but once my mother—" I pause and take a drink of water to clear the lump in my throat since I don't want to cry in front of everyone here. "Once my mother died, I decided to focus on becoming a Ranger." I flick my eyes around to the silent room, feeling my face heat from all eyes on me, including the Warlord.

I take a breath and plunge on. "My people don't worship the Mother, though we're taught a little of her out of respect to those who do. As for your last question... I took my charge to Faurst, and unbeknownst to me... he had hidden motives for going, which led to our hasty exit from the city. I stayed behind to waylay the Monks until he reached our men. I was seajacked as punishment."

Diedra studies me, sympathy filling her lightly creased, sparkling eyes before she sits back and crosses her arms over her ample chest, "It seems like you've been through a lot in your life already. I can understand why Prince Dread paid so much for you."

I frown, but before I can ask to clarify, she smiles and speaks while I finish my breakfast. "I was born in Goldill—Luminum's capital—where we are headed, and since I was young, I have long been curious about how the human body works and those in our world that are gifted. Being fascinated by those blessed with gifts by either the Mother or Ertune, spurred me into the medical field at sixteen after the death of a close family member. I began my residency with the former royal surgeon, earning my full title five years ago." She reaches across the table and squeezes my hand, warm and soft. I can't help but feel my chest ease at the kindness shining in her dark eyes. I return the squeeze.

She pulls away, slaps her hand lightly on the table, and says, "We need to get back in time for Currell, but first, we must deal with the Traitor." Though her words are light and airy, how her body tenses when she says them, speaks volumes. I turn my gaze to Canary, whose jaw flickers. Oh, it's a lover's quarrel if I ever saw one.

The warlord's pearl-masked companion stands. "Rost," he says in a vicious tone directed at Canary.

My heart stops. I look at Diedra, who pales slightly at the word, but everyone's moving. Through the clamor, I find confirmation of my thoughts. Her pulse is rapid at her throat; her pupils are wide.

Fear. True fear. Diedra has feelings for Canary.

I glance at the Warlord, whose supine body reads he isn't concerned.

From what I can tell, Diedra is furious with Canary but still has strong feelings for him. Now, the Warlord's companion is challenging him to a death duel—so perhaps the pearl-masked man is the one with an ax to grind? It's all too confusing to muddle through.

The Prince must not personally know Canary, or else he would've been wise enough to stop his investment from slaughtering one of his most valued companions.

The Azure Warriors file out the front door onto the rust-colored dirt road and form a circle about twelve paces apart, close enough to hear and see the fight. The pearl-masked Azure Warrior paces inside of it like a prowling Deysik. I slip forward and grab Canary's arm as more Warriors push past.

"Who is he, and why's he calling Rost?" I hiss.

I feel Canary's jolt of surprise in his pulse under my fingers as he looks to where I'm touching his arm. I quickly remove my hand, my gut twisting with trepidation. I realize I'm out of line, but I don't care.

"He's Prince Dread's General. Rost has been called," Canary says grimly, "Satisfaction must be made."

"For what?" I demand. "You're already banished. Did they pay all that money just to kill you?"

Canary looks at me, then his metal eyes flick up behind me and mutters, "The payment was intended solely for you." The blood drains from my face, and a dozen questions flood my mind. Why would they pay so much for me? The only thing I can think of is they will want me to handle some sort of task nobody would willingly risk. Something a female warrior can accomplish. But what would it be?

"I'm here to pay for another crime," he says before stepping away.

A deep voice cuts in, "In Luminum, Rost is not like on Captain Nash's ship. My General will not kill the traitor." Shivers run down my spine—the Warlord is speaking to me. His mask distorts his voice, but the cadence and accent are achingly familiar. My heart hurts, and my eyes sting. I clench my jaw, breathe deeply, and watch my friend as he walks to the center of the ring.

The Warlord Crown Prince of Luminum has an expendable General. Or he believes he can take Canary. I wouldn't have to spend more than five minutes with Canary to know he is not someone I would want to battle. Then again, Calix was a formidable opponent. Perhaps his General is equally skilled?

The Azure Warriors stand shoulder to shoulder as villagers and travelers stare curiously. Diedra moves between me and the Warlord, and I glare at him, upset he's allowing this.

Canary removes his tunic and shirt, carefully folding his clothing, and I step forward to take it from him before he can set it on the ground, moving back next to the Royal Surgeon, who I sense shudder beside me. I take in an image that will haunt me for a long time.

Canary's chest is covered in thick puckering scar tissue, and his abdomen's flesh is in swirls from healed burns. Diedra covers her mouth. His arms... It's beyond brutal.

Long clawing marks run down his skin, ruining the tattoos once gracing his body. I have my share of scars and have dealt some scars, too, but never to the extent of suffering Canary has been through.

"He'll be fine," the Warlord sighs, assuring myself or Diedra.

"And which, 'he,' are you referring to?" I growl for Diedra's sake. The Warlord chuckles, and I dislike him.

The pearl-masked warrior faces Canary and takes a defensive stance, wide legs and arms raised. "First blood, and judging from the looks of your chest, you've had experience in this," the man croons through his shimmering white mask.

Cruel bastard. My nostrils flare. His words reveal a streak of underlying anger and aggression, so different from his Prince next to me, who doesn't seem nearly as hostile towards Canary.

"I have, but fighting me won't make her come back," Canary sings back with a vicious, wicked grin. "You could never have made her happy."

Diedra sucks in a short breath, and the Warlord stiffens. Even I know he's poking a raw spot based on everyone's reactions. Fight dirty, indeed.

It works.

The General's body bulges, and he attacks, punching and striking with such intensity it would have crumbled a building. Wherever the pearl-masked warrior attacks, Canary is there a half a breath earlier. I lift the balls of my feet in reflex. Canary dances around the military leader, moving like the air, blocking his strikes with precision and ease. For the scars the Prince mocked, Canary earned and learned from them.

I'm waiting... the Warlord leans forward, whole body tight, just as Canary makes his move.

One strike to the jaw, right behind his pearl mask, and the General drops unconscious like a fallen log. Relief hits me so roughly that my body nearly relaxes into a puddle. The fighting pit champion, cold-eyed guard, gazes mercilessly at the downed General for a moment. A flicker of disgust crosses his face before he turns and walks to me, taking back his clothing. Diedra stares at him but doesn't move, as if startling him will place her in harm's way.

His rough hands shake out his tunic, slipping it back over his head. He nods to the Warlord as he pushes through the men and their stony glares above their golden masks. Diedra leaves me to tend to the General, pulling out smelling salts from her bag, and I see Canary finish wrapping his tunic around his waist before running a hand through his brown hair, watching her.

The Warlord shifts his weight, so he's leaning closer to me as he sighs, looking at his companion, "I was expecting worse. I'm just glad he left him in one piece."

I move a few inches away from him. "Agreed," I say, surprising myself. I snap my mouth shut. This is the leader of my people's enemy. He's not Calix, even if he does treat me kindly out of respect for the feminine kind, not to mention pay what I imagine is the cost of a small country for my services.

"We better move on. We have a long journey ahead of us," he glances at me and where I was before moving away, and I can almost feel his amusement at my petty behavior. "At least the river will be free from traffic heading into Luminum. Most will have already arrived by the time we get there, leaving the Commanders and their Champions to join us for the voyage."

I stifle a groan. Another ship? Mother help me. The goddess has a wicked sense of humor. How else would a defunct Deysik come to serve her favored people?

"Do you not like water transportation?" the Warlord asks, picking up on my discomfort.

"As long as I don't have to sleep in a hammock, I'll be fine. I'd rather fight than sway in a curved bed for another day."

The Warlord throws his head back and laughs, exposing the thick, strong, column of his throat bobbing with movement. "Would you rather I give you the floor for your bed?"

I stare at the man before I answer seriously, "If it means the flat surface is behind a locked door, then yes."

He holds my gaze, and not for the first time am I annoyed his mask hides the color of his eyes. They're the gatekeepers to what males are feeling. Their micro-expressions giveaway too much they'd like to keep hidden.

"You will never be in another hold like the Ravager again, Alana. I swear on my title."

For the first time in months, I'm feeling hopeful I'll survive my indenture based on the mountain of gold Calix paid for me. I suppose Nash was right.

But the skeptical part of my brain won't be convinced.

"For the next five years, I'll believe you. But you can't control what happens to me after that Warlord."

The Crown Prince of Luminum and the man holding my contracted services stare back until my heart begins to beat rapidly. I tell myself it's the stare of an authority figure curious about the newcomer questioning his power, but deep down, I know it's something different.

I just don't know what.

Chapter 3

Hours later, the sun beats down on my face, and I study the pleasant but bland landscape. I grew up with vast mountains, valleys, waterfalls, rivers, trees, and forests. This flat grassland, combined with the heat, is too much for my apathy, and I drift. Occasionally, I doze off and lean against the Warlord's firm back when I do. The crown Prince never complains. When a horse nickers or a sharp swish of a tail snaps at the flies, I startle awake, feeling a flush of embarrassment being caught sleeping.

I had balked when it was discovered there weren't enough horses, and the Warlord demanded I ride with him. I grudgingly rode with him when the warriors left before I could ask to ride with them. Even Diedra and Canary doubled up. I had sensed a mischievous smile behind the golden mask when he said, "I don't bite."

I had snorted at that and climbed up.

The Warlord now speaks in a voice that causes my heart to sting. "Relax. Your body's still recovering from your injury." He sounds so much like Calix.

"What's your name? Or am I supposed to call you Warlord?" I ask, trying to keep myself awake.

"Prince Dread is fine," he says with a bit of laughter in his voice. I roll my eyes. Fine. At least he isn't a hard ass like my father and Drake. Perhaps it would have been better if he was. I know how to guard against those types of men.

"What will you require of me for the next four years and nine months, Prince Dread?" I want to get the awful news over with sooner rather than later.

"That's for my father to decide ultimately, but in the meantime, we'll show off your fighting skills in Currell. Think you can take me?" he asks. Is he being serious?

"You want me to fight you?" Is he mad? Touched in the head? His laughter prickles down my spine because it's not Calix's.

"Who better?"

"I'm skilled, but I highly doubt I can defeat your Imperial Highness," I say drolly, earning a belly-deep chuckle from my riding companion.

"Somehow, I think you're lying through your teeth." There's a smile behind his words, and I can feel my cheeks heat.

I shrug, "I suppose we'll have to see."

***

By the time it's too dark to make out the road, we set up camp next to a stream far enough away from the road that nobody will bother us. The Azure Warriors create a wide perimeter with four watchful guards.

Diedra pointedly keeps her back to Canary, and the scarred male remains close to the healer, pretending not to watch her every move. They're like two magnets, always close but never touching. It might be amusing if it wasn't heartbreaking.

Diedra sits by me as we eat our meal of boiled chicken, rice, and vegetables.

"How's your face feeling with all of the sun?" she asks, sidling up closer to me, leaning her thigh over to touch mine the same way Calix used to when he'd sit with me for our meals. I clear my throat and blink rapidly, pushing the memories away. "It hurts, but I suppose I'm used to it now."

"I'll give you a hood tomorrow. I apologize for overlooking it until now."

"It's that bad, huh?" I tease, and she smiles a brilliant white grin. I can't help but chuckle. After spending eight weeks at sea with minimal shade, my skin has taken a beating. "I appreciate any covering you can offer me."

"Do Rangers wear hats like we wear hoods?"

My smile dims as I think of the typical Ranger attire and answer her, "It depends on the region of Panthum you're in."

"Oh, do tell."

Her smirk is as sly as a fox. I grin. "I can only tell you what I've worn, which are wide-brim hats, leather protective gear, rain slicks, packs, and that sort of thing. The other regions vary but are roughly the same."

"Intriguing. Do you have different climates in Panthum?" Diedra asks and the question isn't unfounded, but I've already said too much.

"We do but I'm not overly familiar with them. What about Luminum? Is the whole country like this?" I ask, gesturing to the plains.

She leans back, inhaling, eyes sliding to Canary who eats mechanically while staring at the fire. "To the west are mountains, which is the bulk of our mining operations, to the north are forests where we develop building materials. To the east and south are a mixture of industrial and agriculture complexes. The temperatures will cool the further north we travel but will still be considerably warm compared to Faurst."

"Faurst is warmer than Rising Pass," I say, taking in her information of economy. No wonder Luminum is an empire of wealth, based on the size of their operations.

"What are the Rangers like there? Handsome?" She asks. Canary doesn't pause, stiffen or so much as blink, and I feel proud of him for not falling for her bait. Whatever their history is, she's enjoying poking him. Every time Hagatha and Everett would get in a spat, they would do something similar.

"I haven't been able to see the faces of your warriors here to make a valid comparison. Why do your Azure Warriors wear masks? Are they ugly?"

Diedra glances at the Warlord, who turns his attention to me, and I furrow my brows. "Is that not a question I'm allowed to ask?"

"We wear them for protection and intimidation," the Warlord answers in his distorted voice. "Would you agree that if you can't see the face of the man you're fighting, you wouldn't know when he feels fear? Wouldn't be able to mark him for death."

I angle my head, "Mark for death?"

Diedra inhales sharply, and answers, "Here in Luminum, Deysik mark their enemies for death—"

"Don't *your* Deysik mark their enemies?" the pearl-masked general sneers. I raise a single brow, uncomfortable with the topic and take in the large male, standing shoulder to shoulder with his Crown Prince. The two are a formidable pair, and I feel a prickle of unease as the attention of the other Blueys land on me.

"*My* Deysik don't mark others for death." But they do know how to track. I always attributed it to their heightened senses, but perhaps it was more than instinct but rather a gift given by Ertune?

"Your Deysik are peacemakers, are they?" the General snarls, and I simply stare at him. He doesn't realize how close he is to the mark. We stare at each other in silent challenge. His for dominance, mine for antagonization. I take a breath to say something, but the Warlord moves away from his companion and lays his bedroll next to mine. I break away my stare, startled and annoyed.

"What are you doing?" I ask quietly. I'd ridden in front of the man for the past ten hours. Wouldn't he want some distance? Diedra stands and takes my empty plate, leaving me alone with the Warlord.

"Making sure you don't run away in the night," he says calmly.

That hurts.

"I'm not dishonest, Prince Dread. I'll honor my agreement, even if I'm not happy about it," I grumble the last to myself, shooting a glare at his General. Azure Warriors' hearing must be as sensitive as a Deysik's. "What are you not happy about?" he asks. "My General?"

My thoughts turn to Calix. He should be here. His family will be devastated when they find out—but how would they know? My stomach tightens, and I feel like I am going to vomit.

To cover my grief, I say coldly, "Your familiarity."

I'll have to find out who Calix's family is from the men. If he is—as high-ranking, then perhaps I can find another full-masked Azure Warrior to ask—one that isn't a Prince or general. Diedra's across the camp, talking to a few of the men, one of whom is washing dishes from dinner, I wonder if she left on purpose or not.

"What about just a physical relationship? I can remove years from your service," the Warlord says boldly. I slowly stand, body quivering with rage as I stare at the Crown Prince with a look promising spilled blood. Does he think I'd be so desperate? A Deysik would be able to smell the seething loathing I feel for the Imperial Prince.

Canary sits up.

"I must admit, I am disappointed at your behavior. I was told Azure Warriors treat the females of this country with devotion and a sort of sacredness. I suspect you manage them that way only to make them pliable to your pithy offerings. It will not work on me, and as my contract states: if you touch me, I'll remove your hand, followed by the part of you that's currently doing the thinking, Warlord, Imperial Crown Prince or not." My chest heaves with fury, and I tremble with it.

"My honor means more to me than my life. Unfortunately, you've revealed your lack of it by making the offer," I say with such quiet, lethal calm all conversation dies down in the camp, and all eyes turn to us. Diedra whirls, eyes wide with alarm.

The tension is so tight I half wonder if it will snap and lash one of us. Canary stands to help or intervene, but I don't find out because the Warlord Prince bows his head and places his large hand on his broad chest.

"I apologize for offending you, Ranger Alana. On my life, I promise it will not happen again," he says with lowered eyes, ever hooded behind his mask.

It's a cheap apology, and I'm too upset to look at him, so I turn and walk away, feeling tears prick my eyes.

The tension breaks, and the rest of the camp resumes their regular activity. Diedra takes a step towards me. "Alana."

Canary holds out a hand, stopping her from following me as I stride to the perimeter guard. "Is there a spot to relieve myself?" I ask.

He points to a lone tree a hundred yards away. I nod my thanks and walk out into the softly hissing grasses, the day's heat still clinging to the night air. I inhale deeply, smelling the dust and bite of dried greenery, and my chest eases with every step further away from the Warlord. I hate him. Did Calix know the Prince? Had they been friends? All I remember is his home of Heviin. I don't know where that is, but I'll ask Diedra and have her help me.

Maybe he'll still feel apologetic enough tomorrow, so I can ask him about Calix's family. Knowing of his death will cause them pain, but it will be better than spending forever with the unknown. Rangers know this all too well when dealing with victim's families.

As I thread the grass tips between my fingers, walking onto the soft, rolling ground, my mind turns back to Panthum and the Riband. This place is so different from my home. I gaze up to the stars and find two Star of the Gods swirling high above. The galaxy's Isili and Kitoa, the Beast and the Jewel, have thinned in their appearance. From this spot in the world, I'm only able to see the outer edges of their rings. Tapato, the Loyal Friend galaxy is missing completely, having gone too far southeast to see her guiding light. I suspect if I move north, Tapato will make a reappearance.

I miss my family. My parting words to Drake sour my gut. I'd happily hear him holler my name and have him chase me through the camp to give me a public and humiliating punishment if it only meant I could see him again. If I were home, Everett and Hagatha would likely already be telling everyone about their first child. Has it really been four weeks after their Summer Solemat wedding?

Wet tears streak down my face, and I hate it. I hate this feeling—this need for others, of my family.

Of Calix.

The anguish is terrible but I know that it meant I loved irrevocably. I just wished I had told him sooner. I miss him so much. If he'd been here, he could've helped me navigate this new Empire and Warlord.

Sweet Mother, I hate his arrogant Prince and malcontent General.

Frustration stiffening my muscles, I trudge through the grass, reaching the tree. I lean back against the rough bark as sobs wrack my body, my cheeks and neck streaked with tears, leaving the Uria cloth tunic wet.

My gasps are hard to keep quiet, but I'm alone so what does it matter? I tell myself the feelings of grief will pass, but deep down, I know I'll love Calix until my last breath. I wipe my tears away with my forearm and tell myself the Warlord now knows where my boundaries are, along with anyone else who heard. That's a win in my book. One has to take the wins when they can.

When I finish my personal needs, I breathe deeply, taking a few moments to clear my head. How long can I stay here?

Will the Azure Warriors think I ran off?

Perhaps their guards' eyes are as good as their hearing, and they can find me out here even under a half-moon.

I sigh and step forward when I feel a prickle on the back of my neck. I swallow and immediately search for danger. Were there wild beasts out in these lands I wasn't warned about? I feel a heavy, unnatural breeze blast my head in a downward thrust. When I peer up, I find an Ariportia staring down at me with a crooked grin on his plain face. Fear coils in my gut like a viper ready to strike.

"Hello, pretty. Why are you crying?" his raspy voice whispers loudly, breaking the tense silence. He's wiry, with dark hair, his eyes taking me in. What did Canary say about their attack on the Red City? They stole women and gold. "You look like you could use some different company."

My heart roars, and conversance keeps me frozen, remembering my fight against his kind in the pit. My muscles coil and wind, preparing for a fight, even if, logically, I know I won't be able to win. I quickly take him in. His black wings are tucked tightly against his body, and I don't fail to notice the weapons strapped to it. Running would be a safer option if only because I imagine it would be hard to fly while carrying a female trying to snap your neck.

I breathe out my nerves, swallow, and take a step backward. His smile drops.

"I wouldn't run if I were you. I'd hate to ruin your pretty face."

"My pretty face is the last thing you should be concerned with, Ariportia," I say levelly. Drake would be so pleased I was caught unaware.

He freezes and cocks his head to the side, eyes narrowing. "What's a Deysik doing in the company of Azure Warriors?"

"*Think! You don't want him to kill you, do you?*" snaps Drake in my head. His voice startles me enough that I blink. I remember how quick they are, knowing there's no way I can outmaneuver this Ariportia, not when he's at his full strength and covered with weapons while I don't have a single blade on my body.

I try a different tactic.

I give him a thin smile and step forward, "What do you think I'm doing with them?"

My stomach twists at my innuendo, my heart thudding in my chest. I dig my boots in the soft red dirt and cross my arms, raising a brow, trying to suck back my snot as subtly as I can.

His grin returns. "You, Deysik, really are evolving. No longer running through streets, bare-bones stealing for your family or murdering anyone who slights you. I think it's a wise decision my Night Queen made to ally with you. It won't be long before we have more of your kind in our ranks. In the meantime, slag, you'll have to find a new Bluey to bed."

"What do you mean?" A sick sensation crawls over my skin. Who is the Night Queen?

"So long, slag. I'd run if I were you, but if not... we'll meet again," he says before launching into the colorless sky.

I don't like the warning in his tone. Not at all.

The pounding of horse hooves beat like a quiet drum vibrating through my feet, and I turn to discover Prince Dread and a dozen Azure Warriors riding at full speed under the waning half-moon, cutting their path through the grass toward me.

Questions flood my mind as they pull their horses to a halt, sending clouds of thick dust into the air. The Warlord is off his horse in an instant, halting inches in front of me, gold filigree mask roving over my body, I assume, checking for any damage to his investment. He must have seen the threat of the Ariportia, and came running.

"You're not hurt," he states, his voice tense and breathless. "What did he say to you?" He's looming over me, and I step back to give myself some space to breathe. He lifts a hand as if to stop me but quickly drops it.

"No. He didn't have time to say much before you came," I said flatly. The crown Prince pulls back a step and speaks sharply in Luminum to the pearl masked Prince, I notice circling on his horse, scanning the skies. A single Azure Warrior takes off back to camp, kicking up dust and dirt in his wake.

"What did he say?" a rough voice asks from the quiet brooding General.

"He asked me if I needed a change of company," I said. "Then he suggested I abandon you, sooner rather than later. I assume he's planning some sort of an ambush." I angle my head. How much of a mess are we in?

Tension ripples through the men and a sense of urgency roars in the silence.

"How far away did you say we were to the nearest fortress? I have family I'd like to return home to in five years," I say in a low tone of voice. I'm his mercenary, not his dog and will not be without any necessary information.

The Warlord and his General share a look, and the tension thickens like a pail of milk on a hot day.

"We have at least a two-day ride before we reach safety," the Warlord says, his voice dropping dangerously low. "You don't need to worry, Alana. No harm will come to you."

I snort. "As much as I'd like to believe that, it's not what either the situation or the contract tells me." I cock my head and say with a little bit of vicious bite, "I don't need anyone protecting me Bluey, least of all you. That would defeat the purpose of my presence here, correct?" I stare hard at the Warlord still furious over his earlier proposition.

The pearl-masked General cuts in, "We need to leave."

The command is said with the force of a blunt object, and the Warlord jerks his chin for me to get onto his horse. Irritation prickles down my spine. I move quickly, noting Diedra, Canary, and the other Azure Warriors arriving from camp.

Once the Warlord Bluey is seated behind me, the whole group takes off, heading further into the grassy plains and away from the road.

It's going to be a long night.

Chapter 4

We stop only to rest the horses and allow them to drink from passing streams as we rush across the landscape, saved from being wholly categorized as uninteresting by its spectacular sunrise hours ago.

My body aches from riding for so long, not having used those muscles in two months. I have no choice but to bear it as we race to safety. When we stop for lunch, the sun is high in the sky. Digging through our saddle bags, I make my way to sit under the shade of a massive, thick-leaved tree—a rarity on the plains.

Above me, white fluffy clouds drift high with a cooling breeze, teasing my Uria clothing away from the sweat coating my skin for a moment. I'm relieved to be away from my human furnace. I rub my neck and shoulders, attempting to ease the tension in my muscles, noticing the clouds swirl in a strange pattern before I enter the cooling shade.

I roll my neck as Diedra pats an empty spot between her and the Warlord. I have the worst luck. I wave her off, choosing to stand before them both. I blame the heat for my irritation, which causes me to ask her, "How long have you been in conflict with the Ariportia?"

"Two years, *Moskazi*," the Warlord answers calmly. I flick my gaze at him before turning back to Diedra. That name—it shaves off more of my thin patience, kindling my rage. I belong to this man.

"*And he belongs to you*," Drake's voice whispers in my head. I shake it off.

"What began the provocation?" I ask Diedra, stubbornly ignoring the Warlord.

"Their attempted sack of the Red City. We rely too much on the port and its commerce with the lower continent to allow it." Again, he answers.

Diedra watches me carefully, and I suspect she worries about the new tension between myself and the Warlord. If he wants to speak to me, then I might as well ask him about Calix.

"I met one of your Commanders on my journey," I say, pausing as the Warlord tenses. I notice a flicker pass through his chest down to his thighs. There's no hiding it. "I survived my journey due to his convictions, and when we were shipwrecked, I'm afraid he and his twin brother were lost at sea before one of your ships could intercede." I inhale a relieving breath as I swallow, attempting to hold back the sting behind my eyes, my voice thick. "I'd like to inform his family."

"There is no need, *Moskazi*. Their family is aware." Short, succinct sentences meant to cut me off. I blink.

Nash must have told him. From the way he answered, he must have been friends with them both.

"When are you allowed to remove your masks?" Nash knew Calix's importance based on the lack of pigmentation on his whole face rather than just the lower half.

Canary begins to chuckle, and my confusion takes off like a bird in flight when I hear his raspy voice gurgle with delight. I blink, I'm so shocked hearing it.

"*Moskazi* has only to ask for my mask to be removed, and I shall," the Warlord replies, his voice distorted and low as if annoyed. I frown, especially hearing Canary's laughter. He must have a reason to hide. Perhaps he truly is ugly? Most likely so. I stand and turn to face him, shifting my weight to one leg.

"Please remove it." I don't like the sense they're playing a joke on me. Canary starts coughing with tears running down his face, earning a glare from Diedra, who flicks a worried glance at her gold-masked Prince.

The Warlord sighs. "Yes, Moskazi." No argument. No protest. Nothing. Just obedience. I pause, wondering why the concession to an indentured servant. Before the Warlord, Prince Dread, Crown Prince of Luminum, can move, the back of my neck stings sharply in warning.

Acting on instinct, I dive for the Warlord, tackling him sideways right as an arrow strikes my Uria cloth tunic, sending a sharp pain through my ribs on impact. I grunt as I land on top of him, hearing someone cry out, "Ariportia attack!"

Canary yanks Diedra towards him as an arrow slices through the fleshy part of his shoulder, sending them both tumbling into the grass. "I'm wearing Uria cloth you idiot!" I hear Diedra yell to, I assume, Canary.

"Shields!" another voice yells, and the Crown Prince reaches over his shoulder, ripping his from his back and holding it over our heads along with the rest of the Azure Warriors as whistling arrows rain down on our group.

In the relief of the first volley, the Warlord and I pull each other to our feet, and I reach for where my sword would be before I realize with frustration that I hadn't been given any. *Mother's braids.*

Several Azure Warriors fall to the ground with arrows sticking from their bodies like pins. They had no chance to pull the shields from their backs. Why do they not wear full armor when traveling? I snatch a dagger off the Warlord's weapons belt, and the overwhelming scene floods through me.

Bucking, screaming horses wounded with arrows crash into a group of Azure Warriors, knocking them down. A thick dust cloud envelopes the troops making it impossible to see more than five feet before us. The Warlord grips my arm, yanking me out of the way as a horse runs past in the dust, sending us both stumbling sideways. I hear more pings of arrows smashing into shields, and grit stings my eyes.

Urgency pulses through me. We have to get out of here.

The Prince roars orders in Luminum, which are quickly passed through the air, and the scent of blood mingles with the dust. His meaning is clear. Gather to the tree. Make a stand. My heart pounds and my skin heats. A whistle sounds through the choking dust, and he grunts.

He's been hit. The hissing of arrows slows as the Ariportia are unable to see their targets through the dust, but they can hear them.

"Stay silent," I hiss.

My blood rushes with the reassuring sound of thrumming from the Blueys' bows returning fire. I hear Diedra speaking rapidly, and my stomach turns to a ball of knots. I can't see her, but it sounds like she's talking to someone, helping her with an injury. Canary? Someone else? She's going to be a target. I move in that direction, wondering where the pearl-masked prick could be.

The Warlord grabs my arm, stopping me. "We need to move while they're blind."

"We need to get back to the tree. I don't want to die before I can return home, Bluey. You're going to have to fight your way out of this ambush."

"We'll need more weapons. They're on the horses," he says quietly.

He turns his gilded mask my way, his hand grasping mine. He pulls me forward, keeping the shield above our heads. Showing no sign of injury, we take off after the bleeding horses. We pump our legs, toes digging into the fine dust choking the air, filled with snapping deadly shafts.

All around us are cries of death and metal striking metal as Ariportia land, kicking up more dust while battling with the Blueys. I swallow down the memory of my fight with the Ariportia in the Red City and how he used the wind to his advantage.

A thrashing horse runs into view, and instinctively, I pull free from the Warlord's grip, lunging to snatch up its reins, being yanked away from the Crown Prince. I slow the terrified horse just enough for me to rip free a sword strapped to its saddle. My muscles scream in protest, and when I turn, I'm faced with the night-shade wings of an Ariportia raising a sword. I whip my weapon in two practiced moves, and the Ariportia falls dead at my feet, where in my periphery, I make out blue and gold mixed with black feathers littering the red-flecked ground.

The music of war echoes in the gritty air, and rage snakes through me like a thunderstorm.

From the flashes of color breaking through the clouds of red dust, we're outnumbered four to one, but that doesn't stop the Azure Warriors from fighting with a ferocity and obduracy that's terrifying to behold.

I've lost the Warlord.

I swing and stab, fighting my way back to where I last saw him, praying to the Mother he won't be hurt. I have too many years ahead of me to deal with someone new, or Mother forbid, the General.

I stumble and crash into another set of soft wings. I stab behind me blindly, lifting my heavy sword with every sore muscle in my arm, anticipating the blow that falls with so much power I drop to my knee, sweat lining my spine as I meet the furious gaze of the dark-eyed Ariportia, his skin nearly as dark as his wings.

I swipe at him with my dagger, and he rears back, pausing with a jerk as a blade stabs through his abdomen from behind. A flash of pearl and the blade cutting through the Ariportia is ripped free from his body. Without a word, the General moves on in his fight.

I follow his retreating form and catch sparks of sapphire blue and gold through the clouds of dust.

The Warlord.

What I witnessed in Faurst when Calix had taken on five men at once was child's play. It appears the Warlord is in a league of his own. His reflexes are honed more than the other soldiers.

His battle cry echoes from his mask in a horror inducing keen, which sends a skittering of fear down my belly, rattling my very ribcage as he swings and attacks, killing four Ariportia in one swing. Their deaths only incite our enemy warriors, and they converge on the Crown Prince. With speed as their greatest asset in their arsenal, it's no match for the Bluey's strength in hand-to-hand combat.

He disappears in a flurry of Ariportia, blades, and black wings, and my chest tightens with urgency as I fight; my reflexes, improved from training with Canary these last few weeks, are the only thing keeping me alive in this fight. I dodge a blade to my neck, stabbing the Ariportia in his thigh to allow me enough time to slice my sword across his neck.

His wings whip around, encasing me, blocking my view for a moment, throwing me off balance as he falls.

Every fiber of my body pulls me towards the Bluey to help him as a ripple of something pulses through the air, sizzling against my skin.

A roar hacks the air, followed by an explosion of blood and bone, taking me back to the Giant's death.

Time seems to slow, and I gasp. For the first time in my life, I'm afraid for myself. The cloud of blood and feathers drift through the dust-filled air, and Nash's words haunt my mind. The fighters would be nothing but blood and gore if he weren't chained.

Is this the gift the Mother gave her Azure Warriors?

Glowing eyes of azure blue, filled with malice and lethal rage, fall on me, crimson blood dripping from every inch of him, making him appear as a god of war come to life. I can't help but swallow and take a step back. All I can make out is the shadow of his brow furrowing before he blinks, reigning in his blood lust.

It's enough to reveal how the man earned his title of Warlord.

A sharp stabbing sensation strikes the back of my neck, and I duck, whipping out my sword blindly, with one hand and with the other, twist my dagger into the heart of an Ariportia who approached from behind. The brutality of this battle strikes me as the warrior's headless body falls slack, dropping at my feet.

In an instant, the Warlord slices and cuts his way to my side.

"You need to run." His voice is hoarse as he presses his large body into mine, herding me to the edge of the battle. His words turn my blood into shards of ice.

"No, I won't, Bluey. I don't run from fights. Not when you're out-numbered," I protest, trying to clear the fear from my throat as I choke on thick red dust, ignoring the lump forming in my throat.

"I'm ordering you to run."

"Diedra—"

"Diedra will be fine!" he barks. "Go, Ruby."

Confusion roils through me for half a moment before I remember Nash used his nickname in front of the Warlord. I attribute the disruption for imploding my decision making ability.

I don't want to leave. I can't explain why desperation clangs through me, but I refuse to abandon him. I recognize it for what it is, loyalty to Calix, and how I felt for him on the ship when it was sinking, as well as panic of trying to stave off death like bailing an ocean away with teaspoons. The Warlord and I continue to swing and defend, stabbing Ariportia as he successfully pushes me to the outskirts.

A wonderful, familiar growl travels through the air, level with my feet. It comes from the right—out in the plains. My lungs ease before they still, going taut as a weaver's loom.

The hair on my arms stands on end as I realize I'm not on the right continent for that particular growl to bring comfort. Horror floods over me, chilling my body at the sight of the Ariportia's smiles as they retreat a few steps, pausing the fight.

Deysik.

At least two.

The Azure Warriors turn to the noise, and instantly, as one they press backward into a tight circle, their shields form a wall of impenetrable steel. The Warlord's intentions quickly shift as his broad back shoves me towards the circle. I'm about to be swallowed up, along with our only chance of survival. I quickly scan our surroundings, taking in the settling dust.

Twenty Azure Warriors left. Thirty Ariportia.

Against the Ariportia, they can make it.

However, with the enemies' ranks, combined with two incoming Deysik... death.

Our story will not reach its zenith today.

I dart under the Crown Prince's arm, shoving his chest back towards his men, who pull him to safety as I bolt for the plains, dropping my sword and keeping the dagger in hand. The Warlord roars my name in a command I ignore. "ALANA!"

I plow past Ariportia, meeting only grunts. They don't bother chasing after me. Why would they when they can carry me away in a few moments when the slaughter has ceased?

Without looking back, I tighten my fingers around the worn, smooth leather of the Warlord's long dagger hilt and flee the fight, cutting through hip-high grass.

Towards the familiar growls.

I swallow down my anticipation, which rattles my ribs, as I hear the Prince call out orders to his men. Together as one.

I don't have time to worry about what he thinks of me running away from the battle he's waging instead of towards the one which will tip the scales.

Two large felines, the size of mountain cats, lope through the grass, both with thick, darker fur around their necks. Lions. I'd never seen these forms of the cat before, but I'd heard stories of how Ertune selected the deadliest animals for his Generals to take as their second skin. The Deysik at home are of a different variety.

I whistle sharply, two notes gaining their attention, twirling the dagger in my hands as I cock my head to the side, exposing my neck. I wink at them with a mischievous smile and take off, running down into a hollow where I spy a copse of trees fifty yards away. Everything down here is hidden and out of sight from the battle behind me. Their guttural bellow has me pumping my legs harder, feeling the wind slice through me.

Adrenaline courses hotly as my feet speed up with the decline despite the grass trying to slow my steps. Thirty yards, and I detect their paths diverging from the targeted Azure Warriors and split from one into two as they flank me. I grit my teeth and push harder, sweat stinging my eyes.

"You're too slow. You'd be ripped to pieces if a monster was on your tail," Drake's welcome sage advice springs in my head, sparking anger inside me, adding another burst of speed, drawing up from a well of nearly depleted energy.

Twenty yards. I can see them in my peripheral vision. I have to run faster, or I won't make it. My toes burn in my boots.

Drake trained me for this, and I'm the best at it. I think that's why he hates me, because I showed him that a human can kill a Deysik.

Ten yards. They begin to close in. The sun scorches down on me, burning me up.

Five yards. My whole body is lighter than air as I fly over the thinning grass, my steps barely touching the ground.

One yard.

I'm out of time.

The back of my neck prickles. They leap. One aims low for my legs, the other high.

I leap horizontally, twisting in the air between the lions, throwing my dagger hilt into a tree trunk. I roll on the ground, creating another thick cloud of red dust all around.

I sit where I roll and cross my legs as I hear them scramble. I close my eyes and lower my head in supplication, waiting for the dust to clear. Their recovery takes a moment. Sweat beads down my face and spine.

Huffs of breath blow across my legs, originating feet away. I keep still, not moving a muscle, keeping my breathing forcefully slow, my lungs screaming for more air, more life, as every part of me calls out for me to inhale more breath to the point of pain. Instead, I slowly retain the oxygen, my ribs expelling it from my body, fighting against my burning organs.

The key to stopping a Deysik attack is surprise. But not surprise by violence. Surprise with acquiescence. To show no fear. To display peace.

Creatures of violence are triggered by violence. But my people have learned over the last four hundred years that even when confronting a Rogue Deysik, the only thing to stop them from attacking is to fall still.

I hear one of them Shift, four steps becoming two as the other flops his lion body on the ground, his heavy pants stinking up the air.

The human Deysik's voice is rough and nodular when he speaks in Luminum, and I cock my head and frown to show him I don't understand. He switches to the common tongue. "Who taught you that trick?" His voice crawls over me. "You a Mother's Monk or something? Those fanatics trying to keep us from killing Blueys?"

I slowly raise my head and open my eyes to find a whip-lean man with thick brown hair dressed in threadbare clothing. He inhales deeply, his cruel eyes glowing brightly as coals against his fair skin. His head cocks to the side.

"You're... Deysik."

My lungs freeze, and my heart stutters. "And you're not a rogue," I reply.

He sneers, and his lion companion chuffs. "Rogue would imply we lost our minds."

I cock my head to the side, "Would ambushing Azure Warriors be something one would do in their right mind?"

He snorts and spits in the dirt, tossing me a scathing look. "You're the one who must be rogue, thinking what you're doing is living? It's disgusting. What? You don't like the likes of us soldiers? Don't like men who do the dirty work?"

My face heats with anger at what he implies, and I glare. "What exactly do you think I'm doing?"

"I can smell them all over you. The Blueys," he spits again, "Don't take no thinking. What are you?"

I soften my tone to borderline condescending, "What do you mean?"

He sniffs again and glances at his companion before facing me. "What's your second skin?"

Embarrassment and shame pour over me. Deysik can smell lies. "I don't know."

The lion snorts again, but the man's lips are thin, and his shoulders stiffen.

More slowly, he asks, "Where are you from? Your accent. You roll your letters funny."

I slowly rise to my feet, allowing my lungs to open up, taking in more oxygen, saying, "Why does it matter?"

"It matters," he says harshly, cocking his head. My heart lurches, and both of them sharpen their focus on me. They can hear everything as clearly as my Deysik back home. Especially heartbeats.

"You've told me what you think of me, and by the sound of it, I think you missed the fight," I say quietly, breathing evenly. Indeed, the metal clashing in the background stopped completely, and I'm not sure who had lost.

The lion turns behind him toward the battle and growls low and deep, sending vibrations through me again, rattling my ribcage.

"We'll bring home their masks after the Ariportia do their job."

My stomach twists. So, they coordinated with the Ariportia to ambush the Azure Warriors.

The Deysik man jerks his chin towards the dagger in the trunk behind me. "Where'd you learn to do that, slag?"

"Practice," I say, shifting back to lean against the tree he gestures to.

He smiles, showing off teeth that are all too white. "I know when you're not answering my question, slag. I'll show you what happens to traitorous whores, if you don't answer me. And to warn you, none are left breathing. Now I'll ask again. Where are you from?"

That word. Slag. My whole body burns with rage, and I know he can smell it by the way his eyes burn brighter, a silent signal.

"You're asking the wrong question, Rogue. You should be more worried about what I'll do to you with this dagger." I move my head to touch the blade sticking out of the trunk.

"That dagger isn't going to pierce my skin, so why should I worry?" He takes a step closer, and I move without remorse, ripping the long dagger free and flinging it right into his eye, killing him instantly.

I break forward, feeling my fingers grip the hilt just as the lion launches into the air, tackling me. My back slams into the red dirt, the powerful Deysik on top of me. Panic lay in the back of my mind, wiggling like a worm underneath the calm of my training.

How many times had Baylor shifted his body and pounded me mercilessly into the dirt, his fur smothering me?

Before I can lift the dagger, one paw slashes its dark claws across my forehead and down the left side of my face, searing pain slicing down my eye and cheek, turning my head, and exposing my neck. I breathe out the pain in a silent scream but don't utter a sound. Nothing sets off the blood frenzy more than a scream of pain.

White and yellowing fangs in a black mouth snap forward. I throw my left forearm up in time to stop him, feeling every individual tooth in his wide mouth clamp down, pushing through the muscles and tendons.

I hiss in agony, pain sharpening my focus and rage. Blood pools in both eyes as its sticky rivulets pour down my face into my hair and the neck of my clothing.

The Deysik's weight bears down on me, his claws attempting to rip through my flesh, but the Uria cloth prevents it. I keep my breathing even as my muscles strain against him. I jerk my leg up quickly so that instead of gutting me, his paws slip down the side of my leg. He whips his head to the side, trying to rip my arm from my body... to splay me wide open.

Frustration threatens to rise—

"Knees and elbows," Drake's voice stabs into me, pushing back the surfacing panic. Once again, I thrust my knee up, only this time making contact with his lower extremities. His eyes flare wide before he jerks his head back with my arm in it.

A loud pop cracks in my ears.

I suck in another silent scream as agony shoots through my left shoulder. Stars blur the vision of my right eye, and a sudden wave of weakness passes through me. Mother's braids. If I don't get up, I'm going to die with a blade in my hand. I can't feel my fingers and I grapple with the hilt, feeling it wobble in my hand.

"FIGHT!" Drake roars, returning me from the clawing emotion threatening to overtake me. I breathe out and focus on my next movements to end the fight, and with my inhale, consuming power returns.

A burning spark spears down my veins, searing my shoulder and fusing it back together. The blade I'm holding in a death grip drops into my waiting right hand, and I swing with all the force I can muster to shove the dagger deep. Enough to kill.

Once, when I was sixteen, it was all the lesson I had needed in my lifetime to learn.

The Deysik lion sags, pressure releasing from my forearm, dropping all his weight on me as blood trickles down his large tan face.

I grunt, heaving him off me, coughing for breath, staring up at the puffy clouds that are no longer swirling with descending Ariportia through my eyes before they're drenched.

Blood pulses in warm rivers down my face. The clash of swords from over the rise is silent, and I grunt in pain as I grip the dagger hilt and yank it out, breathing through the dull pain in my left shoulder.

I stand looking down at the dead bodies, blinking the blood away rapidly. They attempted to kill Diedra and Canary, along with the Warlord and his soldiers. I clench my teeth, holding back the bile as my spine solidifies to steel.

Did they live? I start running, pumping my limbs like pistons, focusing on my future as I cut back through the pale grass.

Back toward the battlefield.

I'm a Ranger and will not abandon my honor or the Warlord.

As I run, my blood flows down my face, and I use my forearm to wipe my eyes, keeping away from the left side of my face, but it's impossible. I stumble, and all I can make out from beyond all the blood are black feathers fluttering in the air and twisted, broken wings pointing to the sky amidst a battlefield decorated with arrow shafts. Azure Warriors weave with black-clad mercenaries, whom I recognize as belonging to the Black Fox. I find the mercenary kicking over dead Ariportia, either checking for a specific one or making sure they're dead.

The Black Fox must have arrived to help while I was gone.

Dozens of injured Azure Warriors are moved into the shade of the tree, Diedra helping the worst ones with Canary and others by her side assisting. Knee-shaking-relief tears through me, seeing both alive. I won't have to deal with more uncertainty.

There... the Warlord sorts through the Ariportia almost frantically, pulling bodies aside.

Who is he looking for?

The wind blows at my back, and my feet kick up red dirt, carrying it toward the group. Two black, armored mercenaries whip towards me and freeze. My head starts to feel light as if it will float away, walking through the scratchy grass, blood dripping into my eyes and off my face. A sound of frustration builds in my throat, and I grunt, making another futile attempt to wipe my face free.

My face throbs and stings, and I'm bleeding heavily. The blood won't clot. I close my eyes and breathe through my nose, attempting to focus on breathing to calm my mind, but the adrenaline is still flowing.

I hear the sound of feet racing toward me—two of them.

My steps become clumsy as I push through the foliage. I have to make it back to Diedra and Canary.

The logical side of my brain wonders why the men are running. The back of my mind screams incoherent thoughts, and my body is slow to respond. I shake my head, trying to clear my mind, but it only serves to make me dizzy. I tip to the side and throw out a steadying leg.

I blink rapidly, trying to clear the blood and focus my gaze on the approaching males. I hear another rush of footsteps bolting in my direction, calling out something I fail to hear with the wind tearing over the plains against his voice, pushing the sound away from me.

What is he shouting?

Based on the sound of their approach, two large males rush closer, and my instinct pieces together what my brain can't.

"Ruby!" someone bellows in panic.

A warning.

My heart rate spikes and panic begins to set in. Instinct drives my defenses back up, and I draw from my well of energy, pushing it out as strength into my veins once more. I raise my blade, not sure what or who is approaching me.

This damn injured arm and blood! I'm disoriented and vulnerable. A combination I detest.

The males are steps away when I raise my dagger defensively, causing them to slow. I take a breath, grinding my teeth, hoping the pain in my face will sharpen my senses.

I blink rapidly, clearing the flow of blood as the mercs pause. Through my rapid blinks, I make out two large black-clad mercenaries with their hands out as if taming a wild animal. Perhaps I look deranged in my bloodied state, but I'm alive.

I want to laugh.

"Alana," one of them says soothingly, while the other lunges for me—for the dagger. I don't register he's used my given name as muscle memory guides my body to duck and twist under his long reach, stumbling away from him a few steps when my vision fills with more pulsating blood. I whip the dagger blindly in front of me, trying to lift my injured arm to wipe my eye, but it refuses to cooperate.

Mother curse this blood loss.

"Alana," one of them hisses, and I shake my head, trying to clear my mind. They're trying to say something to me, but I can't make it out. I don't know them. I don't know what they want with me.

"Ruby!" a commanding and dominating voice shouts across the expanse between us, and I shake my head once more. I move my blade in front of me, stepping further away from the males. My mind is playing tricks on me.

My legs shake, and my battle rage gutters when I sense the Warlord's approach. I swipe my fisted hand across my eyes, the dagger making it an awkward effort, but it's enough for me to make out the glowing turquoise eyes behind a gold mask. The power radiating off of the male is nearly tangible.

Mother help me.

He's going to kill me.

He's covered in gore still, and I don't want to die.

I skitter backward, my dagger swiping in front of me to keep the Warlord from coming closer. His expression is full of wrath and violence. A glowing ember burns brighter inside me.

I open my mouth to threaten; Mother only knows what, but before I can, he surprises me.

"Lay a single hand on her, and I'll slaughter you without a second thought," he snarls roughly, power lining every word. My body trembles, and my dagger wavers. I can't seem to release the grip of the hilt as his words send my stomach spinning.

Why would he say that?

My heart rate takes off at a gallop, and I think I'm going to pass out.

"Then you'll have to pay for them, and I don't think your father would be pleased as we're honored guests for this year's Currell, Prince Dread. Your Moskazi needs medical attention," the Black Fox cuts in as she ambles forward out of nowhere, her thumbs tucked into her belt as her silver fox mask turns to where Diedra is busy helping the wounded men.

The Warlord steps closer, and I whimper in fear. The hot wind whips around us, beginning to dry some of my blood. His body and mask are covered in blood and bits of Ariportia.

"Ruby, it's me."

I tremble, and a sob threatens to rip up my throat. No. It can't be. Why would the Warlord say that?

My brain doesn't want to comply with what my heart is hearing. I step back once more, unable to accept the truth of it. The grass crunching beneath my boot. Why would he—

"Ruby," the Warlord says again. That familiar cadence. That familiar command. His turquoise eyes dim their eerie glow and soften as he approaches me, and it's the only thing I can focus on through blood and blurred vision.

That word. That name. He holds his open palms out to me, showing me he has no weapons, before he pushes his hood back, revealing the rounded edge of his mask. I focus solely on his eyes, my body frozen in place. If someone were to attempt to take my life, I wouldn't be able to stop them as his blood-crusted hands remove his filigreed, golden mark of status.

My heart stutters.

"Bluey?" The question is a supplication for the man I know as the Warlord to make sense of my struggling thoughts, attempting to absorb the male before me.

Calix.

Blonde hair, slick with sweat, tops the handsome face coming into view. His skin is tan, not pale, with full lips, high cheekbones, and a broad brow with a straight nose I know to have a bumpy profile, between blue-green eyes I had grown to love and had mourned clear down into the depths of my soul these past few waking days.

Once more, his hands extend towards me, fingers splayed wide as he approaches slowly.

I don't move towards him.

His chest rises and falls in measured exhales while the pulse at his throat beats wildly. His expression flickers with remorse before his jaw clenches and his eyes harden, and I know, I know, he's expecting the hammer to fall. Expecting my anger, waiting for what he thinks he deserves for keeping his identity from me. He expects me to react the way I have with Nash and the fighters on the ship when wounded. Lash out with violence.

But I don't have a dew drop of vitriol for this man who has shown me nothing but kindness in the face of my prejudice. I had spent it all on the ship, and my reservoir was depleted.

Joy, heart-tearing relief plows into my chest at viewing Calix's face since I thought he was gone forever. I can't breathe, and I'm so overwhelmed. I blink again, making sure my eyes aren't playing tricks on me, but my eyelid sticks with coagulated blood as the hot wind seals my clothing to my skin.

"Bluey," I breathe out.

"This isn't how I wanted to show you—" he begins. I waver, and before my legs buckle, Calix catches me, pulling me against his powerful body and wrapping his arm around my waist. Without breaking my gaze, he slowly peels my fisted fingers away from the dagger as if he knows I can't do it alone. I can't take my focus away from him. It must be a dream.

But it's not.

He made it out alive.

I tuck the unwounded side of my face against him as a lump clogs my throat. My legs tremble as the adrenaline wears off, and I never want him to let me go. All I can focus on is his heartbeat against mine. He's *alive*.

Cries of pain and the movement of Azure Warriors helping those injured come from behind us, but I don't care about them. I don't care about anyone other than the man holding me to him as desperately as I feel.

Hot tears cut down my filthy face, sluicing the grit and blood with it. My vision blurs around the edges, and my legs shake violently. Without hesitating, Calix sweeps me up in his arms.

He's warm, solid, and secure. Oh, how I missed him. The old familiar sense of safety falls like a cloak over me.

"I couldn't find you," he says lowly, his voice pleasantly rough. I squeeze him tighter.

"I'll fight death himself to return to you, Bluey," I whisper. He carries me near where the others are being treated and settles us in the grass, holding me in his lap.

The Black Fox speaks to one of her men in a language that sounds like the sister to Luminum. As she gathers the supplies from her saddlebag, I observe the aftermath of the battle. There are more Blueys alive than I expected. Those uninjured help those with wounds, while some gather bodies, and the rest ride the Black Fox's horses to round up those who fled out of injury or fear before she and her men arrived.

He cradles my head, fingers slipping through my gnarly hair. The other clutches me tightly to his firm body. He tucks his nose against my head and breathes me in.

I'm safe. I'm here and able to take in the soothing undernotes of cinnamon and leather.

"Calix?" the question is a whisper, and his body stills. I gently pull back, and he uses his thumb to sweep away the blood on my eyelid, carefully avoiding my wounds.

Not for the first time, I'm in awe of his gentleness after what I've just witnessed. He's alive. The thought comes again on instinct. I swallow before leaning back to stare at his handsome face under the grit and grime of battle.

"Don't ever hide from me." My tears continue to fall as shock begins to claw its way through my body in the form of tremors. He remains silent as he pulls me to his chest, his reassuring heartbeat beating under my ear.

He's alive.

He rubs my arms, keeping me warm. I allow my head to loll once more against the thick column of his throat. My body sags, and I burrow against his skin, breathing his addicting scent, knowing I'll never recover if I find this is all a fever dream.

"I missed you. Mother, help me; I missed you." A thick sob escapes me, my stinging shoulder allowing me enough movement to wrap it around his shoulder, holding him tightly to me, never wanting to let go.

"You'll stay by my side at all times, Moskazi. If anyone tries to take you away from me, I'll put their head on a pike," Calix—the Warlord—says, his voice dropping dangerously low.

Reassured is the only word I feel as I dive back into reality.

Calix is alive, and he is mine.

"I'm trained in healing if you'll allow me near her without removing a limb or my head," the Black Fox says, her two mercs nowhere to be seen. Calix's threat to their lives must have been enough to put some distance between us.

But a question clangs through my head, and I can't shake it.

How did they know my name?

Chapter 5

I wake, cradled and wrapped in Calix's solid arms, riding towards the nearest fortress city. My shoulder and face ache from the attack, but it is expected. With the pain-killing powders the Black Fox administered under Diedra's supervision, and poultice the merc wrapped on my face, I was able to sleep for a few hours.

Thankfully, Diedra and Canary survived the battle, the latter unscathed beyond his initial wound. The pearl-masked Prince—Calix's taciturn twin—Vasilius, took an arrow to the outer thigh, missing anything vital. He killed a dozen Ariportia alone to match his brother's number of kills. I decided that he saved me out of duty to his brother.

He now broods in silence, his hands flexing over his reins in such a way I wonder if he imagines strangling his foes with them. I know I would after the short memorial and burning of the bodies of their fallen. It was a war burial with no time to dig graves.

We ride in silence, and though I know Calix's processing this attack, I'm aware he's giving me time to sort through the revelation that he's the Warlord.

He is the one who paid *one hundred thousand* gold coins for me.

It would have been nice had he said something earlier, but I don't have the will or time to be angry with him for keeping his identity a secret. I'm only grateful.

After several hours of a grueling trot, Calix breaks the silence. "You mentioned protecting your country as a Ranger once. What does that entail? What exactly do you protect them from?"

I inhale deeply and realize he's processing the information I exposed when killing the Deysik. *Deysiks. Two. Not Rogue.*

"We learn to hunt game and apply the same principle to criminals," I say simply. Somehow, I don't think explaining why we hunt *monsters* would go without probing questions.

"You're not a soldier, but a guard?"

"I am anything my King wishes me to be and serve at his command, whether to protect our people from criminals, wildlife, or our land from any threat."

"Are there many Deysik in Panthum?"

He may be Calix, but I'm *very* much aware of the Warlord who sits behind me. He leads those who slaughtered my people four hundred years ago, and who are also currently at war with the Deysik on this continent, now including the Ariportia.

"There are enough to be familiar with them." A non-answer, but I will not disclose our numbers. "It's a large country and heavily populated in certain areas. They are peaceful, skilled, and dutybound. They've long understood it's easier to ask for help than to suffer the consequences of Rangers by doing anything illegal. Only those mentally deranged commit serious violent crimes."

I wince internally at my veiled inference to the character of my people. *Who I am.* The Mother truly does have a twisted sense of humor.

"Have *you* hunted many Deysik?" Vasilius asks, breaking his silence.

"What do you think, Bluey?" I say with a wry smile, knowing it would infuriate the Prince.

"I think you were Mother's blessed to survive, Ranger."

I shrug my shoulders, pulling in the fresh air of the grassy plains, watching the sunset paint the sky a pale gray.

"It's unusual for warriors, let alone females, to survive an attack," Diedra says softly. "I believe it will take General Dread time to wrap his head around your skill set, Alana." This is the first she's spoken since doing her best to save the injured Azure Warriors, many of whom she knew.

Perhaps it's for this reason I don't allow her statement to bother me. I sense Calix nodding in agreement. I'm relieved they think this. I don't want them to know I'm versed in killing my family's kind. *My kind.*

It will take some time getting used to thinking of myself as Deysik. So many years were spent in denial after my mother died. My revelation during the Mother's Storm four weeks ago rocked my identity.

The Azure Warrior's deity—my mother's deity—wants me to acknowledge my Deysik heritage. I just don't understand why. Why would she want me to admit a part of me I can't access? There is nothing inside of me.

If there is, it's dead.

It died the same night as my mother.

Calix shifts his long legs against mine. His whole body is practically stuck to me. His hand resting on my thigh gently squeezes, and I sink into his chest, earning another squeeze, making my insides squirm. I want to be alone with him, but it will have to wait.

I'm not unaware the sensation is vastly different than what I was experiencing twenty-four hours ago. I twine my good hand through his and distract myself by glancing around at the silhouettes of the trees, both lonely and crowded together on the morning horizon. Besides the sound of horses creating a path on the land, it's soft and quiet. I miss my mountains and streams.

"Are you hurting?" Calix asks, leaning in just enough I can feel his stubble brush my temple.

"No. My body is tired, but my mind won't shut off. The typical after-effects of battle."

"Do you have many battles you participate in?"

Homesickness hits me once more for the Ranger's trials and hunts. "Not like what happened earlier."

"Tell me more about it."

"It's not something I'll speak about."

His sigh is weighted. He is disappointed, but he moves on.

"What does your family do?" he whispers against my neck, his hot breath kissing the sensitive skin, and I suck in a sharp inhale. He's unfair and relentless, and I adore it. This is the playfulness I missed most from *my* Bluey.

"We're all Rangers but also merchants." I wince internally. My father is *much* more than that. I shouldn't have added he's a merchant. Still, I don't want this Crown Prince who arrived in Faurst with intentions of finding a way into Panthum to believe our people are incapable of different interests or capabilities. The weapons we export are limited in number because the bulk of our resources develop items the King and Queen do not want the world to know about.

Panthum's Deysik are intelligent and thoughtful, and we've brought with us a vast array of knowledge that we've built upon. Our country has evolved leaps and bounds because of the efforts of our Deysik ingenuity in combination with the native population.

I want Calix to know the pride of my country, but I am limited in what I can say. Vasilius angles his head enough to clue in that he's listening intently. Diedra, riding with Canary, mimics the movement, eerily similar in mannerism.

"Really? What business does he run?" Calix keeps his tone light, but that's also telling. It seems he hasn't given up on his interrogation from the ship.

"Manufacturing."

Canary glances my way and raises a brow. He most likely knows very well what the answer is but blessedly remains silent. I'm eternally grateful.

"Manufacturing, what exactly?" Vasilius cuts in as sly as a fox stealing into the hen house at midnight.

"Things." I throw a glare at the brooding Prince. Where did the hostile Bluey go? He was annoyed every time his brother interacted with me on the ship. He should be putting a stop to this instead of encouraging it.

"What types of things? Are they used for illicit purposes?" Calix teases, but it's also a prod. Mother, help me, these twins. I want to laugh, but I hold it in.

"Are you looking to get knocked off this horse?" I ask, turning around to glare at my Warlord, who I'd wager is pulling an innocent face behind his Mother's cursed mask.

"Can you blame me for trying to get to know you better?" He angles his head to the side.

"You're not asking about *me*, are you?" I glare balefully, lips twitching.

I can hear his grin. "No. I'm not, am I?"

I flare my nostrils and face forward. He sighs heavily. "Fine, your family is off limits, though I don't know why. Perhaps your father would want to bring his manufacturing of *things* and merchant skills to Luminum? We would pay him handsomely, and you can have your family close to you."

He doesn't add, *"for the next five years."* I suppose he's trying not to rub it in my face, but I'm indentured. To him. His *Moskazi.*

The thought sends a pang of homesickness through me. Being rich in time spent together as a family, you don't realize how wealthy you were in love until you're staring at an empty vault. Having someone who knows what I'm thinking without me having to say anything is a comfort I'm bereft of, and I hate it.

"Are you open to the idea?" he asks softly.

I can't blame their intention to have access to local weapons manufacturing as their war is escalating. Part of the Ranger's job is to ensure our merchants who travel to and from Faurst aren't spying on behalf of other countries. The crown is very selective with those they choose for the positions, which means their methods are effective in keeping our secrets.

"I don't think you'd... get along with most of them. Besides, they'll never leave Panthum," I return firmly—a little dejected. Connor would love it here, though. He loves wide-open spaces to wander and get lost in. The Riband isn't big enough for him. I swallow the lump forming in my throat, which tightens to nearly strangle me.

I clear my throat, shoving down the homesickness, and take in the waves of the grass in the searing wind. It's somewhat soothing, reminding me of the mountain aspens when their leaves rub together.

"Why? Do they love their country more than their family?" Diedra asks. Not only is this the first she's spoken since the mourning ceremony, but she's also riding behind me and unable to pick up on my sudden change of mood. I wonder if maybe she needs distraction from her feelings.

I don't doubt she knows it's a loaded question. She's the better interrogator.

I internally sigh. *Fine.* I'd give them something to swallow.

"We value family more than everything except one—duty. They will not leave Panthum even if they wanted. Honor is tied to our very fiber. Abandoning our post would be akin to death. You will not find anyone coming to look for me. I made my decision, and now I'll suffer the consequences of separation from my family."

Calix leans in, and I breathe his warm cinnamon and leather scent. "We can always return to Panthum."

"I can, but you wouldn't be allowed over the border," I turn to face him so he can see my face clearly, even if he's hidden behind a mask. "I'll not be separated from you." Not again.

Despite my homesickness, I have the man I love and my friends around me. It will be enough. His offer is tempting me, and the thought settles in like a bird over her nest.

Calix's strong fingers press into my hips in approval as I *feel* him mulling over my words. He hums softly in response as if to say, *we'll see.* There's a difference between merchants born in Panthum to trek over the mountains, shuttling goods and stories back and forth, and a Crown Prince.

The rest of the day, the Azure Warriors speak in Luminum to pass the time, and occasionally, Vasilius contributes to the conversation. The

General has a quiet but looming presence that resembles a dark cloud. I don't know if I should pity him or ignore him.

I glance back to view the Black Fox, who chose to ride behind our group with her mercenaries.

I don't want to think about what would have happened had she not been there with her men to save my Bluey. I flick my gaze to the men behind her, trying to find the ones who reached me before Calix, but they all blend with their black masks and hoods. The endeavor only serves to distract me from my discomfort temporarily before I give up my curiosity.

If they're guests of the Emperor of Luminum and will be competing in Currell, I will speak to her and find out what the Emperor uses mercenaries for. Then I'll know if I have a chance of surviving my five-year tenure, or if I'll be going on impossible missions; an Emperor wouldn't want to expend his men on.

Either way, I'm still in over my head, bound by duty to my country to harbor our secrets and caught in a land that will most likely force my hand into revealing them.

I just pray to the Mother that the consequences don't end in death.

Chapter 6

We travel on until the evening when a thick, bubbling gray storm rumbles overhead. The air thickens with humidity, and I bite back a groan. The one thing I hate more than anything is being wet, though growing up in the mountains, it's something you become used to. I hope we can find shelter before it rains.

Calix runs a broad hand over the curve of my injured shoulder, gently massaging the ache. "Have I ever told you one of the many things I admire about you is that you don't complain? However, *Moskazi*, I'd take complaining if it meant you would *speak*. Don't you want to know about Luminum or Goldill, the Capitol City where we're going?"

"To complain means to focus on things I can't control. Tell me about Currell, and I'll listen. Diedra tells me it's quite the party for Luminum." There, that should make him happy. I turn to look at his face, but I don't know why I do when only unmoving gold is all I see.

"Better?" I ask sarcastically.

"I'm disappointed. You didn't ask about Goldill." His grave tone has me cracking a smile. I can never resist his humor. It draws me in like a light in the dark.

"Currell sounds more interesting. Does it take place only in Goldill or the whole country?"

"I'm afraid I can't tell you that," he says with mock sadness. Irritation prickles, and I whip around. "Why?"

"Because we're stopping for the night," he says as he halts his horse and dismounts. The act is so sudden all my air freezes in place. I watch as he speaks rapidly to his men in his native tongue. Because I was so focused on Calix, I failed to notice the cluster of mud huts hidden behind the small copse of trees, beyond our riders.

A group of horses split from our group, and I watch the Black Fox ride away with her men. "Where are they going?"

"The Black Fox is superstitious of the *Maage* and refuses to stay here. They will meet with us in the morning." He sees my frown and says, "There's no need to fear an attack. The *Maage* is deterrent enough for our enemies. She obliterated hundreds of Deysik in the last war, and it's rumored she received her gift directly from the Mother."

Obliterate Deysik? Much like how Calix exploded the Ariportia around him? How old is she? If she can destroy hundreds of Deysik in battle, then why does Luminum need war weapons?

My mouth dries over the news, and I move the reins off my lap, making to jump down when Calix appears, his strong hands gripping my waist. Desire spikes, my mind singly focused on the sensation of those hands—Calix's hands on my body. I swallow and croak, "What are you doing?"

"You've been riding for hours, and you're injured. I'm sure your knees are numb, and I don't want to see you land on your ass," he says, his ever-present humor rumbles down my spine. Heat flares inside of me, enjoying his brand of flirting.

"I'm used to riding for hours. I don't need your help," I challenge, ignoring all of my sore muscles, moving my foot to wiggle, pushing him back.

"How am I supposed to know you're used to riding?" he chuckles, watching me. Heat flares in my belly, sending waves of fire burning up my veins with need, as I remember the feel of his *very* firm body underneath mine that night in the Floating City.

I can't help but laugh. I'm going to punch him. I really am.

"Were you listening on the Ravager when I told you about my horse named Windrunner and the scars on his haunches?"

"I was listening, but I was paying more attention to the fact you weren't glaring at me with hatred in your eyes when you spoke to me."

I roll my eyes, flattered, but not wanting him to know it.

"So, you like to ride?" he asks.

I hold his gaze for a moment before jerking my chin, inviting him to step towards me. I reach out, placing my hands on his thick shoulders. I may be prideful, but I'm not stupid. I pick and choose my battles. And having an excuse to have him touch me is better than not.

His hands quickly grip my hips, and while locking eyes with him, I lean into his wide chest, finding the pulse fluttering rapidly on his neck. I bite back my grin, delighted he's not as unaffected as he makes out to be. I take my time, sliding off the horse, making sure my legs slide against his abdomen before they layer together. His fingers dig in, bordering on painful sending ripples of heat down my belly.

My victory is short-lived as pins and needles stab viciously when my boots hit the ground, beginning with my feet and moving up to my backside. I grit my teeth as I press my face into his chest, breathing in his cinnamon scent. I stomp my heels into the ground as a painful shooting sensation snakes up my sore muscles, all the way to my left shoulder.

"Are you ready to admit you're in pain?"

I grunt, and he sighs as if exasperated. "Stubborn woman. One of these days, you'll allow me to take care of you." His tone of voice brightens, "If you do, I'll show you to your quarters."

I chuckle and roll my eyes. "I'm used to sleeping on the ground."

Calix throws back his head and laughs, his muscular throat bobbing as warmth swells in my chest, making him laugh. Calix tilts his head in the direction of the trees. I am in pain—a lot of it—but his question distracts me.

"That's beside the point. What I'm trying to say is," the Crown Prince bends, lifting me off my feet and tilting his mouth against my ear to whisper, "Our quarters."

I close my eyes to take a moment as I grapple with the heady sensation of his desire, with the same feeling rising in me. I have to think straight, and everything is moving at a rapid pace. Of course, I want this, but I can't help but wonder if he'll still want me when he finds out I can't have children.

His demanding voice breaks apart my panicked thoughts. "Open your eyes. I want to see how wide I can blow your pupils when we finish what we started five weeks ago."

Heat explodes in my body, and I lift a hand to his filigreed mask. "Take this off so I can make sure you're the right Prince and kiss you again. Twice was not enough, Bluey."

Calix's long strides quicken as he carries me past the other Azure Warrior's dismounting. In my periphery, I notice Diedra's hand clasped in Canary's as he leads her through the trees next to us. The yellow-necked warrior must be familiar with this place.

Calix's head dips toward mine. "It will never be enough Alana."

I nod as we enter a small village, greeted by people dressed in purple robes, which contrast beautifully with their olive and dark skin. I don't find anyone who stands out as their leader, but the villagers bow to Diedra first, before repeating the gesture with Calix and Vasilius as he comes to stand next to us.

A knot forms in my stomach as something clicks in my brain as Diedra exchanges a few short words with the purple-clad members.

Diedra turns to face us. "The *Maage* will return in the morning. Let's clean up and allow me to reapply her poultice before you turn in for the night."

I don't have time to be relieved that the Deysik killer *Maage* is gone as Calix carries me into a small mud house on the outskirts of the village. Inside, the tiny building is lit by a large lantern, which illuminates the space to reveal a wide cot with thin bedding pushed against the far wall, with a single window above it and curtains drawn.

"Take a shower in there," Diedra points to a small doorway, and a delighted laugh bursts out of me when I spy a real flushing toilet and a shower. They look like the first ones ever created but they *work*.

"How's this out here in the middle of nowhere?"

Diedra pats my forearm playfully. "The Ikpeazu people may be humble, but not when it comes to their plumbing. As hot as it is, I don't mind, the well water's colder than ice. Thank the Mother! You use it now, while I gather supplies. Prince Dread, keep your hands to yourself until after I return," the Royal Surgeon warns. A puff of breath hits my collarbone as Calix snorts.

When Diedra closes the door behind her, I say, "She's your sister, isn't she?"

Calix freezes, and I turn back to face him, wishing he would take off his mask, so I can study his features. His chest rises quickly, pauses, and sighs, "She is. She refused the crown when Oliana died."

"I'm so sorry Calix," I remember him telling me that his eldest sister was murdered with her husband, leaving three nieces orphaned.

I can hear the wryness in his tone, "I certainly didn't expect the responsibility of protecting the entire kingdom. I prepared myself only to defend a part of it." Defend it from Deysik.

"I'm here if you ever want to talk about it." I know my words aren't sufficient for the loss he feels, but he squeezes me in appreciation all the same. He nods and gingerly sets me on my feet, his hands never leaving my body, following me into the tiny bathroom, where I spot soap and a towel on a narrow shelf.

"Diedra ordered you to keep your hands to yourself," I remind him.

I can hear his grin, when he asks in a low tone, "You like to follow orders?"

Blushing from my roots to my toes, it causes my wounds to throb, and I groan. He's going to give me a heart attack.

"Remember, no questions about my scars." I swallow as I stare at the man I love. He steps forward, and I hold up a hand. "Take off your helmet. I can't do this if I can't see your face."

Ever so slowly, he lifts those scar-flecked hands to his golden helmet and mantle of power, lifting it from his head.

The sight of his handsome face in the bathroom's candlelight nearly brings me to my knees. I forgot how devastating he is. The top of his blonde hair, shorn so closely on the sides that it beads with sweat, his sharp turquoise eyes hold mine with an intensity that sends my heart racing with need. His jaw is rough with stubble, and my hands ache to pull him towards me.

I clear my throat and unwind the bandage from my face. My heart pounds in my chest, and I fear for my ribs as the filthy, bloody, grit-covered bandage falls away. His eyes rove over my face, and it's as if he is touching me.

I smile nervously. "You're staring. Is it bad?"

I lift my fingers to my face, dipping my head sideways. Like lightning, he gently encircles my wrists, stopping me from touching my wounds. His jaw clenches, and his throat bobs as his eyes narrow on mine in a fierce frown.

"Nothing will ever remove the hunger inside me that aches for you. *Nothing.* You ensnared me, Alana, and I am yours until the Mother takes me."

Wet warmth slides down my cheeks, and I inhale with a shaky breath. I've never felt more loved in my life. He said it once before on Nash's ship, but now we're free from the unknown. I'm willing to dive into the ocean of his eyes, his hope, his possibility and drown.

He wordlessly helps strip me of my sweat-crusted Uria clothing, making sure to hold my gaze, never letting go. Gently guiding me into the shower, he pulls the lever for the water. I gasp when the blessed cold water falls over my heated body and find myself fascinated with the look of voraciousness growing in intensity. He begins to speak in Luminum in rich deep tones causing my breaths to exhale out, shallow and hot.

Without breaking eye contact, he picks up the lavender-scented soap, lathers it with the washcloth, and begins the sensuous task of washing my body, all the while speaking in Luminum. His fingers send shivers through me as they slide up and down in gentle strokes, cleaning away the dirt, blood, and grime of battle before moving to my limbs in breathless torture. Heat builds underneath my skin, and I swallow, trying to control my desire, but it's a war I won't win.

My thoughts are consumed by this Warlord. He terrified me, pushed and pulled me until I attacked, and he loved every minute of it because he was testing me. He wanted to see what I would do in the face of the unknown. On the Ravager, I was trapped with death every waking minute of every day, forced to kill people in cages. Here, I have the freedom to fight in the open and move as freely as I can.

I wonder if Calix will ever know the real me and still desire me the way he does now.

When he is done, he cradles my neck, pushing with his thumbs under my chin, guiding me to lean my head back. I can't help the groan that escapes me as cold water surges over my hair. His face becomes pained, but he continues to speak through clenched teeth, and I want nothing more than to drag him into this shower, but there's barely any room for one person, let alone two.

I sag as the water provides rapacious relief, rinsing away death and the smoke of burned bodies. Flowing water courses over my face for a moment. I sense Calix's searing gaze remain on my face as he gently scrubs my forehead, nose, cheeks and jaw avoiding my injuries, allowing the water to debride the wound. Diedra told me to expect stitches when we reached the fortress.

Calix's hands gently guide me to turn around before sliding into my hair, his strong fingers massaging my scalp, building up a mountain of suds. I savor his hands on my body and ache to be with him when I'm not injured and hurting. His hands work in my hair for a few more minutes.

"You have no idea how long I dreamed of doing this." His voice is lilting and soft. A whisper against my skin as he guides me back under the spray to rinse before shutting off the water, leading me out, drying my hair with the towel before wrapping it around my body.

A soft female voice breaks through our moment. "Alana, I'm ready for you."

Calix curses under his breath and kisses my injured shoulder with feather light lips before I feel a burst of warm air. I turn, watching his broad form escape the small hut.

On the bed sits Diedra, freshly bathed and in a deep purple robe, her long braids falling over her shoulder. She smiles and motions for me towards her, where she picks up a similar robe and helps me out of the towel and into the robe.

Next to her is a pile of medical supplies. It's not just the dim light but rather the events in the last thirty hours weighing on my new friend. Calix's sister. Though their coloring is vastly different, they have the same eyes and commanding presence. But what gave it away was the villagers bowing to her.

"I'm sorry you had to live through an attack like that." I know she did her best to patch up the injured, including trying to save two before they bled out.

She gives me a sad smile. "Thank you. It puts things into perspective I hadn't realized before now." She shakes her head, clearing out the heavy tone in the hut. "Now, tell me about how you and Prince Dread met. I heard you two had quite the adventure crossing the sea."

I chuckle and tell her the story as she mixes up a more potent poultice and applies it to my face, wrapping my head in gauzy bandages.

"I'm sure Prince Dread was grateful for the chance to have uninterrupted time to court you. And he must have been extremely smitten because if someone tried to take my hammock, I don't care how much I like them; I'd flip them out of there."

I laugh. The sound comes deep from my belly, releasing most of the tension in my body that I hadn't realized I had pent up like a wild horse ready to break loose. For the first time in two months, I feel a genuine connection with a female. There's something about being in the presence of someone who understands, on a deeply rooted level, what it's like to carry heightened emotions in the presence of men that helps lighten the weight hanging around your shoulders.

"Canary saved my life more times than I can count, you know." Diedra freezes before she hums as if disinterested and begins putting her supplies away. It's not my business, but I thought I'd offer a piece of information I know I'd appreciate if I was in her situation. "Captain Nash told me he never once looked at a woman, let alone speak to one before me, and now I know a little of his history; I know why he did."

"Because Prince Dread was interested in you," she answered with tear-filled eyes before giving me a sweet smile. On instinct, I pull her into a hug, the both of us gripping each other tightly. She smells of lavender soap and mint. For all her luscious curves, she's strong.

"He must have felt hope for the first time in years, seeing Calix, knowing it could potentially lead him to you."

"You're a fire jewel, Alana." She laughs suddenly, and her smile sparkles as brightly as diamonds in the sun. "Currell will be so much fun with you. My favorite part is witnessing the matchmakers at work."

With quick fingers she brushes my hair and braids my long brown hair into two plaits.

"Why do you call him Prince Dread and not Calix?"

She frowns and opens her mouth before closing it again. "Out of respect. Only those close to the Crown Prince are allowed use of his given name."

Her explanation doesn't make sense, but the customs in Luminum are unfamiliar to me, proven when I asked about the masks. There are some things that are known but not talked about. Panthum certainly has them. I can only imagine Calix witnessing our Deysik games during the Summer and Winter Solemat.

She angles her head and offers one last piece of advice. "Prince Dread is a good man, and he needs a strong woman to advise him of his blind spots. You're in a unique position to offer it with your indenture, *Moskazi*. Because no matter what, he can't remove you from him."

I nod as she stands. "Let's eat; the villagers have prepared a feast in your honor. The *Maage* will have returned by morning."

Chapter 7

The stars are splashed against the deep blue of the night sky when Calix pulls me into his lap and captures my lips with his. The bonfire sparks and pops, the embers rising to the heavens with a cheer from the villagers and Azure Warriors. I laugh, which makes it harder for Calix to kiss me. His hand skims up my arm, cradling my neck as he angles my head to deepen the kiss. Fire licks my veins, and I try to suck in a cooling breath to quench the desire threatening to consume my very being.

He pulls back, picks up the last piece of meat with his fingers, and brings it to my mouth, holding my gaze with scorching heat, causing me to squirm on his lap. As I eat what's offered, his eyes darken with unadulterated desire, and I chew slowly before swallowing, his gaze flicking down to the swell of my lips.

His nostrils flare, and before I can process what he's doing, his arm is underneath me, and he's carrying me to his hut. More cheers shout into the night sky, the sound diminishing as he kicks the door closed. The lantern, the only light source in the space, illuminates the cut of his jaw, the dip in his throat, and the love and desire he has for me. What we're about to do will forever shift our relationship the way a seismic event rearranges the landscape.

That's what Calix has done to my heart. I love him, and there is no one I'd rather spend the rest of my life with.

He lowers me to the bed, falling to his knees before me, eyes tracking over every curve on my body.

"How are you mine?" he murmurs quietly, shaking his head as if in a dream. "Demand every shred of my soul, and it's yours. Tell me never to see you again, and I'll rip my heart out of my chest and hand it over before I follow your wishes."

My breaths are heavy, my blood lines of flame under my skin. The depth, the intensity is consuming, and I want to burn with it. His turquoise eyes are filled with a love so deep, even the trenches in the sky above our world could not hold what I find there. But he has to know I'm not what he should have. Not what a Crown Prince would want.

"I can't have children," I whisper, closing my eyes, not wanting to find the disappointment there. "If you want to rescind—"

"Alana," he says in a tone I've only ever heard him use twice with me. Once when he tried to pull me from the depths of my self-destructive spiral and the other to get me off a sinking ship. It's the same voice I've heard him use to command his men. "Look at me."

I squeeze them tighter, phantom pain over the loss of a potential future with this man aches inside my heart, worse than the lakeroot poison.

"My fire jewel, my love, look at me," he says, no less commanding but softer.

It takes me several tries, but I push the pain down and open them to find Calix's face unchanged. A thumb strokes the tears from my right eye away. "You are who I'm in love with; there is no part of you that cannot satisfy every one of my desires and needs." He smiles and kisses me lightly on the lips. "Do you know what we both want?"

I nod, an overwhelming shyness coming over me.

"I need to hear you say it because once I have your permission, I'll not stop unless you explicitly demand I do so."

Again, I nod, and he kisses me once more, building the need inside my body until I want to split at the seams. He murmurs against my ear, "Say it, my *Moskazi.*"

"I want you, Calix. I want you more than breath, and if I don't have you, I'll die." I pull back and say with a fierceness that emboldens the confident part of me hidden behind uncertainty. "Save me from this torment."

With a tug of the knot, he unravels my robe and all shyness from my mind, leaving only a woman with the pure knowledge, she is loved. His eyes drink in what I was conscious of, what he respectfully refrained from looking at when bathing me by keeping eye contact the whole time. Scars given to me by a monster adolescent set upon me as a diversion attempt. Scars are proof I survived. I survived the agony, and I'd suffer from it all over again if it brought me to Calix.

The Mother, indeed, has a twisted sense of humor. A defunct Deysik in love with the Crown Prince of the Azure Warriors.

Perhaps I was meant to bridge the gap between our two people?

His calloused fingers touch the top of my breast where the scar begins and skim along its raised webbing down to my abdomen. His hazel eyes snap to mine, and I whisper, "Your tongue will feel better."

A wicked grin slashes across his handsome face, and he lays me back before standing, removing his clothing at an unhurried pace. I grin, crossing my arms behind my head as I take in all of him. I've seen many male forms, but Calix's is a masterpiece of masculinity.

He lowers himself to the bed, hovering over my prone form and does as I request until I'm devoured by fire.

***

After waking, I find I feel immeasurably better, proof of Diedra's skill as a medical professional. My face no longer aches with the sharpness it did the night before. Diedra knocks. "Prince Dread, the *Maage* has returned and is eager to meet your *Moskazi*. Time to make her debut."

Calix and I dress, kissing as we help each other into our freshly laundered clothes left outside our door. Butterflies riot in my stomach as nervousness takes over. Calix leads me out to where Diedra stands by the bonfire, light flickering across.

The villagers are about twenty feet away, surrounding us, and the Azure Warriors stand behind them. All eyes are on me, and I swallow as a short, gray-haired woman stiltedly waddles through the parting crowd toward Calix, Diedra, and me with the help of a wooden cane, stopping only when her toes nearly touch my own. I catch a whiff of sage, smoke, and promise.

The *Maage*. This is the destroyer of Deysik? She doesn't look capable of sitting and not falling asleep, much less killing nearly indestructible enemies. Her bright yellow robes wrap around her slender, slightly hunched body, and her regal face holds clear black eyes that slice right to the center of my soul.

"*Ah, Weok imma Moskazi?*" the aged female says in Luminum—or rather Ikpeazu, the dialect named for the mountain range that curves across the continent, Diedra had informed me yesterday.

I'm lost as to what she says and turn to Calix, but he shrugs his shoulders. I wait patiently for several long minutes while the old woman studies every inch of me making small noises of approval before she takes in the bandages on my face, earning a *humph*. Whatever her grunt means, Calix's lips fight to quirk upwards.

I raise an eyebrow. It seems she's impressed with my injuries.

With a smile full of warmth, she says, "Smart. Strong. Good for him." Her speech is haltingly accented as she stabs her cane in Calix's side. I pull my lips in, biting down to stop my smile. Calix's deep chuckle warms the blood in my veins, and I can't help but like that this ancient woman teases him.

Calix speaks to her again, and I spend the time admiring her heavy beaded jewelry, draping over her yellow wrap and gracing the top of her head in a circular design I've never seen before. I can't help but wonder if it's a mark of importance like jewels on nobles.

Calix says something and gestures to the Azure Warriors, Canary, and even Vasilius, who stands on the fringes, the latter, with massive arms folded across his muscular chest, his pearl mask firmly in place. The old woman shakes her head, and Calix gestures towards me with a broad hand, "Alana."

The woman pauses, and her clear eyes sharpen as she takes me in, she holds out a slender hand gesturing for my own. I place my right hand face up in hers, and her papery thin grasp tightens like a vice and pulls me in. She breathes in deeply, maintaining eye contact with me before she releases it out in a great whoosh.

Eyes flicking down to our hands, she spreads my palm flat by sliding her soft thumb over my much rougher one, running her nail down the lines in my palm. She bobs her head side to side as if whatever she's seeing could go either way with whatever decision she's building to entrap my future.

"*Reeve toka imma Moskazi,*" the woman says, bobbing her wizened chin, stabbing her cane into the ground, dropping my hand.

Everyone around the village falls still, and Vasilius drops his arms, straightening from his leisurely position. Diedra swings her gaze between the *Maage*, Calix, and myself.

My new friend turns beseechingly to her brother, but Calix shrugs his wide shoulders.

Whatever *reeve toka imma Moskazi* means, it's incendiary.

The woman shuffles closer and lifts a wrinkled, crooked hand, gently placing it over my bandages, and all sound ceases around me, leaving only a clear, gentle, voice, in a tone I had long forgotten, speaking in my mind.

Do not waiver and you will not fall. If you forget, he will die. Life is yours to return to the captive.

The *Maage's* paper soft hand slides down to hold my cheek as she holds my stare, unblinking for several long moments before she smiles. "*Moskazi* is a Fire Jewel, Prince Dread. Cherish her as she deserves."

Turning away, she waddles back into the village, leaving me stunned by the entire exchange, wiping the hand she touched me with onto her canary yellow robes.

It was my mother's voice I heard.

***

Sunlight brightens the hut, entering from the window above our bed, through the cracks between the curtains. I groan as I press my face against Calix's naked chest as someone pounds on the door. "Prince Dread! Our escort will arrive in a few hours."

"Be out in ten minutes," Calix calls with a rusty voice. Two hours was not enough time to nap. It didn't help we slept for only fifteen minutes before we were interrupted. I try to rise, but his arm wraps around my waist pulling me to him, kissing my neck, sending fire through my belly.

Fifteen minutes later, Calix pulls the brush through my hair until all the worked-up snarls are untangled.

He kisses the side of my neck and stands, allowing me to admire the grace with which he swaggers out the door, calling over his shoulder, "Diedra will be by to change your bandages."

I quickly braid my hair and am pulling on my boots when Diedra enters the hut, hands filled with supplies, her face flushed. I narrow my gaze, smiling. "It seems I wasn't the only one who was kept up all night."

She chuckles and taps my knee. "It was worth the wait."

She peels back the bandages on my face and pauses, a confused expression crossing her face. She pulls the rest of the material away, and I find there's no pain. I wonder when it stopped hurting.

"You're completely healed." Her voice is threaded with awe and disbelief. She shakes her head slowly, "That's not all, there's no webbing from the main scar."

I blink. "No webbing? How? I have them on my chest." There are no mirrors here in this village for me to see for myself, but I feel three ridges cutting down the left side of my face.

Diedra shakes her head, and asks, "When did you notice you were no longer in pain?"

I think back to last night. "Since you last gave me more pain powders. Could it be something the *Maage* did when she touched me?"

Diedra bobs her head side to side as if unsure, shrugging, "That's probably it." I can see she's still unsettled, and I wonder if it's because she's a surgeon, and the gifts of the Mother don't carry an explanation. I'm only starting to accept the possibility that there are forces of nature I'm unfamiliar with.

Canary and I make a pair; both indentured servants with scarred faces.

Diedra sits back with a thoughtful expression on her face. "Now that you're healed, we have time to do a little maintenance for the soul. Would you want to join me? Have some girl time alone?"

I grin. "You'll soon find out you don't ever need to ask that question. I'm always up for time away from the men."

Chapter 8

"I promise you will enjoy it," Diedra says as she guides me through the village to another small mud hut. It was after lunch when she informed me, she was taking me somewhere special. She closes the door behind us, sending us into darkness, save for a small lantern casting low light.

"Why are there no windows in here?" I ask, hearing a loud plop that has me jerking my head to the unexpected sound. Diedra laughs.

"It's a mud bath. It's good for your skin, and it will help our bodies recover from the ordeal we just went through. It supposedly has healing properties."

"It does? I've never heard of such a thing."

"I'm sure there are places or things on your continent that I've never heard of before."

"Mud bath?" I pull a face, and Diedra begins to remove her clothing freely, uncaring if I'm here watching. It's fascinating to see a woman be so confident in her skin. She moves to a handrail leading to the bubbling mud and descends to a spot where she clearly sits, the mud reaching her neck.

I can now make out the ground in the low light. Stones in a strange puddle-like shape mark the borders of the warm bath. I follow suit and hiss when the mud, bordering on skin melting hot, absorbs my toes. The mud is as thick as pudding and just as smooth.

Diedra smiles, "Now comes the fun part." She proceeds to take the mud and smear it across her neck and face. I just stare.

"Can you not feel hot or cold? Like is there a connection missing in your brain?"

Diedra's laugh grows into a deep belly laugh, and I begin to chuckle. I lift my hand out of the mud, with a glob of it on my hand, and I slowly bring it to my cheek, testing the heat radiating from it before it touches my skin.

I decide it's cool enough and mimic my new friend's actions, covering my exposed skin. She's right, it does feel good.

"If you say we're going to put this in our hair, I am now informing you, I will not partake."

Diedra's voice is relaxed and soothing when she answers, "No, the next stop will prepare you for what type of pampering you will receive while as Prince Dread's *Moskazi.*"

"I don't know what you mean by pampering, but if it's putting slug slime on my skin—"

"Why would we put slug slime on our skin? They're no medical benefits!" Diedra flicks mud at me, and I feel some land in my hair, and I smile. She breaks out laughing, catching onto my joke. "You're a tease!"

"Don't tell Vasilius, or it will ruin my fun with him."

Diedra sobers, and my laughter dies down as a pang runs through me. "I'm sorry. I understand he's in a difficult position."

"You have no idea, Alana. He's been holding up, not just those he loves but the rest of Luminum. He's doing the best he can."

"How can he hold up Luminum if he was gone for three years?" I ask, a little bit of bitterness rising. Calix has been searching for him for that long. Diedra doesn't answer, and I sigh, "He just makes it so easy. It's going to be hard to resist."

She agrees with a slight nod of her head, unable to move as the mud begins to dry. It feels so good to be able to rest and laugh with Diedra. I rest my head where there are slight dips in the outcropping of the ledge. "May I ask why the shape is the way it is? Is this man-made?"

"It's the location of a fallen general from the ancient battle between the Mother and Ertune. No one knows why the mud is this way but—" She stops talking when she takes in my horrified, widened eyes before laughing, cracking the mud on her face.

"You're worse than me!" I chuckle and flick mud back at her, hitting the piled knot of braids on top of her head.

"You made it so easy!"

"Ignorance will do it!" My laughter grows until tears flow down my face, and then the thoughts of the battle and loss hit me like Drake's punch to my gut. Diedra sits quietly, tears of her own coursing down her cheeks, cutting rivers through the mud. I suppose what bothered me was less about what I witnessed in the fight and more that my family wasn't with me to comfort me in the way I was familiar.

"Does it ever bother you, after battle? Or stay with you?" I ask after I collect myself.

"Always. There isn't a single person it doesn't alter. Some are affected worse than others. We have trained assistants who can talk to you if you wish."

I shake my head. "I have Calix."

"For which I'm grateful. Don't go too easy on him. Like the *Maage* said, you're good for him."

The *Maage*.

The old woman still troubled me. I couldn't make sense of her actions. It was as if she was pleased I was with Calix but disgusted by me. Perhaps she knows I'm Deysik, but a broken one, so she didn't announce it. I picture her wiping her hand against her yellow dress.

It brings up old memories from when I was little, of a few boys who would wipe their own hands against their pant legs if they touched me while playing chasing games. It was as if they didn't want what I had to contaminate them.

I couldn't blame them. I wouldn't want anyone to be the only one with Deysik blood but unable to Shift into their second skin.

"Why did you give Canary his name?" Diedra asks, effectively shifting my thoughts. "It can't be because of his singing voice."

I smile. "His scarf reminds me of home."

"I gave one to him the first time when we were five. It was before he left to begin his training. Then I replaced it at ten years old. We wrote to each other every day while he was away. At fifteen we vowed to spend the rest of our lives with each other. The last yellow kerchief, I made sure was Uria cloth. By accident, I figured out I could re-shape it with steam. I fabricated his scarf from the sleeves of a tunic my parents had purchased for me.

Despite the near scalding mud, I freeze as ice flows through my veins. Mother help me.

"Did Canary tell you what material it was?" she asks in a thin whisper. I shake my head, and she nods. "Yellow bounces the light to hide the faint shimmer you'll notice in the clothing Prince Dread gave you."

I know this too; I just hadn't expected anyone else to realize it as well. Or pick up on it for the two months I spent on the ship next to him, training with him.

Diedra gives me a knowing look. "Remember, I studied anatomy and noticed what it was the first time I saw it. No one else had, at that time, because no one with medical training was wealthy enough." She moves her arm, sweeping mud into her palm and filling in the empty lines on her cheeks.

She turns a haunted gaze towards me. "My family has never conceived what I've done Alana. I want to caution you. I've never witnessed this sort of push for entry into your country. We're preparing for war, and we intend to win, and that type of determination can breed irrational liability. Do you understand what I'm saying?"

I nod. Luminum needs Uria Cloth. They may not know *what* it is made out of, but Diedra does, and it scares her, as it should. She's also heavily implying that their Azure Warriors will breach our borders if diplomacy is futile.

"It was what kept him alive in the Red City Pits. I hated him for his betrayal, and I was glad he suffered." She sucks in a breath and closes her eyes. "How wrong I was."

I didn't speak or pry more confessions or admissions from her. She'd finish talking when she's ready.

It just isn't today.

My mind whirls with all she's told me. Luminum wants more of Panthum's goods; there's just one problem. Diplomacy will never work because Panthum's King and Queen have deep-rooted beliefs. Materials may leave the country but not its people or its processes. It doesn't matter that Fidir is the first Royal to want to leave and explore.

Some rules of law cannot be broken when tied to anchors far heavier than a single person's wishes.

***

After rinsing the mud off, I feel physically rejuvenated. My mind is still spinning, but I set it aside and focus on what's ahead of me. Five years as a mercenary in Luminum, currently in conflict with Deysik and Ariportia.

When we leave the cool shade of the hut, I find over a hundred mounted Azure Warriors surrounding the village, armed to the brim. A child hands us large leaf platters of food, before running to the group of children laughing out in the field.

As I eat the marinated goat, salad, and vegetables, I track the kit away from the Blueys and smile, my cheeks and brow free of pain as well as tighter. I watch the pearl and golden-masked Princes play with the village children. Vasilius tosses something curved into the air only to have it come flying back to him, his swift hands snatching it out of the air to squeals of delight. Small arms reach up to grab it with one succeeding. The kit runs off, throwing it in the air, and the other colorfully clad children follow.

A pang hits me, I'll never be able to have children, but I decide not to dwell on it. All I need is Calix. As if feeling my eyes on him, he turns, catching me with a bright smile, sending my stomach flipping over itself. His grin falls when his eyes settle on my fresh scars. He jogs over, pulling me into a searing kiss. I melt against him as his soft lips move to feather-light kisses over my three scars.

He tucks me under his chin, holding me tightly, and I study the object the children are bringing back to Vasilius to launch in the air, trying to figure out the simple mechanics of the wood.

"What's it called?" It's curved like a bowed triangle, tapered on both ends in opposite directions of the blade.

"A boomerang," he explains, releasing me to rush forward to snatch it out of the air before the kits can. With a powerful throw, he launches it, and the children giggle and scream with excitement.

"Get ready to catch it," he calls.

"No!" I yelp and duck, dropping my empty leaf platter. The children roll with laughter, and I join in, my ribs no longer sore as I chase a few of the kits, tickling their sides once I reach them, trying to understand the language they speak as they chatter at me, telling me stories and things I have no hope of figuring out. After a few minutes I return to Calix.

"You feel better," he says, pulling me to him once more, whispering against the sensitive shell of my ear, sending shivers of desire through me. "Ride next to me?"

My cheeks warm, and I nod. With a look of pure male satisfaction, Calix slips his hand in mine, guiding me to the horses. I take the time to search for Canary, his intense gaze locked onto Diedra like a starved man.

We wave goodbye to the villagers and the children, the *Maage* is nowhere to be found, and we leave the safety of the village territory, making our way north, cutting across the plains.

The Black Fox and her mercenaries meet up with us but remain far behind the rest of our newly arrived cavalry. I pity them for all the dust they will eat as heat waves sear over the grassy plains.

It's going to be a long, hot journey.

Chapter 9

"Which province do you think will place first in Currell this year?" Vasilius asks his brother, and I hide my shock he would genuflect to speak in front of me.

"What is Currell?"

"Diedra didn't explain it to you when you were having your one-on-one time?"

"Jealous Vasilius?" I chuckle before I remember Diedra's caution. I sigh and roll my eyes. "No. We spoke about other things."

"Like what?" he barks.

"Like what ornaments she likes to put in her hair, what tunic styles look the best on men. How to slice a man from navel to throat without getting blood all over you. You know, the usual sort of thing."

I can't tell what his expression is because of his mask, but I'd bet a year's salary he's glaring at me. I grin and relent.

"You'll never get a straight answer from me, Vasilius, if you don't ask kindly. Learn some manners and I'll think about being generous with my complicity."

"You're a mercenary—"

"Technically, your father owns my contract, or so I've been told," I cut in.

A guttural sound comes from his mask, and he snarls, "And by law, *ours* to command."

"Oh, I belong to Diedra as well? How delightful." I grin, goading him.

Diedra continues with exasperation, "I rescinded my right to the throne and have only honorary status in our country."

Before either Prince can speak up, I ask, "What does that entail?"

She gives me a disapproving look but answers, "Perks of being a royal without the power to order anyone about other than medical staff."

I nod and stay silent, counting in my head. I get to twelve before Vasilius asks—I suspect based on his tone—through gritted teeth, but in a polite tone of voice, "What did she tell you about Currell?"

I don't goad him further and answer honestly, "That it's a cultural celebration of the Mother's victory over Ertune. Azure Warriors from all over the Empire compete in their territory for months leading up to Currell. The territories with the highest statistical wins per capita will arrive in the capital city of Goldill to compete on an Imperial scale."

I slide him a look, "Did I miss anything, Prince?"

"No." a short, succinct answer.

"Yes," Diedra cuts back in. "All the Azure Warriors competing are unwed, and the celebration is used as a time for matches to be made."

"Fascinating. Tell me more about this?"

"Do they not have matches in your country?" Calix asks quietly, and I suspect he was asking to protect me from his brother, who is leaning forward on his horse, adjusting his seat.

"No. Not even royal ones. There are other methods used to find the perfect partner."

"Which are?" This from Vasilius, again in a gritted teeth, polite voice.

"If they want to marry, they're put through three trials together to see if they support each other or push the other away. Their joined families decide what the trials will be."

"Truly?" Calix asks. I turn and meet his hidden gaze. Three trials.

What were ours? We've been through so many… The time when he was injured, and I stayed up all night to protect him. When I unchained him from the humble. When he saved me from the lakeroot poison. Even the battle days ago.

What more would we experience? A lifetime's worth, I hope.

Deysik don't matchmake. They *know* when they've met their mate. Baylor's daughters informed me, it's all in the pheromones; biology does the matching.

"Who do you think is favored to win, Currell?" I ask, bringing the topic back full circle.

Calix shrugs. "Toriey is the favorite, but I hear Teegu has given his men additional training."

"And what makes these men the top favorites?" I ask.

Based on their conversations, Toriey is a Commander from the south, and Teegu is from a central territory. Both are longtime rivals for the championship, with usually one of them winning every few years. The winner will be crowned the newest Champion of Luminum and placed in the territory with the fewest points—a high honor. One Calix informed me he reached his eighteenth year and Vasilius the year after.

There was only one who competed at sixteen years old and won. Canary.

"Toriey's men are closest to the Deysik borders and have more action experience than Teegu's, but I know that Teegu pays his mercenaries to bring Deysik prisoners to his Fortress for training."

My stomach sours, and I ask, "Is that why Nash sells so many mercenary contracts to your kingdom? Because so many die attempting to capture Deysik?" I know enough that no matter how skilled the fighter, their chances of survival are slim, especially with how Calix and his men reacted when they heard the insurgent Deysik's growls.

I had only a dagger and Uria cloth, not my usual gear.

"Yes, but you won't be tasked with those sorts of assignments," Calix says reassuringly.

Vasilius looks to his brother sharply, and Calix turns just as fast, and I detect they're having a silent exchange. Tension coils around the group, and I want to move on from the subject.

"What happens if you win?" I ask as I adjust my hood, making sure to shade my face, feeling Vasilius's stare like the change of temperature from sunlight to shade on a hot day.

"The top ten runners-up become Sapphire Warriors, trained to protect the Imperial Family for at least a year before deciding to take a prestigious position in the Empire or continuing their tutelage in war and battle, which takes years. But will earn them a higher position as a Commander over a Fortress," Calix answers.

"Is that what you two did?" I ask, knowing their full masks must have been earned beyond their bloodline.

"Yes," Vasilius answers. I wonder why he speaks at all; he's so irritated.

"The law applies differently to those particular warriors as well. They're able to physically harm women, if needed, under extreme circumstances. Their punishments are also more severe," Vasilius says before throwing a meaningful glance to where Canary rides on my other side, next to Diedra; his cool gray eyes meet mine and hold them with a reassuring steadiness.

Diedra cuts in with a sharp voice. "Despite Canary's past, it doesn't take away from the fact that he's the youngest Azure Warrior to compete and win."

Canary remains silent. I'm guessing he's at peace with his choice. He'd have to be to not react over Vasilius's slander.

"Maybe if you're nice to Canary, Vasilius, he can tell us who will win, and we can earn some spending money," I say. "He's more practiced than all of us combined."

Canary gives me a look, clearly saying he doesn't appreciate my praise, and I toss him a wink.

They launch into a discussion on the various territorial allies and gambling, which will partake during the next two weeks during the celebrations, leading to the championship week in Goldill. I should be paying attention, but there are too many people and strategies I don't have context for, and it all becomes noise I drown out. I'm sure over the next five years I'll become more familiar with who they are speaking about.

***

Later that night, while lying on bed rolls under the stars, holding each other, surrounded by the safety of a hundred Azure Warriors, I ask Calix a question that had been plaguing me.

"What will your parents think of me?" I slide my hand over his firm stomach, feeling his heartbeat begin to pick up its pace.

"They'll dislike you."

I sit upright and stare down at his face, seeing if he's teasing, and only find a steady, serious expression on his handsome face. I'm not surprised by his answer but just making sure it wasn't a fluke.

"Once we reach Toriey's fortress, I'll send them a message explaining everything. They will not be pleased you're my *Moskazi* because you are not someone of Luminum noble birth," he says before continuing quickly. But once they meet you and see the noble character and honorable woman that embodies who you are, they will love you."

I understand all too well the expectations of Princes and who they should wed. Fidir's letters lamented the fact. Yet another clue he wanted out from under his parent's rule.

"And if it doesn't work, I'll tell them about the *Maage* being taken with you," he says.

I chuckle and pinch his side, causing him to jerk away from me with a mock warning glare. "You may be her new favorite person since Oliana." His voice drifts off as melancholy takes over his expression in the firelight. The sister who was slaughtered with her husband by Deysik.

"She loved my sister too," he adds softly.

My heart twists in my chest for his loss. When my mother died, all I wanted was to talk about her, but no one wanted to except Master Baylor, his wife, and his daughters. They saved my memories of her.

"What was she like?"

He smiled slowly. "She was regal, dutiful, lighthearted at times but knew when to be serious. She took care of Vas and I, always making sure we were paying attention to our tutors, reading, and training. I was worried when she married, her husband would change her, but he fit right in, training beside us and giving us pointers before our competition. He was a friend to everyone, a wonderful father, and a masterful General; he would have made an excellent Emperor Consort."

By the time he had finished speaking, his body had hardened. The pain in his voice slipped under my skin and settled there like nesting snakes. I didn't like it.

"What are your nieces like?"

He flexes his hands before taking a deep breath and lightening his tone. "Pippa's the oldest at fourteen, Olga's twelve, and Vivian's seven. To let you in on a secret, they all adore their uncles," he says with a tender smile.

"That doesn't surprise me, seeing how charming you can be," I reply wryly.

"This will be their first time back in Goldill for Currell since their deaths. It will be hard to witness the Battle for Justice at the end, but it will be good for them."

"What's that?"

"An opportunity for criminals to fight for their freedom."

Something twists in my stomach. "Will Canary be fighting in it?"

His mouth thinned, "No."

"Why?'

"He'll be going on a mission for the Emperor."

"How do you know that?" I say frowning.

"Because I was meant to purchase a mercenary specifically for it."

I sit up again and stare at him. Me. He paid so much for both of us. Did Nash know this?

I can't imagine he would because, for as horrible as Nash is at times, he clearly was fond of Canary. I glance to where Canary sits with Diedra, quietly whispering to each other and laughing. My friend's scarred face is twisted into that beautiful grin I had worked so hard for but came so easily in Diedra's presence. Everything in me rebels.

"You can't ask to send him, Bluey." My voice is low and dangerous.

"I don't plan to, but it's going to take time to figure out a way out of this mess."

"What mess?" I whisper hiss, glaring at him. "I didn't ask you to pay so much money for us—"

"Money has nothing to do with it, but rather my father's feelings over the Sapphire Warrior who abandoned his post and led to his brother and his family's death. Some actions can never be forgiven. When you take the position of Sapphire Warrior, you are held to a higher standard, and Canary knew that. I'm asking you not to say anything until I come up with a solution."

I work to control my anger as we silently hold each other's gaze for several long moments. When I feel Diedra's and then Canary's notice, I relent and nod sharply, looking away up to the stars and swirling god galaxy above, clenching my teeth. I'm infinitely irritated over the guilt that creeps up over having Canary unwittingly take my position for the assignment simply because I'm Calix's *Moskazi*.

"Why do you do it? The Battle for Justice?" I shift back, so I can see him better, bending my elbow to rest my head on my hand.

"They do it for the sake of the Mother. She wants peace for all her children—or so the Mother's Monks say—but also demands justice from those who have wronged innocents."

"And the Azure Warrior's give it?" My voice turns slightly bitter.

He frowns. "No. The other people in the fight do."

"And how's it won?" I swallow knowing I won't like the answer.

"Last one standing," he says with finality.

"How are you eliminated?" I breathe. "First blood?"

"Yes, but most don't stop there—most *won't* stop until everyone's dead."

I need to confirm my suspicions. "What criminals would risk it?"

Calix muscles flex. "Deysik. They're given a choice to stay in prison and wait to be executed or fight. It shows the world what happens if there isn't order or defense for those who can't defend themselves. Chaos and death. What Ertune desired most," he answers. "I know the Deysik here aren't like the Deysik you're used to, but after my uncle and his family's murder, and especially after Oliana and her husband, we had to stop it."

Sickness roils in my stomach. "Where's the mercy in that?"

"Where's *their* mercy for their victims?" He counters evenly. I inhale, not liking his logic. I can't argue the point. If the Deysik have already had their trial and sentenced, who am I to say what they choose to do with their lives after?

"Luminum is vastly different from Panthum, isn't it." Calix's blue-green eyes rove over my face, studying my inner turmoil. It's an honest question.

"Yes. We have the benefit of not having people who attack and kill us, so I realize I'm more biased than I should be, but it doesn't mean we're without our own hostile problems."

"Which are?" I hear the smile in his curious voice. I smile and say, "Our Rangers are trained as thoroughly as your Azure Warriors for good reason."

He raises a blonde brow and demands, "Tell me about this reasoning. You can't hint at that and not say." He laughs, and I grin, shaking my head.

"I made a vow, Calix, and my honor is paramount to all else."

"Even me?" he asks with mock horror.

"Especially you."

He pulls me towards him and kisses me quickly before pulling back, meeting my eyes. "Will your loyalty ever shift from your country to me?"

"You already have my loyalty, Calix, but there is nothing about my country that you *need* to know. It is all wants and wishes."

He rolls his eyes, "Fine, but I won't be able to tell you where the family gems are."

I smirk. "Who has need of family gems when I'm a fire jewel?"

He throws his head back and laughs, and I laugh with him.

"Well played, Ruby. I walked right into that one. Don't think this will stop me from wanting to know, what about your country made you who you are."

"Fair enough," I answer. There are really only a few things I can't speak of, but I enjoy playing these games with Calix and Diedra. Canary is more of an observer. He'll most likely figure out things faster than the others because of it.

I just hope he doesn't tell Diedra.

Chapter 10

By late afternoon the next day, we finally arrive and enter To-riey's Territory and its southernmost city, which surrounds a star-shaped fortress at its center. I admire the rounded and geometric architecture of the pale and red granite stone and stained glass-covered buildings, some ten stories tall. They're small mountains in their own right amongst the immaculately clean streets, crisscrossed with blue and gold streamers and music playing somewhere in the distance.

I can practically feel the joyful energy pulsating in the air.

Currell is in full swing.

We ride down the wide main thoroughfare, under cheers of people in the street when they realize the return of their Prince Dread. News quickly spreads and we're soon surrounded by throngs of people as we pass a large central square, which is cordoned off for entertainers, performing for the crowds.

Some people dance, and others eat from tables set with food of flaky pastries, sliced meats, vegetables carved into figurines, and towers of fruit with whole displays dedicated solely to desserts. The cakes are layered with frosting, chocolate, fruit, and flowers. I wish I had more time to study the edible works of art before we pass them by.

"Don't worry, Toriey will have the same food for us when we arrive," Diedra promises, and I meet her smile. I've never seen so many beautiful confections, and it causes the red crystal-like rock candy on sticks in children's hands and mouths to seem out of place.

The fortress entrance comes into view, the focal point a twenty-foot-tall iron door depicting figures on a plain. As the doors open, the sun shifts across the images, and I catch a glimpse of Deysik being speared by Azure Warriors on horseback. Above them, a woman wreathed in armor battles a monstrous man, their swords clashing fiercely.

Cold sluices down my spine as I brace myself for the unknown.

In the main bailey, we're greeted by the infamous fortress Commander, Toriey, a chiseled and stark older gentleman who appears to be in his sixth decade. The town mayor and other council members are also in attendance, wearing varying degrees of bold, dark colors. They eye me suspiciously, their focus lingering over the new scars on my face. I don't shrink away from their scrutiny. To give them credit, neither do the rest of my audience when I do the same.

Canary dismounts, assisting Diedra, and I find Commander Toriey staring at the traitor with piercing blue eyes that remind me of Vasilius'. Canary freezes for half a breath upon seeing the Commander before Diedra tugs him along inside, not bothering to stop for a proper greeting. The Commander says nothing, but the muscles around his mouth tighten, and his jaw flickers as his muscles flex.

He knows Canary, and he isn't pleased. But Canary's pause is more telling. He once respected this Commander and cared about what Toriey thought of him. Vasilius comes to stand next to Calix and slips off his pearl mask, hanging it from his belt. He looks so much like his brother it's startling at times. Toriey raises a silver brow, looking unimpressed, "Welcome back boy."

Vasilius nods, and the Commander's gaze shifts to me, and the urge to allow my familiar, cool mask of indifference to fall over my face is overwhelming, but I shove it to the side and instead deliver a practiced smile I typically reserve for formal occasions at home. I want Luminum's first official impression of Panthum to be kind, warm, and guarded. Even if they're lacking warmth themselves. When Calix glances at me, a flicker of assessment flits through his expression. "Join me?"

Vasilius whips his head to Calix and glares, but I ignore him. It's a request I can't deny. Though I want nothing more than to follow after Diedra and Canary inside the building, where I assume a room is waiting for me away from the sun and heat, I'd rather be by my Bluey's side.

I nod, and his solid hand touches my lower back. Calix introduces me. "This is Ranger Alana from Panthum and my *Moskazi*. Please use the common tongue for our conversations in her presence." A swell of pride rises through me.

No asking.

No cowering.

A simple order that brooks no room for argument. It's the order of a leader, and it melts my insides and heats my blood. *He is yours, and you are his;* Diedra's explanation of what we are to each other returns to my thoughts.

The blinks of surprise and sharp glances of the fortress and town leadership are expected—in fact, I've been waiting for their judgment of an outsider with a claim to their Crown Prince. The title of *Moskazi* seems to cause a stir wherever it's heard. The group collectively is brightly dressed in simple yet expensive clothing, their only embellishment are the jewels stitched subtly into their clothing, belts, and weapon hilts.

Except one; Commander Toriey is dressed in matte black leathers, matching his expression. He takes me in, his wizened gaze giving nothing away. He reads like a true battlefield commander. One who knows when to wait until the right time to strike. He's patient and cunning. I like him instantly, though I'm reserving my full verdict until after I speak with Canary.

A man and woman glance at each other with high brows and frown before the female Mayor turns to me and bows, though she doesn't look happy about it. "*Moskazi*." I imagine how painful the word must be to spit out for her. After that acknowledgment, she straightens and turns to Calix and Vasilius. "Princes Dread, we have an urgent matter to discuss. There was a Deysik attack three days ago. Fifteen people have been killed, including four children."

The news twists my stomach in knots, and Calix nods gravely. I, along with the group of men and women, move inside the fortress, and cold air blasts over me in instant relief. Their cooling system is similar to the Red City's Master's throne room.

I take in the peaked arches, blue mosaic tile on the floor, and potted plants lining the wide hallways. It's beyond impressive. Azure Warriors and servants are everywhere, busy preparing for the winners' journey to Goldill with us in two days.

We move into a large room with a massive oval table and padded chairs surrounding it. Calix pulls a chair out for me in the center of the table with him on my left and Vasilius next to him. Despite having ridden for hours, I sink into the chair and hold back a groan of comfort.

Once everyone is settled, Vasilius says in a confident, serious voice, focusing intently on the Mayor. "Tell us what happened."

The Mayor responds, "The attack took place in the early hours of the morning while the families were asleep in their beds. Those cursed Deysik fled before our men arrived, but they tracked the insurgents back to the base along the border, ten leagues from here, before they were forced to turn back as one of their patrols spotted them."

She shifts slightly, flicking her gaze to my scars before turning back to Calix. "Every member of those homes was ripped apart, and the carnage was more than just destructive."

She dives into further details, and my emotions plunge with them. Hearing the gruesome details is all too familiar from what I've seen when I was training as a Ranger for the past four years, as we responded to Rogues on a rampage. My training takes over, leaving only numbness in its wake. Toriey's eyes flicker as if reading every feeling I carefully guard.

Calix glances at me and frowns.

The Mayor finishes her report, "It was clear the Deysik were retaliating."

"What were our recent violations?" Calix asks. I'm grateful to him for wanting to clarify.

Her lips thin, but she doesn't look at anyone other than Calix before she answers. "The homes belong to those who killed the Deysik livestock that came over the border onto our territory, in addition to burning their alfalfa and wheat fields on the Monk's farmland four days prior."

I tense and grind my teeth together. Killing livestock and burning fields is a vindictive way to treat neighbors. When you destroy crops, you're starving people who rely on those things for their income or food.

I blink when I feel Calix's rough hand slip into mine, giving it a gentle squeeze. I exhale my tension and sense his shoulders relax; I'm relieved

I can remove one worry from his mind. I'm curious how this situation will play out.

Vasilius speaks. "How are the families nearby holding up? What assistance has been provided, and what else can we give them that may have been overlooked?"

Toriey straightens taller. "Our protocols have been followed through, along with grief responders made available in addition to their appointments with the families."

Calix continues to ask thoughtful questions about the families in the community, those injured, and the people there to witness the attack in tandem with his brother.

Removing my own bias from the issue and Vasilius's attitude towards me, I ponder the facts and come to the conclusion that this is the tip of a mountain of burden Calix carries, and I love him all the more for his genuine interest and awareness of his people. He and—I grudgingly admit, Vasilius—aren't absent rulers, but ones who are involved and follow up on problems rather than blindly trusting the job will be done and blaming others when it fails.

I'm hit with stark clarity, what a poor ruler the King and Queen of Panthum are.

After three hours of meetings that are both intriguing and make my eyes want to bleed, we move straight to the dining hall with no break. I remind myself that I'm living their customs, and a guest of their country, therefore I should not complain. I've been made to endure physical hardships for extended periods of time, hours long meetings should not eliminate all practice of placidity.

At the edge of my patience, we move into the white dining room decorated with macrame, dark wood designs along the wall, and textured fabrics and statement pieces. Only Commander Toriey, the Mayor,

Vasilius, and Diedra join us with the promised meal of culinary delights on the table awaiting us.

My stomach is practically eating itself and goes ballistic when I smell the cuisine. I refrain from touching the food as Calix once again seats me, with Vasilius on my right, Commander Toriey sits directly across from me, flanked by the Mayor and Diedra.

To distract myself from my aching hunger, I lean closer to Calix and whisper, "Where is Canary?"

I catch the Mayor's eyes drill into me as if I'm breaking social protocol. Calix whispers back, "He's in the barracks, reacquainting himself with all of his childhood friends."

Surprise flits through me, but I'm glad for my friend. He should be reunited. Though based on Toriey's reception I wonder how well his reappearance will go over with his friends. Calix must have read the question in my eyes because he says, "They have different feelings than my family," his eyes swing to Diedra, "Or her."

I straighten and wait to eat until the others begin. The delicate sniff of the Mayor causes Toriey's lips to quirk as he begins spearing his green salad with vinaigrette, candied walnuts, and apple slices topped with goat cheese. I may be a grunt of a soldier, but I was taught table manners.

"*Moskazi*, how far back does your history go? As a civil servant, I would love to know more about Panthum," the Mayor says.

"Our history pre-dates the Mother," I reply before taking a bite of the savory-sweet salad. A visible pause from the table.

"How far back before the Mother?" Vasilius asks roughly as if annoyed he was curious to ask at all. My eyes flick to him before resuming stabbing my food. His hand clenches around his utensils.

"Since the written word, our records have been kept on thin plates of metal and stone in the old language. It was difficult to read, but after a month or two of tutelage, I was able to translate a few pages when I was allowed."

Vasilius refrains from snorting his disbelief, but his face screams his feelings about the matter. I don't really care if he believes me or not. This isn't new information. The Mother's Monks have always been curious about the Royal Library in our Capital and have been given pencil scrapings.

"How far back does your history proceed?"

The Mayor answers in a soft voice, which is much different from the stronger tone she used in her report and what she labeled as civil duties. "When Ertune reigned, he destroyed the great Library of Luminum after his conquest. All of our history is from after the Mother's invasion and liberation of this continent."

"Fascinating." I haven't heard this before, but Vasilius clearly doubts my sincerity and glares at me. I want to stab him with my fork, but I don't think I'd be allowed back to dine if I did that, and I'm too hungry. Instead, I stare at him while I spear an apple.

He holds my gaze with a sneer and blazing blue eyes. I half wonder if he will start glowing if I provoke him to unleash his killing power. It's a compulsion I've yet to master well. In battle and with friends and enemies, yes. With Drake, certainly not. Perhaps Vasilius reminds me of my oldest brother, which is why I'm unable to rein in my incendiary side.

Their conversation, which I'm slowly putting into context, turns back to Currell. I have a thousand questions, and though most were answered in the efficient meeting, there's subtlety and craft underlying the conversation I'm curious about. Politics. It's fascinating because in some ways it's the same in Panthum but weighed differently on the scale of importance.

It's apparent, Panthum in comparison is equal in size to Luminum but half the population. Our Deysik make up a quarter of the total number. It was somewhat reassuring. We may not have a higher number, but we have a higher concentration of war weapons at our disposal.

"Toriey, I believe I heard your grandson won his competition last night and will be joining us on the journey to Goldill as your territory's Champion. How long have you been personally training him?" Calix says, smoothly transitioning the conversation to one more malleable for Vasilius.

Toriey smiles. "I don't know what you're talking about, Prince Dread."

"Perhaps our Ranger would like to spar with him while on the journey to Goldill," Vasilius suggests, and I slowly blink.

"No," Calix snaps.

"Worried about your *Moskazi's* skill?" Toriey asks curiously, studying us with a narrowed, hawk-like gaze.

"My Ranger's extremely lethal—"

"She killed *two* Deysik with only a dagger," Vasilius cuts in scornfully.

The Mayor and Toriey whip their heads to me, and I want to glare at Vasilius, but I just shrug. "Had to be done."

"Had to be done," Toriey repeats with a disbelieving huff as if the thought can't be grasped but studies me with more calculation than I'm comfortable with. I'm hit with exhaustion, not just physically but mentally as well, and I feel that invisible string of my patience wearing thinner and thinner.

"Like I said, she's lethal. Vasilius knows no one else could have killed them—"

"The Ariportia could have, by covering their tracks, and she's taking credit—"

I stand, shoving my chair back, done with this conversation, and the room falls silent. From the way Calix is fisting his cutlery, it looks like he could murder his brother, and I wouldn't stop him if he wanted to.

"Thank you for the company, but I've had my fill of this excellent meal and steak. Did it by chance come from one of the Deysik's slaughtered livestock?" I say with an inflammatory grin when I see the wide-eyed blinks from the Mayor and Toriey.

I don't look at Vasilius while I turn and walk out of the room, not caring that I threw all manners out the window. Baylor's daughters would beat me senseless if they saw the way I handled the situation. Not only that but knowing that the prick wormed his way under my skin with his disbelief of my capabilities, throwing his theories out in front of others I just met, reminded me too much of Drake.

I burn with fury and embarrassment as I storm down the beautiful passages, now lit with lanterns in even intervals, until my Warlord catches up to me, wrapping his hand around my waist, tugging me into him, brushing his cheek to my temple and says with a heated low voice, "Do you want to fight it out?"

"No," I hiss, still feeling annoyed.

"Perhaps I should show you our bedroom, so I can put you to bed?"

I look at him as his deft fingers slip over my hip, pressing into my flesh, causing desire to spike through my veins as a servant appears and motions for us to follow them, guiding us through the halls. I sag against Calix's warm body, eternally relieved he's not angry with me for my bad behavior.

His body is relaxed but exhausted, just like me. I'm grateful we're finally retiring for the night. I subtly pick up the pace, and Calix quickly matches my speed.

We arrive at a private room that's large with an immaculate wide bed with delicate cream-colored bedding. To the right is a partially open door, leading to an ensuite bathroom, and to the left are table, chairs and a seating area with sand colored fabric. The simplicity of the furnishings like the nobles we just met, don't conceal the luxury of the space.

Calix orders the servant that we're not to be disturbed before locking the door. Drifting to the bed I pick up a corner of the sheet, the smoothness unparalleled to anything I've ever felt, different from silk as the texture is too thick to compare. I wonder how it would feel tangled around Calix and I.

His heavy tread approaches, and I turn, heart beginning to pound in my chest as he saunters closer. He takes his time, roving heat filled eyes over my body, sending my pulse skittering faster. My breaths grow heavy as I take in every line of him moving towards me until his body heat mixes with mine.

Towering over me, his hands rise to softly rub my shoulders, and I can't resist the groan that leaves my body as he digs into my muscles. Concern flashes in his steady gaze. I marvel that this magnificent male could be mine and worry about me. It's unusual for a man to be so perfect, but I know his flaws.

I just can't think of them right now.

With my fingers, I skim the dip in his throat above where his two collarbones meet before rising to the blond stubble lining his defined jaw. Warmth seems to stem from those sensitive nerve endings, traveling down my arm into my chest, sparking a fire of want and need under my skin until I can think of nothing else but my desire for him.

He presses a thigh between mine, pinning me against the downy bed as he leans down, pressing his cheek, rubbing his stubble over the softer skin of my neck and cheek. My heart pumps in a rapid staccato, fire licking through my body. His breath warms the delicate flesh of my neck, and I inhale sharply, arching against his chest and urging his touch to expand beyond my shoulders. His finger slips underneath the collar of my tunic wrap, burning the skin at the base of my skull with intense heat.

This is a game we play. A game which pushes the boundaries of our desire, intensifying the inferno blazing inside us.

He pulls back enough for his eyes to flick to my lips, and when he speaks, his voice is dangerously low. "Are you sure you're fully healed? Because what I have planned for you, my *Moskazi*, will leave you still feeling me for a week."

It's enough to snap the leash of my lust. Leaning up on my toes, I pull him down to my lips as they clash and dance in a fiery and hungry passion. Mother, help me; I want him. Heat sears up my veins, raising the temperature of every part of my skin under his touch. His firm lips coax mine open, and I taste his sweet flavor as our tongues battle for dominance, our breaths heavy and deep. His hands slide around my back and down my spine, sending me gasping for air. He moves his hot mouth to the side of my neck, and I transform into a blistering inferno.

"Answer m—," Calix breathes against me, teasing my throat with the tip of his nose, but I cut him off, hissing out, "My answer will never change. Ruin me, Bluey."

He doesn't act immediately, and I realize this will be a long and torturous night of lust and need, sating our love. His calloused fingers mimic my earlier movements and skim along my collarbone, sending shivers down to my core. Forever a tease, he plays with the collar of my tunic, taking time to fiddle with my ties.

He takes his time once more undressing me with shaking hands, trembling fingers reaching for each other, exploring the expanse of skin, counting each other's scars. He lightly touches the three large ones across my torso, trailing kisses along their thick ridges. My breathing turns heavy as his lips move down my stomach and across my hips, and I can't stand it anymore. I want him *now*.

"Calix," I plead, and he kisses me before answering, "Say it, *Moskazi*," he demands, his voice rich and smooth like velvet against my breath.

"I love you, Bluey."

He doesn't disappoint, and our body's meld into one, and I know I'm not the same person I was when I left Panthum all those weeks ago. I've never wanted anyone as much as I do him. No one can make me laugh like he can. No one knows who I am as a person like he does, and no one is as attentive as he is. He has ruined me for anyone. He is not my enemy.

He's mine.

***

That night, I dream of a Rogue Deysik attacking me, its searing claws raking down my face. Dark, glowing, coal-like eyes bear down on me, and I scream as pain slashes across my skin.

You hide behind mountains and monsters. You hide behind your human skin. You're a coward. Do you think learning how to fight will save you? You think serving the Warlord who slaughters your kin will save your friends and family? He will kill them all. Massacre them in their sleep.

My throat burns hoarse, and I feel large hands grip my arms, shaking me, but I can't pull out. The clutches of the dream refuse to release me from their grasp. The dream is so vivid... agony spreads like blood across my face. Panthum burns, and a jagged line of fire and destruction spread across the Riband as though across my forehead, eyes, and cheek. My father's home, the royal palace, Drake's new fortress—all reduced to rubble and ashes.

Battle for Justice? It's only an excuse to kill Deysik. They're defined as violent criminals. Ertune's soldiers. Wild animals needing to be put down. Your family and people won't be looked at any differently. They will be treated like refuse.

The Rogue Deysik slashes my chest.

I scream.

A voice breaks through like a sliver of salvation.

"Alana."

The Warlord will kill you if he knows. Kill our *people,* Drake's voice warns. *Nothing will satisfy his bloodlust. Not even you. He will kill you. I promise you he will betray you and turn away from everything you gave him. You will be his prisoner. His tool. He will use you to gain entry into Panthum, slaughtering them all. Hagatha and Everett and their unborn child. Dead. Killed by your Warlord.*

He lunges for my throat, and I scream, "*No!*"

"*Moskazi*!"

You are nothing more than his whore. Nothing!

"*RUBY!*"

The hold on my mind releases, and my eyes fly open. Calix is above me. His face is tight and heavy with concern, and his eyes burn a bright blue and green in the candlelight. I squeeze my eyes shut, attempting to turn away as a sob escapes me. The nightmare is a new kind of torture, like a seed of rot planted in my head.

"I have you. You're safe. They won't touch you again," Calix's deep voice caressed over my cheek. His arms sweep behind my back, pulling me upright.

I wrap myself around him, not caring if he's the cause of destruction. I need him and want his comfort. The images flash again through my mind, and I shake my head trying to clear them away.

"Calix," I sob. "They were trying to kill me again. Kill my family. Please make it stop." I was babbling nonsense with no clear meaning. I was terrified of him and his warriors coming to my country, and want him to stop it from happening. I know he could stop them. He's never fought a battle he hasn't won.

My throat tightens, and I squeeze his strong body, burying my face in his chest, breathing in his cinnamon and leather scent. His hands rub my back, and one hand wraps around behind my neck, cradling me to him. He kisses my head. "Alana, I'm here. It's just a dream," he murmurs against my hair. "You're safe. You're safe with me." His lips travel from the top of my head, trailing down to my cheeks, causing my body to shiver and shift against him. I need more. I need him.

I fight against the seed of doubt and fear, scooping it out, ripping up all the black filth, and flinging it far, far away. I cling to him as my sobs quiet, and a sense of safety calms my racing heart.

I swallow back my tears and breathe, reveling in the soothing strokes of his hand across those little, thick cicatrices across my spine and ribs from the injuries I sustained in the Floating City. I slide a hand over Calix's chest as he throws a leg over me, tugging me closer. I can't help but feel safe and protected.

Feeling tiny thumps of his heartbeat increase in pace underneath my hand, causing something hungry and desperate to awaken inside of me.

My fingers trail over his shoulders, and I push him back down to the bed and move to straddle his body. There's something about being on top of him which settles my fear. It's a power lending to the control he gives me. I run my nose along his jawline, across the blonde stubble on his neck, and I press a kiss to the underside of his throat before pulling back enough to gaze at his handsome face and eyes, holding mine in the dark. My heart erupts. *He loves me. He's here. He's real, and he's mine.*

His rough fingers touch my throat, sliding down to the beating pulse at its base. My hands move up his chest and rest there.

"Make a vow with me that no matter what happens, we'll always fight for each other," I whisper, "That we won't allow anyone to hurt the other." His face softens as he nods before sitting up, wrapping his arms around my back, kissing me until I'm breathless and writhing against him. He pulls back and smiles in a way that shatters my soul and pieces it back together. "I'd think breaking free from my chains and risking death was vow enough."

With those words, the last bit of mist from a dream evaporates into nothing more than a memory. I kiss him, savoring his lips, hungry over mine and roving hands. He rolls over me, shoving those soft sheets aside, his weight perfect and heavy above me.

I wrap my thighs around his hips, pulling him closer as love pours through my heart, tunneling down to my soul, consuming every ounce of passion, devouring any lingering doubt about his love for me as our bodies join together, over and over, until we are both spent.

I believe the Mother did, in fact, know what she was doing when she sent me on the voyage across the ocean. It led me to the one person who matched my soul, unlikely as it was.

She only had to pull back the veil for me to see it.

Chapter 11

I wake long after the sun glimmers above the horizon, stretch across the soft sheets, and feel for Calix, only to find a cold bed where he lay hours ago. Did he train without me?

I quickly shower and dress in a black sleeveless tunic, cut for a female's figure, and a cream skirt I discover in the wardrobe. I make my way through the halls until I find a harried Diedra with a frown on her beautiful face, ordering servants to prepare her surgery. She's wearing an emerald jacket and fabric hat covering her braids. More people rush around wearing those same colors—medical colors.

"What's wrong, Diedra?"

She turns to me and blinks before taking me in. "You didn't hear the cannon's going off?" I shake my head no, and she continues. "There was a report of an attack party of Deysik just beyond the boundary of the city, and Prince Dread led a war-band to kill or capture them. Canary went with them. Messengers just arrived, they're returning and have a few critical injuries."

My stomach twists into a furious knot. Calix. Why did he go without telling me?

"Why are you upset? He isn't titled Warlord without reason," Drake hisses in my head. *"I warned you."*

I swallow, "What can I help with? I know how to triage."

She angles her head regretfully, "There is a competent medical staff here. I've worked and trained with them frequently." She squeezes my arm, "Thank you for offering." I nod sharply, grateful and regretful I can't be more help. I hate being left behind, and I hate even more not being useful. She slips her steady hand into mine and together we go out to the bailey where more servants come, carrying medical supplies as we wait for the men we love to arrive.

I used to think I was accustomed to battle with my experience and training, hunting criminals and monsters, but nothing could prepare me for the sight I witness as the first group of Azure Warriors enter the bailey. My whole body tenses as cold fear creeps down my vertebrae. Every single Azure Warrior is wearing full silver and gold body armor covered in dried blood and gore.

My feet are glued to the spot where I stand out of the way, and in the back of my mind, I realize they're exactly like the men from my dreams, butchering my people. My breaths become low and shallow, and the edges of my vision begin to blur.

Where is Calix? I take in a big breath, clearing my sight as I swallow.

Two men are wrapped in field bandages and barely alive with their entrails and partial limbs hanging, and once I see neither are Calix, Canary, or Vasilius, I move my gaze away from the medical personnel, including Diedra, as they administer help, carrying them inside the fortress.

My eyes seize on a steel wagon, encasing an enraged, snarling tiger, being shuttled to the back corner of the large courtyard. His orange and black stripes are drenched in blood, his eyes orbs of amethyst flame, glaring at his captors as he rakes his claws over the bars of his cage. I don't know how they brought the Deysik back; I'd have thought it impossible for the Blueys since they send mercenaries to trap them rather than do it themselves.

I can't help but keep my jaw from clenching. The sight is repulsive and goes against every fiber of my body.

What happened?

They're all too similar. Where is Calix? Electricity buzzes underneath my skin, snapping and sizzling, begging me to find him as my eyes pass over each one, looking for a familiar trait. I find one warrior who holds my gaze before he nods. Canary's gesture is familiar, and though a part of me is relieved, he's informing me Calix is alive; all the questions I've been staving off in my panic for news about the man I love rush to the surface.

I can't believe he would leave without me. Not only that, I'm furious he wouldn't discuss his plans with me. When *did* they plan this? How did they know the Deysik band was a war party? How did he know—

My thoughts are cut off as Calix rides through the fortress gates, whole, and maskless, bringing up the rear with the rest of the Blueys, and servants rush forward to take their horses as he dismounts and shouts orders in Luminum. My relief unlocks my knees. I take a step from my spot on the fortress, moving towards him, only to freeze as something large and black on wheels rolls inside behind him.

Unbidden words fall from my lips, "Mother, help me."

It's a cannon my family designed and engineered. It's the same ones the Giant Hunters commissioned. *The Waste.* My stomach twists into a knot as I realize why they're covered with body matter. The Blueys move apart, creating a walkway for their Crown Prince, and for a terrifying moment, I'm transported back to my dream.

He cuts through his men, his intense gaze burning right through me as his long legs carry him towards me. His gold mask glints from where it hangs from his hip, covered with blood splatter. He stops feet from me, and servants hurry forward, removing his armor, leaving a sweat lined tunic and black pants. Anger and relief mingle and twist together like writhing eels.

I'm self-aware enough, I know not to speak in anger in front of others, but the way Calix is looking at me like he can't wait to reach me, leaves me feeling off-kilter. It's common knowledge one of the strongest emotions after a battle is a renewal of life by way of intimacy, and with the way I'm seething inside, I don't believe Calix and I'll share that until we come to terms.

His eyes ask for me to reveal my hidden emotions, but I refuse. I stare back unflinchingly, silently telling him how furious I am. He must read it because the burning of his gaze dies down to embers. Vasilius descends the steps, pausing next to me before he takes in our silent staring contest and heads towards the other men, and I don't have time to wonder about why he didn't go on this mission. Maybe he too slept through it.

When the last piece of armor is removed from Calix, I turn, walking back to our room, making sure I'm several steps ahead of him.

When the door is shut behind him, I breathe in the floral-kissed air from a fresh bouquet of pink and white dahlias someone must have brought this morning before I turn slowly and drop my mask.

"Explain," I demand with a snarl. I don't care if I'm not in a position to be ordering the Crown Prince of Luminum to do *anything*. I'm his *Moskazi,* and if our positions were reversed, I'm sure he'd be doing the same thing. He pauses, and I can practically *feel* the energy buzzing in the air around him like a swarm of bees. A muscle feathers in his jaw before he speaks.

"After you fell asleep, I couldn't rest." He shakes his head and begins to pace, running a large hand over and back through his blonde hair. His energy intensifies. "I went for some air and found Toriey receiving a report of a Warband riding nearby, and I decided to command a company of warriors to execute them for their treaty violation."

"You must have accomplished your goal based on the state you arrived in, not to mention returning with one in tow."

"He'll be interrogated." He pauses to turn his head and takes me in. "You're angry."

"Of course I am! Why didn't you tell me, let alone take me with you?" I snap. "You left me behind! What if something happened to you?"

His nostrils flare, and I know I've provoked either his ego or male pride. "*My sole* purpose is to keep you safe," he grinds out a flash of warning in his turquoise gaze. A commanding gaze that threatens provocation.

Too bad I've never backed down from a challenge.

"That's not what the contract says," I return with a low, steady voice.

"I don't care what it says. You will not be put in harm's way." Instead of erupting in anger, he buries himself in a trench of it, and it only infuriates me further.

"I'm not one of your females that need protecting, Bluey."

"We made a vow last night. I will not willfully put you in harm's way," he returns, his voice lowering dangerously.

"So, I'm to work off my years on my back?" I regret the words as soon as they leave my mouth. His body flinches before his expression darkens.

"If that's what it takes to keep you alive, then yes, that's the position you will find yourself in," he snarls before storming to the bathroom and slamming the door behind him.

Pain spears my chest, and I turn away from the closed bathroom door before I pick up the vase of dahlias and smash it against the wall in a cry of outrage. When it shatters, tears prick my eyes.

Why haven't I learned by now to shut my cursed mouth when I'm angry?

I push out the doors, and three female servants scuttle backward, their eyes bulging with fright as I glare at them as I pass. "*Veshti yo sem*," I curse at them in Panthese, unable to hold back my temper enough not to speak my native language.

Nosy biddies. I stalk the halls until I find a quiet library with tall windows and find a seat overlooking a stone courtyard, centered around a water fountain and thick green vegetation. I unbraid my hair until brown and golden strands fall around me like a cape and pull my knees up to my chin, my cream skirt flowing over the side of the chair.

I brood in silence, turning over my argument with Calix, wishing I could have changed things. I'm sick of making the same mistake over and over again. I need to stop speaking when I'm angry. Why can't my mouth just stay sealed shut?

"Oh, hello," a younger male voice says, and I look up to see a man as large as Calix holding a book, wearing spectacles with boyish features in such stark contrast from his warrior frame it steals all my anger, replacing it with surprise. I blink, quickly observing the man-child, who's wearing tailored, expensive clothing that strains against his shoulders, biceps and thighs. He looks familiar, but I can't place him.

He appears to be my younger brother Connor's age, and when he smiles, he reveals deep dimples. I realize I'm staring, but it's hard not to when it's the first time I've met someone who isn't openly hostile towards me.

Introducing themselves.

No one has done that since Diedra.

"Hello," I murmur quietly, turning my head to look back at the window, trying to dismiss him without being rude about it. I'm not in the best mood. Despite my annoyance with myself and Calix, my curiosity is piqued, and I steal a few peeks to watch the newcomer with a bit of wariness. He's the definition of juxtaposition in male form.

He moves to a couch a good distance away from me for my answer.

"Are you the Ranger from Panthum?" he asks softly.

"Yes."

His brown eyes meet mine through his lenses briefly before going back to his book. "Panthum is nearly halfway around the world from here. You had a difficult journey and on a mercenary ship no less?"

Again, those brown eyes flick to me, and I nod. I can't make him out or get a read on him. He's curious and intelligent. But what I don't know are his intentions.

"You look like you can survive anything if pushed to it." The comment surprises me more than anything. The observation and his sharing it with me. He's someone of importance, or he wouldn't be in here. I didn't see him out in the bailey this morning when the others returned from their assault, which means he's being saved for something else.

"Why do you say that?" I ask, my curiosity getting the better of me.

"Because you haven't killed the pearl-masked Prince Dread yet."

"You mean Vasilius?"

He pauses and nods. Their lack of use of their Prince's first names will always baffle me.

"What are your thoughts about him?" I challenge, asking what others think of their dear Prince.

He turns back to his book, his eyes moving over the pages before he pauses and takes a breath, looking unseeing into the room as he collects his thoughts.

"He's an Azure Warrior, and all of us Champions hope to surpass the records he set in Currell." That's why he's familiar. He's Toriey's grandson. The Champion of this territory. Those large fingers slide under a page and turn it over. "You're going to want to be on his good side."

"He doesn't have one," I answer without missing a beat, but the youthful yet wise Azure Warrior doesn't react beyond a slow nod. He angles his head, taking me in, focusing on my unbound hair before looking out the window.

"I have a feeling you have a lot of friends back home?" He flicks his gaze to me quickly before looking back to the courtyard, the gurgling fountain, and the birds that land on its edge.

Again, I nod.

"You might want to try being a friend to those who don't deserve any. The hardest won loyalty is one that doesn't falter."

I stare at the young Warrior.

"There you are," a deep voice calls, and I turn to find Commander Toriey filling the doorway, grinning at his grandson, before his gaze finds mine. Didn't take the servants long to tattle about our fight. I'd have thought the Commander would be as wary of me as I am of him. I don't trust outsiders by nature. But perhaps he's here to protect his grandson from me.

He turns to the young Azure Warrior. "You have enough time for one more training before dinner."

The young man stands, his tall, large frame dwarfing the book held in his hand, tapping against his large chest. "Good-bye, *Moskazi*. Think about what I said."

Make friends with Vasilius. I'd rather fight an Ariportia. It'd be easier.

He leaves, and Toriey stares after him for a moment before turning back to me, and I wonder if I traded out opponents without realizing it. Toriey's grandson and Champion didn't ask intrusive questions but rather ones that asked about my mental and physical endurance.

I have a feeling that my impending conversation with Toriey will be interesting to say the least. During our meeting, he gave short, distinctive reports and didn't expound on any topics, and I heavily suspect that was because of my presence. He's cautious, and I admire that.

Calix is a Bluey I'm familiar with. This one isn't. I take in the details I observed from yesterday. He's shorter than my Warlord but not by much, and based on the way his tunic hugs his muscular body, age has not stopped him from training with his men. Another admirable quality.

My eyes cut over him, head to toe, noting he's relaxed with a hesitant smile on his face. "Prince Vasilius informed me you're familiar with Deysik, and I wondered if I might have a conversation with you about them."

I don't know what to think about the fact it was *Vasilius* who said I was familiar with Deysik, but my first instinct is to think it's a lie, especially with what he said last night. With those thoughts whirling through my head, it takes me a moment to process what he's asking.

"What exactly do you want to know?"

He gestures to a chair not far from me, silently asking if he can be seated, and I nod. He moves with the same grace as a king, his spine straight, fingers gently clasped. I face him and drop my feet to the floor and cross my ankles.

"I'd like to know what your experience has been with the Deysik of your country. Prince Vasilius told me they are... quite different than the ones here."

"Did he now?"

If I were a functioning Deysik, I could smell the truth in words and their intentions behind them, but I don't have those gifts. I may be a Deysik without a second skin, but my skills to read faces and body language were hard earned.

The micro-expressions on his face whisper he's intrigued and concerned. But by what? His sworn enemy or me?

"I don't know anything about *your* Deysik to tell you what's different from mine," I counter.

He smiles, and a spark ignites in his eyes as he leans forward, settling his elbows on his knees. "Counter Intelligence is something I'm keenly familiar with, Ranger Alana."

I angle my head. "Are you? Is that what you assume my question was?" I smile. "Is it not logical I'd ask for information to base my answers against in order to provide you with what I'm allowed?"

"What you're allowed?" He laughs, his throat bobbing with the movement. "You, Alana, are quite skilled; I'll give you that." He smiles as sharp as razors.

I mirror it with one of my own. "I'm a mere foot soldier, Commander; you flatter me." My heart begins to pound in my chest, and it's a beat I'm keenly familiar with. It's not of terror or nervousness but the challenge of facing an opponent.

"You are Prince Dread's, *Moskazi*, a position of significance; many would argue you're legally bound to Luminum over Panthum."

Calix said as much, and I wonder if it's because of their desires to enter into Panthum, or at least have unfettered access to our Uria cloth and weapons.

"Titles do not erase obligation and duty, Commander; I'd think you, of all people, would agree with me."

"Perhaps." He belabors a sigh and gives me a look as if he realizes how far down the detour I led him. "My sole role is to protect this Empire, and the fact remains that two Deysik fell by your hand with a single dagger. The Black Fox confirmed it."

I blink. I had completely forgotten about the mercenary and her men since I hadn't seen her since we entered the city.

He shakes his head. "It's unprecedented even for an Azure Warrior. When the cannon came back with the men, you recognized it as one of your own. That's the impetus with which we are forced to resort."

I blink slowly. "Then why are you asking for my help? It seems you discovered a way to deal with them." I brush invisible lint from my skirt before looking at him once more.

His voice deepens with emotion, but I still don't trust him. The sun's reflection illuminates the silver in his brown hair as the man's dark eyes flicker, and he sits back, his nostrils flaring before he says something I'm not prepared for. "Because I'd like to cease making orphans of Deysik children and sending my men to drug water sources so we can safely retrieve them from their hollows."

I flare my nostrils, not liking what I'm hearing.

Not. At. All.

"What do you do with the kits when you've retrieved them?"

He narrows his gaze when I say "*kit*," and his face hardens to granite. "We send them to the Mother's Monks townships on the border, where they are educated and cared for until they are able to find work in the mines if they don't return to their territory. Monks don't replace parents. And there are too many orphans on both sides of these skirmishes."

"My guess is there will be more after their fields have been burned. Is that something which occurs often?"

"Because the weather is mild this far south, they grow all year long, and right before harvest, there seems to be an increase in violations."

This wasn't something that was discussed in the meeting because I understood it to be a common occurrence, but I'd wanted it confirmed.

I inhale and switch my legs, silently agreeing with him. I shift tactics, taking a calculated risk. "To answer your question, the ones I know are loyal, kind, compassionate, and hard-working." I make sure to hold his gaze when I say, "And the Rangers of Panthum will go to war to protect them, should once more, a misguided attempt be made to commit the genocide of Ertune's descendants upon our soil. There is a reason why Rangers forbid the transaction of our weapons to Luminum. That policy will never change."

To give Toriey his due, he doesn't blink, but his face shifts into one that's softer and nods respectfully. "Is it a Ranger policy or Panthum's?"

The sly fox.

Canary's admission of Fidir and his family's betrayal, strikes my chest once more. The bastard knows how they worked around our legal contract. I shrug. "Like I said before. I'm a mere foot soldier. I'm not allowed to discuss our foreign policy with any authority, let alone divulge information beyond a friendly warning as Prince Dread's *Moskazi*. Any breach of our borders, well intentioned or not, will be met with the expulsion of those who violate our laws." I inhale before I hit him with one last barb. "We've found diplomacy is more effective than death."

I drum my fingers against my thigh as he studies me, taking my measure. If anything else, I respect this commander. He seems honorable, yet he is an Azure Warrior and loyal to his Empire, the same way I am loyal to my country.

"I apologize if I upset you with my questions, *Moskazi*. I wish to only understand better how we can improve relations with the Deysik bordering our Empire."

I rise and angle my head, "Is what you did this morning? Improve relations? You asked about our weapons."

"Weapons to protect our borders."

"You cannot control other countries' citizens, but I suggest trying harder with your own."

His powerful body stiffens, and his nostrils flare as his eyes cut to me. He doesn't respond because he knows I'm right and refuses to say anything about his Prince being the one who led the attack. It's a topic I plan to discuss further with Calix.

"Thank you for the conversation, Commander. This country is lovely when its neighbors are not trying to kill you." I dip my chin in dismissal, turn away, and exit the room, calling over my shoulder, "I've heard you're favored to win over Teegu. May the Mother bless you."

He barks, "Do you even believe in the Mother?"

I laugh as I round the corner. I do *now*, but he doesn't need to know that.

I return to our bedroom, hoping to find Calix. My conversation with Toriey cleared my head enough that I am drained of my anger for a reasonable discussion.

When I enter the room, there's no sign of the mess I made in my fit of fury. Calix stands at the window, his shadow lengthening across the marble and rug-covered floor. He doesn't turn, and somehow, it makes it easier for me to speak to him.

"I apologize for the manner in which I spoke to you but not for the question." His shoulders tense, and I press on. "One hundred thousand gold coins would feed my entire community for six months." I swallow, my throat thickening with emotion. "You have so many things I've never dreamed of, so please do not take away the little value I hold for myself. I've trained half my life attempting to scrape enough respect in the eyes of my family by becoming a Ranger. You didn't compare my worthiness based on skill." He says nothing. I swallow and plow forward. "I realize it's because women are revered here in your Empire, and there is efficacy in that, but it pains me that it's also not the intention with which you purchased my indenture. *You* did not think I'm capable—"

He whirls, a look of fury flattening his lips, his square jaw tight, before cutting me off, "Of course, you're capable, but that does not mean you should *have* to. It should not mean more scars on your skin when mine will do. You have survived *enough,* Alana." He exhales, and with it, his fury leaves him, softening his features as he approaches me, his turquoise hazel eyes pained. "You are *mine* to protect. You are *my Moskazi.* My fire jewel." He cups my face, running a thumb over my cheek, wiping away a tear that slipped out at his impassioned speech.

"I won't lose any more family or men to their unprovoked attacks, to pass by without retribution. I'll not *stand* for it. Not against the one person I found halfway across the world." He presses his forehead to mine, his blue-green gaze capturing my own. "Not against the woman who forced me to work harder for her respect than any position or championship. I'll not lose you too."

His voice falls to a whisper at the end, and I know he's thinking about all his lost family: his uncle, aunt, and cousins, his sister and brother-in-law.

It strikes me, what the immense pressure to live under the threat of an attack or assassination attempt would be like for him. I never thought of it in compassionate terms before now because he was once my enemy, and those people were distant strangers. Now, they're not.

I wrap my arms around him and pull him flush against me. There are many things to discuss in the way of differences and concerns over Luminum's Deysik neighbors, and I realize not everything will be solved in a day. I've learned all my life that trust, faith, effort, and action are what it will take to chisel away at the hardened walls of those entrenched in their ways.

"If you fear something, you only manifest it sooner." I push a lock of blonde hair back from his face before cupping his cheeks and pulling him in for a kiss. The feel of his full lips against mine stirs a need inside.

His hands slip to the ties, holding my tunic wrap together. With deft fingers, he unknots it, before warm air touches my skin, and his hot hand slides underneath my tunic.

"You have a forgiving heart, Alana, but I do not." He pulls back, holding my gaze fiercely. "I'll slaughter anyone who has ever hurt you." He kisses the scars on my face before moving down my neck to the white line on my collarbone. "This is too thin and straight to be an accident." I arch into him as his words, though promising violence, send a thrill through me. His breath heats my flesh as he murmurs lowly, "You harbor your secrets like a dragon does treasure, but I can be patient." He picks me up and lays me back on the bed, his eyes sliding across my body, mesmerized by what he sees. I've never felt more beautiful.

He scrapes his scruff along my body, and I'm gripping the sheets with my head thrown back, gasping for breath.

He murmurs against my belly. "One day, you will tell me, and there will be nowhere for them to hide from my reckoning."

His vow surges under my skin and along my bones until I'm wreathed with electric desire. I'd do the same for him. He removes our clothes and takes my body, all the while whispering his love for me.

He is mine, and I am his.

Afterward, he drags me into the shower and begins the process all over again, after I attempt to wash him the way he did me, two nights ago. He's insatiable, and I don't think I'll ever be rid of the need that spikes in my belly whenever he shoots me heated looks, promising nothing but pleasure for both of us.

No relationship is perfect, and I know it will only fail if one of us stops making an effort.

And it will not be today.

Chapter 12

At midday, I hold Calix's hand tightly as he leads me onto the vessel that will take us on the next leg of our journey. I glared at him when he informed me that we would be spending the next fourteen days on a grand steamer named Grace. It's at least larger than the Ravager.

Calix leads me to our gilded private suite with an adjoining bathroom and says, "There will be no waves or swells, endless amounts of food, and two large training pitches for our journey to Goldill." He laughs when I give him a baleful look.

"If there's a storm, I'm swimming to land and riding to Goldill," I grumble. "What's this river called?"

"Safa River, it's fed by the Ikpeazu Mountain Range glaciers. It cuts west before it splits, snaking north and south across the Empire. On the north Safa, after Goldill, it tracks west to Heviin, my seat of command. The Grace is a fine way to see our country without ever stepping on land. You'll see dozens of cities, fortresses, farmlands, and forests."

I sigh, convinced this will be the better, faster, and safer way to travel. "When do we train again? I'm curious how the Black Fox will do with their mercenaries against your Azure Warriors."

Calix smirks. "They're well paid for a reason, but I doubt any of their men can defeat Raine."

Raine being Commander Toriey's grandson and Champion for his territory.

"I was informed the Black Fox will be using the front training pitch on the steamer so as to avoid any conflicts before the main events. They're not allowed to practice together while on the trip."

I nod. It makes sense for the Champions and Mercenary guests not to train on the same pitch. Less chance of "accidents."

"Would you join me for our meetings?" Calix asks, and I give him a look, "For all I love you, I don't think I want to suffer through endless scrutiny and try to interpret comments made. It will only serve to confuse me. I'm not ruling it out entirely, but give me a few months to acclimate before throwing me in with the wolves."

"But that's where you thrive best."

I roll my eyes. "I wouldn't say I thrived on his ship but rather, survived."

"That's not what Canary said." His blue-green eyes sparkle as he crosses his arms over his chest.

"What did Canary say?" I ask quickly, wanting to know.

"He didn't actually say it to me but to Toriey and Vasilius," he clarifies, leaning a hip against the dresser.

I raise an eyebrow. He smirks, "He told them, that if you had three more weeks of training on the ship, no one would be able to best you, and that included him."

I blink. That's the highest compliment anyone has ever given me.

Calix pushes off the wall and strides towards me, pulling me into a hug, kissing the top of my head. "I'm off to my meeting. Diedra and Canary are waiting for you upstairs on the top deck restaurant for lunch."

***

"Is there anyone else with the same amount of killing power as the *Maage*?" I ask Diedra. We're sitting under a wide shade umbrella, eating a lunch of grilled chicken, vegetables, and fruit lemonade. Both of us are wearing white sleeveless sun dresses with eyelets in the material in sun and star shapes. Canary's tan, scarred hands set down his utensils, having finished eating much faster than Diedra and I. My friend has barely taken her eyes off of him, and I'm sure she's noticing everything about him that hints at what his time in the Red City's Pits and Nash's ship were like all those years he was away from her.

I'm sure lack of food was one of Canary's many hardships he suffered. Now, he's in a light brown tunic and pants with sleeves hiding the mangled skin of his arms. He doesn't seem bothered by the conversation.

"I've witnessed the Warlord's and his General's killing blow. Do you not have it, Diedra?"

I'm still horrified to think a single woman could destroy hundreds of Deysik in a single setting. It's a power that troubles me.

Diedra sits back in her chair, her long-braided hair falling over her voluptuous body and grins. "You haven't figured it out?" She glances at Canary who smirks. "I would have thought with how observant you are that you'd guess."

My expression falls flat. "She's your relative, isn't she?"

She throws her head back and laughs before propping her chin on a hand, elbow resting on the arm of her chair. Canary sits solemnly, staring at Diedra as she replies, "My fortieth great-grandmother, I believe."

I stare at her, knowing that she's speaking truth, I just don't believe it. She continues, "Deysik have heightened senses and impenetrable skin, but Azure Warriors have the ability to heal quickly. Certain bloodlines have other gifts, but they're rare. Like the killing power. I've been studying bloodlines and can't make sense of it. It seems to follow people in line for power, not necessarily age or gender."

"Does it dissolve with each generation?" I ask frowning.

I remembered how Calix healed rather quickly while on the Ravager, but I didn't think twice about it; I was so used to Deysik's recovery times. His was still slower than I was used to.

"It appears so. Oliana and myself didn't receive it," she answers before switching subjects. "How are you doing with the cultural differences? Toriey told me you refused a maid?"

I roll my eyes. "I don't need a woman helping me dress every day. I didn't use one in Panthum either, in case you were wondering. If a formal event happens to be on the itinerary, then perhaps I'll reconsider for that evening only. As to the cultural differences, I've been taught not to have any expectations when introduced to something new. That way, you can't be disappointed."

Her face falls. "Are you disappointed?"

"Aside from political tensions with your neighbors trying to kill me, it's been wonderful," I smile wryly, not admitting to the staring I've encountered from most women.

Canary moves his arm to rest against the back of Diedra's chair as she replies, "What a diplomatic way to say it. What about with Prince Dread? Did you resolve your tiff?"

Canary's eyes narrow on Diedra in disapproval. She ignores him and studies me curiously. Diedra is the boldest of everyone when it comes to asking me questions, I can forgive them because they're personal in nature. In Panthum we rarely have to ask because everyone can sense those feelings. Nothing is hidden unless you've practiced it your whole life.

I wonder if her skill came with her profession.

"He knows how I feel." The blank statement answers nothing, and Diedra smiles, knowing it. I turn to observe a passing town with white stone buildings with blue domed roofs.

"Would you like to know what I think of you, Alana?"

My stomach twists, and I slide my gaze to her. I like Diedra, but my protective walls immediately rise. Toriey's grandson Raine simply spoke his observations. There's something terrifying about someone asking if you want to know their opinion of you.

She waits for me to respond, so I inhale and nod, wondering what criticisms she will lay at my feet.

She leans forward and grabs my hands. "You're loyal, kind, passionate, and thoughtful. You were betrayed by your friend in Faurst, and it's natural to hold part of yourself back, but you're intelligent enough to know Prince Dread will die to defend you. You're a part of our family, Alana. We adore you. When the *Maage* met with you, it was to confirm what he already knew but what my youngest brother and I didn't fully realize."

Her answer wasn't what I was expecting. "What's that?" I swallow, a lump of fear lodging in my esophagus. A prickle of awareness creeps up my body, wrapping around my throat like a specter's hand. Diedra's eyes soften in a small encouraging smile.

"Prince Dread's success or failure depends on your position by his side. A royal family is only as powerful as those close to them. Your indenture is his excuse to keep you by his side, but by the end of it, he will ask you to stay. You will have to decide then if you will abandon him or remain in Luminum."

After a moment she releases my hands and sits back, winking at me. "You better choose to stay, or I'll sic Canary after you, and we both know who'll win that fight."

Canary and I share a look before I throw back my head and laugh.

***

The next morning, Calix, Vasilius, Canary, and I train in the rear training courtyard while Toriey watches from above like an eagle picking out his prey. He barks commands in Luminum to the two princes, and I wonder if it's because he trained them when they were younger. He completely ignores Canary and me, when we spar with blunt-tipped spears, though I feel his gaze on my back like a brand. Raine is training next to us, but Calix made it clear to everyone that only three males are allowed to enter the pitch's borders with me.

Raine doesn't let on that he's familiar with me or that we even had a conversation let alone his advice to me in befriending Vasilius.

Canary gives me a little nod with his chin, and I attack, whipping the weapon that I'd always choose last when given a choice of weapons, which is probably why Canary picked it. In minutes, I'm soaked with sweat, and my chest is heaving.

"Give her a break," Toriey calls from above, but Canary ignores him, slamming his spear against mine as I block his attack, twisting my spear shaft on top of his, forcing one side down into the sand, before cartwheeling over the two shafts, kicking out at his face, forcing him back only to bring my wooden dagger against his neck before he could recover.

He glares at me. "Cheating."

"Winning." I smile. He drops the spear and tries to grab me around the waist to throw me on the ground, but I expected his counterattack, being this close to the warrior who trained me to fight dirty.

I twist my leg around his, pushing him backwards and off balance, and we both fall into the sandy pitch where he easily pins me, holding a dagger to my throat.

"Dead." His gravelly voice echoes with a hint of victory. I smile brightly, and tap the inside of his thigh, where I hold a second dagger against his femoral artery.

"At least I won't be alone," I laugh.

Canary rolls his eyes and climbs off of me, yanking me to standing. I catch movement above and I find Toriey folding his arms across his muscular chest, a deep frown wrinkling his brow.

I'm not sure who he's more disturbed with, Canary or myself. My guess is it's an equal measure.

***

The next morning, with still no sign of the Black Fox and her mercenaries on the ship, Canary pushes me to train with Vasilius. Calix nods his agreement, and I brace myself for the acidity of the youngest prince before Commander Toriey pulls my Bluey from the training courtyard to have a quiet word.

With Canary overseeing our sparring session, the man who saved my life in the cage in Floating City has no interest in showing mercy. I'm out of breath and sore.

I love it. He is nearly as brutal as Canary.

"Tell me, Ranger, why do you want to train with us? You don't *need* to..." The way he dips his chin and the malice lining his eyes, his meaning is crystal clear.

I only smile and surge forward, feigning an attack on his weak side before I smack the flat end of the training sword into his hip. He hisses in pain, and I smirk, dodging his next assault, my body relaxes, moving like a serpent back and forth, stepping backward until I reach the edge of the pitch. I risk a glance at Canary and wink, all thoughts of listening to Raine's advice to make friends forgotten with Vasilius's innuendo.

Vasilius snarls, dropping his sword, and lunges forward, snatching the front of my tunic with his left hand, and in a move taking less than a second and has become second nature, I slip my right arm underneath him, grabbing my left bicep. Then, bringing my left hand over the inside of his elbow, I twist my right elbow up and over his hand to break his grip on me by folding his bent arm into a stress position, folding him over. Finally, I twist my body next to his and slam my knee into his arrogant face before slinging him to the ground, stunned.

Canary's cackle fills the room, and I stride away calling over my shoulder, "The better question to ask yourself prince Vasilius is, how can I not enjoy it?"

I hear him push up and spit out the sand I'm sure he swallowed, but he makes no move towards me. His voice cuts the distance all the same, "You're not good enough for him."

Canary's laugh cuts abruptly, and a whisper of movement from behind carries through the large room. I angle my head only slightly to find him seething in my periphery, Canary's blade at his throat, as the older warrior snarls in Luminum to the Prince.

"Perhaps, but I can be improved upon." Then I turn to face him fully. "You, Vasilius will slowly poison him until he withers into the man you've become and from what I can tell…" my gaze drifts over him slowly before meeting his furious, glacier-blue eyes. "I'd sooner remove your head than allow that to happen, because my contract is to protect him regardless of my worthiness. I'll have no regrets killing you."

We glare at each other, and I know that my response purges any hope of friendship between us. But I don't care. I'll protect Calix before any amicability or alliance in this country.

Canary steps back, taking his dagger with him, following me out of the training courtyard. I move to the deck railing of the ship, breathing in the morning heat. My gray-eyed friend moves to stand next to me, and we both rest in silence. I expected some resistance from Vasilius but not this much. I rub my hands over my face and sigh.

"You did well."

I glance to Canary before looking at the passing landscape of green wheat and corn fields, thinking about the amount of food it produces and the number of people it feeds. The thought does little to distract me from my worries. What I said was true. I won't allow Vasilius to poison Calix. He needs to know where I stand.

"He'll go and tattle to him."

"No, he won't."

The confidence of that statement… What did he say to him? I frown and look at him, finding only steady confidence. I open my mouth to ask, but Diedra's voice breaks the moment.

"What are you two doing?" she asks, walking towards us. "Hurry and clean up, it's lunch time, and I'm famished. Alana, it's your turn to tell me about your customs. We need to expand our culture in the Imperial Court."

Canary's lips quirk, and I glare at the man. He knows how much I hate dodging these questions. The woman is persistent and charming at the same time. I have to last five years and perhaps a lifetime of inquiries. It will be difficult, but not impossible.

Chapter 13

"If you come to one meeting, I promise I'll give you something you'll enjoy," Calix says from the bathroom as he shaves his morning stubble.

"Time alone with you?" I counter and give Calix a quick grin so he knows I'm teasing. He's gone quite a bit planning, and I know it's a strain for him to have me parted from him during the day. Yet, I'm keenly aware of the suspicious natures of the Generals and Commanders. I cross my ankles from where I lounge in the bed, enjoying the view of my Warlord's upper body that's been honed by combat and is capable of giving so much love and devotion to my wounded soul. I can't help the pleased smile creeping on my face. A white towel is the only thing keeping him modest as it's wrapped low around his narrow hips.

He turns to look at me, the morning light from a high window, setting ablaze his golden hair and the smattering covering his chest and arms. "As my *Moskazi*, you will be offering me counsel and a different perspective than my Generals or myself. I'll be able to reach a conclusion faster, so yes, more time alone with me."

I watch as his straight-edge blade runs up his throat, scraping across the skin I breathed in the night before. "I don't think you'll like my council."

"Perhaps, but change often comes with a fight and dislike."

He's not wrong. I stand and move to the floor-to-ceiling slider doors near our stateroom balcony. It's not Calix I'm worried about. Each day we pick up more Commanders and tension mounts, but what I've found from them so far has been interesting. They're subtleties with their masks. The more ornate, the higher rank, and Calix's is exquisite. Vasilius's pearl mask represents his rank as general in the Luminum Military. There is no other like it.

"I'll come with you today, but please don't tell them to speak in the common tongue if they're not fluent. I don't want to have someone annoyed with me because they can't articulate their thoughts."

Calix smirks in the mirror. "You hate being the odd duck in the pond, don't you?"

"If by odd duck, you mean predatory eagle, then yes."

His laugh is deep and throaty, and it sends a jolt of pleasure through me. Done shaving, he strides towards me, and I squeal with laughter as he lunges for me, pinning me to the bed and kissing me. His lips are full and soft as they work over mine, teasing me to open up for him before deepening the kiss. I sigh against him and wrap my legs around his waist, pulling him towards me. He runs a hand over my bare thigh and squeezes gently.

He pulls back from my swollen lips and says, "It's going to be hard to concentrate in those meetings."

"I'm sure Vasilius will find a way to keep you on task," I mutter.

Calix frowns and rolls to the side, propping his head up with his hand. "What do you mean?"

"I mean his hostility towards me. Will he ever stop doing it publicly?"

I lament his observance, but it's what makes a skilled commander—someone who pays attention to detail. I debate telling him what happened yesterday but decide against withholding information only because I want to be as honest with Calix as I can. I tell him about our confrontation, and he bristles, rising to sit up and staring down at me, his body no longer relaxed. It's as though someone dumped a bucket of testosterone and fury all over him.

"You train as much or as often as you desire, Alana. No one will dictate otherwise." His voice is commanding and brutal, bordering on vicious. "Your value to me is more than physical."

I raise a brow. "Really? Do tell, Bluey."

He glares at me, meeting my smile before huffing a breath. "You challenge me in a way I haven't experienced yet and impress me with how quickly you can decide on the outcome of a situation, I never thought possible. What you did out on the plains—" He shakes his head as if he can't rationalize the outcome of my killing two Deysik. "I never would have believed it."

I blink, not expecting that answer. With a straight face, I say, "Thank you, Bluey. Wish I could say the same, but it's just physical—" I peel with laughter as he once more descends on me, tickling me until I have tears rolling down my face, and I'm begging for mercy.

Once I can breathe again, I say, "I've never met anyone quite like you, Bluey. If you were a grunt foot soldier, I'd be just as happy."

His muscles flex. "You're happy? Being here away from your family?"

I sober instantly, but hold his intense gaze. "You're my family now, Bluey."

I hadn't realized how true those words were until I spoke them. Calix is mine, and I am his. He lifts my hand and kisses my inner wrist, sending want shooting through my veins. "You didn't answer the question, Ruby."

"I'm happy. My family will keep."

Something behind his turquoise eyes flicker. It's the best I can offer. I don't like disappointing him.

"It's not good enough for my Moskazi," he says, and my cheeks ache from smiling so much. "My darling, Calix, you spoil me." I reach over and pat his firm pectoral. "It's a nice thought, but trust me in this. It's better to let things settle rather than kick over a second hornet's nest. One thing you should know about my kin is they're resilient and patient."

It's not the answer he wants to hear, but it's the only answer I have to give.

It will just have to do.

Chapter 14

"How many times are you going to suggest a diplomatic solution to one that doesn't exist?" One of the Commanders snaps. Webbed scars run over his exposed biceps, and out of the new arrival of leaders, he is the most taciturn. When he speaks, I know it's out of his love and pain for his people who have been suffering from Deysik attacks these past twenty years. I can't remember his name.

"More and more are sneaking over the border. Reports from Red City are that they've seen a massive influx of Deysik sailing out to sea."

"Good riddance," someone mutters, and the others grunt their agreement.

The Deysik in Floating City said that there was going to be a gathering. I say nothing. I've already decided I'll only help these Deysik. I will not interfere in their conflict.

"Our spies tell us there is a group making for Faurst to plead with the High Monk to sway the Emperor to allow provisions and merchants into their country, but of course this is just rumor. There's nothing concrete other than speculation based on these few facts."

"Why not interrogate the Deysik you captured for information? Why are we waiting?" A low-ranking commander asks levelly. Pei is his name. Tattoos are thick and black across his exposed skin, eloquent and violent.

Toriey doesn't move from his position across from me, but his eyes shoot to me before flicking back to Calix on my left. Vasilius once more is on my right side, and we've yet to acknowledge each other. For the past two hours, they've debated the merits of the options presented on how to stand against the Deysik threat near their southeastern border.

"We already tried. We're waiting until we reach Goldill before moving forward." Vasilius answers, frowning in Toriey's direction. Interesting. I wonder if the two are at odds with that plan.

"After Currell, we need to send reinforcements to Toriey's territory. I've already sent—" he cuts himself off, pausing, flicking his gaze between the Prince and me.

The Warlord stills and says, "My *Moskazi* is allowed to hear our numbers, Commander Pei." The commander nods curtly, continuing. "We're sending ten thousand, and that is all I can manage."

I keep my face from falling slack. Ten thousand spare Azure Warriors? From one territory.

"I'm sure those numbers don't impress our Ranger," Vasilius says with a smoothness, which hides his hostility as frigid eyes fall on me, burning as coldly as hoarfrost.

"Ten thousand warriors with one purpose are formidable in any re-gard, Prince," I reply just as smoothly. He holds my stare before turning away.

Toriey's face softens as he drums his fingers on the table. "Is that considered a high or low number where you're from *Moskazi*?"

The tension in the room thickens as twelve military commanders' attention veer like a blade toward me. I angle my head. "Why do the numbers of Panthum's population interest you, Commander? We will not come to your aid should you ask, beg, or threaten. Panthum will neither provoke a war."

"Are you diplomatically telling us you know how to de-escalate situations between two conflicting parties?" Pei quips. Instead of laughing at what could be construed as a joke, the Commanders wait for my response. I nearly break a smile for the young Commander. He's quite crafty.

"It depends on the willingness of the two parties. I would think that in your circumstances, death would be a strong motivator. However, from what little I've witnessed, it will not sway them. You will have to change your approach as I only know one side of the conflict."

Toriey leans back in his chair, studying me, and Calix's expression is unreadable. I hold his steady gaze for several long moments until Toriey says softly, "Perhaps we should take you down to interrogate the prisoner?"

"No," Calix and Vasilius snarl at the same time. The tension once again spikes as the two brothers glare at Toriey, who stares back just as calmly. His suggestion isn't unfounded as he's attempting to find a solution. Neither side appears to back down, and from my right, I feel a subtle prickle on the flesh of my neck. It's a new sensation I've not yet experienced before, and I turn to look at Vasilius, studying his harsh features.

I would never have thought it possible for him to speak in defense of my physical safety based on training with him alone, but some part of it must be ingrained in him enough he assisted me out of the cage in Floating City, killing the Deysik before he could kill either of us. I reason it's most likely because I'm his brother's *Moskazi*.

I shift to take in the table and inhale deeply before I say softly, "I do not think a conversation with your prisoner would give me a clear perspective on conditions of the Deysik community. Though I am intrigued by your idea, Toriey. Would you perhaps offer to escort me into Deysik territory, so I may have an unfiltered view?" The smile I give him is full of razors and sweet as honey.

His nostrils flare, and I shrug my shoulders. "If you would like my *biased* opinion," I offer to the room at large, once again arresting their undivided attention. "Which, I will add, does not take into account the differences between your Deysik and the ones I'm familiar with. If you're going to place your men on the border, do not provoke your enemy. Keep your people on their side, and away from the Deysik's property or potential food sources." I sweep my gaze around the room. "Protect them in a sense as much as show them your force, your weapons, your might, but sit long enough they make the decision for you. If there are small-party attacks, defend but do not retaliate. They will want to test you for weaknesses. Show them none. The more controlled you are, the more they will fear you."

I shift in my seat. "Time will determine their willingness to open lines of communication. Offer a missive one week apart, four times. Don't expect a productive reply or response to the first two as it will be full of threats. The third will be full of insults. On the fourth, if they use any language offering solemnity, amongst the insults and threats, take it; whatever it is and build from there."

I stand. "If your goal is to stop this war from escalating, you both must make peace with your past and move beyond the small cuts along the way. Each incident should grow further and further apart, until they will be but a distant memory."

"How do you know this?" Pei asks, narrowing his gaze.

The men shift, and a few sneer over the thought. I look at Vasilius. "If you want peace, you must make concessions. A flexible tree survives the windstorm. It's the unmoving ones which break." The younger Prince clenches his fist and glares. I should have taken my own knowledge and applied it to Drake. But family tends to be our blind spots.

I move to Calix and bend down, kissing his cheek before whispering softly, "You have my wisdom and counsel with what little knowledge I have. I trust you will do what is best for your country and your Deysik neighbors."

I leave the room, inhaling a lungful of air as the door closes behind me. I can't help but wish I could speak with my father or Master Baylor. Part of me longs for their sage council for myself and the situation I find myself in. I was supposed to be a simple mercenary. Not the council on how to de-escalate tensions between Azure Warriors and Deysik.

I just hope I didn't make things worse for the Deysik by giving them that advice. Calix is a good man, and I trust he won't manipulate them with the information I gave, but it doesn't mean his commanders wouldn't.

I rub the bridge of my nose as I make my way down to Diedra's office, hoping to find the two people I trust won't trick me into giving away state secrets, just personal ones.

When I arrive, Diedra is pulling out the intestines of a pig and plopping them onto a stainless-steel tray. I pause and look for Canary, not finding him in the room that smells like cleaning solution.

"Put some gloves on and help me, please, Alana."

I do as she instructs, noting she's wearing black medical clothing. "Please tell me you're conducting an experiment or making sausage and not something like witchcraft."

Diedra whips her head up to me so fast, her large curls bounce. "There's witchcraft in Panthum?"

I chuckle. "No, but a merchant told us stories he heard from one of the long distant traders from the south. I don't believe in something I can't see." Except for the Mother and her wrath. I know that power all too well.

I still dream of waves the size of mountains bearing down on me.

"Oh. Well, I'm not making sausage but I am conducting an experiment by trying to determine if a new surgical technique will work or not." She pulls out more slippery pink organs. "I have to remove the intestines first."

I move forward to help her, following her guidance. "Don't you have specially trained assistants for this work?"

Diedra's face flickers for a moment before she answers, "They refuse to work with the *Traitor*." I don't see either assistants or Canary.

"I thought Rost had given leniency until your father makes a decision."

Her dark eyes flick to me, nodding her head. "Yes, but they don't wish to be tainted."

I snort, and she replies with a quirk of her full lips, "Not everyone can be as rational or intelligent as the two of us. Tell me more about Uria cloth, Alana. I would like to know your thoughts on how, if metal cannot pierce or cut the—fabric, why scalding steam can be used in creating its form."

I tease, "You haven't figured it out yet?"

She gives me an annoyed look, not appreciating my turning her own words against her.

"I can't tell you the exact process because I've never seen it done," I lift up my elbow, looking at the slightly shimmery material of my red tunic.

"But my guess would be the chemical makeup elicits a reaction, allowing it temporary malleability."

"Well, it certainly must be extremely difficult to come by... " she glances at me, and I smirk.

"You have no idea."

"You can't give me your best guess?" she whines. "I've examined it under a microscope, and its webbing is flawless. I've never seen anything so pristine. It makes sense that it cannot be cut."

"Why are you trying to find a weakness in the material? You already know how it's formed."

"I don't actually. Mine was discovered by accident, but I haven't been able to recreate it with any of the other materials that we've received from Panthum." She maneuvers her hands inside the pig and says to herself. "That won't work."

She quietly works for a moment, figuring out a way around the problem she's presently dealing with.

"It's almost like the material became more resistant. Nothing I tried has worked. It's as though the steam isn't hot enough."

I look up to the ceiling. No, not with the amount of heat they enjoy already.

"How much longer should I expect to be your assistant today?" I ask, hoping, but not anticipating a favorable reply.

"Three hours more. I'm reaching the spine now." She digs around inside the pig carcass, and I'm eternally grateful I don't have a Deysik's sense of smell. I begin translating everything she says into Panthum's old language just to keep it fresh and my mind off of the heavy secrets I'm holding, knowing no help will come to carry it.

I just need to find a way to endure.

Chapter 15

The next day we stop at a city, and more commanders arrive, but with them in tow are females. A lot of them. All wearing dresses of different cuts and designs, it's hard to decide which one is favored above the other. There doesn't seem to be fashion trends like there are in Panthum that shift and ebb with each year. Three things are made apparent.

Most are around my age and younger.

They're dressed in gowns, covered with jewels from head to toe, with their hair and makeup done to perfection.

Calix and Vasilius flank me as they arrive with Diedra and Canary who stand on Calix's right as they trail past.

They all react to my appearance as though I'm a monster. I can't decide if it's my scars, casual dress, or the Prince's by my side that cause their jaws to fall slack, but Calix, my casual laid back Bluey, wearing his golden mask, glares at anyone who looks too long.

They speed along and from across where we stand are Raine and Toriey, with the other Commanders greeting the leaders as they board the ship. Both males glance my way, and the younger man looks from me to Vasilius before continuing his conversation with his grandfather by his side.

Vasilius too is wearing his pearl mask, and now I envy the ability to wear a facial expression other than boredom.

Calix turns to me, "We're heading into our lunch meeting. You're welcome to join us if you wish."

That will only be more practicing keeping expressions off of my face and dodging more inquiries about Panthum in comparison. I don't want to make myself an object of resentment. I shake my head and feel Vasilius's glance. I'm sure he's relieved.

"Diedra and I are going to the top deck. We'll meet up with you later during your break."

Calix's sister slips her arm through mine, and she smirks at her brothers. "Good luck, Princes' Dread. You know who to call if you're suddenly feeling sick to your stomach." She gives them a wink, and together we leave with Canary trailing behind, acting as Diedra's shadow.

Once settled under the shade of the umbrella, I select a new item off of the menu, and Diedra launches into the specifics of dancing for the opening ball. "What dances do you have in Panthum that are similar?"

I smile, but before I can say anything, I hear laughter from a nearby table and turn to find several women looking at us, with their heads close together whispering. I'm reminded of my old schoolrooms when I began taking classes with the others at nine years old because by then, the other children had a better leash on their emotions and controlled their second skin from making an appearance. It was a difficult year until Baylor's daughters took me under their wing.

"Our music is played mostly with different instruments, so I can't compare. But it's like a storm building before it breaks across the Mountain sinks."

"Which are your favorites?"

"The faster-tempoed ones because I never had anyone to dance with—"

"I can see why," a voice from behind me cuts through the air and laughter erupts. I roll my eyes.

"Why didn't you have anyone to dance with?" Diedra asks while frowning at the woman. Canary outright glares at the table.

"Because my brothers scared off anyone who tried."

Canary glances at me and raises a brow. Oh, right, I haven't outright told them about my family. I smile sheepishly. "I have two brothers. One older and one younger."

Diedra smiles like a feline, and I hide my internal cringe from letting that slip. She's going to hound me for details.

"Tell me all about them. Are they as handsome as you are beautiful?" she asks. Canary smirks, leans forward, places his elbow on the table, and presses his cheek into his hand, staring intently with wide eyes.

I swat at him. "Stop that, or you'll make me choke on my food."

"Spill the tea, Ruby," Canary says in his gravelly voice, and I can't help it. I burst out laughing and can't stop. My whole body shakes, and my abdomen hurts. Diedra and Canary join in, and soon, we're all laughing so hard we have tears running down our faces. Then Diedra notices the women staring and points her finger, and when I look to find their horrified faces, we all laugh harder.

I'm sure Canary and I, with our scarred faces, are a sight to behold. Even the sound coming out of Canary is similar to the barking cough of a sick child. It draws every person's gaze to the restaurant, politicians and citizens alike.

Only, every horrified face we find, sets us off so much that we can barely breathe. I bend over, grab a napkin, and press it to my face, so I don't see Diedra and Canary leaning against each other.

"My, my, I missed out on all the fun," a soft male says, and I turn to find the Champion Raine standing near, gesturing to the empty seat at our table, and while mine and Canary's laughter takes a minute to slow, Diedra nods for us.

Raine takes the seat and quirks his lips in a crooked grin before settling his gaze on Diedra. "How are your surgical experiments going?"

"Well, thank you. If you have any more ideas, send them my way."

"That was your idea?" I ask Raine, crossing my legs as I pull a face.

He turns his upper body to face me and smiles genially, his spectacles glinting against the sun's reflection. "Medical innovation is a hobby of mine." He turns his attention to Canary and nods politely. "It's nice to know there's another person with similar tastes. I'd appreciate any discussions you'd like to have."

He's friendly and has a calm presence, and I don't fail to notice the gazes of the young females drift over him more often than not.

"How goes making friends?" he asks me, and I allow a slow grin to cross my face. He's sure persistent.

"I'd say as well as can be expected."

"Whose expectations?" he responds without missing a beat. Mother's braids, he's sharp.

"Yours," I answer just as fast.

"Mine?" The lines between his eyebrows appear as he frowns. "What expectations do I have?"

"That I'll do it at all. I don't like being nice to people I don't like."

He laughs at that, and Canary looks at him as if he's puzzling out this Champion. Raine smiles and casts his gaze over the restaurant. "I appreciate your honesty *Moskazi*. Is that a commonality among Rangers?"

"Yes."

He nods his approval. "I'm glad to get to know you then. Your opinion will be refreshing, to say the least."

"Be careful what you wish for boy, her tongue is as sharp as her blade," Canary says, and I raise my eyebrow, and Diedra and I share a look before laughing.

"If I'm asked for honest feedback, I give it constructively with positive suggestions for improvement. If someone demands it, then it may sting."

"So, Prince Dread has found out," Raine chuckles.

"Which one," Diedra laughs.

Canary asks Raine about his training and what he's eating, and the two make plans for Canary to critique the Champion. I meet Diedra's eyes, and she gives me a wink.

So, this is how you build alliances and safeguard any bets placed on the Currell fights. I have a sneaking suspicion that Toriey put Raine up to it.

I'm sure this won't be the last of the Champions who will approach us, but only if they set aside their prejudices against the Traitor if they want to win. I certainly wouldn't bet against anyone who trained with him.

Chapter 16

A week passes quickly, with more nobles and supplies added each day, and I wonder how this steamer doesn't sink with so many people aboard. In the mornings, we train in rotations with Canary, and I go first so while Vasilius and Calix train together he can coach Raine, fine tuning his techniques.

Diedra, the minx, has taken to observing our sessions, pretending to read her medical books but really, salivating over Canary. The rest of the space is taken up by other Azure Warriors as they maintain their skill and calisthenics. The familiar sound is relaxing, but I don't think I'll ever be entirely comfortable being surrounded by the enemy.

Once training is finished for the morning, Calix and Vasilius return to their meetings with the commanders. Raine and a few of the other Champions move to a different part of the ship specializing in recovery.

With Calix and Vasilius occupied, Diedra heads to the infirmary to work, and like a barnacle, Canary goes with her, leaving me blessedly alone to train on the empty pitch. After assisting her in her surgery, my fingers wanted to fall out of their joints, so I politely declined her return invitation. My formerly cold-eyed friend is fascinated with her work, and I've seen Raine join them a few times.

Alone, I stretch and move my body in restful, slow motions, returning to something more familiar than the time I spent on the Ravager. I wonder briefly what Nash is doing, now that he's retired. I'm sure whatever it is, he's imploding more establishments and overturning stability.

I hate to admit I miss the bastard, but I do.

***

"Have you ever fought for someone you loved rather than gold?"

Vasilius's sneer cuts across the air, and I come to a halt next to the training pitch where I had just finished my solo training. I'm covered in sweat with my tunic in hand, not wanting a confrontation with the General. I look to the second exit, and before I can take a step towards the door leading to the outside deck, a second voice carries through the door before me, keeping me in place.

It's been a while since I've heard its garbled tone. "You know, I don't think I have. I don't even remember the last time I thought about someone besides myself either, if you can believe it."

The sarcasm is so heavy I can hear the plops of it dripping from where I'm frozen in place. What are those two possibly fighting over?

She continues, "I can see why your betrothed fled her wedding if this is your true nature."

Vasilius's voice takes on a lethal quality that sends a shiver crawling down my spine. "Do not speak of Svetlana. You know *nothing* of why she ran."

"And you do?" she sneers.

"Yes."

The Black Fox's voice takes on a surprised tone that perks an awareness in me. "Is that why you're still looking for her?"

Vasilius snaps, exasperated, "If I don't find her before her brothers do, she'll be executed, mercenary. Perhaps I should ply you with enough gold to convince you to stop your activities for my father."

A heavy pause before the Black Fox speaks again, "What exactly is your disagreement with the arrangement I have with your Emperor, Prince Dread?"

"I don't like you capturing Deysik and bringing their filth into our cities. I don't care what my father or my commanders are paying you. It's dishonorable."

"What's dishonorable about earning money?" She asks. "I have men who rely on my income. Men who are paying for their crimes with time, which I've purchased. Your commanders have lost their skills to kill Deysik and are trying to regain it. Do you think this might be a reason for the escalation in this war?"

The question is one of logic, though she may as well have thrown kindling onto a fire for asking it.

"Of course, it's the reason!" he hisses. "I don't care about your mercenaries or any savage Deysik that crosses our border, only the cause with which it brings about my people. Death."

"Unfortunately, Prince Dread, I didn't start this problem, nor was I the first mercenary to take advantage of the situation. I just happen to be the best at surviving and collecting on it."

"I wonder why that is—"

The Black Fox cuts in, but she's no longer gloating; rather, she is caustic in her verbal assault. "You know why; you just refuse to accept the answer. Much like the *Moskazi's* honor."

"What do you know of her honor?" he snarls.

"I know that she's loyal to your brother, and you choose to ignore the gift the Mother gave you in her relationship with him. I heard of your fight in the Floating City. Why do you think she drew the Deysik away from you? It certainly wasn't to kill you but to protect you. You just happened to be quick enough to strangle it first."

"You speak as though you were there," he growls.

"I heard about it a day later. Word is quickly spreading about her killing Sharksong. The old siren's reign is over. For that alone, her contract purchase would have doubled what you paid had Nash held off its sale a day longer, and you know it. With how secluded their country is, she's your only window into the character of her people. Besides, you don't sacrifice yourself for a nobody, the way she did on the road to Rising Pass."

I hear lighter footsteps walk away, and her gravelly voice drifts back toward me, "If I were a gambling person, I would guess that she's worth more as your ally than your enemy. You may need more like her."

The door opens, and Vasilius plows into me. I fall backward, but he snatches my biceps, throwing out a leg to keep us from slamming into the floor. The unexpected jolt sends my heart galloping in my chest, and it's as if I sprinted for my life. My thoughts spin as he swears and yanks me into him while righting our position. We spring back from each other, glaring as if it weren't an accident. His icy blue eyes bore into me, and his muscular body vibrates with barely constrained fury from his conversation with the Black Fox.

A slight pang of sympathy shoots through me, and I remember Raine's encouragement to make friends. I clench my jaw when I bear down on the knowledge that Toriey's Champion, like my younger brother Connor, is right. I need to take the first step. Kill them with kindness as Hagatha and Baylor's daughters would tell me.

"How much of that did you hear?" he growls.

"Enough to know you care about your people and will slaughter anyone who threatens them just like I would."

He sucks in a breath, his shoulders rolling back, but he bites his lips together to keep from saying something rude, and I blink. He probably didn't expect the compliment but it's true. He takes in my sweaty state and those crystal blue eyes narrow in curiosity and confusion, rather than anger.

"The Black Fox was right about one thing though," I say more to distract him from my second workout. I feel a tremor of nervousness lance through me as I extend an olive branch, knowing it could very well be broken and tossed aside.

"I wanted to protect you in the Floating City because I couldn't bear the thought of Calix suffering another loss. He doesn't deserve anymore."

He places his hands on his hips and looks down at the floor. "You don't either, Vasilius. I apologize for not thanking you when you saved me in the cage and assisted me out of it. It was an oversight I won't make again."

His chest under his black tunic rises and falls with shallow breaths as he gathers his emotions. I'm suddenly ashamed of myself for not having thanked him sooner.

He raises his blonde head, and for the first time, his blue eyes lack all hostility when they meet mine. It's like a punch to the gut, and I swallow, shifting the weight on my feet. I make to move past him but pause at the door, turning to see every muscle in his back flicker with movement as he runs a hand over his face.

"My responsibility in Panthum was training other Rangers." Not quite the truth but it was true enough. "You need to relax your shoulders more when facing off with your opponent. It makes it harder for your body to compensate when you need to move your feet."

With that advice, I leave. There's no way I can tell everyone I'm not important in the grand scheme of things other than reiterating my lowly position. I'm a mere Ranger. It's my friends and family who are important.

However the Black Fox isn't wrong. If they're to win this war with the Deysik, they're going to need more weapons and skills they're clearly clawing for by trafficking stolen Deysik to their fortresses to train against. My stomach twists into a knot, and I'm sick to my stomach. I need to come up with a way to encourage Calix to stop the practice. It's not right. I weigh my options of offering to train them how to kill Deysik to save a few or say nothing and leave the Azure Warriors defenseless.

It's getting harder and harder to adhere to the old opinions I held before I left Panthum.

I don't want either side to suffer, but I have a strong premonition that it's what it will take for either side to bow down to peace.

Mother help them all.

Chapter 17

On the morning of the seventh day, we arrive in the second largest city in the Empire, home to a grand fortress, Commanded by Toriey's rival, Teegu. It guards a school for the Mothers' Children.

Orphans.

This school is nothing like what I know in Panthum. I'm told the children here are given the best education, care, and attention, with every opportunity available to them when they reach their majority at eighteen.

It's vastly different from where the Deysik children of this continent go.

When I wake, nerves trickle through my limbs. I begin to untangle myself from Calix's hot body that's wrapped up around me like a protective beast, only to have his hands reflexively tighten around my waist. For all he's busy during the day, he never fails to find me during breaks to pull me into an embrace, leaving me aching for our nights together. I kiss his shoulder, causing him to relax his grip before I slide out of bed.

After showering, I finger-comb my blonde-streaked brown hair. My skin's coloring has deepened into a dark tan, earned under the light of the sunroof over the training pitch. When I train alone, I remove my tunic, leaving only a single band around my chest for modesty's sake.

Under the prismatic light of the bathroom, the appearance of my body's definition is sculpted. It's hard not to be aware of the painful difference of my physical form compared to the women of this empire and those filling the ship. They have plump curves, and I have hard muscles. I realize now why Diedra asked about refusing a maid. All the women onboard are primped, scrubbed, and glistening from body oils. They're feminine and delicate, without scars on their face or body.

When I return from the bathroom, Calix is lying on his back, staring at me, his hands behind his head, his glorious biceps on display. He rakes his eyes over my body from head to toe. When I drift close enough, he reaches for me, tugging me across his chest, dragging his lips across my collarbone, effectively banishing any insecurity over the way I look, and whispers, "Do you know what you do to me? How I want to drop to my knees and worship you when you gaze at me like that. Like I'm the only thing you'll ever need."

"I don't need anything but you Bluey."

We grasp for one another, hands moving across our bodies as our lips collide in passion, tasting each other, all of it burning as hotly as our desperate breaths. How does Calix do this to me? I don't know when he became my obsession, but I regret I didn't give in to him sooner. He is everything I could ever want in a man.

A knock on the door interrupts our exploration of bodies.

"We've docked." Vasilius's voice cuts through the door, and we hear his footsteps fade down the hall.

A hot sigh blows against my stomach before a kiss meets my abdomen. Calix pulls back and says while looking at me with those fiery turquoise eyes, wearing a smirk that sends a shiver through me, "Tonight, my Ruby, I'm going to make you scream my name."

"I already did that this morning," I hum as his hands slide over my sensitive skin.

His tone shifts, turning tentative. "Maybe you'll help me come up with a plan to convince you to stay here when your contract is officially over?"

He's too close not to feel my body tense. His expression swiftly falls serious, with no trace of a teasing grin on his face. "I want you to stay Alana. I want a life with you, and even if you don't think I'll succeed, I want to at least offer an open invitation for your family to visit or move here permanently."

I shake my head in bafflement. How can this perfect man see right through the cracks of the walls around my heart? Cracks he's caused and chipped away at until there's a Bluey sized hole for him to burrow inside.

He rubs a calloused hand along my waist. "You would be able to get the message to them because you're Panthese, and if it means breaking through hundreds of years of tradition just for you to see those you love again—no blocked pass, and no number of Rangers will stop me from giving it to you, Alana."

I can't help the tears from slipping down my cheeks. He moves back, so I can sit up and wrap my arms around his neck, burying my face in the strong column of his throat, breathing in his soothing scent of cinnamon and leather.

"I love you, Calix."

"My *Moskazi*. My fire jewel." The reverence he speaks, is his way of saying, I love you, back, and it sends a shiver of deep emotion down to my toes.

He's spoiling me with love and worse... possibility.

Chapter 18

We're escorted by hundreds of Azure Warriors while we are driven in an open-topped carriage from the Safa River through Azure City, the streets teaming with cheering people wishing to catch a glimpse of their Princes and Princess. Calix holds my hand, giving me the occasional squeeze as the crowd practically pulses with excitement that ramps up when they realize I'm sitting next to their Crown Prince.

Instead of the leather vest and blue hood of the other Blueys, both Princes opt for a solid blue tunic wrapped in a darker blue sash around their waist, fitted black pants, and tall boots reaching past their calves.

I'm dressed in a similar fashion but in red and black, representing Panthum's colors with gold dangling earrings. Diedra gave them to me this morning, before slipping several flowers into my braided crown. The two accessories add a touch of feminine to my otherwise masculine appearance. I think the maids were horrified when I once again politely declined their help.

Spectators' fingers point, and gasps are thrown into the air. Vasilius studiously ignores me, waving and nodding to the people as we pass, Diedra sits next to him grinning. I find a smile on my own face. It's hard to keep the contagious feeling of welcome at bay.

Calix leans over and says loud enough to be heard over the cheering crowd but quiet enough for the guards on horseback not to overhear, "They love you!"

"They love their future Emperor. I'm the novelty." I return with a grin, and when I turn away, Calix's hand cradles my cheek and turns me back to him, kissing me with a passion that sends the crowd into a frenzy, rippling through the streets. His tongue demands entrance, and when I open for him, I melt against his firm body. Vasilius clears his throat and grumbles, "You've made your point."

I pull back and swallow, not used to displays of desire in public. "What Vasilius said." Calix doesn't smile and whispers against my lips, using that commanding tone which sends my heart into an arrhythmia.

"Never diminish your worth. Not to anyone, especially me." His lips brush mine softly again before he pulls back with a smile. I blink and catch Diedra's subtle wink.

We enter the fortress, and while we pass under the shadow of the walls, I ponder on how far I've come from the broken outpost of Rising Fortress and even further from the Riband.

I take a breath, reminding myself I have five years before I go back and not to think of problems ahead, rather focus on what's in front of me. I have my promise from Nash for free passage, but I doubt Calix will allow me anywhere near the seajacking Captain.

We drive to the entrance of the Mother's School, where we enter an elegant formal lobby, dripping in wealth, which surprisingly holds warmth. Greenery and light gray tile underneath cut-colored glass chandeliers hang in a brilliant display above the towering entryway of the building and courtyards beyond, drawing me in. It's a curious contradiction and I like it.

Statues and works of art decorate the white-washed walls. Servants, tutors, and students flit about from hallways to rooms, peeking through interior windows. It lends a sense of life in the large building as I hear the rustle of clothing and giggles.

I roll my shoulders back as I walk, smelling the freshly baked pastries and flatbread in the air from a nearby kitchen. The main stone courtyard is rimmed with potted ferns and brightly colored exotic plants I've never seen before.

Two people stand in the lobby waiting for us. As a custom, Calix and Vasilius are greeted by the infamous fortress Commander Teegu. He exudes power the same way Calix and Vasilius do, reminding me of my father. His intricately designed, full face mask hangs from his belt, his hood back, revealing thick brown hair over a face with blunt features, enhancing his four-decade old appearance. His eyes flit from my boots to my face and linger on the scars there. He flares his nostrils and quickly turns away to face the headmistress of the school.

The woman is in her sixties, tall, and wears a fitted black dress revealing an hourglass figure I could never hope to achieve. I don't miss the way her critical gaze flicks over me and barely veiled smile wrinkles her nose. The two are on opposite sides of the pendulum from each other.

I murmur a hello and look away from the haughty Commander in time to see Diedra disappearing with Canary down a hall. I fight back a smirk, keeping my face passive as the courtyard fills up with bodies. Calix's hand rests on my lower back in a familiar claiming gesture, settling my nerves. Vasilius stands like a dark pillar of power, exuding it in waves I would never have expected to come from him in this place. I peek a glance and find his face tight with displeasure. He focuses his attention on Teegu, but the Commander ignores the Prince, choosing to direct his concentration on Calix and myself.

This is the man the Black Fox has been bringing Deysik to in order to train his Champions.

"A Ranger from Panthum," Teegu says, and I dip my chin in a polite acknowledgement. His gaze turns sharp. "I'm sure you're aware of how valuable your weapons have become as of late."

Another dip of my chin and his eyes narrow. "You have nothing to say?" Vasilius bristles. I've come to the conclusion he does this when he feels a need to protect the honor of his brother's *Moskazi*. It's the image rather than the person he guards. He's still kept me at arms length since my apology but less antagonistic.

"If you ask me a question requiring more than a yes or no, I'll respond. I don't waste my breath."

Teegu shifts his weight, and Calix chuckles. "Alana is not like the women from Luminum, Teegu. You'll have to apply more effort than that for her to reveal anything about herself. She's not one to offer up information freely."

"I see. My apologies, Ranger Alana."

"Just Alana. You don't call yourself Azure Warrior Teegu, do you?"

Vasilius smirks, the Commander blinks, and the Matron raises a thin gray brow, her lips thinning into a smile before quickly covering it. I gather everyone here with exception to Calix, doesn't get along with him. They must not appreciate Teegu's blunt personality.

Calix laughs and squeezes me to him. "She demands respect the same way an Azure Warrior would."

I slowly look at him, and it's my turn to raise a brow. "You're saying your women don't demand respect, Bluey?"

The majority of the Azure Warriors stiffen, and if looks could slice and dice, Teegu would have me dead. The Matron's eyebrows pull together and taps her finger against her elbow. Vasilius blows out a loud sigh as Calix turns his hazel-bright eyes down to me, and I hold his stare unflinchingly. I'll not back down from this. I half wonder if he'll rebuke me for his nickname.

"The opposite, my darling Ruby. They already have it and know it. It's the Azure Warriors who fight for dominance." He smiles warmly. "You don't back down for anyone, even me. It's why you're my *Moskazi*."

His words have a calming effect on the room around us, yet I hold his stare, trying to decipher any hidden slights in his words, finding none. Calix doesn't hurt those he loves.

"It's a pleasure to meet someone from another country, *Moskazi*," the Matron says warmly. "What do you think of Luminum in comparison?"

I soften my features as I respond, "It's beautiful, and the company never makes for a dull moment."

"Which company would that be?" Teegu asks, his voice deep and sure.

"The Princes Dread, the Royal Surgeon, and the Traitor," I respond evenly. Teegu's eyes flare wide and shoot to Calix, his face darkening with shades of red as blood flushes his skin with fury.

He barks out a harsh sentence in Luminum, and Vasilius cuts in, his own tone filled with restrained anger.

After the tense exchange, I remain silent as they speak, comfortable with being studiously ignored. I observe the other Azure Warriors in the distance greet friends who have come to visit. When the conversation reaches the inevitable point where the others would like to leave to discuss sensitive topics in private, I dip my head in a respectful gesture.

I would rather peel off my own fingernails than sit through endless meetings. That's the benefit of being a mercenary. I smile at Calix, letting him know I'm fine, surrounded by his men. They disappear down a hall, the matron moving in a different direction.

I don't see Vasilius. The younger Prince is who knows where. The man has a knack for disappearing and appearing like a ghost.

I shift and peruse the art gracing the walls of the courtyard, finding it entrancing.

As I move under the arches and study the various styles of landscapes, stills, and portraits, something on the far wall catches my attention. The design is set with precious stones: ultramarine, amethysts, jade, turquoise, zircon, moonstone, tiger's eye, howlite, and mother of pearl. It's a mural of the world map.

The map is painted in rich detail with images representing what each of the ten territories of Luminum is known for. Farming and ranching comprise the bottom four to the south above the Red City. Running all along to the west are hundreds of leagues of coastline and three territories of fishing and manufacturing near the larger trading centers. Stone quarries, mining, logging, and so on to the east along the Ikpeazu Mountains, and the north to the northwest are weavers, tradespeople, and more manufacturing. The towns are larger and closer together the closer in proximity to the Capital of Luminum. At the heart of it all to the North, set in gold, is Goldill. A shining beacon to the world and former home of the Mother's Heir before she disappeared four hundred years ago.

My eyes search further out to a long cluster of large and small islands off the coastline to the North of Luminum's borders. Surrounded by Siren Waters is Nakka, Nash's home.

Nasheer.

The crowd of Azure Warriors laugh and continue speaking to one another, glancing at me, but no one approaches to speak. It's hard not to feel like a fish out of water. I wish Hagatha or Everett were here. The two could start a conversation with a rock.

Refocusing on the map, my eyes fall to the southern border of Luminum next to Deysik Territory. Slate is outlined in obsidian, naming the country along the eastern border before the Ikpeazu Mountains. Chips of volcanic glass, emeralds, and rubies mark the crags, trees, and mines.

I trace my finger along the jewels to the center of the vast ocean and find the Floating City Island chain. Further west, Faurst is bright and colorful, as if the artist included the launching point of the Mother's battle against Ertune as notable. More countries are to the North and South, but I'm not overly familiar with them yet.

At the edge of the map, I'm disappointed to find a gray empty smear beyond Rising Pass, showing the artist's contempt for what lay beyond the mountain entrance. They clearly know little of Panthum and the monsters lurking there. Where Panthum and the Ikpeazu Mountains sit on opposite sides of the map, it appears as if they'll forever be on the outside of the world's focus.

Unfortunately, I know that to the very western border of Panthum lies barren volcanic rock and black sand dunes, with a distant twin-peaked mountain jutting out majestically against the blue sky, only visible on a clear day from the highest ridge with a spotting scope. We've pushed the monsters back to the borders, choosing to stop there as there aren't enough natural resources to justify expanding the borders of Panthum.

"The map reveals how little we know of the world, doesn't it?" a soft, raspy voice asks me, causing me to startle. I notice the courtyard is nearly empty with a small group of Azure Warriors, I recognize from the Grace, remaining on the opposite side, quietly speaking with one another.

"Where's Diedra?" I ask.

"Gathering the Princesses' things," Canary says as he stands next to me, looking over the mural. His gray eyes travel east to the unknown, where the Ariportia make their home in the Ikpeazu mountains.

Canary points to the land of the Ariportia. "My father visited it once in his youth and came back with me a little over a year later." His voice drops low. Barely a whisper. I blink at the knowledge he handed to me. I'm not sure what to say about his honesty, recalling what Nash said on the ship... that his father beat him in a fight and gave him those scars. My heart aches for him and for all he's suffered in his lifetime. No one should've ever had to go through what he has.

And to be tasked with an impossible mission he's yet to know of. It's one of the many reasons why Calix is attending so many meetings. He's trying to come up with a solution so as not to upset Diedra when she finds out about his father's plans.

He's half Ariportia. No wonder he's so fast.

"Are you afraid?" I ask him, curious if his feelings have changed about coming back to his home only to be given a death sentence twice over. Canary faces me, his stone-colored eyes are no longer cold but placid.

"No. Because I know what I'm fighting for," he says. Hope, I realize. Diedra.

"Do you know what *you* want, *Moskazi*?" he asks, angling his head, his brown hair shifting with the movement.

I inhale, "I haven't decided." I wince, realizing what it sounds like. He shared something deeply personal about himself. My heart pounds in my chest. "I'm like you—"

"I hear his *Moskazi* looks like a hideous wild animal trying to dress as a human," a small child's voice says, coming from around a corner into the main courtyard. I'm grateful they interrupted before I did a colossally stupid thing like tell Canary I'm Deysik. I don't know what came over me.

Canary and I both turn to see two beautiful girls with dark skin and tight curly hair. One is older, about fourteen, and the youngest—the one who speaks—is about seven.

Sisters.

Both have Diedra's piercing dark eyes. They wear light pink dresses so delicate and detailed that I know they have to be Princess Olianna's daughters, Calix's nieces, Pippa and Vivian.

Horrified doesn't begin to describe their faces when they find Canary and me. I hold back my laughter. Unmoving, we stare at each other, and I wonder who will break first. Both girls' faces flush with color, and I take pity on them and smile, remembering my own blunders as a child. Especially with Deysik's hearing, I got away with nothing, even under my breath.

"I suppose you will have to tell me what you think *hideous* means," I say, tapping my chin with my pointer finger. "Does it mean something different here in Luminum than it does in Panthum?"

They jerk back when *Panthum* crosses my lips. My smile falters when the older one shoves her sister behind her, eyes wide with fear. My heart seizes. "I'm Ranger Alana. You must be Princesses Pippa and Vivian," I say, forcing warmth into my voice. I'm your uncle's *Moskazi*." I hope the information will settle their fears, but it does the opposite.

Vivian, the youngest, seems duly embarrassed with high color in her cheeks, staring at the floor, but Pippa... Pippa regains her composure, cutting her eyes over my body with the regality of a queen in a sneer worthy of Drake. Those damn scars.

"I don't know what my uncle sees in you. You look just like a man and sound like a bleating sheep. He could have picked a better-looking slag."

Canary stiffens at the delivered insult, but I'm too stunned by her vicious words to react. Pippa snatches Vivian's arm and tugs her away across the courtyard, their feet barely touching the tiles. As if I'm diseased. As if I'm less than.

Slag. Whore.

Hurt settles under my skin the way a tick would.

Leave it to children to find the same weak spot my eldest brother often targeted—my appearance.

Stares and embarrassed glances are thrown my way by the Azure Warriors in the courtyard, and my skin feels like it's going to peel. I turn to leave and find Toriey's tall form amongst a group of staring Azure Warriors. He must have come in while Canary and I were talking.

I ignore his frown, and I angle my head differentially to say, "Please inform the Crown Prince that I don't wish to be a distraction from his family reunion and will be returning to the Grace."

His brows pull together, before dipping his chin in acknowledgment. I depart and am grateful Canary's unassuming presence follows me out of the building and back to the massive river steamer. My muscles loosen somewhat, being back to a space where I'm less of an odd duck.

Canary drags me into the empty dining hall where the majority of Azure Warriors eat their meals rather than the top-deck restaurant where the citizens and nobles of Luminum dine. I'm grateful for the silence to untangle my thoughts.

My weapons tutor drills me with a hard stare until I sigh and eat my simple lunch before he takes me to the forward training pitch. The sounds of weapons clashing carry down the halls.

Canary and I enter the observation level above, finding a sea of black-clad mercenaries utilizing the space. In the week aboard the ship, I haven't seen a single one and nearly forgot they were here.

"Ranger Alana," a garbled voice calls out. It's the Black Fox. She angles her head, silver flashing across the elongated nose of her mask. "Would you and the Traitor like to join us for a sparring session while we warm up?"

Canary and I share a look, and I can swear on the Mother the corner of his mouth twitches up. I know he's doing it for my sake, but I nod. Descending the stairs into the training courtyard, the glass sunroof allows natural light to brighten the space but casts the areas below the observation deck as dark as my mood.

Four walls are filled and lined with weapons of every kind. The Black Fox's mercenaries have already paired off. Two are in a corner battling it out, and I admire their techniques. I never grow tired of watching masters at work. It's a good thing Raine is training with Canary because the Black Fox Mercenaries are highly skilled. More so than one would think.

Perhaps that's the reason for her success and invitation to Currell.

The lanky female tosses me a staff and one to the man she was sparring with at the very center, under the sun, shining through the glass roof.

I twist my staff, growing accustomed to its weight and feel as I observe my opponent. He's as tall as Calix and just as big, his black tunic stretching over his thick muscles. A spark of trepidation of the unknown and the thrill of the fight bursts inside me, shifting my wounded emotions into a frozen tundra of icy determination.

The man's onyx mask matches the color of the Luminum style of shortly cropped black hair so unlike the long braids of Deysik back home.

The mercenary and I circle each other.

I can hear the smile in the Black Fox's rough voice from the sidelines. "I've heard of the infamous Rangers growing up and was on my way to Panthum when I was informed of the avalanche blocking the pass."

My opponent swings, and I barely catch his staff before he swings again.

She is speaking to distract me, but the two can play a game.

I defend before attacking, moving faster thanks to Canary's training he drilled into me over the past two months. The large male meets my pace, staff clicking rapidly with each strike, but I sense he's holding back... testing me.

Circling the center pitch like two sharks, Canary and the Black Fox miss nothing.

I decide I've judged my opponent's skill enough to split my attention and reply, "I thought I recognized you in Faurst, slipping between buildings. Perhaps you're avoiding a certain someone who has an affinity for insults?" I toss her a smirk as I whirl my staff, meeting her mercenary's ducking and spinning under his forceful swing.

It's just a guess.

The merc shifts his arm in an attempt to trick me into the wrong end of his staff. My face and midsection have experienced enough welts growing up, to fall for it.

The Black Fox pauses. "What do you mean, 'avoid?' All I do is see Vasilius wherever I go," she says lightly—too lightly. *Bingo.*

"And you don't think that's by chance?" Another guess, but based on the conversation I heard the day before and the few tells she revealed, it wasn't their first encounter. I dance back and spin the staff, tossing her merc a mocking grin. His eyes are set too far behind his mask for me to make out the color, but if he's anything like my opponents in the past they're probably narrowed to slits.

"Possibly. But what does a Ranger know of it?" She taunts from behind her silver fox mask, her black gloved hand sliding along the edges of her dark hood, covering her head.

My voice takes on a sing-song tone. "The best way to hide is to be right under the nose."

She calls out, waving a gloved hand to the other mercs, "I grow bored of this. Swords."

Oh, I made her mad. I bite back a smile, pleased to ratchet up my practice.

The male and I exchange our staffs for blades, and I ignore the audience of Azure Warriors as they return for their afternoon practice, beginning to crowd the observation deck above. Their presence stings my insecurities, painfully pointed out by the Princesses.

I want a real fight.

I'd been a novelty all my life. A human training with Deysik, and then a female among a ship full of men. The courtyard is soon full of warriors, mercenaries, and other guests, and I can feel the eyes of the Black Fox's mercs like patient daggers in shadows.

On the second level vantage I glimpse Calix and Vasilius with Commanders Teegu and Toriey.

The back of my neck prickles, sending a warning as the mercenary strikes. I duck and spin under his arm, cutting the man's sleeve as my sword follows, passing over his skin.

No blood drips from my weapon, and I note all the Mercenaries collectively pause, but none of the Azure Warriors notice, surely thinking I missed him. I keep my surprise to myself as I shift back, not finding a glowing light burning behind his mask.

Deysik.

One well trained.

It seems the Black Fox has been hiding more than her gender. Under their noses indeed.

She tenses, waiting for me to expose her Deysik in the heart of a steamer full of Azure Warriors. I'm not an idiot. I won't start a blood bath, especially when Deysik blood runs through me. She certainly isn't an assassin because she has had plenty of opportunities to end the Royal line.

But why would she help capture other Deysik and deliver them to Teegu?

I glance at the silver-masked woman. "Is that all he's capable of? He seems a little slow."

The comment breaks the tension, and she snorts and nods. My neck doesn't have to warn me this time before I spin out of the way of his blade and begin a dance of death, gliding past his thrusts, our swords striking together with the sound of clashing bells.

There he is.

I love it when an opponent doesn't hold back.

The merc unleashes all of himself on me, and it's beautiful. My muscles burn, and I grin, grateful for Canary teaching me new techniques and maneuvers this summer. With a few moves, I slap my opponent with the flat of my blade on his waist and laugh.

"Mother's mercy. That's a *Ranger*? And she's a *girl*!" a little girl—Vivian—says, her astonished voice carrying over the training yard. "Look how violent she is; she likes it—she's laughing. She'll hurt us!" the girl cries. Some Blueys exchange glances and shift on their feet as if the little girl points out something wrong—something they should defend against.

I'm stunned. Mother's braids, how can she think that? My smile dies, and I want nothing more than to disappear.

I don't like hurting people. I like besting them.

My neck prickles sharply, and I dodge a blow that, three months ago, would've sent me flying. In a maneuver learned from my Bluey, surprising the merc, I quickly disarm him, ending the training.

Above, Calix bends down, picking up Vivian. Her small arms grasp him tightly around his neck, and he pats her back with his large hand, taking her away. Teegu stares with a calculated look on his smug face, and I imagine he's devising a way to acquire more weapons from Panthum. Vivian's whimpers of fear sour my gut, and my teeth ache from grinding down so hard.

I move off the pitch, handing my weapon to the Black Fox who remains silent. I duck my head and leave the courtyard, ignoring the stares from all the men who back away when I walk past.

I'm used to that sort of movement from other warriors. Only this time, it's for a different kind of respect—fear and not love. Or maybe only outright fear.

Alone, my feet carry me to the lower hold where our horses are stabled, and I don't stop until I find Calix's mare. I miss Windrunner. The soothing scent of horse, hay, feed, and musk help a little to calm my racing heart. A lump lodges in my throat, and I pick up a brush, hoping to work my body as I process my feelings.

Footsteps sound along the wooden floor, and I find Canary on the other side of the horse, feeling along the mare's back, rubbing near the hump where her neck meets her shoulders. He's here to make me feel better, but I can't shake the seeping hurt bleeding inside, tainting my confidence. "Why can't I be good at something and have people admire me for it and not be repulsed? If I'm not a Ranger, I don't know what I am." The admission surprises me, and I look away, tears falling down my cheeks.

What I like about Canary the most is he doesn't try to fix my problems. We stand silently for five minutes, breathing in the scents of horse and leather before he responds, "Who hurt you when you were young? Made you feel like you weren't enough?" His voice is quiet, almost lethally quiet.

I look up to find the left side of his face puckered with scars and his gray eyes softer than I'd ever seen them before. His expression relaxes something in my chest.

"My oldest brother. He was angry with me for not saving my mother. She died protecting me, and he's never forgiven me for it. As if an eight-year-old can fight against three full-grown men."

"If he's as smart as you are, then I'm certain he's aware of the fact. From what I know, siblings have a way of wounding each other with more precision than anyone else. I'd imagine now you're gone he'd take it all back if he had a second chance."

It reminds me so much of what Connor would say, and my eyes begin to water yet again. I miss my brothers.

"I'm sure your father would be proud of you," he says as softly as his gravelly voice will allow.

Would he, though? I've avoided thinking about him for too long because I didn't want to bog myself down by what I'm sure would be his reaction. Mostly because he's been my greatest champion. My advocate. He's my best friend. What would he say if he could see me now? Would he be ashamed?

A shift in the air has Canary and I turning our heads to the disturbance, but neither of us can see what it is. Canary goes so far as to step out into the aisle but frowns before shrugging his shoulders.

"Perhaps it's just the intake on the air ducts," I suggest, as the vents leading to the outside open, bringing in outside air. He turns back to face me, and I ask the question Diedra has been avoiding: "Do you know what your mission for the crown will be?"

"I'm to meet with the Emperor during Currell to find out." He strokes the horse's coat in long sweeps of his hand.

"Are you frightened?"

Canary resembles a tree in the dead of winter, seemingly lifeless, but underneath is a dormancy of emotion. Now that he has Diedra again, budding life seems to appear on his branches.

"It doesn't matter if I am or not. If that's what my Emperor asks of me, I'll do it."

"Why?" I run my fingers over the horse's warm, sleek coat.

"Because I'll be forgiven if I am successful."

"And will you and Diedra be together after?" I know I shouldn't ask this, but Canary nods.

"She has been the only woman I've thought of every day since I met her. I'll do the impossible if it means being free of my life sentence, and I'll always be grateful for you bringing me back."

I wasn't sure if he meant emotionally or physically, but either way, I don't think his words could have struck more deeply, replacing all the hurt.

And to me, it's worth more than earning Ranger.

I just wish I didn't have the guilt of knowing he was going on the mission that was originally meant for me.

Chapter 19

"Alana, would you join me for a moment?" Calix asks.

Coming up the companionway from the stables, I find him striding towards me on long legs, his golden mask bobbing against his narrow hip. My heart lurches with uncertainty as I notice his narrowed gaze on the stairs behind me.

Every line of his body radiates power. It's captivating. Entrancing. A Warlord approaching a Deysik. I blink, curious about what caused the shift in his mood. Is it from how upset his niece was earlier?

"What were you doing down there?" His voice is deep with displeasure.

"Horses," I answer. "I needed to think." He furrows his brow, and I crane my neck when he prowls closer. He slips a large hand around my lower back and pulls me against him in a tight hug that slightly melts my hurt.

"I don't like you being near the prisoner," he says against my hair.

Oh. I raise an eyebrow. "Why is that?"

He pulls me in for a searing kiss, and I dissolve into him, before he pulls back.

"Because he will smell me all over you and mark you for death. You have no idea how vindictive they can be. I don't want to risk it with your proximity to me."

That's right. I forgot their Deysik have that ability. I slide my fingers over his soft tunic. "It sounds reasonable."

He frowns, his body stiffening as he pulls back, and his voice drops low. "I'm serious, Alana. Once they have your scent, they can track you anywhere."

"Anywhere? What do you mean by that?"

"It means they will follow you to the ends of the world if they want to kill you badly enough."

My stomach drops, and I can feel the blood drain from my face, leaving me cold. I blink rapidly as I think about my mother and the three Deysik who attacked her. It certainly seemed personal. But how can that be possible? Master Baylor and my father never said a word about it. Wouldn't they have known?

I've never heard of that particular gift in my Deysik. But perhaps that was something we left behind when we became more civilized.

Calix mistakes my reaction for fear and wraps me up once more, rubbing my back soothingly.

"No one will ever touch you, remember? I'll remove every one of them off the face of the earth if they try."

My breath hitches. "Don't overreact; there are innocents who don't deserve that promise. Not for me, Bluey."

He angles my face up to meet his shimmering hazel eyes with lips mulled tight before he says gruffly, "Only you. I love you, *Moskazi,* in this life and beyond."

I blink. "That sounds really serious. I'll have to think it through before I commit—"

Before I know it, I'm tossed over Calix's shoulder and delivered a playful smack to my ass. I laugh as my Bluey hauls me in the direction of our bedroom. "Think about it? Sounds like I need to remind you how much you love me."

My toes curl in my boots as I gasp, catching sight of flowing skirts and feminine voices gasping and whispering furiously. I glance up to see spot Raine amongst the gaggle of females, a smirk on his face.

"You're going to cause gossip!" I hiss to Calix. I secretly don't care because mercy is a rare thing when he sets his mind on something, and I know I'll thoroughly enjoy it.

"No one will question how you feel about me when they hear you scream it."

I pinch his firm backside and chuckle, "Ah, my plan has fallen into place." That earns another playful smack, and my peals of laughter meet his hum, rattling deep through my ribcage.

***

The next morning, Calix and I join his family for breakfast in a private room off to the side of the main dining hall. I spent all morning bracing myself for the worst, and I'm grateful I did. The room's utilitarian nature is oddly comforting, as it's what I've been used to for the past several years. It's a more quiet and intimate setting without hundreds of eyes staring at me, studying and picking apart everything I eat.

"*Why* must we have *her* as our guard? Everyone will be staring!" Pippa whines. Last night, my Warlord asked if I'd guard the girls as an excuse for them to get to know me. I begrudgingly agreed, and it seems I wasn't the only one not exactly riveted over the idea.

"As opposed to you, Pippa?" Olga teases. At least the middle niece is decently behaved, with manners as she picks up her second cinnamon roll from the food spread across the center of the table, with different types of fruit and all sorts of sweet and savory choices.

"Shut up, Oink," Pippa snaps.

All the adults whip their heads to Pippa, Diedra's mouth hanging open as Olga drops her cinnamon roll onto her plate. Vasilius and Calix bristle. The young girl shrinks into her seat. Unlike her older sister, Olga's body is round, typical of a twelve-year-old youth, not yet a woman. In stark contrast, the fourteen-year-old, Pippa, dresses more stylishly like the rest of the women aboard the ship.

The tension is ripe with Olga and the adult's embarrassment and Pippa's callous attitude.

It's concerning that the older girl has such an influence over seven-year-old Vivian, talking like that. The animosity between the girls is tangible, and I now realize what it must be like to experience myself and Drake constantly at each other's throats.

"When a girl resorts to name-calling, it's usually because she has no alternative argument," Diedra recites through clenched teeth. Olga's face darkens with embarrassment, and she's on the verge of tears as Pippa glares at her aunt. I didn't think it was nearly a scolding worthy of the hurt Olga was experiencing. I'm tempted to wash her mouth out with soap the way my father did to me when I was younger than Vivian for name-calling. Once was enough to cure the problem.

"Olga, I hear you love horses," I insert, using some information Calix gave me about the girls last night to change the subject. "I used to have a speckled-gray mountain stallion named Windrunner. I'll have to tell you the story of how he saved my life from a predator once, leaving long scars along his haunches."

"Was the predator a filthy Deysik?" Vivian asks. Her little face scrunches in disgust and confusion directed at me. My spine goes rigid at the insult.

"And what do you know of Deysik?" I ask the little girl, curious to know what she's been taught. I keenly feel everyone staring at me, surprised.

"That they're animals who live in a human shell. That they steal things and murder people, like my mama and papa!" Vivian says.

Her words punch me in the gut. "They can do those things, but it's important to remember not *all* of them are like that. I was reminded of something similar—"

"Prince Dread tells me you're an experienced fighter. How many have *you* killed?" Pippa interjects, cutting me off. I hold her stare, refraining from outright glaring for several moments until she realizes I won't back down and shifts uncomfortably in her chair.

"Five Rogue Deysik," I answer, "fourteen men and seven Ariportia. Do these numbers satisfy you in my qualifications, girl?" I stare at her without a flicker of clemency on my face. Pippa swallows but shows no other signs of unease before she blinks rapidly, shaking off her surprise, and flicks her gaze to Calix and Vasilius, who nod in confirmation. Calix has already heard my body count while on the Ravager and saw how many men I killed in the cage.

"What are rogues?"

The question piques everyone's interest, and Calix can't hide the smirk on his chiseled face. I suppose a definition wouldn't hurt.

"Deysik who lose all control and fall into a blood fury. When they reach that state, Ranger's put them down."

Vasilius glances at me, and I clear my throat and try to lighten the mood. "I may be *hideously* scarred, but nearly every single one I have is from saving a life. If not my own, then others."

"Nearly? You mean you have a scar from your own stupidity?" Pippa pounces.

I smile, finding her hostility somewhat amusing now. Pointing to the scar along my collarbone, I answer. "My queen gave me this as a punishment and warning. Do my duty or lose my life. That's what a Ranger does. I'll hold the same standard in my duty to you and your sisters."

Olga's jaw drops open. "She gave you a scar as punishment? What did you *do*?"

I shrug. "Didn't stop her son from being foolish." I pause, realizing the irony of my failure the second time. Olga is quiet momentarily, her icy blue eyes staring at me thoughtfully. "In your country, you hurt women as a punishment?"

"Not as punishments, but as reminders. If kindness doesn't work, then pain will. Nothing overly violent as my scar, which is... a consequence for an extraordinary circumstance," I say. Calix reaches under the table and squeezes my thigh gently. I have not told him any of this, and I hate I'm doing so now, but they asked, and I want to put them at ease.

Pippa's eyes narrow, but she raises her chin like a queen and nods. Vivian mimics her movements, adding, "Kind of like the Mother and how she first went to war with Ertune."

"Oh? I've never heard your version of this part of history," I prompt, curious.

"It doesn't surprise me you know *nothing* of the Mother in your backwater country," Pippa snips. Diedra shoots her a warning look, and Calix stares her down until the girl slumps in her chair in a sulk.

Calix adjusts his seat and says calmly, "As you know, the Mother isn't the first deity to rule this world. Ertune came before her—a fiery god of war, who bestowed powers upon his three favorite Generals and their armies; Deysik, the gift of changing skins; Ariportia, the gift of flight, along with a third General, whom history no longer remembers. Their armies brought about this land's destruction, enslaving people and the three reigned, causing terror and suffering wherever they conquered. The Mother in Faurst heard about the atrocities occurring from the refugees fleeing to her shores. Her desire to stop Ertune's soldiers became her war cry."

Vasilius adds, leaning forward on the table with his forearms, "She possessed the fire jewel which gifted similar abilities to her followers—her children—to unite and go to war against Ertune's dark soldiers to save the people of this world. A great battle was fought. Ertune and his favored Generals were vanquished by the Mother as she sacrificed herself to save her warriors."

Diedra sets down her spoon, pushing her plate away and adds, "The Monks of Faurst have a sacred statue honoring her." Calix and my gazes lock across the table, keenly aware of how sacred. "The Monks claim it changes to show the mothers who sacrifice their lives for their children. And only her true heir can kiss the statue to inherit her powers—whatever they are and the city with it." The blood in my veins turns to sludge as what she says reaffirms the purpose of Fidir's foolish journey to Faurst.

With my unwitting help.

Calix squeezes my hand. "The empire has lived in peace until four hundred years ago, when the Empress of Luminum lost her life, protecting her child from a Deysik. The Emperor commanded his soldiers to wipe them all out, and he nearly succeeded."

And the *Maage* helped him.

"Over two decades ago, they started the cycle all over again," Vasilius sighs, rubbing his temples, "They should've been happy with what we gave them four hundred years ago."

I frowned, "What is that, exactly?"

Vasilius peers at me, his solid blue eyes cold as a winter storm. "Their lives."

I say with a soft facetiousness, "How ungrateful of those born after your purge to want a better life or a chance to learn from their ancestors' mistakes."

Vasilius's glare dies before he turns away from me, staring at his calloused hands folded in front of him. Calix frowns at his brother.

"The Mother loves *all* people in this world, not just her children," Diedra reminds the table, sitting back in annoyance. Canary is half Ariportia. From what I gather, Diedra follows the Mother's Monks' urges for Deysik to be treated equally.

A hard thing to do when the relationship between the two communities are fraught with hostility.

"How do you communicate with the Deysik?"

"Usually, the Mother's Monks on the border are our couriers, however the past several years—"

"Since you started using the weapons from Panthum on them," Diedra cuts in for clarification.

"—has been tenuous at best."

"Tell me about your predators—the ones who attacked Windrunner," Olga cuts in, changing the subject, eagerness written all over her face. Her skin is a few shades lighter than her sisters, and it's glowing with enthusiasm.

"No horse could survive an injury that severe," Pippa snaps at her sister, her curls falling over her face. She shoves away her plate as if the topic sickens her, so I change the subject, while refraining from rolling my eyes.

Turning to Olga I say, "I'll teach you how to wield a dagger. Every girl should know how to defend herself. Do you have one?"

Olga's smile brightens once again. "We'll scrounge through the weapons cache to see what's free to take."

"Your uncle has a trunk full of weapons in our room we can sift through," I say, and Calix smiles, settling his hand on the back of my chair before leaning in to whisper in my ear, "Is the same trunk—."

"—Stop flirting in front of your nieces," I hiss.

He leans back, tugging on my braid. Pippa glares, and Vivian joins in when she sees her older sister doing it. I have to stop myself from sighing heavily.

"Aunt Diedra, I'm surprised to see you with the man who betrayed us all," Pippa says with sweet venom, causing Diedra's face to fall. The girl is skilled at cutting open old hurts. I wonder where she learned that from?

"If another vile word comes out of your mouth, Pip, I'll make you recite comportment lessons for three hours before you're allowed to drink anything," Calix snaps, and the girl shuts her mouth with a click, before shoving back out of her chair and sashaying out the door. Vivian follows suit, their blue and pink organza dresses swishing furiously.

"I'm sorry Diedra," Calix says, nodding to his sister. "It seems the Matron hasn't helped. Pippa's not been the same since her parents died."

"That's no excuse. You don't see Olga behaving that way," Vasilius interjects.

I was like Pippa once, and I remember the anger storming inside me like a hurricane, and nothing could stop it until I learned how to channel it. Then I was able to control my grief better.

"No, but I eat everything I see," Olga says before bursting into tears. My heart wrenches for this girl who's a little older than I was when I lost my own mother. I leave my seat and kneel down to her level, the way Master Baylor did when I was young and needed comfort.

"There are lots of different ways to handle grief, Olga. When my own mother died, I fought with my older brother so fiercely my father sent me away for a year," I say softly. "I was a lot like Pippa." She pulls back with tear-stained cheeks, locking eyes with me and a buzzing sounds in my head, and I'm unable to look away. "You're right. Your grief presents itself differently, but the solution is generally the same."

"Really?"

I nod. Hurt people, hurt people. Once I was able to control my body, my mind soon followed.

I only hope that if it works for Olga, then Vivian and possibly Pippa will follow suit.

Chapter 20

I wake earlier than I normally do, leaving Calix's sleeping form to head to the bow side training room where I find Canary sparring with the Black Fox's mercenary I fought with yesterday. The merc's companion sits against the wall, sharpening the blade of a sword. He's larger than the other men here, but his movements are measured and at ease. He drops it, and stands when he sees me, signaling the end to Canary and the merc's fight.

Disappointment floods through me as I wanted to see how someone else fairs against my friend.

Canary and I spar for thirty minutes before deciding to go find the girls. While I'm wiping my face free from sweat, a male voice carries down from the second-floor balcony. "Tell her it will be a marriage in name only if that's her desire, I don't give a damn." Vasilius snarls. I glance up to see the hostile Prince facing the silver mask of the Black Fox.

"So ready to fall on your own sword, Prince Vasilius?" the Black Fox growls.

Vasilius laughs bitterly. "More like slit my own throat. We don't need the alliance. Her country is between the Deysik and Ariportia, meaning her people will be slaughtered first if this comes to war. The Emperor was just as humiliated by Svetlana's disappearance as her brothers. He will not come to their aid even if they beg on their knees."

He's talking to her about the Slate Princess who jilted him on his wedding day. Little does he know who I suspect he's talking to.

I move just under them and drink some water while shamelessly eavesdropping. I can imagine how angry he is with the mess she's left him in, but my logical opinion is he chooses to feel that way. Without the alliance, there's no reason for him to feel responsible for her or the fallout of what will happen to her people. It was her choice to leave.

Perhaps it's the callousness with which Vasilius speaks to the Black Fox that keeps the female silent, most likely mulling over his words. A moment later, his footsteps retreat, and the sound of the door leading outside to the wrap-around deck opens and closes sharply.

It seems the Black Fox is going to hold onto her secrets. It strikes me then that he cares *too* much. It's the cause of all of his anger. He hates he can't help people.

***

The Princes spend their morning meal in meetings, leaving women to have breakfast in the private dining room, with bright light gleaming through the many windows lining the outside wall. Pippa and Vivian completely ignore me as I show Olga two different places to strike a man while Diedra explains the anatomy behind it.

"Did you grow up in the woods?" A voice lashes like an unexpected whip, and I turn to Vivian as she eats a ripe strawberry from her white porcelain plate filled only with eggs and fruit.

"You could say so. My home is in a mountain valley, surrounded by pine trees," I answer with a warm smile, trying to attempt a good relationship with the girl. I walk around Olga and move to snatch her by the collar, and the girl sweeps her hand defensively, hitting the inside of my elbow, effectively causing me to weaken my grip, before her other hand mock strikes my throat. I smile at her and jerk my chin so she can take a breather and grab some water. "What are your favorite subjects to read?"

"I hate reading," Vivian replies offhandedly.

"That's because you're no good at it," Pippa comments with a bland, sort of matter-of-fact tone that's worse somehow. Little Vivian bows her head, fiddling with her fork, making a racket against the porcelain.

I roll my shoulders and hear little cracks between my shoulder blades. "If you like, I can sit with you and read. I can share with you some of my favorite stories—"

"Like how to hunt and gut an animal?" Pippa says sweetly.

If only she knew *what* I hunted.

I can't help my wicked smile from slashing across my face as I give Pippa a stare that causes many Ranger recruits to second guess the human who was somehow faster and more agile than them.

"I don't want you to read with me," Vivian says quickly. My grin falls, and I give Pippa a look. The girl smirks and drinks her orange juice. Was I this horrible to Drake?

I try again, spinning my dagger to give me something to do. "Vivian, my father used to tell me stories of a Princess just like you who tamed a wolf to become her companion. Would you like me to tell you a story tonight before bed?"

Vivian brightens and nods, clinking the beads in her thick, dark braid. I beam, and Pippa opens her mouth.

I cut her off. "Would you like me to select your comportment recital, Pippa?"

She snaps her mouth shut and remains silent for the rest of the meal.

Olga, however, asks me a dozen questions about what it's like growing up in the mountains and riding horses. "Did your father show you how to ride?" she asks. I nod, and before I know what's happening, Pippa bursts into tears and runs from the room.

I turn wide eyes to Olga, whose face falls, looking down. "I forgot. Father was teaching her how to ride right before he died. She still won't get on a horse, though she wants to."

The poor girls desperately need love and attention. I once knew the feeling all too well. Thankfully, I can handle a fourteen-year-old's bad temper, if only so she knows she's worth fighting for.

*****

The moonlight causes shadows to dance in the bedroom of our suite, enough for me to make out Calix's large, powerful form under the covers. My heartrate takes off like a gallop as butterflies take off in my stomach. I'm glad he's here and not attending more meetings. I quickly ready myself for bed, sliding between the sheets and slide over to Calix's warm body, but I find him stiff.

"What's wrong?" I ask, dread pooling in my stomach.

He doesn't move, save for turning his head to face me. It's light enough in our room I can tell his eyes are hard like I've never seen them before. In a cold and calm voice, he says, "Pippa said you threatened her at breakfast. She burst into my meeting in tears. Is that true?"

Tingles of annoyance run down my spine. Why is he taking her side? "Yes, but the threatening and her tears aren't related."

He clearly cares about the feelings of his nieces a great deal, I think bitterly.

"Please tell me. I spent thirty minutes trying to get her to calm down," Calix sighs wearily, turning to face the ceiling, pressing fingers into his eyes. It's difficult not to be irritated over Pippa throwing a tantrum to her uncle about me when he's overwhelmed with the Ariportia and Deysik attack fallout. More reports have come in of assaults at the mines, and outlying townships along the border.

"Pippa was being rude to Olga, and I simply asked her if she would like me to choose a comportment recital for herself, which did the trick. She was quiet after that, and when I asked Olga about horses, she burst into tears and ran out of the room. I found out afterwards why she reacted that way, and I feel bad, but I searched the whole steamer to find her before I discovered her in her room where she declined my apology," I explain calmly, thinking of the hour I waited for her to come out with no success.

"Why didn't you ask the servants to help you search for her?"

I roll my eyes, "How would that look, Calix, if the whole ship knew she was missing while under my care."

Calix exhales, "Why do you care so much about what others think?"

"I don't care what they think of *me*. I care about what they think of *you* with me. I'm an outsider who is looked at with suspicion. The other guests don't speak to me—"

"You're not exactly inviting anyone—"

"Who am I supposed to invite Calix?" I say, exasperated. "The only person I know is Diedra, and she's in her study with Canary. Raine is flocked by females wherever he goes, Toriey is in meetings with you and Vasilius all day. You want me to introduce myself to women who aren't exactly open to making friends with me?"

His body sags, "I'm sorry—"

"You don't need to apologize for being a protective uncle or for Pippa's behavior," I say, keeping my exasperation in, and steadying my tone. I lie still next to him, staring at the shadows the moon casts along the wall, wondering if this type of concern for his niece is more about the grief of his sister and her husband, dredged up with the recent attack. I lay quietly, my mind buzzing with all the stress and worry I've just barely admitted to myself.

Warm hands reach for me, followed by soft lips kissing my neck. Calix's voice is soft and reconciliatory. "Will you forgive me for jumping to conclusions?"

He kisses along my jaw, and I groan and arch towards his fingers as they tease the expanse of my thigh. He runs his hands over my curves, worshiping what little I have. Instant fire sparks in my belly and spreads through every limb and fiber of my body. I never want it to end.

"Possibly, but I'm not quite there yet," I say, pressing against his side, twining my legs through his. I'm absolutely head over heels in love with this man. I've never felt so valued and loved before in my life. It's intoxicating. His strong hands pull me on top of him, a hand sliding through my hair to grip the back of my head, his lips a whisper against mine as he says, "Then let me see if I can help you along."

When he pulls away, I gasp for air, "Don't stop," I demand.

"So greedy," he teases and ever slowly kisses along my jaw and column of my throat and peppers kisses over my scar.

"How old were you when your queen gave you this?" he asks, skating his hand along my abdomen, zig-zagging toward my heart.

"Eight," I answer, mindlessly. His hand pauses for only a fraction of a moment before continuing, but I know my comment surprised him. "I love you, Bluey. So much, I don't know what to do with it." His hands run up and down the backs of my thighs, and I bring my lips to hover above his. "I love that you take care of your family and country. It's honorable, and I'm more enamored with each new quality I discover that you embody."

He stops smiling and brings his hands up to cradle my face. "You will always be safe with me. I know there will be growing pains with the cultural differences between us, but I know together we can handle it."

I didn't think my heart could handle all my love for him, until he said those words. I passionately kiss him again, the scared part of me settles at his declaration. It cements my love, further keeping me where I want to be.

Chapter 21

"Tell me about your family. What are your brothers like, *Moskazi*?" Pippa says slyly. The way she says my new title is as if it is an epithet rather than a title of love and honor. I frown before I decide to ignore the way she tries to sow discord. I figure it will be a very long time before she'll come around. From under the shade of the top deck we pass towns with decorations and enjoy the music drifting across the water from their celebrations of Currell.

Diedra left us just moments ago back to her infirmary, leaving only myself with the girls.

A gentle, hot breeze sends the tablecloth dancing along the legs of our table on the deck of the steamer, offering some relief from the searing afternoon sun. I couldn't stand being cooped up any longer inside with their tutors, who are thankfully now on their lunch break.

I sit back out of the shade and face the sky, enjoying the breeze. "I have one older brother who's six years older than me, and one that's two years younger."

"Describe them, please. I'd very much like to have a firm grasp of your family," Pippa cuts in eagerly. I frown, unsure of why she wants descriptions, and I half wonder if Calix put her up to it so he could send someone to find my family back in Panthum. I lower my head and look to Pippa to study her face and see what I can glean from it. Is she truly curious? Or crafty?

"Are they as—interesting as you are?" She smiles like a cat with a canary, and I grin back. She doesn't know she's dealing with a wolf.

"Much more so. In fact, my oldest brother is just like you. He likes to use words to cut people down and make them feel as miserable as he is. He isn't the only one who lost a mother, yet, he blames others for an unavoidable tragedy." I don't think she would have appreciated being compared to myself. I keep my eyes pinned to her, unblinking, and it clearly makes her uncomfortable. She turns away and raises her chin, shaking off any guilt she may have felt.

"How did she die then?" she asks, barely keeping the sharp tone from her words. If I could see my heart now, I'd find it curling in on itself.

"That's none of your concern," I say stiffly, my hand bunched into a fist on my lap as I look out at the greenery of the trees and flowers between regal stone buildings.

"Ha! Then you're hiding something, aren't you? I knew it," Pippa smirks, settling further back in her seat, pleased with herself.

Ridiculous girl.

I raise a patient brow and continue. "I'll not tell you because you will not treat it with the respect it's owed."

"I'm sorry your momma died," Vivian says quietly, her dark hair braided into a crown.

I remember Master Baylor, the most frightening Ranger I knew at some point in my life, asking me to tell him stories of my mother. It was a balm to the wound in my heart. Perhaps it would help these girls, too?

"I miss her every day, which is why I'm sure you girls feel the same. Why don't you tell me about her? I'd love to hear what a wonderful mother I'm sure she was," I smile warmly at Vivian and Olga. Pippa stiffens.

"She—"

"Don't tell her Viv. For the same reasons she gave us," Pippa turns her slitted blue eyes toward me, and I frown wearily.

"I'd never speak ill of your mother. You have my honor," I promise.

Olga glares at her older sister and speaks with defiance, which makes me swell with pride. The middle sister is taking a stand. "She was the most beautiful woman in all the Empire—at least that's what everyone says. She read us stories and played dollies with us. She danced with Father—"

"They gave the best hugs!" Vivian interjected gleefully, wanting to add in, her face bright. I smile and warmth fills my chest, seeing it work so quickly.

"She convinced Prince Dread to find a female warrior to teach women of the Empire how to defend themselves. And he found *you*," Olga adds, cheeks rosy. I swallow.

I had no idea.

"I'm glad he did," I reply softly.

"*Of course* you are. Any woman would be with how rich he is, *Moskazi*. I'm sure you'll be gifted with all sorts of things soon enough.

Just like his other slags," Pippa snarks, her light eyes peering in my direction, spitting with venom before she turns away in disgust.

What? I catch myself, barely keeping a reaction off my face. I don't want the girl to know how painful her words hit. My temper begins to simmer, yet, I take a calming breath. She thinks you're here to take advantage of Calix.

"There are more important things than gold, Pippa," I say softly. "Do you really think so little of your uncle?"

Her cheeks flush, and she shifts in her seat. Lifting her chin, she looks out to the glimmering dark blue river and says, "Men can be fooled by deceptive women."

My face flames with how closely she has hit the mark. I *am* being deceptive about what's in my blood, but not *who* I am as a person. However, Pippa catches my expression and narrows her eyes.

"That's true, but not with your uncle," I assure, taking another calming breath to smother my growing anger with myself. I haven't yet resolved what to do about omitting such key details about myself to Calix.

"We don't even know you, yet he's *trusting* you to guard us," Pippa argues.

I lean forward, placing my arms on the table. "Because I *earned* that trust, Pippa. I'll never be cruel to you. What is it about me that bothers you? Is it that I speak differently? Is it that I don't dress as the women here? Is it that you think I'm taking away your uncle's attention from you? *What?* Because I don't back down from a challenge, and believe me when I say you would be no match for me, girl."

With every word, my anger hones like a blade, and when I'm done, I know it was the wrong thing to say, especially to Pippa with how she twists whatever I say into a threat of violence. Vivian pulls her legs up and tucks herself into a ball and Olga swallows, eyes wide.

Mother's braids.

I close my eyes and breathe, forcing quiet into my tone. "I didn't mean *'challenge'* as in I'd hurt you, but I can spar *words* with you as long as you continue to cross them with me. I don't harm kits… " At their scrunched faces, I clarify, "Children. I've hunted down people for that very thing." Vivian's body relaxes a little, and Olga nods. Pippa glares unrepentantly, fear still in her frigid eyes, but I know it to be false.

"Are you afraid of your uncles or their Azure Warriors?" I ask the younger girls.

Vivian shakes her head, and Olga replies, "No."

"Then you shouldn't be afraid of me. The only difference is I'm a female from a different land. My honor is my life, and I vow to protect you, no matter how poorly you treat me, because that's what Rangers do."

I can see from their faces the younger girls understand, but I find Pippa plotting away, and I know it won't be just a battle of will or words.

It will be a full-scale war.

***

"If she isn't replaced within the hour, I'll run away!" Pippa yells from inside the room, where I know Calix to be holding meetings with the commanders we collected on our journey.

I freeze in the hallway. Apparently, Pippa is lobbying her uncle to remove me from watching over her. Publicly. *Again.*

"You will do no such foolish thing. Besides where would you go?" Calix asks calmly. I walk to the door. It's cracked a few inches, and I see Pippa launch herself into his arms sobbing. Commanders Teegu and Toriey are in the room, further back talking amongst themselves, casting furtive glances at Calix and his distressed niece.

Wonderful. I'm the villain again.

"To Heviin, where Mama met Papa. She scares me. What if she betrays us like the Traitor before he was banished?" Pippa wails. His fingers tighten for a moment on his niece, and I know that disloyalty still haunts him. Pippa's playing on his fears, and I can't stand it. Protectiveness rises in me, and impulsively, I push open the room, all eyes turning on me.

I try not to wince when the commanders frown in my direction, but on some level, I understand I'm an outsider who's frightening a young girl.

"I've vowed on my life, Pippa, that I'll never hurt you. You insult me when you question my honor," I say, deciding to lean against the door frame to not overwhelm the situation. I'm done being kind to her. The girl needs firm consequences like I did when I was young. Calix looks at me and from his torn expression, I know I won't win this argument.

"Would you excuse us, Alana? I'd like to speak privately with Pip," Calix says softly. I gambled it was coming, but the hurt still cuts deep, foisted, and I hate I feel it so keenly over something so silly. He sided with her last night, but after our talk, I'd have thought he'd side with me.

My thoughts darken. I did it to myself. He doesn't value me enough to stand up for me against his niece.

Pippa turns her head away from the room and smirks. I keep the glare off my face. She plays as dirty as a spoiled child, and they're no Deysik to smell her vile intentions. I must figure out a new strategy in dealing with her. Teegu crosses his arms across his wide chest and narrows his eyes.

This rejection and embarrassment is worse than Drake not awarding me my Ranger in front of the other recruits. It's one more hurt piled on top of a mountain of cuts.

My father foisting me onto the Panthum Royals. Deysik not wanting to play with me because I was human. Drake not wanting me to join the

Rangers. My chest hollows out as I push off the door frame, trying not to wish the same amount of pain I'm feeling on the manipulative girl.

"Take all the time you need," I say evenly with every fiber of control in my possession, leaving the room, and closing the door softly behind me. He'll need it. One can't reason with a girl who's gone too long without consequences for her behavior.

I stalk down the hallway, past curious servants and Azure Warriors, seething with anger and humiliation I brought upon myself when I entered the war room. I was thoughtless. I make to go to Calix and my shared quarters, but I pause to think as women and Azure Warriors brush past me, staring and whispering.

I have nowhere to go that's my own. Calix has provided living quarters, clothes, food, and transportation, but nothing is outright mine to possess. Pippa's toxic words from before ingress upon my thoughts. Just like his other slags.

A tornado would be less destructive than my anger right now. I'm too upset, and I know if I see him, I'll blurt things I'll regret, just like I have in every interaction with Drake growing up. I don't want a repeat of our previous fight. I'm not in a state fit to be around people, let alone provide fodder for the servant's gossip. I'm keenly aware of their eyes as they sweep past me in the corridor, taking in my clothes, my scars, my expression. All of it's most likely funneled back to Teegu, Toriey, or worse, the Emperor and Empress.

Instead of traversing to our bedroom, I aim for less eyes and descend down a companionway to the very bottom level of the hold, and make for the stables.

Being on the opposite end of the Grace from where they're housed, I navigate the narrow halls until I'm greeted by several Azure Warriors guarding a door.

I slow my steps, the lamp light casting long shadows against their gilded masks, covering the lower half of their face. I slow my approach as a creeping sensation buzzes underneath my skin.

"*Moskazi*," one greets politely, earning a nod, and as I pass the door, I glimpse into the barred window into the prison and cell beyond. Glowing purple fire in the shape of eyes blink open and hold my stare. Something sharp stabs my belly. The eyes blink, and a guard clears his throat.

I realize I stopped. I should move and leave. Calix's warning of Deysik marking their enemies for death clangs in my brain, but I ignore it all, irrational hurt and anger riding my decisions. I have no idea what to ask this Deysik because there are too many questions bunched behind my tongue and too many ears.

The Deysik rises to stand, and the Azure Warriors move next to me, one saying, "You need to leave, *Moskazi*."

"*Moskazi*?" the Deysik says in a low, gravelly voice, rife with emotion. "You're a warrior. I smell the shards of metal and the sting of death on your skin. Do you delight in war too? Are you and the Prince well matched?"

All the hairs on my body stand on end. I say nothing, still frozen to the ground as my heart takes off like a startled horse running at full speed. Perhaps it's been too long being away from my family and their heightened senses, but the astute description is disserting.

His amethyst eyes shift as the Deysik angles his head again in the dark, drawing closer to the door. He's so quiet I can't hear his footsteps.

"*Moskazi*," one of the Azure Warriors hisses and nudges me to leave.

It's enough to break my concentration, and I turn and walk away, ignoring the guilt gnawing at my insides.

I'm a Deysik by blood, if not by gift. One soldier can respect another, and I don't agree with the fate of this Deysik. I can no longer ignore the difficult conversations I must have with Calix.

Once I arrive at the stables, I help the baffled stable boys, clean stalls, the smell and work helping in clearing my thoughts. I pull down and carry over fresh straw to each stall, before playing a game of cards with them. I lose miserably each hand, before trouncing them at the last, winning the game. I tell them to take the night off and to give them credit, they only protest once before I cut them off and demand they leave me in peace.

Once they leave, I allow my tears to fall in earnest.

I'm furious with myself. How could I be so stupid? How did I put myself in this emotionally precarious position? I hate it. I hate that I *feel* so much. Everything is amplified, and I can't stand how this hurt seems to burrow deep. Is this what having a menstrual cycle has reduced me to? Is this why Ranger's drink *chaze* tea every morning? Is this why I'm so broken hearted over Calix's rejection of me over his niece.

Or am I feeling this way because of how deeply I love him?

I don't have the answers, and I'd talk to Diedra but she's Calix's sister. Besides I couldn't open up to her and work through my snarled and twisted feelings, especially when it's tied to all the sorrow from my past.

I take a measured, deep, watery breath and hold it for four seconds... then I let it out slowly. I repeat this, trying to shift my thoughts to things I know. Things are facts.

I'm his *Moskazi*.

His.

He paid an astronomical amount to save me. Despite threat of death, he fought for me when he thought Nash was hurting me. He delayed the Monks in Faurst from pursuing me up the mountain. He swore his undying love for me. He wants my family here for my happiness.

He's not perfect, but he's perfect for me.

***

Sometime in the middle of the night, I hear heavy footsteps approach, and I turn the dial on the lamp to increase the wick, brightening the tack room where I made a bed out of saddle blankets.

Calix's hood is up, shadowing his eyes, and his stubble shadows the lower half of his face. His broad shoulders are stiff and tense under his black tunic. His tan skin glows in the light, revealing the tendons in his neck.

My Warlord grabs the back of an empty chair and slings it around, sitting stiffly, keeping his gaze down, staring at the floor. Trepidation fills me like water sloshing against my feet inside a boat.

Before I can speak, a deep voice fills the tack room. One that does not belong to Calix. He raises his head to look at me and clear-cut blue eyes stare back.

"Pippa is waging a campaign against you, and you're losing sorely."

This isn't news to me. I'm well aware of the precarious position I'm in. I cross my legs and wait.

His blonde brows furrow. "You know this, but you don't care, do you?"

I raise a brow. "I can't change how she behaves or thinks." His gaze flickers, and I continue, "I don't know what boundaries I can set with her because she is mine to protect, not mine to discipline. She's a child who has been emotionally neglected since her parents' deaths."

He stares back. I breathe in and look at the ceiling. "You have not liked me since the moment you laid eyes on me. Tell me, Vasilius, what have I done to earn your virulency?"

His nostrils flare. "You're deceitful, arrogant, and, in my opinion, appear slightly deranged."

I uncross my legs and sit up, "You're right about the first, possibly correct about the second, and mistaken on the last."

He blinks as if surprised I'd admit to his accusations. Then, the muscle in his jaw flickers, and he drills me with his gaze. "You're also honest, loyal, and extremely intelligent. Who uses the word virulency?"

I can't help it, the edges of my lips twitch. I shrug. "I love words," I pause, "and it used to drive my oldest brother crazy when I'd use them on him."

My response earns a huff and then, "Why are you unable to tell us anything about Panthum?"

I twist my lip and rub the back of my neck. He wasn't being a prick; he was asking *nicely,* and that's also my weak spot.

"I am under threat of death by *law* and honor bound to keep information about my country private. For this reason, I am unable to provide you, your brother, commanders or anyone else who asks me with the answers they desperately seek. Calix knows this. He hopes I'll tell him one day, but I can't do that."

"Why not?" Vasilius asks.

"Because my family will be slaughtered if I do, and I'll not betray them, simply because a Prince asks."

"What if an Emperor inquires?"

I shake my head. "He is my contractual owner for less than five years. He can order me to fight for him but not be tasked with suicidal assignments, or he will be in violation of the contract, and that will release me. There's nothing in there about sharing state secrets. Everything else is spun sugar."

"We are at war with the Deysik and you hold information and possible resources that will help us win this war," he says exasperated and frustrated, but I don't think it's necessarily at me, but rather the situation of having an uncrackable safe holding all of the keys that will help save your people.

He pulls a dagger from his boot, and a look of concentration comes over his face as he leans forward, twirling the blade. "What if I put a knife to your throat and demand the information?"

I shake my head, "By your hand, I would only die. If I tell you, all my family dies."

A flash of silver and dirk is pressed against Vasilius's carotid artery.

"If you ever threaten my wife again, I'll gut and skin you alive before I kill you."

Nothing Calix said could have surprised me more.

I blink. "Wife?"

Chapter 22

*W*ife.

I blink, and before I can open my mouth to rectify Calix's misunderstanding, he snarls, "According to the contract Alana signed, saving my life on the Ravager, she is legally and lawfully bound to me, which makes her the Princess of Heviin and Princess to the Empire of Luminum."

All blood drains from Vasilius's face, and he doesn't fight back when Calix hauls him out of the chair and punches him.

I leap to my feet. "We were making conversation, Bluey. Don't over-react," I shout.

The voice he uses sends a shiver of delight and fear down my spine. "If anyone pulls a weapon on you even in conversation, they will pay for it, despite their rank."

If it weren't so serious, I would roll my eyes. I raise an eyebrow at Vasilius as if to say, *you violated the unspoken code.* He exhales, bows slightly to me, and then leaves.

Calix stares hard after his brother until we can no longer hear his footsteps. Then he strides towards me, scooping me up and carrying me back to a soft bed. My boots are removed and my tears are wiped away. I hadn't realized I was crying.

He came for me. I hadn't expected him to. I was nothing more than his slag.

"I've botched it again, haven't I, Alana," he whispers, pulling me to his warm, strong body. My tears are ones of relief. My feet are on solid ground with his security.

Moskazi. Wife.

The lingering ache causes me to hold onto him with a fierceness that surprises me.

"I know I should have told you sooner, but I wanted to propose properly and allow you to make a choice in the matter." Calix then launches into the story of how, when he broke Nash's rule, he was going to lose his life until Canary suggested he marry me, which would excuse the crime as well as ensure the Azure Warriors and Warlord would bid for his return. The one condition was, I was not to be told.

Everything clicks into place; why did Nash tell me he'd cut out my tongue if I asked about it? How Toriey looked at me curiously when I refuted Calix being *my* Prince. I'm technically a citizen of Luminum now.

"I wanted to give you the option to dissolve the marriage. However, I couldn't keep my hands off you, and the *Maage* confirmed your title with her magic." He squeezes me tightly to him and pauses, "If you would like a divorce, I can arrange it."

"As polite and chivalrous your offer is, I'd like to politely decline and threaten you with dismemberment of fingers if you suggest or otherwise ask me again." I burrow into him closer.

Calix chuckles. He kisses the top of my head, "Noted."

"I'm going to wake up and find this a dream; it hardly seems real."

"No dream, fire jewel."

"Calix?"

"Hmm?"

"If I could tell you all my secrets, I'm afraid you won't love me the way you do."

"Then don't tell me. I know who you are, Ruby." He kisses my temple. "I apologize I haven't been handling Pippa very well. Toriey pulled me aside and gave me a tongue lashing for allowing her to cause scenes the way she did."

To say I'm surprised the older Commander came to my defense is an understatement. This is a night full of surprises.

"This is all new for me too, and I'll say I'm trying with Pippa, but I'll no longer try to reassure anyone of my honor," I say quietly. Calix shifts back to look at me, his turquoise eyes staring at me with hurt, love, and the tenderness I need. I run my finger along the cut of his jawline, the stubble pricking my skin as his calloused fingers rub up and down my arm.

"You have always been. I know and trust it." Calix says softly.

"How is Pippa?"

"Diedra is with her." A weighted pause, "I think I like being called spun sugar. Ow—"

***

"My eldest brother is the best Ranger on the Riband. He's the most successful behind my father and Master Baylor. He was always correcting my form or criticizing my efforts. He made things extremely difficult and made sure every challenge he could think of would be strategically placed in my way," I say as I work with Olga the next morning.

Because of the additional people we've collected on the Steamer in the last two days, the training pitch is filled with our Azure Warrior guards and the Black Fox's mercenaries, while the other Champions are moved to the front Training Courtyard.

"It took me four years to pass my trails to join as a Ranger," I murmur quietly, and Olga's eyes flash wide, and she stares at me with her mouth hanging open.

Vivian sits on a bench next to Pippa with her feet curled up under her flowing yellow dress, cradling a book, sounding out words slowly and clearly.

"How old are you?" Pippa asks, still with her head down, to look at Vivian.

"Twenty."

It has been another terse morning at breakfast, but I succeeded with the younger girls telling me about themselves. Pippa has been silently ignoring me all day, until now. I can practically see her doing the math that Rangers start at sixteen.

"How long does it typically take?" Pippa asks again, a frown on her face.

I gesture for Olga to take a break and drink some water before I respond, "A year."

"Didn't he want you to be a Ranger?" Olga asks, straightening her pants. A few of the men glance towards us, and I grin.

"No. He didn't want me anywhere near it and did everything in his power to discourage me enough to quit."

"But you never did!" Vivian exclaims, squeezing her book. I shake my head.

"I wasn't the best sister, though, so I can see why he made it so difficult. I'd get upset with him, and sometimes I'd put dirt in his boots and give him the smelliest blankets instead of clean ones. I loosened the stitching on his sleeves once so when he pulled his shirts on, they fell right off."

I smile, remembering the time he came out of his tent and glared at me while holding twelve pairs of sleeves. I couldn't move for a week after he had me take a full Ranger pack and climb the nearby mountain trail with six thousand feet elevation gain, while timed, twice over.

"What did he do back?" Olga's beautiful round face breaks into a smile, and she nervously tightens the band on her pants.

"He made me train harder and longer and *then* had me assist the smithy with sharpening our weapons." I pause, adding pensively, "I was terribly mean to him, so I deserved it. I realize now that, though he was hard on me, I'm better off for it. I'm grateful to him because I wouldn't be alive had he not been so tough."

"What about your younger brother?" Vivian asks, blushing slightly. Even at seven years old, she's starting to think about boys. Pippa shushes her, asking her to refocus her efforts on reading.

I laugh. "He is shy and loves solitude, so he enjoys scouting when we go on hunting trips. He promises to be better than Drake as a Ranger, and I don't doubt it. He has an uncanny ability to know what's coming before anyone else. He also is the one who taught me how to shoot an arrow with perfect accuracy, though my oldest brother never knew it."

Homesickness hits me hard. I miss my family, friends, and home. I've been turning over in my head how I'll ask Calix to help me send a letter to my family. I believe I could do it through Tuafu, our agent in Faurst if he's still employed. I think more and more about Calix's offer of having them come here, but I know it would be impossible. They would not hide who they are, and they certainly wouldn't hide their disdain for how the Deysik are treated.

Pippa snorts and rolls her eyes, causing me to place my homesickness aside and focus on the task at hand.

I decided to work with Olga on one particularly difficult maneuver, I think she'd enjoy. "Want to learn something my father taught me when I was first training?"

The girl nods eagerly, and I can't help but notice the Black Fox and a couple of her mercenaries watching, along with a handful of Azure Warriors. I place my hands gently on her shoulders and say, "Spin, thrust, pull," as I move her body to follow the actions before stepping away and guiding her through it. Over and over, we work until she finally manages it perfectly.

"Well done, Olga," Pippa cheers, surprising me. Olga's face flushes with delight, and her smile breaks through with such sincerity it's stunning. I mirror Olga's grin and begin again, showing her how to block and strike with the movement, acting as her mock opponent. Not many minutes later, the dark-haired girl is successful, and Pippa claps for her sister. Based on the older sister's enthusiasm, I wonder if Olga's mock stabbing me between the ribs is what makes Pippa cheer.

She finishes the book with Vivian, and the little Princess goes to find another one, picking through the basket their tutors brought. For the sake of getting to know them better I thought they would like to join Olga and I.

I decide to engage with Pippa. "What is your favorite part about Currell?" She blinks, clearly surprised I'm asking her a question. She closes her book, keeping her finger in as a placeholder, and leans forward.

She shoots her gaze to the Black Fox and her mercenaries. "When the Emperor and Empress have guests come and compete against Azure Warriors. It's an absolute delight to see them get beaten into the dust. No one comes close to winning against our own."

That earns the glances of a few mercenaries and smirks of Azure Warriors. I cock my head to the side, saying with a straight face, "So you like boring fights?"

She flushes and pulls back, glancing around, and I continue, "There's no fun if it's not a competition. It's like an adult competing against a child."

Her smile is practically feline as she stands with delicate grace and says boldly while looking down her nose. "Don't pretend to care about us. You're nothing but a prospecting *slag*."

Vivian and Olga gasp, and the urge to grab her jaw and pry her mouth open, demanding to see her forked tongue, is overwhelming. Once again, the men in the room glance at us, and the mercs outright stare. Pippa stands, holding her hand out to Vivian, who curls up tighter, eyes flicking between us, unsure what to do. I jerk my chin for her to go with Pippa and turn back to Olga, whose mouth is still gaping. My ears burn. I inhale and release it slowly, knowing there's nothing I can do about it. I'm not able to discipline the girl.

Because I'm her protector, and she is a child.

My job is to guard her, even if it is from myself. I don't think I've ever felt so humiliated before. Drake couldn't hold a candle to Pippa when it came to insults. I need to get out of here, but I won't leave Olga alone. She's as horrified as I am, but I do what I've long ago learned. I put on a mask of indifference while reminding myself only time can heal Pippa.

And only if she decides to heal herself.

Turning to Olga, I ask, "Would you like to go for a walk?"

We docked an hour ago for supplies, and Calix has *more* meetings to attend in the city.

The girl nods, and after we put our training weapons away, she slips her new dagger into her slender sheath made out of stamped leather that's buckled around her waist. We leave Pippa and Vivian to their tutors.

Chapter 23

"Do you know where we're going?" Olga asks as I place a stylish wide-brimmed hat over her head before adjusting my matching one.

"Diedra says I'd be an idiot if I got lost, *and* I have an excellent sense of direction." The edge of the river is lined in a wide riverwalk, and bridges intermittently close and open for passing vessels, spanning the length of the city, growing gently in elevation on either side. Like Diedra said earlier today, I'd have to be missing feeling in my limbs, blind, and deaf not to find my way back to the river and her royal steamer.

When I stopped by the war room to inform Calix of our plans, he kissed me swiftly and with more passion than I'd expected from him with a room full of battle-hardened men witnessing it.

His kisses are delightful.

The city of Illalangi is stunning with its pale stones and terra cotta red roofs, with flowerpots and shrubs gracing the doors and windows of each home, reminding me of Nash's neighborhood in Red City. The streets are clean and not overly crowded because most people are heading up to the top of the hill on the opposite side of the river where the Currell arena is. Tonight will decide their territory's Champion.

A hot breeze kisses my face though the sun is on its descent. Olga and I walk companionably, exploring the city's window displays of art galleries, jewelry, and clothing stores. After examining some of the items closer, I find the price tag on a few pieces of clothing. The whole ensemble cost a fraction of what Calix paid for my indenture.

After that I stop checking the prices. The value of things here pains me over how little we profit from our merchandise. Being so secluded is a disadvantage. I realize now, especially because the royal family has been taking advantage of our business and wealth—keeping us at their feet. What does it matter to them if our country is secluded when they have all the opulence of the world brought to them through their merchant supply chain, paid for by our products?

We spent the morning at the library, where Olga found books on history, warfare, and different novels.

I'm unable to read Luminum, so I have her read me passages out loud that she finds interesting. She finds one about Deysik and reads out loud in a clear voice. "A Deysik's second skin is nearly impossible to breach, though luckily for the Azure Warrior's, their people fight amongst themselves with such commonality they often have wounds, which are used as an opening in their armor. A skilled Azure Warrior will be able to find those healing wounds and, with enough force of their weapon, can pierce the skin, fileting—"

"That's enough." My words are sharp and brutal, and Olga frowns, looking at me.

My stomach roils and goes hot, hearing the means these Deysik have been killed off all these years. Their own lack of control and injuring others is their death sentence.

"You personally know Deysik don't you?" The question catches me off guard, taking me a moment to collect my thoughts. I look out over the balcony where we sit, viewing the rows and rows of shelves of books. So much knowledge, so much wealth, so much death.

"Yes," I say softly.

"The ones you know aren't monsters, are they? Not like how Vivian describes them?" she asks so gently I wonder if she thinks she will get in trouble for this question. I see curiosity lining her brown eyes, and it causes me to wonder if Calix or Diedra shared with her what I told them about the Deysik I know. I look out over the library again and the few workers below carting books back to their homes.

"Not the ones I know. I can't speak for the ones on this continent. Then again, I've known monsters to be within every group of people," I say, my blood heating with anger. If only they knew the Deysik's potential, perhaps, they wouldn't be going to war.

It's so different here; it's hard not to feel that way. I feel something brush against me like a cat, and I turn to see Olga staring at me with a strange look—almost like she's not present.

"You defend them because you love them, don't you?" Olga's tone is flat and all heat in my blood turns cold as ice.

The sensation is coming from her.

It's similar to Nash's pulse of power and to Calix's during battle. It's also very much like the *Maage,* only hers is gentle and quiet. I swallow, fear pulsing through me and wonder if anyone else has noticed her strange gift. Her gift of what though?

Does Calix know? Diedra?

Olga blinks, and I can see she's coming back to herself. She closes the book, stands and adjusts her belt, holding onto her dagger handle for a moment. "A Deysik killed my parents. They are vial and—and evil. I wish they would all die!"

I stand, my fears over her powers forgotten, and Olga lunges forward and wraps her arms around my waist, burying her head in my chest, squeezing me in a tight hug. I return it, holding on to her until she lets me go. My heart swells with empathy and warmth for Calix's niece.

"I'm so sorry, Olga. The pain of losing a parent will always be a heavy weight to bear. It doesn't go away, but we become stronger and better equipped to hold it, but you can't wish death on those who haven't harmed you. Where would the justice be in that? You would just be repeating the cycle."

She wipes her tears away with the palm of her hand. "You're nicer than Pippa. I wish you could teach her the way your family did you, so she'd be kind," Olga mutters under her breath.

My heart twists for her. I pull her to my side. "I'm sure she loves you. She perhaps needs more love in return. At least, that was the only thing I failed to try with my oldest brother. I was too angry and bitter with his treatment of me that I gave as good as I got. It didn't make things better between us," I say sadly, wishing I could have done things differently with him. Regret nips away at my mind. Connor had always been kind to Drake; in turn, he was treated with more tolerance than my oldest brother ever gave to me.

We leave the library and find the museum, exploring the various artwork in sculptures, artifacts and paintings. A whole section of the museum is full of small pieces from the ancient war. A shield, a spear head, a chariot, replicas of the style of their day, and a replica of a large red jewel seems to glow from the inside out. It is so arresting I stop and stare.

"They use lights to make it appear alive, but it's not," Olga says from beside me.

"What is it?" I ask, unable to keep the awe out of my voice. She huffs and laughs and glances at me to see I'm serious, and all amusement falls away. "It's the Mother's Fire Jewel."

I look back to the jewel and I inhale. "*This* is the famed fire jewel?"

Olga giggles. "No, it's a replica."

She comes to stand by me, resting her head on my arm. "It's how the Mother was able to gift her Azure Warriors their powers to rival Ertune's. It disappeared from Goldill along with the Mother, a hundred thousand years ago." She shifts to stare between me and the replica with a bemused expression on her round face, the braids of her hair moving like strands of hanging rope.

There's something about the replica that communes with something deep inside of me. This piece inspired my mother's pet name for me, including Nash and Calix's.

Precious. Rare. I don't feel like I'm any of those things.

I pull myself away, and we finish exploring, learning about Ariportia and how Ertune's soldiers were convinced to turn against him, changing the tide of the war and how they were once allies with Luminum. They have two different major clans, one with white and gold feathers and one with black. The Mother's Heir was their intermediary, and the one who kept communication lines open. When she disappeared, neither side spoke officially again.

I remember Canary telling me how his father had gone to their lands and came home with him. There's so much of the world I don't know.

We learn about Naaka, the great island chain nation that is notoriously neutral in all wars, instead profiting off of trade and transport.

The Slate Empire is a coin in size compared to Luminum, bordering the Ikpeazu mountains and Deysik territory, landlocked between them all. Their people are known for their infamous archery skills. I wonder if it's been honed from the Ariportia and Deysik. From what little I've overheard from passing conversation, their country is brutal and proud, making them notoriously difficult to deal with.

Chapter 24

When the sun starts its descent, we leave the museum and make our way down the hill, back towards the river with thoughts of my mother, wondering why she left her country and traveled to Panthum.

As we walk down the hill, the stars begin to emerge, and the lamps on the street are lit, lending a soft, welcoming feel to the city. Across the river, we see people leaving the stadium as Currell ends, making their way down the main thoroughfare as the evening fight finishes. Mirroring their movements, Olga and I are near to the riverfront where Diedra told us she would meet us. If Calix isn't occupied with his commanders, I'll be able to enjoy dinner with him.

My thoughts are cut short as a scream pierces the air from behind us on the street we just turned from, the sound cutting off shortly after it starts. In warning, my whole body feels like a thousand needles are stabbing me. I tightly clutch Olga to me.

There's only ever a reason for my senses to be sharp—*Rogue* Deysik.

I grab Olga's hand, pulling her towards the river. "Run!"

People's terror-filled cries rent the air behind us, and our boots hit the cobblestone path at a furious pace. Chaos and people running, falling, and sobbing move around us. Olga tries to turn her head. "Don't look back!" I bark, pushing my legs faster and dragging the girl along with me.

My heart thuds in my chest, and my mind turns vengeful with fury. I must keep Olga safe. A couple runs past us with horror stark on their terrified faces. One crashes into a decorative fire pit, scattering a pile of coals. The prickles feel like needles again, this time deeper—no time to run. I reach over and snatch Olga's dagger with one hand.

How can I be unarmed, again?

My churlish older brother's familiar cadence answers my thoughts, *"Because you're a city away from the Azure Warrior's capitol. Their arrogance is their weakness."*

I yank her to the ground, throwing my body over hers.

Sharp claws swipe past our faces, and I shove the dagger's blade into the spilled coals. A snarling, ragged wolf the size of a small horse lands ahead of us, attacking one of the couples and shredding them apart. A second Rogue, a twin to the first, plows into another group of people across the street, clawing and biting viciously. Through the beast's fur, I can make out each rib and hip bone.

They're not just rabid; they're feral.

I hold Olga's head to my body, covering her ear with my hand while her body shakes in sobs of dread. Murderous rage fills me as the streets grow slick with blood. There's a business, feet away from where we lie, but with Olga, we won't be able to reach it before we would be ripped apart.

Not unless there's someone in the way.

"Get into the business behind us," I say to Olga.

"No. They'll get past you—"

"They will *not* get past me, Olga. Trust me." I can feel Olga's surprise as I keep my eyes on the golden-eyed wolf when it turns its malice-filled eyes on us. I roll off the girl, grab up the dagger, yank her behind me, and bear down on the burning pain in my palm as I breathe to calm my heart.

The Rogues both turn towards us, narrowing their gaze with precision. The wolf closest to me flares its yellow burning eyes in surprise—it must have caught my scent. The other one drops what was in its mouth. A hand with a sparkling ring on one of its fingers.

I know I have a few moments.

"Leave now!" I hiss, but Olga is frozen. Bullocks. I'm out of time.

I spin the dagger in my hand tauntingly. This isn't on a plain with clear-headed and single-minded warriors. These are Rogue Deysik, incredibly difficult to subdue because of their unbreakable bones, unpierceable thick skin, and reckless nature. One disadvantage I've brutally learned growing up is while in their animal form they move more quickly on four legs instead of two.

The wolf growls with a blood-covered maw and takes a step towards me. I know they're wondering what to do with me, and that's a boon. The girl's my responsibility, but with two Rogues I can't guarantee her safety with a dagger alone.

"Olga," I warn. The Rogue to the right lowers itself into a leaping crouch. I grip the dagger tighter, sending festering pain in my hand, knowing I'd die before it leaves my fingers. I focus and feel the energy surge inside me and draw it up.

"Go, now!" I cry, shoving the girl towards the business. In the time it takes her to reach the door, the wolf is already in the air, red froth flying from its maw.

The impact of the Deysik hitting me in the chest isn't as powerful as I was used to, but it still sends us rolling. As we tumble, I slam the blade into the soft spot under its jaw, before yanking it free to slam it into the open mouth of the second Rogue that joins the fray, plowing into us, launching us further over the cobblestone street.

Their hollow, unmoving bodies lie in the street, and I push to my knees, sitting back on my heels. I tug the dagger out, chest heaving, and blink, surprised at how easily they went down. Much easier than the two warrior Deysik. I stand, step back, and turn, glancing around the empty street, and notice a few people looking out of their windows.

I look back to where we were moments before and find dead bodies littering the blood-soaked street. They were here to deliver death and nothing more.

Silence.

No more screams of terror, only distantly, and those are the aftereffects of an attack—ones of mourning.

"They're dead," I call, trying to slow my breathing. I try not to stagger as Olga slams into my body, squeezing me in a bear-like hug.

"You're alright," I wheeze. "You're safe. They won't hurt you."

"They were going to kill me! I knew they would! I hate them! I wish they would all die!" She echoes her words from inside the library. "How did you do that? They're impossible to kill," Olga sobs.

"Clearly not," I say through a heavy sigh, soothingly patting her back while staring at the two wolves' bodies. So thin and ragged.

"I wish my parents knew what you do!" she wails.

I squeeze her tighter and cover her eyes, walking and angling her away from Deysik and human bodies. Four men, two women, their forms no longer recognizable in their shredded clothes and I'm so grateful Calix dressed me in Uria cloth, or I'd likely be joined with them.

Olga needs to get away from this, and I stumble with her holding onto me tightly, not allowing me to loosen my grip to walk properly. I don't mind.

My brain processes just fine during a fight, but afterward, it shuts down, only working on basic instinct. I head to safety—to Calix. I hang onto Olga tightly, dagger in hand, not wanting to let her go. She does the same.

Pounding feet come to my attention, and I'm relieved to see Calix, Vasilius, Canary, with Commanders Toriey and Teegu, racing up the street with a dozen Azure Warrior's and the Black Fox's mercenaries behind him. The mercs slow only marginally when they take in the scene behind me. Probably because at least one is a Deysik.

When I see my Bluey, I want to fall to my knees. I'm so relieved. Reaching us, he wraps his big arms around the two of us, and I sigh. The Azure Warriors and mercs form a perimeter while the others investigate the carnage, but there's no use. "They're dead."

"Let's get back to the steamer," Calix says tightly, before jerking his chin to several soldiers who tend to the frightened people emerging, now the threat is gone.

As we walk, I can feel Calix growing stiffer, his anger radiating from him in waves. I'd be angry too. This is the second time in as many weeks of an attack, both involving Deysik.

He doesn't look at me once, even after we reach the ship, and Diedra tends to Olga who rightfully appears shocked. Calix wraps her in a blanket, his large hand rubbing soothing circles over her back.

By the time the others return, she's done checking over Olga, before Diedra kisses me on the forehead. "I'll stay with the girls tonight. I'm sure this will bring back painful memories." She turns, squeezing Canary's bicep as she passes him to leave the room, taking Olga to stay with her sisters. The girl will need the love of her family to help her feel safe.

I nod, distracted by Vasilius and Teegu entering the infirmary, the latter leaning in to whisper into Calix's ear. The two brothers have seemed to work out their feelings over the other night, and the unique feeling of peace between the three of us has been pleasant to say the least.

Whatever Teegu's saying, Calix doesn't like hearing it. His heavy stare shoots to me. Vasilius leans against the wall, crossing his arms with a look that screams disapproval. I'm tempted to toss him an insulting gesture.

Once the door closes behind Diedra, Calix demands, "What happened with the Deysik?"

I've never heard this tone of voice directed at me. I stiffen as his disdain cuts deeper than any other rebuke I've ever had in my life. Canary's eyes, glittering like shards of smokey quartz, bounce to the crown Prince. "*Rogue* Deysik," I correct automatically. His nostrils flare with annoyance. Vasilius raises a brow and Teegu snorts, but Calix doesn't take his gaze from me. His handsome face is set in stone, rocking the ground underneath my feet. I refrain from swallowing but my throat is suddenly very dry.

"Olga and I were walking back to the riverfront to meet Diedra for dinner when I heard the rogue's rampage. We tried to run, but they caught up with us and attacked. You could tell from their bodies how it ended."

Canary's face remains passive and unsurprised, and Teegu leans back against the wall, throwing a look to Calix, who stares hard and unmoving at me.

Teegu's dark voice cuts through the tension, adding to my irritation. "Why didn't you take Olga back to the steamer?"

I blink and refrain from scoffing. Is he really this dense? "I already told you. They caught up with us and attacked."

Why is he interrogating me? Deysik don't look ragged unless they're neglected—lack of food, water, shelter, and being treated like animals will push them to continue to be the worst parts of themselves.

Calix lowers his voice and practically spits venom as he says, "Answer me, Alana, did you taunt him like you did with the one in the cage with Vasilius to draw their attention?"

I shoot accusing eyes at Vasilius, but his face is a mask of stone. Calix continues, "Deysik don't usually stop their senseless slaughter unless a challenge is thrown in front of them. It's not like you have defensive wounds."

The leash on my anger snaps.

"Because of the Uria cloth," I snarl back, "I won't apologize for doing what I have been trained to do." I hadn't thought twice about it, and he knows it. "Perhaps if it wasn't mistreated its whole life, it wouldn't have attacked people," I shot back with quiet venom.

The whole room falls still at my assault and defense of the Rogue Deysik. Calix shifts and stands taller, his shoulders thrown back, and he gives me a look that reminds me of a royal speaking to one of his lowliest servants.

"That's what you are," Drake's voice burns into my mind like a thousand coals.

"You're tasked with protecting my niece; instead, you put her life in danger by challenging an enemy," Calix growls. Cold sweeps over me at the rebuke. Canary's steady gray eyes flick between Calix and me, and the room's warm air licks at my skin, but I can't feel it.

"Are you upset about your *Moskazi's* facial scars Prince, or that she killed not two, but four indestructible foes with a mere dagger?" Canary asks.

"Even the best of Azure Warriors has a difficult time doing it. Look at her face and her hand. Her arrogance put Olga in harm's way," Calix snaps at Canary. I freeze and go numb all over, unblinking. So, Vasilius has been continuing to feed his brother reasons to doubt me.

I thaw and sit up slowly so the blood has time to regulate, and I stand, ignoring Teegu while glaring at Vasilius first before I turn to Calix, meeting his steely turquoise gaze, his jaw tight as a drum.

"I'm not an Azure Warrior, *Warlord* Prince. I'm a Ranger," I say tightly, staring him down. "My honor demands I protect *all* life as well as your niece. We ran, and when we couldn't, I did the next best thing; I drew their attention away from your niece so she could escape to safety, and so I could kill them before they slaughtered anyone else." Something cracked in my chest, and the crevasse slices to my soul. "Ask the people who witnessed the fight." His nostrils flare as if the thought hadn't occurred to him. Teegu certainly didn't bother investigating.

"If you don't like how I behave, find yourself a new guard for your nieces. I'll not change who I am for you no matter how much Mother's damned gold you paid for me, *Moskazi* or not."

Calix blinks with surprise as if my words deflate all his anger.

I've never been so furious in my life. I was saving Olga and others, and he's livid with me? If I stay, I don't know what I'll do. I turn and find Vasilius blocking my path, and I feel inner energy surge with my rage. His eyes shoot to the hand still holding the dagger as if I'm going to stab him with it. Everyone tenses, and I want to laugh bitterly.

How quickly they turn on me.

"Did anyone ask her if she's capable of letting the weapon go because of the tension in her body or *because it is seared to her hand*?" Canary says slowly, with rough anger.

Vasilius jerks back, and I see Calix flinch. I'm so livid I don't *care*. Canary continues, "Diedra was too worried about Olga to notice the burns on Ruby's hand."

While staring at Vasilius, furious with him for blocking my escape, I extend my arm with the dagger and bear down, clenching my jaw and *will* my fingers to open, sharply inhaling and exhaling air as pain powers through me. My fury is the only thing surpassing my pain. The dagger clatters to the ground, and Vasilius's eyes go to my hand, flaring wide and horrified at whatever he sees.

I'm beyond feeling.

"Alana," Calix says, his voice trembling with regret and something else I don't care to name. "Your hand. We need to bandage it." He makes to move towards me.

"Don't touch me," I bark, pausing him in his tracks, not ready to hear what he has to say. It hurts to hear him speak.

Canary continues to rebuke him, "If you want women to defend themselves, expect injuries to occur, just as they do with men. She's alive is she not?"

"Olga's the Princess. Her safety is paramount," Teegu snaps out, and my anger intensifies. He is clearly digging in deeper with his argument. And as I stare at Calix, battling with myself to stay silent, waiting for him to defend me. Waiting for him to dispute what Teegu has to say, it's much, much worse, because he's not worried about *me*.

"Get out of my way Vasilius," I grind out, my voice ragged with rage. He must see violence in my body because he steps out of the way.

"Alana's your *Moskazi,* not a Sapphire Warrior." Canary speaks with razor-sharp steel behind me.

When I open the door with my good hand, I startle Pippa, who leaps back, eyes wide going to my hand, cringing away. I scoff with disgust at her fear and stride down the hall, my back stiff as a blade, injured hand cradled to my chest.

I need to find Diedra.

Chapter 25

Before I see my friend, I need to work off my temper, I've never felt this out of control. If I had the Shift, my eyes would be glowing right now.

How could he be so callous? How could he not see there was no other choice than to kill them? They didn't go after Olga. They went after me like I knew they would when I antagonized them. If I hadn't been wearing Uria cloth, I'd be enduring a slow death right now.

I go to the stable of the steamer and pace its dark aisle so furious I don't know what to do with myself, not knowing where else to go.

After twenty minutes, I'm no longer furious, just hurt. Not just physically but emotionally. I hate this.

I look out the portholes to the sky, observe the clear blanket of onyx, broken up by stars so bright they look like gems in sunlight. I cradle my hand, the pain nearly unbearable now, I don't have my anger to help keep it at bay. My chest is so tight with heartbreak and grief; it's hard for me to breathe.

I wipe away my tears with my forearm before I make for the girls' room where I knock. Diedra answers the door with a look of alarm, relaxing immediately before her eyes dart to the hand cradled to my chest. She gasps and tells someone inside—a motherly looking servant—that she'll be back.

She wordlessly leads me to her bedroom that's identical to Calix's and pulls out her infirmary bag.

"May I stay here tonight?" I whisper, feeling like I want to claw away my skin. Shame seems to try to seep into my very pores over how Calix attacked, not only my honor and choice to end the rogue Deysiks, but my face.

I know he's under overwhelming pressure, but you don't turn on your *wife*. You lean on them. I'd never thought of the label before. I just continued on with how things were, but after tonight, the label makes the situation worse.

Master Baylor always said tragedy reveals true character, and it should never be used as an excuse. I wonder if he meant it when talking about my father and how he turned his pain inward, instead of lashing out at friends and family.

My father never turned away from his duties but rather threw himself into them. He was involved with Drake and Connor's training. He was concerned about my safety and delivered me to royal care, until they proved to be untrustworthy.

He could barely look at me after that for a year, and it's only now I realize it's because he was ashamed of himself for putting me into that situation. He made up for it by keeping me by his side until I joined the Ranger recruits. He didn't try to talk me out of it but told me I could make it if I never gave up. I think part of him wanted me to, but he never said it. He missed me being made Ranger, and my thoughts shift to Fidir and how the young Prince arrived on the final day, but my father didn't. It's not in my father's nature to miss important events for his children.

Diedra sits beside me, gently taking my injured hand, bringing my thoughts back to the present. Her brows pull down into a concerned frown, her beautiful brown eyes roving over my hand. "Of course, you can stay in my room. I don't stay in here anyway."

There's a lot of meaning hidden behind the soft words she just spoke. I shift and clear my throat. "I'm happy for you." Indeed, Diedra has been glowing these past two weeks.

She opens up a jar of salve and begins rubbing it into my hand, immediately taking away the sting. "You are gifted with speed, correct?" I nod.

"Everyone *with* a gift has the ability to heal. It flows through their veins. It's only a matter of identifying the gift and commanding it."

"Oh."

She looks up to me and angles her head. "Do you feel any sort of warmth or light inside of you? Something you can draw from?"

I think about the energy I pull up before I fight, giving my body extra speed and bursts of strength. "Yes."

"Are you practiced in using it, because if not, it will take some time, but I want you to explore gathering it up and moving it to your wounds."

I nod, closing my eyes and focus on the inner ball of energy—the Mother's Gift, I realize—and draw it up and will it to my injured hand.

Diedra gasps, "Mother bless you. Alana look."

My skin is pink and healthy instead of swollen and white with blisters. The pain is even gone.

I turn to Diedra, and an unexpected sob bubbles out of me. My whole body is wracked with them, and I find myself in Diedra's arms as she holds me, patting my back murmuring words of comfort.

It causes me to cry harder. She is so kind. It should be Calix comforting me.

She pauses. "I have to get back."

I give her another squeeze, and she holds me a little longer. "I'm not sure how you were raised back in Panthum and as a Ranger, but it's healthy for you to cry. You're still a woman who has emotions like the rest of us."

I nod. Diedra gives me one last squeeze on my shoulder before she leaves the room, popping her head back in, "Oh, and just know, the door has a lock, and I won't tell Prince Dread you're here. He needs to sit in his guilt for whatever he said to you that has you in my room rather than in his."

She tosses me a wink and closes the door firmly behind her.

It takes me nearly half the night, but I finally succeed in falling asleep.

In the morning, I allow myself to sleep in, waking near noon. I test my hand. No pain. I don't have an appetite, so I decide to skip lunch, showering and dressing in the clean clothes Diedra must have put out for me. Fresh Uria tunic and pants.

After I finish dressing, I find Canary on the training pitch with the tall Black Fox's mercenary. I've fought against him a few times since discovering he was a Deysik.

The Black Fox has made herself scarce since she and Vasilius had their argument a few days ago. It reminds me I need to confront her. There are too many Azure Warriors and Sapphire guards around for an assassination because the mercs are not allowed to carry weapons outside of the training courtyard.

I hadn't realized they were on the steamer until Diedra pointed out that the Sapphire guards' vests are a deeper blue than the others.

Canary sees me, turns to his opponent, and jerks his chin to the big merc who nods and moves away to sit and begin oiling the training blades. Despite the sun coming through the glass roof, the air is cooler in here, thanks to the cooling vents.

He bows his head and points to the swords on the training rack. A grin hovers over my lips as I pull two free from the wall and toss them to my silent friend, who swings with precision. He knows how to cheer me up. Swords are my favorite weapon.

I grab my own pair, and for the next hour, Canary and I create the music that soothes my broken heart, ringing through the steamer.

My muscles are screaming, and I'm covered in sweat when I finally slip past Canary's guard and slap his waist with the flat of his sword. In return, he backhands me, reminiscent of our time on the ship, and I'm so startled I burst out laughing, doubling over.

Canary gives me a wry look and we both smile.

"You only did that because you think I failed to appreciate the gesture of your kindness in training with me this afternoon. I promise you I didn't," I chuckle.

He raises a brow and pulls me up before whipping his gaze to something over my shoulder, a look of startled terror on his face. Pushing me away, he extends his sword upward. As I stumble away, I find the Warlord charging the pitch and watch in horrified bafflement as he brings his sword in a great arc down on Canary's so hard the former guard drops to his knee from the impact, straining to keep his sword from snapping in half.

I step back, moving away as Calix and Canary clash like thunder. The impact vibrates through the ship's walls as tangible as an attack.

This isn't training; this is a battle.

Their blades clash like massive bells. The violence is so similar to when Calix burst in to attack Nash when I fought him in his cabin, it jars me to my core.

This is the Warlord I feared would come for my people. It flays open my memory to the nightmare I had several weeks ago.

I bump into Diedra, who wraps her arms around me tightly, and I cling to her. Azure Warriors pour into the yard and observation deck above with excitement to watch these two infamous fighters combat. The Black Fox mercenaries fold their arms while spectating, the merc leader herself coming to stand by them, joined by Vasilius.

Canary is exhausted. His pants are heavy, and his tunic is soaked in sweat. I hear him speak to Calix in taunting bursts in their native language. Diedra squeezes me and holds her breath.

"What's he saying?" I ask.

"Your self-loathing from your treatment of your *Moskazi* makes you sloppy. You're not really defending her honor, but rather soothing your guilt from how you degraded her yesterday. You mistreated her for doing her duty and failed in your own," Diedra interpreted.

Calix roars and swings faster, leaving a gap in his side open. Canary dodges the attack, spinning and slapping Calix's side with the flat of his blade harder than he'd ever hit me. I lurch forward instinctively, wanting to protect my Bluey as much as I want to punch him, but Diedra holds me back, "Wait."

The Warlord turns, ready to jump back into the fight, but Canary snarls at Calix, freezing the Luminum Crown Prince in place.

"What did he say?" I ask, but Diedra shakes her head, tears filling her eyes. All eyes in the room shift to me and sense their surprise. What did Canary say that Diedra doesn't want to tell me?

Calix drops his sword to the ground and turns his blue-green gaze to me, and that hurt once again, slices deep. I swallow when he approaches and feel a twinge of dull pain in my face from my scars, hearing his words from last night. *Look at her face...*

Diedra releases me, rushing to Canary's side, and I lower my gaze, staring at the leather of his vest as he approaches. It hurts too much to look him in the eyes. I ask the question I previously didn't dare voice, but anger and hurt are riding me hard. "Would fighting in Currell satisfy the debt of my indenture?"

He sucks in a sharp breath, "That is not a requirement, Alana—"

He reaches up his hands to touch me, but I cringe back. He freezes, and I dare meet his eyes, finding devastation on his face. I don't care.

"I want to be free from you," I say. His throat bobs, and a sort of panic crosses his face. It hurts so much I can't stand to look at him—at what it means. It hits me in the gut like a punch from my brother. My face crumples as I turn, fleeing from the room, not wanting him to see my tears.

∗∗∗

For two days, I avoid everyone to keep my sour mood to myself. I don't watch over the girls; I don't join them for family meals, instead taking them with Canary in the stable where I spend my days—the only person who doesn't try to speak to me or broker peace between Calix and myself.

Calix, in turn, patiently bears my slights, pleading with his eyes for me to forgive him when I see him in the training room, until I move to train with Raine.

What I'm scared about is how much I'm terrified of myself. I thought Nash broke me on the ship, but it was nothing. This. *This* is what will break me. The power my Bluey has over, not just my life but my heart. I have taken to calling him Warlord instead of the more respectful title of Prince Dread when I'm forced to speak to him, to keep him at bay.

I refuse to be someone who is to be verbally, publicly assaulted if I do something he disapproves of. I'm not a soldier. I'm not his warrior.

I'm his wife.

And I'd rather be his indentured servant, because then I'd be expecting his verbal lashings.

If this is how it will be as his wife, I don't want it. He must do better.

Chapter 26

I wake before the dawn breaks, head down to the training courtyard, and study the intricate mosaic tile designs and colorful details of the walls and ceilings people take for granted. Tall, dark green plants give life to the otherwise rather stark and empty space. The morning is quiet. Not a single Azure Warrior awake yet.

The Black Fox is wearing her silver mask in the ring with one of her bodyguards. I wince as she's slammed to the ground, hearing the whoosh of air leaving her lungs, echoing throughout the courtyard.

"Your merc is as ruthless as a Ranger," I casually say as I approach.

Her silver mask flashes in the low light as she turns to me, snapping, "Coming to avoid your *Warlord*?"

I press my lips tightly together. *She isn't wrong.* I can tell it irritates and hurts him. It sours my belly, and I can't stomach it myself anymore.

"How can you tell?" I reply with a heavy sigh.

"You realize despite you being his *Moskazi*, women will still try to seduce him. Currell is for the warriors, but the match market is competition for women of a different sort. You would be wise—"

So, women here don't honor commitments between couples? Deysik are coupled for life. Indiscretion is extremely rare because they can scent it, and the consequences are dire.

I didn't consider before now.

"Thank you for your advice," I say sharply, turning away. I freeze, finding Calix standing feet away, staring at me the way a starved man does a meal.

The overwhelming need to speak with him hits me. Not just because of what the Black Fox says, but because I miss Calix. I want him to apologize and promise to do better. I want *him* to hold me. I know he's a good man.

But will he be a great one and change?

We stare at each other, eyes roving hungrily over each other. He's still tall and proud, his posture straight, but his face is slightly haggard with dark circles under his eyes and his blonde hair mused as if he's been running his large hands through it.

The thought of anyone touching or trying to sway him away from me sends violence to my heart. He's *mine*, and I'm done being full of self-pity. I realize he's waiting for me to speak, and instead I jerk my chin, silently commanding him to follow me. He does, and I can feel those turquoise eyes on my back, watching my gait, studying me as he always has.

I go to his—our room and feel antsy. My eyes ping to the messy bed, empty water cups on the end tables, open curtains, clothes draped across a chair.

I turn back to him as he closes the door and leans against it, large arms crossed over his broad chest, his flat abdomen drawing my eye further down his narrow waist. I shake thoughts about his body away and focus on my pounding heart, opening my mouth before I can clam up.

"Do you find me ugly with my scars?" I ask bluntly, cracks forming underneath my neutral, non-feeling mask.

Calix's face falls, and he drops his arms, "No! I could never think you're ugly. What I said the other night in anger was stupid of me. You're not arrogant. You're right in finding a way to save Olga and other people. It infuriates me they were able to come this close to the capitol. It's as if they have a knack for finding my family." He closes his eyes tightly.

"Please forgive me for my anger overriding my good sense and taking the word of Teegu at face value and not asking for full details. I was wrong—so wrong, Alana. I'm embarrassed I behaved that way. You're my *wife*. If anyone spoke to you that way, they'd be on the ground bleeding. Canary was right in what he said to me on the pitch; I was assuaging my own guilt by ambushing him."

I sit with his apology and admission. I hate that we ended up here, and I realize it was because we never established boundaries.

"Calix, if it ever happens again, I won't be able to survive it." I silently beg him to understand. "You not believing me—publicly—and skewing my actions, which have always been honorable, is something I never want to feel again."

I add again, in a broken whisper so he knows I mean it. "I won't stand for it." A tear escapes, and I brush it away with calloused fingertips. He pulls me to him, cradling my face with his big hands, rubbing his thumbs over the lines on my cheek.

"Of course. Of *course*, you're right." His voice is full of anguish. His lips press against my face, over those three pink lines. "I fought against you and not for you, like I vowed. I'll never do it again because I can't bear to be parted from you. I'm so sorry Alana, please forgive me."

My heart surges with love for Calix, and I move without thinking. I kiss him, and all the pent-up emotions and feelings over the last three days rush to the surface. He must feel the same because his hands find their way to my backside, lifting me up. I wrap my legs around his waist, our lips hot and searching, kissing with desperation until we are both breathless.

His long legs carry us over to the bed, where he lowers me to their downy sheets, covering my body with his before breaking away from the kiss. "You're my wife, not my mercenary. Your contract debt is forgiven."

I stop breathing and blink, not sure if I heard him correctly. "Really?"

"Vasilius and Toriey signed as witnesses, but my father needs to approve it."

I nod as he kisses down my jaw and over my throat, as I touch his body, feeling the rapid thumping of his heart. Something shifts between us, and I sit with the new feeling of hope of freedom from my five-year contract.

It's almost gone, but I'm too much of a realist or skeptic to allow myself to hope too much because the Emperor is an anomaly. In my experience, a royal with power over people will fight tooth and nail before they will give up even an ounce of it.

I realize how terrified Calix must have been when signing for my contract's dissolution. He cares more about me than his fears, and that is the very definition of trust.

Chapter 27

Goldill is as beautiful as its name implies. Pale stone with shining gold dome roofs pepper the city. Even from a distance, I make out blue and gold flags hanging from windows and banner poles. I ride horseback into the great city at the center of our entire entourage of Azure and Sapphire Warriors, the Black Fox and her mercenaries, and the various territory officials and commanders we picked up along the way.

Calix rides next to me, wearing his golden, polished mask and squeezes my hand he refuses to release. After we reconciled, he attempted to once again have me join his meetings, but I refused, telling him I'd only do so if his father gave him his blessing. With the amount of curiosity and distrust sent my way, I refuse to put myself in a position to be used as a wedge between Calix and his family.

I turn my thoughts to the capitol as we begin our parade route. The city sits on a massive hill at the center of a valley where water cascades off a cliff from one side of the hill, with the palace directly above. A second river runs down the gentle slopes of the plains and forest, intercepting the waterfalls and cutting through the city.

"The hilltop is a natural spring and aquifer. It has been the capital of this land long before Azure Warriors and the Mother arrived. Isn't it a sight?" Calix asks. I nod, absolutely speechless. How can this city have so many people living in it?

"A portrait of the Mother's favored people," the Black Fox quips as she rides past, inclining her head respectfully. I can't tell if she's being sarcastic or genuine. "I'll send word when I find Lady Svetlana Brozna. It shouldn't take long. I expect my payment when it arrives," she directs to Vasilius before turning to me. "Good luck *Moskazi*."

She and her men depart down a different road leading into the large city, quickly swallowed up by the people, vendors, and wagons lining the street. Summer heat doesn't stop the citizens from coming out in droves to witness their Princes and Princesses return home. We enter the shadow of the pewter granite walls surrounding the city proper.

The towering decorative iron doors remind me of Toriey's fortress. They swing open as we approach, trumpets and drums announcing our arrival. The tunnel is at least fifty feet wide, big enough for two carriages to pass through with plenty of clearance. The one-hundred-foot journey to the other side, reveals just how cleverly disguised this fortress has been built as a wall surrounding the city proper.

As we pass through the other side, I turn back and have a clear view of their defenses. I find the weapons Luminum purchased from my home on top of the walls and further in the city on roofs, large bows that shoot dozens of arrows at once, which can be loaded and reset moments after firing, with clips of pre-notched arrows.

Those were our most recent and in-demand item.

Now I know why. Ariportia.

The clatter and cheers build and hover over us, and I'm overwhelmed. I lean towards Calix to speak to him, hoping to distract myself from the vibrancy of the celebration.

"What should I call your parents? Emperor and Empress Dread?" I ask to shake the nerves tingling underneath my skin. Goldill is much, *much* more magnificent than Panthum's capital where I spent a year with the Royal family as a child.

I can hear the smile in his deep voice, "My mother would love that. For now, their formal titles will do." His admittance stuns me. I never thought of ruling royals as having a sense of humor. Probably because the King and Queen of Panthum are as crusty as dried bread on a hot day.

The noise from the crowd and city explodes the further we ride, making conversation impossible. Drums pound as quickly as my heart as I take in Azure Warriors lining the streets, holding people back as they cheer, calling out to the Imperial family.

Most gasp and point to me crying out, "*Moskazi! Texui ap e Moskazi!*" Roughly translated, it means *Prince has a wife*. I still don't know enough of the Luminum language to make a conversation. Diedra, Olga, and little Vivian have been helping me, but it's still over my head.

We travel down the streets, swallowed up by Goldill, to greet the Emperor and Empress of Luminum. By the smirk on Pippa's face every time she glances at me from the carriage beside us, I decide to brace myself for a cold welcome.

Somehow, I know Calix bringing home a *Moskazi* will not go over well, based on the surprise of literally everyone who's seen my scarred face.

I'm eager to get out from under the sun and into a cooling breeze, away from curious eyes. Our pace quickens as we ride deeper into the heart of the city, entering a massive square, facing a six-story white, granite building where a dull roar seems to grow from within like a purring mountain cat. Great banner flags hang from the behemoth.

The heat is so suppressive it causes my red tunic to stick to the river of sweat down my back. I breath out any doubts and nerves over meeting Calix's parents and focus on the fact I'm in the heart of Luminum.

The crowd churns closer, and I note bright colors are favored among the women in Goldill. It appears everyone's tunics and dresses are pressed and clean, ready for a celebration.

Those citizens flowing into the white building turn at our approach, catching sight of the golden and pearl-masked Princes. Cries and whispers carry on the air in Luminum's tongue, twined with others in the common tongue.

Prince Dread has returned! Did he bring more weapons? Who's the woman with him? How will he respond to the Deysik attacks? Slaughter them all, I hope.

She has scars on her face. Spoiled. Revolting.

My face heats with every carrying word, and I inhale deeply, smelling roses and cinnamon, reminding myself I'm used to this. Calix dismounts, and my body marginally relaxes as he helps me down from the horse, with a tenderness I can't help but revel in.

I lift my chin and decide to ignore the women's stares in the crowd with their fluttering hands. Instead, I focus on the dismounting Azure Warriors walking their horses inside the stone building through another set of large gates opening for them.

"This is the Arena of Champions, *Egronous*. It's the largest fighting pit in the known world. We'll head up to greet my parents and officially start Currell."

Vasilius walks his horse next to me, peering down his masked pearl nose.

I raise a brow in question. I accepted his apology, but it doesn't mean I've forgiven him quite yet for not siding with me immediately.

His voice is muted and gruff. "My parents will still be mourning the loss of their daughter and son-in-law, I ask only you keep sympathetic comments about Deysik to a minimum, *Moskazi*."

I nod, not bothering to reply. I turn to find Calix waiting for me and stride beside him, looking for Canary.

"He knows where to go," Diedra says, catching up to me, slipping her arm through mine.

Calix removes his mask, clipping it onto his belt before putting an arm around my shoulders, pulling me snugly to his body. "He'll be fine."

My muscles relax with his assurance.

The carriage holding the young Princesses clatters behind us.

"I'll be with the girls," Diedra says, leaving me. "You go enjoy your Prince."

We grin at each other. I'm so grateful for the love and friendship she's given me. It's certainly added strength to enter into the unknown with meeting her family.

My Warlord Prince pulls away to extend his elbow for me, leading me down a dark tunnel, brightened by small trenches cut out of the wall, filled with oil and lit on fire. We turn down another tunnel and eventually move into a small stairwell, passing heavily armed guards, dressed in dark blue, hooded vests—Sapphire Warriors. He nods to the men as we pass. Diedra and the girls appear from behind us.

"I can't wait to see Grandfather's face—" Pippa's voice echoes.

"Pippa, ve shnout victin, *Moskazi*," Vasilius snaps through his mask, and Pippa immediately falls silent. I've never heard him use that rebuke before on the girl, and I feel tingles of daggers as Pippa stares at my back as if I'm the one who snarled at her.

The General jerks his head sharply in acknowledgment when I meet his gaze. He's uncomfortable with the situation but is attempting to broker a better relationship with me.

The staircase isn't as long as I thought it would be to reach the top where bright daylight reveals a landing which joins the beginning of the curved hall that smells of fresh air and hot savory food.

As we walk down the hall, I spy to the left, where the crowd's din echoes the loudest, wide verandas between thick columns, filled with opulently dressed people, heavily armed guards, and more Azure Warriors. The blue-hooded soldiers stand at attention every few feet, light gleaming off their half-golden masks. I count fifteen wide veranda's we pass before reaching our destination.

Calix slows to a stop while his brother, nieces, and Diedra walk past us entering the imperial veranda. It's much larger than the others we passed, filled with bejeweled, important-looking people and twice as many guards.

The lavishness alone sets my heartbeat pounding, and I swallow, resisting the temptation to curl into Calix's broad chest.

"You're going to do great. They'll love you like I love you," he says quietly, glancing to where squeals of delight come from the girls as a beautiful dark-haired woman, with wrinkles around her eyes, sweeps Vivian and Olga into hugs. For all I'm happy for the girls, a pang twists in my heart at the sight. I'll never have that kind of love for myself.

Calix squeezes my arm, releasing me and strides through the open doorway, entering what I assume is the imperial family suite of *Egronous*.

The room is large with columns on three sides and gauzy white curtains hanging in between, giving the appearance of walls. There's a table of grilled meats, elaborately carved fruit, salads, and steaming foods. Frosted cakes, dipped chocolates, and other desserts sit on ice along the opposite walls in a large foyer area above the steps, leading down to three rows of twelve seats. The far side of the room is open to reveal a lower veranda, with potted plants exposed to the entire stadium.

I'm not prepared for the scale of it. *Egronous* is ten times larger than the arena in the Red City, filled to the brim with people cheering for the beginning of Currell.

"Perfect timing," a lyrical feminine voice says, and I tear my attention away from the stadium to the striking, dark-haired older woman who steps forward and pulls Calix into a hug—his mother. She wears a silver gauzy dress with a belt of sapphires wrapping around her waist. She's the most beautiful woman I've ever seen and aside from the creases around her eyes, is untouched by age.

Several other official-looking people in the room wisely step back from the family reunion. Vasilius moves past me to hug his mother, swallowing her in his large arms.

"You've returned at last! I thought you would be at least a month longer—"

"We were unable to enter Rising Pass because of an avalanche, so I brought home a Ranger who was stranded," Calix says to his mother, turning to me with a wink. I try to tamp down the flush rising to my cheeks.

"The mythical Rangers of Panthum are female?" a man asks as he approaches, with a courtly smile. He looks identical to Calix and Vasilius, with broad shoulders, white tingeing his blonde hair, and blue-green eyes, coming to speak to his sons warmly. Power exudes off him in waves, and I suppress a shiver. He's dressed in a white tunic with gold embroidery and a golden circlet on his head—the Emperor.

His hawk-eyed gaze flicks over me, settling on the scars on my face, and I reply in the same tone I reserved for Fidir's mother, the Queen of Panthum, polite and demure. "A quarter of our forces are female."

"Uncle Dread, don't be rude. You should introduce Gran and Tanta to your *Moskazi*," Pippa's voice sounds from behind me. Sweet, false, and full of knives.

I don't fail to notice how his parents stiffen in surprise, their eyes shooting over me in a new light. His mother looks like she might throw up. His father's warm eyes turn to ice.

Heat steals into my cheeks, and an uncomfortable, embarrassed prickle swarms over my skin like a thousand bee stings. I'm *lacking*. Someone always finds me deficient. I shouldn't have expected...

What *did* I expect?

The Emperor of Luminum raises a frosted golden brow, saying, "The Ranger? Her?" He narrows his gaze on his son as if expecting him to say he's joking.

I can hear the strain in Calix's voice as he calmly replies, "Yes."

He doesn't bother glaring at Pippa. By how her grandmother is looking at the girl, Pippa shrinks back into the crowd, rubbing her wrist.

His father says something in Luminum too quiet for me to hear, and his mother directs a sharp glance at her son. I bow my head. "If you'll excuse me... I'll allow you some privacy."

I turn away from their scrutiny, surprised expressions, and the covert glances tossed between the other guests, already grouping and sharing the news, some hiding their shocked and startled faces. I school my features to the familiar emotionless mask I hadn't wanted to wear today.

I realize... I hoped, which was the most foolish thing I could've done, but I had *wanted* to be welcomed—desired to be wanted somewhere. I take a deep breath and remind myself Calix wants me. He speaks of this Empire with love. So, I'll love it, along with the bad.

My feet take me to the edge of the exposed veranda, and instead of going out into the searing sun to view the whole stadium, I keep to the shadows where the stone railing meets the great columns. I run my fingers over the fronds of a potted fern and lean against the smooth, warm stone, crossing my arms. I sigh, ignoring the rapid Luminum being spoken behind me, passing between the guests, but more pointedly, between the Emperor, Empress, and their eldest son.

My eyes rove around *Egronus's* pitch. The field below is nothing like the one in Red City which embodies death, and this field... encompasses viability and achievability. Hope is tangible here with rich, thick, green grass. Thick cabers stand tall in neat rows of three on either end of the oval shape pitch, hanging between them are two rings suspended in the air, staggering in height with a golden object at the center, and behind the rings is a gilded target. Tulle-like protective mesh hangs over the crowd from the rafters, providing shade for the spectators fifteen feet above the grass. Rows and rows of people, hundreds of levels high, sit and wait, most still pouring in, finding their seats. The spectators closest to me appear excited, chatting with one another, while others cheer loudly.

I've never seen anything so grand on a scale such as this. It's truly an engineering feat. I wonder what ours would say if they saw it. I commit every detail into memory. Perhaps I could draw what I see if I can purchase a notebook.

If it's allowed, I'd like to journal my experiences, so I can share them with my family one day.

The conversation behind me has fallen to more normal tones, and the background chatter picks up. I sigh a breath, releasing some of the tension in my shoulders.

Wide doors round the bottom wall of the field—entrances for the fighters, I presume. Each has metal bars and behind the bars a set of doors.

Glowing purple eyes appear from behind the bars of a door across from me. They stare right at me, and I fall still. It's the Deysik detainee from Calix's attack.

This isn't just a field of competition but a prison. Each one is awaiting their Battle for Justice. Two things trickle through my mind. The first is how many Deysik await their fate, and the second is what happens if they are unsuccessful?

Movement to my left draws my attention.

The Empress and Emperor.

Calix's large hand drifts over my lower back and leads me to the front seats. His body is relaxed, but by the feathering in his jaw I know he's annoyed. I slip my hand in his and squeeze. He meets my eyes, and his gaze softens before whispering against the shell of my ear, "You're the most attractive woman I've ever seen, and I'm downright thrilled you're here to witness our biggest celebration."

I smile and whisper back, "Right back at you, Bluey." It earns me a kiss on my temple.

Vasilius and Diedra come to sit next to us, and we watch as his parents hold hands as they enter the bright sunlight. The crowd roars, jumping to their feet as their two leaders walk out, moving to the railing while waving gracefully.

The Emperor raises his arm, and the crowd quiets with immediate silence, allowing the Empress to speak in a clear voice, which carries easily in the fighting pit, "Luminums and honored guests, Welcome to *Currell*!"

A cheer explodes from the crowd and after a few moments he speaks again. I settle against Calix's firm body, his thumb roving over my shoulder.

The Emperor's deeper voice rings out next, "This year will mark the third year since the death of our oldest daughter and her husband." The crowd's quiet transitions to somber at the mention of their loss. "In an act of friendship, we've invited our neighbors and closest allies to participate in this year's contests. As tradition, the participation fees will be divided into prizes for those who win in each feat, but only one contestant will win all of Currell. One contestant will be given the highest honor of Goldill.

"As you know, four hundred years ago, our beloved Mother's Heir and Fire Jewel was stolen away from the Mother's Hall at the very core of Goldill by a Deysik. However, our unwavering faith in the Mother has been proven to be sure. The High Monk of Goldill prophesied the Fire Jewel will return *soon*. The Mother's Heir will once more bless us against our enemies."

The crowd breaks into gasps and shouts. "With this felicitous news, the Empress and I have decided to change how Currell and the Battle for Justice are completed."

There's a collective tension that runs rampant through the first row, the three royal siblings freeze. Whatever it is their parents are announcing, it wasn't made known beforehand.

"With the recent attacks on our people, we have decided that the Battle for Justice winner and the Champion of Currell will face one another in final combat."

"But as the Mother is known for her justice, so is Luminum. We have decided the returned Traitor will fight in the Battle for Justice." I glance back to find Diedra, finding a furious female, sitting in lethal quiet. Calix's gaze is steady, but the muscle in his jaw clenches rapidly as the crowd's displeasure ripples through the stadium. "Only if he wins the impossible, will he be restored to Sapphire Warrior status and forgiven."

Pippa's bright white smile gleams against the sunlight, "As it should be."

Her aunt and uncles glare at the girl until she swallows, before jutting her chin, not backing down from their silent anger.

"Let *Currell* begin!"

Diedra quietly excuses herself not bothering to look at her parents, and my heart hurts for her. I want to go with her to reassure her, but Calix shakes his head.

For the next three hours, I watch the top one hundred Azure Warriors compete against each other in different rounds of various tasks of speed, agility, dexterity, intelligence, and of course fighting. Calix and Vasilius explain the rules and point system they use to determine the winners. It's no surprise, Raine maintains his champion position for Toriey's territory as well as Teegu's.

With glowing purple eyes staring out from his cell, I can't help but think back to the talk of gambling and ensuring outcomes. I glance back to Toriey and meet the steely blue gaze of a man unrepentant.

He's the reason Raine talked to Canary, fostered a relationship with him, and trained with the Traitor. Toriey was shoring up his odds, gambling off of how the Emperor would react to the attacks.

Out of all of the competing Champions, Raine is by far the most skilled.

Perhaps I would have anticipated this outcome if I had gone to the war meetings with Calix. The deviousness of this empire was hinted at all along. I just chose to ignore it, instead focusing on the problems at hand rather than the long-standing issues that would sweep the current problems off the board.

Either way, Raine is meant to kill Canary, but I know one thing that Toriey doesn't.

Canary most likely knew this was coming all along, because Nash told me once that Canary had never taken anyone under his wing until me, and that was because it was going to lead him to Diedra.

In all his years fighting in the Red City's Pits, it taught him one thing.

How to fight dirty and how to win.

Canary took Raine under his wing because the Azure Warrior Champion's death would lead to his freedom and Diedra.

And nothing in this world, neither gods alive nor dead, will keep Canary from the love of his life.

Chapter 28

When the celebration ends, Diedra returns when the guests depart along with the three Princesses, leaving the Emperor, Empress, their children, and myself. While the entire arena empties out, servants quickly clean and rearrange the seating into a more intimate setting with chairs facing each other.

Now seated across from his parents, Calix once more slips his hand into mine, giving it a reassuring squeeze. His mother's sharp gaze takes it in, but her face is nearly unreadable if I didn't know what the tension around her mouth indicated.

She doesn't like me.

Turquoise eyes, below graying blonde hair, stare at me with such intensity, I fight against a shiver. He's a man who wields incredible power, and I sense I'm about to witness some of it directed against me.

"My son tells me of how you were both seajacked in Faurst. I'd like to hear you tell your story."

His words are a simple command. Not an ounce of request in his tone. Calix allowed certain gaps in my story, and I have a feeling the Emperor will devour every single detail. So, I give it to him, leaving nothing out, except Fidir's identity. I explain my agreement to escort my 'friend,' into Faurst not knowing his intentions, and the debacle of our escape of the city, my capture and agreement to indentured servitude as a fighter.

"To sacrifice yourself so they may escape, must mean they're of high rank. Or am I wrong?"

Calix falls still, but I feel his curiosity at my incoming response. Perhaps this is why he never pressed me, either because he thought his route into Panthum lay in me, or his father could intimidate the information from me.

My tone is quiet and resigned. "You are not wrong."

The Empress turns her head as she takes me in, her voice deep and rich. "What is your full title? My son says your family trains Rangers in your land? Is that a prestigious position for Rangers?"

I cringe internally. "My full title is Ranger Alana. I can't provide you with my last name because it will endanger the person I protected in Faurst."

I'm met with narrowed eyes and displeased royals. I pause and face the question I don't want to answer. "I was raised in a household of means with ties to nobility, but after my escape from Faurst, I no longer hold any significance. Any further inquiry, formal or otherwise, will not be answered."

The two rulers share a look, and it's not a pleasant one. The Emperor leans forward, placing his elbows on his knees, steepling his fingers together. "You choose to protect this person even after they betrayed you and left you to die in Faurst?" I can hear the disbelief in his voice.

"I must, regardless of what he has done to me. My honor demands it."

"Why can't you elaborate? We wish only to understand the predicament you are in to help, but you are not giving us anything to assist you," the Empress says, shifting her legs and adjusting her skirt.

Mother's braids, is this how they want to manipulate me? I hold back an eye-roll.

"The political atmosphere in Panthum would be placed in jeopardy if I reveal the name of my charge in Faurst or my own given name. This will be the last time I say these words, but I don't wish to keep these things from you, but rather I am following my duty to protect my people. These are laws I abide by, whether in my country or outside of it. I won't give up my integrity for the sake of curiosity or other's problems to be solved, including my own. This is the consequence of my choice in Faurst. My duty dies with me. I may be Calix's wife, but I am also a Ranger of Panthum."

They collectively sit back, processing what I've said, and Diedra leans forward to say, "That's very admirable Alana."

The Emperor's eyes shoot to his daughter with anger flaring in their turquoise depths but does not speak against her. Why would he, when he has sentenced his daughter's love to what he thinks is his death.

Calix's father leans back in his chair. He's not as muscular as his sons, but he is equally fit with a flat stomach and thick biceps. "You mentioned a quarter of your Ranger forces are female. About how many would that be?"

I dip my chin in acknowledgement but keep my face neutral. "Unfortunately, it is not a question I'm permitted to answer."

A raised brow and a slight smile meant to disarm but Calix falls still, and I know it's in fact the opposite. "Am I to understand you refuse to answer your new Emperor? You ignore the opulence I extend by allowing you privileges no other mercenary has ever dreamed?"

A simple question and a loaded one. I cross my legs and meet his eyes with steel lining my own. I will not be intimidated.

"You are not my Emperor, but rather the owner of my contract. Like I've informed Calix, you're free to give or take away anything you like. I'm used to possessing nothing, it won't be hard to sustain once more."

He scoffs, but doesn't deny it. "My position leaves me in constant defense of my family, especially from assassins who disguise themselves as damsels in distress."

Calix snorts, and I raise both brows at that, though it would have been wiser not to. My Bluey leans forward, matching his father with a flicker of anger on his face. "Alana did not *need* rescuing. Not the entire eight weeks on the ship, saving my life and Vas's multiple times, not when she fought against four men and an Ariportia in the Red City Pit. Not when she killed four Deysik saving your children and grandchild. She has done *nothing* but save our family from death. Your accusation is insulting."

Calix's mother looks me over with eyes not as laced with misgiving as before. She angles her head in the same way Calix does, and her braids fall over her silver dress.

The Emperor glares at his eldest son. "Perhaps, yet I'll not trust her until I know her full background, including her *family name*." He turns those hazel bright eyes on me.

"I understand your position and respect it immensely. With the tragedies your family has suffered, I don't blame you for your suspicion. I'm not here to harm or destroy anyone. I wish I could improve relations between our two countries, but it will never happen, unless Panthum dissolves ingrained traditions that have nothing to do with outside pressure."

The Emperor angles his head, his circlet shining in the indirect mid-day light. "How old are you?"

I don't hesitate. "Twenty years old."

He sits back and looks to his wife, "Will your family be looking for you?"

I swallow, and Calix gives my hand a few gentle squeezes. My voice is low. "No. They will not leave Panthum and their duties there."

The Emperor opens his mouth to ask a question, but a soft voice cuts in. "I heard of your defense of my granddaughter in Illalangi, and I want to thank you. I'm sorry you were injured in the ambush two weeks ago." Her brown eyes travel to my face and linger where the pink lines mar my skin. "I heard you met with the *Maage*?"

I nod, and something flickers in her eyes, but I'm unable to interpret what it means.

"Is that something you do? Kill Deysik?" Her question is more dangerous than all the others.

"No, though we have experience. Our relations are peaceful and what negative experiences we have, are with *Rogue* Deysik." I glance at Calix. "Much different than the Deysik here."

"In what way? They should *all* be put down. Filthy murdering thieves." The Emperor barks, causing me to blink. His face is fierce, and with the loss of so many close family members and his child, it's understandable that he holds a deep hatred for them.

One can't reconcile with it. Calix's hold on my hand becomes nearly painful.

"The ones I know control their emotions and rarely Shift into their second skin. They are not violent. If they become so without cause, Rangers execute them."

I feel all eyes on me, and the Emperor shakes his head as if he can't believe it, and the Empress regards me steadily as if searching for a lie.

"Easy to say such things without any proof to back it up. You'll forgive us if we refuse to believe you."

I shrug, half expecting this reaction with his deep prejudice against Deysik. "I'm the only person from Panthum you've ever met. We do not leave our country."

He narrows his eyes, somewhat menacingly. "Why is that?"

I can't help but smile. "Because we love our country so much… and because if we did, a law older than the gods will be broken, and the fallout will be existential."

That earns me curious looks from Diedra, Vasilius and Calix, but I couldn't resist throwing the truth at them. Judging by their expressions, they don't believe me. His father outright fumes. "Prince Dread is to take responsibility for you as your husband." He turns to look at his oldest son, before leveling his cold blue eyes so like Vasilius's on me. "You are family now, whether I like it or not. I'll make anonymous inquiries and if I discover you've lied to me at all, the consequences will be dire, *Moskazi* or no."

"As I've told your son," I say with an even tone. "I'll not jeopardize my—"

"Do you think I care about your peace when I am grasping for my own? I don't. You are my daughter by marriage and a citizen of Luminum. If you haven't answered honestly with the questions I've asked, your life is forfeit."

I sit up and hold his gaze, using cool logic with an even colder voice, burning with the energy buzzing inside of me, unleashing it to see what it would do. "If you will not see reason, then hear this. If you ignore me, Luminum will never receive your precious weapons of war. If you upset the balance of my country, the production will cease as those inside of it will tear each other apart, and you will be Mother's blessed if it stays within our borders, because if it spills out, the world will never recover and Luminum especially, will fall and fall the hardest."

Everyone in the room is silent, and all but Calix have leaned away from me.

I angle my head and soften my tone to a lethal vibration just above a whisper. "How far have your engineers succeeded in trying to recreate our designs?"

The Emperor's nostrils flare, and his jaw flickers as he grinds his teeth together. He knows as well as I do the boxes holding the mechanical parts of our weapons are unbreakable. My father designed them as such, so no one could plagiarize our goods. If it's breached, all the pieces inside are disintegrated.

It was the only way, we as a community, could agree to sell our weapons to the outside world.

The Emperor of Luminum seethes until Calix clears his throat to which the older man holds a hand out to his wife, and they both rise and depart, my threat hanging in the air like a challenge.

The High Monk will have already tried to find out who I am. Fear slices through me even though I know I can't control other people from searching for the information. It's Fidir's mess, but it will be my family who pays the price for it.

Calix releases my hand and rubs his across my shoulders, pulling me towards him, kissing my head.

"You did well. I'm proud of you."

I laugh bitterly. "For brokering a stalemate? I'm not lying. There are things I can share and things I can't."

Vasilius stands and looks down on me. "Good, because at this point that would break our trust irrevocably. The consequences would be your death, and Calix would be forced to deal it out."

I suck in a quick breath. There's nothing I can do but nod, though my heart breaks for Calix to ever be forced into that position. Diedra stands, "Let's get back home and rest so we can get tonight over with."

Right, the dancing and celebration.

The two siblings depart, leaving my Bluey and I alone for a moment, before he stands, pulling me against his firm body.

"You're not lying? Even about the law older than the gods?" he asks, his warm breath blowing over my forehead.

I sigh, exhaustion lining my body. "Especially that."

"Tell me about it."

I close my eyes. "I can't, but remember the monsters I told you about?"

"*Drakes*," Calix says, cutting in. "I remember."

My face falls slack with shock, and he grins, "Uria cloth is one of the many reasons we're trying to open up trade with you. It was a fluke discovering what it was, but I had some of our experts research the cloth, and they came to the same conclusion. It's molted drake skin."

I flush hot. Diedra said as much, and hearing my Bluey's description, it's disgusting to think about, but if it protects the person wearing it, who cares?

"Monsters—or *Drakes*—have plagued Panthum for millennia, which is why my family developed the weapons we now sell. It's part of the reason we cannot leave. They're one of the things we protect our people from."

Part of being the keywords. There are many different varieties but they're all covered in scales. When they molt, it's collected and shipped to the South where the textile mills are operated. They are soaked with a brew to create Uria cloth. I didn't lie to Diedra when I told her I hadn't seen it done.

I read about it.

"Any more secrets you're willing to part with?" he asks, raising a blond brow. I realize he's using humor to deflect all that I've given him, but he's handling it and respecting my boundaries. When I shake my head, he tugs me out of the veranda and down the darkened halls, meeting Vasilius and Diedra in the tunnels.

"Let's get back home, I'm exhausted," Diedra says, and I hug her. She squeezes me back, and I whisper to her my suspicions about Toriey and Raine. She nods her head, sighing.

"He told me as much, and I don't like any of it, but this is the life we're made to bear in order to be with one another."

I nod and give her another hug before we depart for their palace and the beginning of the celebration of Currell.

Chapter 29

Our open top carriage winds up the hill to the magnificent palace, with its curves and golden domes above guard towers like gilded confection. The waterfall's roar, a soft white noise as Calix escorts me into his family's crowning seat of power. Diedra and Vasilius follow behind. My friend's shoulders slump and mutters something about work and leaves quickly, still upset about her father's plans for Canary.

Vasilius follows suit, saying something similar before disappearing, as well.

Canary's confined to the bowels of *Eregonus* until the Battle for Justice at the end of the week, and I imagine how painful it will be for Diedra this week while we celebrate. Canary had become her loving shadow.

Inside, the granite walls are decorated with carved murals depicting animals, people, and landscapes. The high open windows allow mist from the waterfalls to waft inside and cool the empty hallway but dissipates before reaching the rug covered tile floor.

Alone, Calix leads me inside the palace, turning down grand corridors and hallways, past servants and guards until we reach a quiet level, arriving in front of tall wooden doors—our suite.

The marble floor is covered with colorful rugs and leather couches, mirroring each other, flanking a low-lying table. Shelves filled with books line one wall with trinkets such as a colorful collection of enamel covered coins.

I walk over to a portrait of a beautiful woman and a handsome man inside a gilded frame on one of his many shelves. Princess Oliana and her husband. I can't remember his name. Pippa, Olga and Vivian's parents. I set it down and turn, finding Calix, raking his eyes over me, sending butterflies into a whirlwind.

For all our hardships and trials, he has always loved me.

He strides slowly forward, wrapping his muscle-corded arms around my body, his lips nuzzling my neck, before whispering in my ear, "I think my memories of our last visit to a bedroom are fading. Would you like to help me remember?" He kisses my neck.

I chuckle. "It was only this morning."

I push off his hood and lean in to kiss him, our hands desperate for each other. I'll never grow accustomed to this consuming desire. Never get used to someone who can't keep his hands off of me.

Sometimes, I wonder if the Mother is toying with me. It doesn't seem like this joy can last.

***

I wake with a start, the sound of a door closing softly, jolting me awake. I groan, trying to clear my soggy dreams, taking in the direction of the sun. *Late afternoon.* I napped part of the day away, despite Calix telling me it's custom, due to the celebrations lasting until near dawn the next day. I find I'm alone on the silky white sheets, and in my Warlord's place is a gilded white box with a tented piece of paper on top.

I snatch up the note, running my index finger over the thick velvety texture of the paper.

For the friend I waited thirty-six years for, Diedra

I pull the box into my lap and remove the lid, smiling slowly, my heart stuttering. Warmth spreads through me, clear to my toes. It's a white lace and silk dress. I roll out of bed and shower, taking time to primp before dressing in the fitted gown.

Diedra arrives when I finish slipping into it, bringing with her two servants who begin to set up their supplies. I beam, pulling her into a hug, kissing her cheek. "I loved your note. Thank you for this! It's gorgeous. And I couldn't have survived without you these last two weeks. I wish I could have gotten you something in return."

She waves away my comment. "My treat. If it were up to Calix, he'd *maybe* remember to buy you clothes instead of weapons and Uria cloth."

I pull back, admiring her flawless wrap dress and smile.

"White is what all new couples wear on the first night of Currell. It's a declaration of love." She smiles softly, and I'm sure she's thinking of Canary. The servants quietly murmur they're ready.

"One's for hair, the other is for your nails," she says, sitting herself on a chair beside me. She's trying to smile, but sadness rims her eyes.

The significance of it hits me hard. "He's survived insurmountable odds to come back to you. He won't fail, not when you're the prize at the end of it all."

The servants begin their work, speaking to each other in Luminum, with Diedra chiming in every once in a while. I catch a few of their occasional stares at my scars, and I refrain from snapping something rude, but instead smile at them, even if it wears on my nerves.

In an hour, the women finish and leave the suite. My scalp and fingers ache, but when I examine what they did, I'm grateful. I look somewhat like the women here in Luminum.

Diedra stands and walks forward, taking my hands in hers. "I never told you thank you for not prying or digging into my relationship with Canary. It's complicated, and we both needed time to sort it out. If I were with any other woman, they would have asked me a hundred questions every day, wanting updates, and I wouldn't have been able to bear it." She sighs. "You're the only one who doesn't want to berate me for my choice in men."

"Why would I do that? Not everyone is like that here, right?" I ask, frowning.

"In the imperial court they are. The only reason you weren't grilled by the two servants is because they don't speak the common tongue. To answer your first question, you're not a judgmental moron like the rest of them." Her deep throaty laugh carries through the air, mingled with mine as I hug her soft body.

"Thank you for being my friend, Diedra."

"After tonight you may not think so." She slips her arm through mine, tugging me along. "Time to dance. It's the only thing that will make this day somewhat bearable. The High Monk of Goldill is in attendance, and the man is as stale as pond water."

We walk arm in arm down the corridor. "What's he like?"

"Judgmental," she quips, and I laugh. "Sometimes he annoys my parents, and I like that he stands up to them. He doesn't allow them to sway his decisions."

"Does he want peace with the Deysik?"

"He does, and I wonder if it's because he spends so much time on the border where their orphanage is. I do a clinic there every year, and he still hasn't warmed up to me."

"You? I wonder why."

"Hey, I got you that dress!"

I laugh, "You should have bought him a new hat then."

"You know that's not a bad idea. The man doesn't know the meaning of 'refresh your wardrobe.'"

She turns to me; her dark braids elegantly coiled around her head and gives me a watery smile.

Our conversation's been distracting me from the butterflies swirling in my stomach the closer we approach the ballroom where the string orchestra's music carries.

"Can we go to the balcony for a moment? I need to center myself," I say to Diedra, and she escorts me to a wide veranda, and we walk along the stone railing to a peaceful area. The stars begin to shine bright above, and I look to find the three God Galaxies swirling above. This far north in Luminum I'm able to see them again, though Tapato, the Loyal Friend, is the only one that's fully visible, directly overhead. The others are seen by their outer cluster of swirling stars. Kitoa, the Jewel, is far to the west beyond Panthum, and to the North, Isili, the Beast.

I take a few deep breaths calming myself and smile at Diedra, telling her I'm ready.

As we slip inside, we are washed with a growing volume of music and flowing chatter from people milling about amongst guards and servants carrying food and drink trays. It's overwhelming and stunning at the same time. I allow Diedra to guide me as I look up at the ceiling to where flowers and greenery hang mingled with twinkling lights.

When we near the door, I see a thick line of people, waiting to enter. Diedra bypasses them all, and I feel the stares of clusters of elegant women with voluptuous bodies and whispers follow in our wake, picking out words that set my teeth on edge.

Too bad she's so scarred. The Prince can always find a new one. She's so muscular. Who would want a woman like that?

I tense and clench my jaw so I don't open my mouth and say something cutting.

Diedra squeezes my arm and says, "Ignore them. No one can compare to your capabilities let alone beauty."

We stop where a regal footman bellows loudly to be heard over the music, "Second Princess and Royal Surgeon, Diedra Vivian Crystal Dread and *Moskazi* Alana... Dread, Ranger of Panthum." The pause is pointed, and the smile I give him causes him to blink in surprise.

Diedra laughs, "I don't think anyone has ever threatened him with a smile before."

"There's a first time for everything," I say.

Diedra leads me into the room, and I can't help but take it in. The ballroom is bigger than anything I've ever seen before, filled with hundreds of people. I dare say, over a thousand. Lights dance against shadows on all the walls, near where hundreds of tables are set, filled with guests conversing away from the dance floor.

Couples in white, blue, black, red, gold, and green, swirl and twirl, hop and skip as they dance in a line before spinning around their partner in perfect synchronization with the music.

"It's breathtaking," I breathe to Diedra.

"I'd say the same about you," Calix says as he approaches, his gaze roving over my body with heated admiration. A thrill shoots through me as he pulls me into his tall warm body, and claims me with a kiss. He pulls back to say against my swollen lips, "It was a good idea for me to leave the bedroom before you woke up, because if I saw you in this, near a bed, we would never leave the room."

"Scandalous," I tease. "What would the servants think?"

I run my fingers over his own white tunic, threaded in dark blue with an intricate design. He traded his mask for a golden circlet, and I admire the curves of his cheekbones, strong nose, and the sharpness of his jawline. He's freshly shaven and smells of cinnamon and leather.

For all those women like to talk, they can't say what I can. He's mine.

He presses his forehead to mine. "To new beginnings, Alana, my fire jewel."

He smiles, and it's a stunning sight. He pulls me towards the dance floor where someone has already swept up Deidra—Vasilius. I'm surprised. I wouldn't have thought the youngest Prince capable of knowing how to dance, but he leans in and says something to his sister, which has her laughter ringing in the room as he expertly spins her around.

Something in my heart softens towards the man for that alone. He's not *all* bad.

I spot Raine dancing with a beautiful woman his age and Commanders Toriey and Teegu looking on, speaking with the Emperor and Empress. All are decked out in full splendor and regalia befitting their station. Raine smiles as he passes by me, and I glance to his grandfather who stares at me with furrowed brows. The gray in his hair stands out in the low light.

He reminds me of a predator walking past. Observing but not hunting.

Calix pulls me away and closer to him, and we laugh as he teaches me the steps to the dance. I do my best to keep up, but the steps change too quickly and in a pattern I'm not entirely familiar with. Why didn't I have Diedra show me how to do this before now?

I hear snickering from the guests around me, and my laughter fades. I glance around quickly to see dozens of people staring at me, making mistake after mistake, with a mixture of humor, pity, and cringing into their hands. Embarrassment floods my nervous system, and I smile at Calix. "Can I have a break? I don't want to hurt your feet more than I already have."

He frowns, nodding as he leads me away from the dance floor, and I see various spectators eye me suspiciously before slithering to Calix with blatant greed. It's an odd sensation to be scorned so silently and publicly.

The royal halls of Panthum don't compare to the magnificence of this ballroom. I'm a country bumpkin compared to these women who are dressed in gowns, jewels, and perfect hair.

His fingers touch my chin, guiding my gaze back to his warm, hazel eyes. I don't miss the way his jaw flickers. "Don't pay them any mind. They're only jealous they can't look as beautiful as you." My body instantly melts. All of the tension drains away from me as fast as it built.

Leave it to Calix to have that effect on me. I enjoy his hands holding me gently but with firmness, as if I'm the most precious object in the room.

High above, crystal chandeliers cascade rainbow light onto those of us in white, and it reminds me I have the one person who I'd do anything for. I love Calix, deeply. None of these perfect people have gone through what we have together. They haven't endured storms or battled for survival like we have. They can't take those trials away.

He may not be Deysik, but he's my perfect match.

The song ends, his hand slipping in mine, and a crooked grin grows on his face as he stares at me. Love fills my heart, and I'm so infinitely happy to be here with him. Music swells in another part of the room, and Calix nods to someone before whispering to me. "We will have to practice dancing in our chambers so you don't send me to Diedra for injured toes."

I burst out laughing, "Ah ha! So, your true motives for not teaching me are revealed!"

"I thought your superior footwork in combat would translate!" he says, pretending to be offended.

"Uncle—Oh, Alana!" Olga approaches us. She's wearing a red dress with bows on the shoulders. Her hair is free from her braids, creating a beautiful curly halo around her head, with a sparkling headband made up of pearls and rubies, pushing it back from her adorable round face. She gives me a nervous smile, and I frown. It's so off from her usual demeanor, I'm instantly concerned. She fidgets with her hands. "I didn't think—Oh, uh. Uncle Calix, I need to speak with you—privately." Her troubled dark eyes flick from Calix to myself.

"Olga, are you alright?" I ask, wondering what's bothering her this much. She steps back from me, swallowing. I frown as Calix turns to me with a confused and apologetic face. He takes the care of his nieces seriously, and I understand.

I sigh. "I'll meet you back in our room. I don't feel comfortable out in the open like this with no allies," I say before leaning up and kissing him on the cheek. I face Olga and give her a warm smile. "You look beautiful Olga."

The girl's eyes duck as she blushes furiously, and I slip out of the ballroom and head back the way I came.

"*Texui ipa redoda slag ey Moskazi,*" a woman says to a group of females slyly peering at me. I don't need Diedra to translate what she said. *The Prince picked an ugly slag of a Moskazi.*

I grind down on my molars and remind myself punching a woman is not proper etiquette. Hurt poisons the joyous feeling inside me, leaving it oily and wasted.

Slag. Whore.

I'd like to know if any one of them would put themselves in harm's way for him. If any one of them would face murderous Deysik and not cower. If any one of them would stand up to an Emperor for their people.

Anger burns hot and fast under my lungs, building with each pointed whisper and stare from the women at the party. Now Calix is not here to shield me from it. I walk faster, hoping to run from the embarrassment building with each step.

I want to curl up in our bed and wait for my Bluey. I hate it when he's not here.

Chapter 30

When I slip back into our suite, I take off my earrings and borrowed jewels from Diedra, setting them on the table by the door, slipping off my dancing slippers, making my way to our bedroom when I hear, "Prince Dread, what took you so long? Were you able to sneak away?"

The female voice is husky and calls from behind the cracked door. A painful jab of cold fear and fury leap under my skin, coiling in my stomach.

I push the door open to find a woman in our bed with the sheets pulled up over her well-endowed chest and body. I can't move. A hundred thoughts race through my mind until her voice breaks through them all.

"What are *you* doing here?" she sneers at me. My heart freezes in my chest as a deadly calm settles over me as my mind falls into a lethal quiet, the same way it does when threatened.

"Get out," I say with death on my tongue.

"No. I'm right where I should be and where I belong. *You're* the one who should get out. Go back to whatever backwater slum you crawled out from, you brick of a slag."

That word. *Slag.* My vision turns red.

I didn't realize I'd moved until I'm across the room, grabbing the woman by the hair and dragging her out of *our* bed. She shrieks and screams, hissing like the snake she is. She's a lot heavier than I thought, but my rage floods through every muscle of my body, lending me strength to get this bovine out of my living space.

How dare she call me that vile word? I am no slag! The word eats away at my mind like a worm through an apple. That's all they see.

That's all they see.

I kick open the doors as guards rush down the hall drawn to the commotion. With a roar, I whip her out of the room, watching as she goes tumbling across the hall in a heap of skin before I smash the doors closed, locking them behind me.

My hands are shaking, and I start sobbing as all the bottled hurt cascades over me like a waterfall. I move to the end of the bed and slide to the floor in a puddle.

I've never lost my temper like that. I've never so much as laid a hand on a woman before. I cover my face with my trembling palms, guilt and shame swallowing me up like a great abyss. Drake would be disgusted if he saw what I did. Any Ranger would.

Something crashes in the other room, and I jerk my head up with a gasp. I fly to my feet and rush into the sitting room, finding Pippa on the floor with the pieces of shattered pottery all around her. A shallow cut bleeds on her cheek, and I frown in confusion as she holds a piece of the broken vase. She slides the jagged edge of pottery across her hairline, and

I'm stunned as blood pours down her face. She screams, and it jolts me out of my stupor.

"Pippa!" I cry out, horrified. I run to her. "What are you doing?" I attempt to snatch the shard away from her but she ducks under my arm, twists and stabs me between my ribs, just like I had shown Olga earlier this week.

The piece is not angled enough to cut deeply, and I cry out more in surprise than anything, and out of reaction I backhand Pippa, causing her to tumble to the ground before I pin her, snatching the vase piece away from her hands as the door to the bedroom crashes open.

Her blue eyes widen, and suddenly she's whimpering, scrambling to get away from me. "Help! She's trying to hurt me! Alana, I promise it was a misunderstanding!"

"Pippa, what—" I begin, only to be interrupted by Calix bursting into the room. He halts, filling up the doorway, arms wide, his eyes flicking from Pippa on the floor cowering away, the blood on her face, the blood on my dress, and finally stopping on the piece of broken vase in my hand.

His expression turns from horror, to menacing anger, eyes blazing with fury.

"Alana, what have you done?" he shouts, flying to his niece's side, scooping Pippa up off of the floor.

"She tried to kill me!" Pippa cries as several guards rush into the room, followed by Olga and the Empress, who fearfully grabs her granddaughter's shoulders, hauling her back and away from me. The Sapphire guards draw their swords and the Emperor strides in with Toriey and Teegu on his heels.

"Traitor," Calix snarls. All the blood drains from my face over how the scene appears. I look to Pippa, tucked against him and find her smirking like she did a week ago.

That little liar. My face flames with mortification and humiliation over what I'm silently being accused of.

"You can't possibly think I'd *hurt* her, let alone try to kill her," I stammer, feeling bile rise in my throat. The Empress moves forward, shoving Olga behind her, and pulls Pippa from Calix's arms as Diedra rushes in, gasping at all the blood. The Emperor orders the guards to seal the hallway.

The older girl wails loudly, pointing a damning finger in my direction. "I came to apologize to Alana and found Riki in his bed, and when she walked in, she thought I put her up to it! She threw a vase and then cut me with it as punishment, just like her queen did to her! She's violent when she's upset."

The Empress glares at Calix, and my heart shatters as she silently accuses him of bringing a wild animal into her home. She turns, snarling at her husband, "Have him deal with her."

I wish I could swallow, but there's a lump in my throat at what she's asking him to do.

I catch Pippa shooting Olga a look in askance, and the younger girl nods, twisting the ties nervously at her waist. Mother help me, Olga's involved. It's enough for me to realize the lengths a hurt teenager would go to protect her remaining family.

Based on her howls of pain echoing off of the stone, I know it isn't going to end well.

I turn to Calix, bracing myself. The hate sparking from his beautiful sapphire and emerald eyes confirms Olga revealed her suspicions to Calix that I'm Deysik.

Fear clutches my heart and feet, leaving me immobile. This is what I've always been taught to fear—a Deysik pitted against an Azure Warrior.

It feels as though a blade is twisting in my stomach. Even if Calix were to threaten my life, I don't think I could stop him. I don't think I'd want to. I could never hurt him. We vowed not to.

There's no evidence of the man I love when he stares back with such hate, betrayal, and grief that tears slip down my face.

He's physically different. His tall and broad form is swollen with rage. The glittering of his deadly stare and ticking of his jaw sends terror through my veins. I've only seen him look like this in battle with the Ariportia as the Warlord.

"You betrayed not only me but my family as well. I *trusted* you with my most valuable family members, and you *hurt* her in your jealous anger," he snarls.

I shake my head, and he snaps, "You never liked Pippa."

"That's not true. She's lying. That's not what happened," I defend, but my voice sounds weak even to my own ears.

He didn't believe me a few nights ago. Why would he believe me now? With all the secrets I hold, is it a surprise? I didn't *not* like Pippa, only the way she behaved. She's the mirror image of my younger self.

"Don't you dare speak to me of *lying*! You, who say you value honor—have none! This is a betrayal I cannot stand for. You're probably not even a Ranger! You're a lying *Deysik*." I flinch at the word, and he can see it on my face.

The truth. I *am* Deysik. He shakes his head, spitting disgust. His lip and nose curl in disgust, and he takes a step back, body trembling with repulsion and rage.

I shake my head. I can't get enough air in my lungs. It feels like my chest is caving in. My stomach is sickeningly tight.

"You had so many chances to tell me, but you didn't!" he yells, face desolate and ragged as if my betrayal is ripping him apart. Tears slide down my cheeks, and I grip my dress until my fingers hurt.

I sob, my voice breaking. "I'm not a liar or a violent murderer."

"You are those things!" He roars, spearing my heart with such force, I take several steps back. My stomach drops and my body flushes numb. He can't really think that. No. He can't.

I shake my head, but my denial only seems to enrage him further.

"You aren't what I thought you were. You found out who I was, and you weaseled your way into my heart. You calculated how best to solidify your position by stopping those Deysik. You probably tried to taunt the Deysik to kill Olga, but they most likely turned on you, forcing you to kill them."

With every accusation, I experience how quickly love can turn to hate. I can't stop my body from trembling with shame and guilt. Calix snarls viciously, "Don't you dare cry! You are *ugly* from the inside out, you, *slag*!"

Nothing could have gutted me more. It would have been better had he slit my throat.

He turns away with a look of disgust and speaks to the sapphire guards, "Take her to *Egronous*. She will fight in the Battle for Justice."

"No," I plead. "Please Calix—"

"*Do not speak to me!*" he rages, turning back, his body humming with wrath. He looks as if he's going into a killing rage as he pulls his sword, taking several steps towards me, his eyes bursting into turquoise flames. I jerk back, slamming into the wall, shrinking down, thinking he will remove my head or shred me apart with his killing power.

"Not here," Toriey's voice cuts in, and Calix stops himself short, catching himself. Breathing heavily and brokenly, he speaks to the room, "I can't believe you're my *Moskazi*."

"The marriage will be dissolved, since it was signed under false pretenses," the Emperor says, coming to stand by his son, looking at me not with pity or disgust, but calculation.

Sapphire Warriors grab my arms, hauling me to my feet, and as I pass Calix, I can't help but bitterly whisper, "It won't be hard to find a new whore, Bluey."

I walk to keep from being dragged, but it's as though I'm not inside my body. I feel nothing and don't care what they are going to do with me. I gave everything to Calix, and he cared more about the contents of my blood over who I was. I had told him the Deysik I know are different from those here, but he thinks I tricked him.

He told me he would love me forever, but *he* lied. He was the one who fabricated the illusion we would last forever no matter what trials we faced. It turns out he would fight for me until it came to his family. Only they were worth more than me on the scale of Calix's loyalty and love.

Had it been true love, then he wouldn't have so easily believed Pippa's story and scheme. Not after everything we've been through. My character and honor are nothing in his eyes.

Nothing.

The journey from the Palace to Eregonus is a blur as my mind twists into knotts of seething fury.

Calix gave up on me and won't change his mind about things. He didn't when he was rebuking me over the Deysik attack. Canary had to reason with him and if not for a voice of reason, Calix is lost to his dark thoughts.

And I'm to pay the price.

PART II

THE METTLE

Chapter 31

CALIX

Everything has crumbled underneath me. A Deysik breeched the walls of our home again not by force or ambush, but by my own hand. Fury floods through my whole body until I'm shaking with rage so hard the length of my sword vibrates. The woman I loved more than myself deceived me. Her smile, her laugh, her movement, all of it was used to mold me into a puppet.

The voice of my father cuts through my tumultuous thoughts. "You are responsible for her, and the damage she has done to your niece, and it will ripple through the rest of your life."

The hiss and fury in his condemnation is deserved. I clench my teeth and nod. I failed Pippa. I failed my family. I failed my empire.

I turn around to meet the faces of my commanders, my father, my friends, and people I've known my whole life. How many of them would she have killed had Pippa not revealed her true nature.

I didn't believe she was a Deysik; she bled, and her eyes didn't glow. None of the signs pointed to her being our enemy, but I had to confront her with what Olga told me.

My niece has always had the gift of hearing the truth of people's thoughts and feelings. The *Maage* tutored her in the art of picking apart the threads of those feelings and thoughts to weave a tapestry of a story.

"How did you find out?" Toriey asks me.

I sheath my sword and unclench my jaw enough to confess, "Olga informed me she discovered the truth of her deception the night of the attack in Illalangi, but didn't say anything, convinced that she was a *good* Deysik, because she saved her life."

A scoff from my father and I shake my head as my nostrils flare as betrayal lashes at my skin, incriminating myself until I'm bloody with it.

"The best assassins are beautiful," Teegu says as if he has any idea. The Commander's a snake and does whatever my father suggests.

I think back to the day we first met when the man she was with announced I was an Azure Warrior and the fear and disgust in her eyes. The reaction was so common, I assumed she was one of many who held a longstanding prejudice against the enforcers of Luminum. But I was smitten with the curse of obsession. I couldn't get her out of my head and followed her and distracted the Monk for her, allowing Canary enough time to render me unconscious and seajack me.

On the ship, I was consumed by her presence, like a fawn to a wolf. I did everything I could to win her over, but I realize now, she was reeling me in with mystery and humor. She used the right amount of vulnerability that caused my natural instincts to rise in wanting to protect her, though she didn't need it.

"Did the Traitor know who she was?" Teegu asks, turning to my father who looks at me for the answer.

I shake my head, "No, he only knew I was interested in her and could lead him back to Diedra."

"I would love an excuse to execute the Traitor, but perhaps we can use him for a different purpose? The Night Queen has allied herself with the Deysik. Why not send him to assassinate her?" Toriey suggests, his nose curled with anger.

My father nods. "His skill is unparalleled. If anyone can do it, he can, and he's properly motivated to come back alive."

The thought twists my stomach, but I know that the consequences of my lack of investigation into Alana's background will harm Diedra.

"What are you going to do with the Ranger?" Toriey asks. "She's been announced publicly as Prince Dread's *Moskazi*."

"She'll be forgotten in a few days. No one wanted her," my father sneers, moving to stand by me. His words gut me.

"We need to give ourselves a few days to think about how we will use this to our advantage with Panthum and our needs. I don't believe any woman would hold up under the right... convincing for her secrets to spill. I'm sure she has many. If that is what we decide you will be the one to do it."

My body flinches in repulsion over the idea, even though moments ago I was so furious I could have killed her. When she jerked back and true fear glazed over her dark brown eyes, it broke the killing lust that swallowed me whole, leaving me disgusted with myself.

Now, I shove those feelings down. She *lied* to me. She lied to all of us. I could see the truth of her heritage when I confronted her. Despite masking her feelings well, I've been studying her and learning her body language to compensate for the many things she doesn't share.

She's an artist in deception.

The silver lining in all of this is she refused to attend the meetings I had begged her to join. I had wanted her there to give her opinion on how we can design our own weapons. Every prototype and attempt failed horrifically and with every failure the more obsessed my father has become, putting pressure on his Commanders to develop a solution.

"We need to look at the contract again," my father says, voice firm and decisive.

I growl in frustration and admit my own lapse to my father. "In my rush to save her life I left it with my men in the Red City. I realized it after we departed and ordered them to bring it back to me. It will arrive in three days.

Alana wasn't the only one who lied. I had Toriey and Canary sign a form, stating that they agreed to witness my dissolution of her contract, but I was waiting for the notarized document to make it official.

"Will the form arrive with Captain Nasheer?" Teegu chuckles, and I turn to face him, feeling the skin pull tight over my cheekbones.

"What did you just say?" I reply with lethal rage lining every word.

The three men left in the room stare at me, and my father raises an eyebrow, putting his hands on his hips. "The Captain is a guest of the crown. I invited him to attend last year."

"Did you now?" I snarl, and my father drops his arms, taking a step towards me.

"I know *how* you were caught in Faurst. Be grateful the Captain has never seen your face or you would have destroyed forty years of hard-earned business ties with the man."

In the Red City, during negotiations, Nash slid over the marriage certificate he, Calix, Canary, and Alana had signed, knowing that I would honor the agreement even if the man had supposedly died at sea.

"You need mercenaries so desperately?" I sneer, unheeding the warnings he gives me when he steps closer, his blue eyes flashing in restrained anger.

"They're cheaper than my own men's lives, and he trains the best, which helps get the job done."

"Which would include slaughtering women and children," I snap, pushing forward until I'm inches away from my father.

The Emperor has power, but he knows if anyone outside of this room knew the true extent of what he was doing, he would lose the support of the Mother's Monks, and they hold more sway than my father will ever admit.

"If I don't kill them off, they will reproduce like rabbits. Would you rather have this continent overrun with their poison? Would you rather Azure Warriors suffer? Because that is what I'm doing. I'm making it possible for *your* children to grow up without the threat of death hanging over their head."

Alana can't have children. The thought hits me in the stomach until I find the blood on the floor from Pippa and next to it single drops from Alana. She was injured, and I know how she reacts when physically pained by surprise.

Deadly wrath burns inside me once more.

Regardless of how I feel about Alana, my father is wrong for what he's doing.

"Find a different way," I say looking to Toriey. I trusted him to be the voice of reason in my father's cabinet, but on this issue he's remained silent. Mostly because his sister was my aunt, and was murdered by the Deysik assassin twenty years ago.

"Let's worry about the threat under our noses first," my father says and turns to leave my bedroom suite. "Make sure to wear your mask for the rest of Currell, you never know if a Deysik will be around the corner, waiting to mark you for death."

What my father doesn't realize is that most people think it's better not to antagonize an Emperor.

But truly, it's best not to provoke a Warlord.

Alana will pay for her crimes against my family.

***

"Thank you for the lovely meal, Emperor Dread," the Black Fox says to my father as they sit back in their seats. "You honor me."

The light from the chandeliers hanging over the private dining room casts an ethereal glow over the mercenary's silver mask. The table is full of guests of the crown, our Commanders and my family, except Diedra and the Princesses. The dinner my father is currently hosting is a welcome gift for his mercenaries on entering Currell as participants for the first year.

My father's loyal dog is joined by Captain Nash and two other mercs whose names I can't remember.

The captain sits next to my father and mother, quietly speaking to them, unaware that the men who he kept chained and caged on the ship sit across from him at the same table. He didn't know my name because it's not public record for our protection. Canary gave it to the captain, knowing he wouldn't recognize it.

Only those close to us know it. It's one of the reasons why Diedra doesn't call me or Vasilius by our given names in public.

The past six days have been a flurry of strategy meetings and ensuring each fight has led to the correct territory's champion taking the round and advancing on.

Tomorrow's battle will decide the Champion of Currell.

Everything fell into place with one upset. One of the Black Fox's mercenaries has advanced in each round, beyond all hope, reason, and stumbling block placed in their way. They've avoided eating tainted food, or drinking anything with herbs that would cause severe stomach pain for three days. Quite frankly, I think the man lived off of air.

I'm surprised my father hadn't put a stop to the mercenary's domination in each round. Regardless, Raine, Toriey's grandson, will face off with him in combat tomorrow. And the winner will fight the Deysik who wins the Battle of Justice where my little liar will compete. My heart seizes with fear and fury at the mere thought of it. The guards told me three days ago of her bid to enter and my father laughed when he heard. His response was, "If she dies in the battle, we won't have to execute her."

Six days later and I'm functioning off of rage, grit, and determination to protect my country. Sleep is non-existent, and I'm wracked with icy hate for Alana and all things Deysik. Diedra refuses to speak to me, and Vasilius and I are competing for who has the vilest attitude.

We shuttled the Princesses off to Heviin for their protection.

The Black Fox now takes in my brother next to me, their two companions flanking them haven't said a word all night. I'm curious if they speak Luminum or the common tongue. Most likely neither.

My father is single-minded in ensuring his power will reign supreme. Each territory fights for priority in their bid for their goods to be sold and exported to other countries or inside our empire. Currell is a way to decide who those are, and he's made it clear that it's my job to ensure the outcome.

After Currell, I'm to lead a quarter of our Azure Warrior's to Faurst to gain entry and if they refuse, I'm to bring Panthum to its knees, taking their weapons and Uria cloth. The last order he gave was to burn the country down in Total War and slaughter their Deysik.

It will take at least two months to gather the supplies, order the logistics, and redirect our ships, half of which are currently protecting the Red City coast from the Deysik who are attacking merchant vessels in the area.

"I hear the *Moskazi* is rotting away in a cell below *Eregonus*. Do you know when her torture will begin? I would like to join as an observer, to see how a Ranger breaks."

I'm the only one allowed to lay hands on Alana. "No one will harm her, but me. That includes you, coming near her," I snarl.

"My, my, are you still feeling territorial, Warlord?"

I turn my head to stare down my father's paid servant. They angle their head in response, unaffected. Too arrogant for their own good. I was caught up in the blissful rapture of new love with my little liar to be bothered much by their cutting words before. Now I'm irritated.

"Always. What's mine is *mine* and nothing will change that."

"A contract is law," the High Monk of Goldill says from his seat, three people down from me. "I've reviewed the document this morning. You're unable to touch your *Moskazi*, Prince Dread."

Yes. The stipulation in the contract, which stayed my father's hand from acting against my little liar.

"She's not his *Moskazi*," my father snaps, and my mother lays a calming hand on his, silently commanding him to remain calm.

The High Monk, is a man in his late thirties with black hair and drab clothing in need of repair. He was once a Sapphire Warrior before he resigned his commission and turned to the Mother's Monks for his living. "Then are you formally dissolving their marriage contract?" he asks, turning cutting blue eyes to my father.

I can see why my father hates him. Burning fury over my manipulation by Alana hasn't banked, and I don't see it ever doing so.

"Yes," my father says decisively and what he says is law. A part of me recoils and howls at the thought of parting with my legal ties to her, but I grit my teeth and bear the pain of her betrayal. I tell myself I would have liked to have her completely at my mercy.

This is her doing, not mine.

Vasilius looks at me, and I snort and shrug my shoulders. There's nothing I can do about it. If my father says she's not my wife then she's not.

"Now that that question has been answered, you will need to release her." The High Monk's words resonate, and the whole room falls silent.

"What do you mean, release her?" My father fumes.

"I mean, when you annulled her marriage, you rescinded her citizenship as a Luminum, and the death sentence you gave her, forfeits the contract altogether."

My heart thunders in my chest. No. No, she can't be free.

"You can't do that," my father fumes, his entire being swelling with rage. The table rattles with his power as it spills out. My mother grips his bicep, hissing his name.

The High Monk smiles. "I didn't do anything. I simply stated the facts of the case. You did it yourself, Emperor."

My father snarls, "The girl will pay for her crimes and assault on my granddaughter."

"She will not." The High Monk stares down my father, and I wonder if the rigidity of his stance is for power or pleasure against my father.

Either way, I don't care.

Captain Nash remains silent, taking in the table at large and the drama playing out before him. As old as he is, I don't doubt he's amused. No one has been able to pin his age, and the Maage doesn't know or won't answer.

My father sits back in his chair and turns to his favored mercenary.

"The Black Fox, will you be so kind as to kill our Ranger?" my father asks smugly.

"No." The word whips across the room, and my father's hostile gaze flies to his favored mercenary, but they continue, "I was witness to the contract being sold, and I cannot break it by carrying out your orders to kill her."

"That's a conflict of interest."

"I didn't know you wanted her dead when I signed it. One could argue the conflict of interest is yours, not wanting her to be your son's *Moskazi*."

"You legally can't order your mercenaries to kill her either," the High Monk says with a chuckle. "Unless you want to lose your crown? Besides the Black Fox was witness to the contract. They know the consequences."

"You sold out your honor to save a Deysik?" the Emperor rages, his face turning a dark pink with his fury.

The Black Fox stands and removes her mask, and my gaze shifts to Vasilius next to me, who freezes, his pearl mask hiding his expression, but I know for a fact, he's either furious or murderous. Her white blonde hair and pale skin and eyes give her the appearance of a ghostly specter hidden underneath all that black.

"I found your Princess, Prince. I take my payment in gold."

My stomach drops like a stone into a raging river. This is one surprise I don't think my brother will recover from. Svetlana Slate, Princess of the immensely wealthy and deadly region of Slate, southeast of us, has returned. And has been here all along. For three years to be exact. I look to her men. They must be the Slate Knights that fled with her. No wonder her man is undefeated. He is death personified.

Vasilius stands and says in his garbled voice, distorted by the mask to protect our identities, "You'll have it within the hour."

Then he turns and leaves.

She sits back down and turns to my father. "Captain Nash has politely agreed to command my men while I fulfill the contract *you* signed with my brothers." She angles her head and a piece of white blonde hair falls onto her dimpled cheek. "I do not lie when I say I witnessed her contract and if you threaten my country, your people will suffer."

"I'm surrounded by deceivers and liars!" my father snarls, shoving back his chair and storms out of the room, my mother following after him.

I look to Nash and snarl, "Did you know who she was?"

The captain shakes his head, "I must confess I didn't, though it seems quite a shock, no?"

"Everyone out but you," I point a finger to Svetlana who stares at me with a nervous expression on her pale face. She glances to her men and nods her head. They pause and stare at me until I snap, "She's legally family, I'm not going to hurt her."

"But you tried with Alana," the slate Princess says, flinging the truth at me. I hold back my flinch. The other guests leave, and I'm alone with the mercenary who fled my brother three years ago on the eve of their wedding.

"Yes I did."

"You still want her dead for her deception?" the woman asks, her pale violet eyes glitter with disgust.

"Of course I do. She betrayed me, just like you did with Vasilius!"

A bitter laugh escapes her. "As you say. What does Vasilius think of Alana? Does he hate her like you do, or did he learn his lesson the first time she scolded him for his lack of inquisition?"

Cold fury and fear rattle inside of me like a war cry.

"Funny how as smart as you are, you allowed a fourteen-year-old, bitter, hurt girl to spin a story without picking it apart by asking the simple question, why would she be in your bedroom?"

She drills those ghostly eyes into me, and I feel the impact.

"It doesn't change the facts."

"No, but it should change your perspective, Prince Dread." She cocks her head again. "Or should I call you Bluey?"

She grins at my flared nostrils and the porcelain plates rattling with my swelling power as she stands to leave. I've never been this uncontrolled before.

And it's all Alana's fault.

Chapter 32
ALANA

They toss me into a cell, deep in the roots of the *Egronous* pits and give me a plate of food and a cup of water. I don't bother touching it. I'm nothing but an empty husk. The only light is from a torch right outside my iron door. I can't even work up the energy to cry, I'm so devastated.

My once-white dress is now stained with dirt, blood, and sand. I don't think I'll live long enough for it's filth to bother me.

What hurts the most is I grew to love the Princesses, and they returned it by twisting truths and lies, destroying the love of my life. I refuse to feel guilt over my actions. I did nothing wrong.

The *Mother* knows I did nothing wrong. Yet why would she place me on this continent with Calix if it wasn't for some purpose.

Unless I was the sacrificial lamb. Perhaps that was her plan all along. I was supposed to admit I was a Deysik so that Olga could use her gift to discover my secrets, and the Azure Warriors could use it as an excuse to go to war with Panthum.

Based on the threats of the Emperor earlier today, I know my fate is sealed. He doesn't seem like a man to back out of a promise.

My cell is twelve feet long, and the door leading to the fighting pit is warm to the touch from the heat of the sun lingering long after having gone to bed.

That night I don't sleep because I'm too busy focusing on the wracking agony of heartbreak, thoughts spinning and twisting into an ugly monster that consumes me.

The next morning, I'm brought another plate of bland food and a cup of water.

No one has come to speak to me, and the indignity of it all, rakes its claws down my back, and I feel like I'm going to rip my skin off if I'm cooped up in this hole without some sort of explanation of what they plan to do with me. Will Calix kill me? Will they put me in the Battle for Justice?

An hour later, a loud clanging sound rolls through my cell, and the large door leading out to the grassy pitch opens, the metal bars with it. I slowly near the door, checking for danger, and I hear a guard call, "You have two hours before you're back inside."

Lovely. I might as well walk the pitch and look for anything hidden or missed by the servants who clean up after battle.

All I discover is an arrowhead from a broken arrow and shove it deeply into the grass by my door underneath the royal box. My guess is they placed me here so Calix wouldn't have to look at me while watching Currell.

The same meal arrives for lunch, and I'm infuriated, but there's nothing I can do about it, so I set aside my anger and focus on all the ways I'm going to dismantle the empire of Luminum. I only get about ten minutes into that project before I give it up, too upset with myself for not sitting in on meetings all day, so I could have used the information from them to wound the country that was to be my new home.

Instead, my thoughts shift to the battle ahead. That was what was promised, and that is what will happen.

It's easy to keep time as the meal delivery is always the same. It reminds me of when Calix once said they punished women by skipping meals. I suppose I don't need to skip any when they're planning on making a spectacle of me.

From the door leading to the pitch, I hear the cheers and screams of Currell. The second night is as long as the first with my anger setting into something solid along the edges with a churning center.

***

On the third day, Vasilius visits my cell, standing outside the barred door. "My father is ordering a quarter of our forces across the sea to broker a deal with Panthum for your weapons and Uria cloth."

"My family will burn our warehouses to the ground before we'll manufacture them on your behalf." My voice is dry and raspy. He cocks his head, crouching down to my level, his face even. No hint of gloating in his micro expressions.

"Perhaps, or maybe they already have leverage over your family... in the forms of debts, or lives, and if that doesn't work, they will invade Panthum and burn it in Total War, taking everything they can."

I'm so far past feeling anything other than cold calculation, his inference doesn't glimmer against the hoarfrost of my rage. They will all die before my Rangers allow that to happen...

He looks down, "I do not believe you harmed Pippa." My eyes flash to meet his, and I find shame contouring his face. "After the last time I doubted you, I promised I'd not do so again, so I dug deeper. Pippa's story and injury don't add up. Diedra agrees her injuries were self-inflicted."

"Did she tell Calix or your father?" I know not to hope. I *know* not to. But I do. If anyone could convince them it would be Diedra.

"It still changed nothing."

When Drake taught that hope is the difference between life and death, I had listened. I just never thought I would experience its complete loss until this moment.

I turn to face the wall, shattered once more, my insides and heart cut up with the pieces of a bloodied and broken vase.

"I'm sorry, Alana. Neither will listen to reason," he sighs. "But I thought you should know."

I will not get out of this place, but my Rangers have been preparing for this moment all their lives. Before he can walk away, I say, "When you stand at the doorstep of Panthum, Vasilius, if you happen across a warrior with long black hair and emerald eyes, larger than the Warlord... don't engage."

"Who is he?"

I turn my head to stare him dead in the eye, letting him see my lack of empathy, lack of life, lack of soul. "The Lord of Rising fortress. He'll pick up my scent off of you and not think twice before he'll splay you apart."

"Calix will be leading our armies across the sea."

His words kindle my rage, "I suppose a good General would have to follow the command of his Emperor, while the Crown Prince stays home in safety."

He clears his throat. "What?"

I slide my dead gaze up and down his body, pausing on his iridescent mask hanging at his hip, before finally stopping on his churning ocean blue ones. "Only Commanders wear gold, the more filigree, the higher the rank. Even Toriey's isn't as nearly as exquisite as the Warlord's. Your pearl mask is deceptively plain and the only one like it. Calix told me once that age doesn't determine the next in line to the throne but power. I did not see any Azure Warriors near you when fighting the Ariportia, because you had no need of them."

He stares in silence until I turn back to the wall and mutter, "Your secret is safe with me. I'll die in a few days."

"I wish things were different, Alana."

I say nothing, and after a moment, he leaves me to my thoughts and roiling pain.

***

On the fourth day, I resolve I'll never love again.

On the fifth day, I despair, sobbing until there are no more tears left to shed.

On the sixth day, I determine to never be another's pawn, or hold my true-self back so as not to cause waves.

On the seventh day, I know what I have to do to earn my freedom.

Only my freedom comes in a completely unexpected way on the evening of the seventh day, long after the crowds have gone from *Egronous*.

With a grunt, a guard opens the door. I don't bother standing or hoping. My love has tipped over the cliff to its death and splashed into a raging river of loathing for Calix.

He failed me. He didn't come for me the next morning. I *knew* he wouldn't come, but I still held out foolish hope, but Vasilius confirmed his betrayal. How had he not realized Pippa's lie or grasped the *thought* I'd never hurt his nieces? Or grasped his reasoning was flawed?

The signs were there, and I missed them. He was too busy convincing me to come to his side of thinking, he never truly came to mine.

"Mother, help me, you stink!" Nash's cheerful voice calls. The thick cadence of the sea Captain's lyrical voice stirs nothing inside of me. I sift the sand and grit through my fingers, imagining it's the ground from home. I am determined to see the pine trees and mountain valley's of Rising Pass and the shining capital of Panthum. Fidir has much to answer for, but after he protects our people.

Nash's boots appear in my line of sight. I don't bother looking up at him. I don't speak. I'll be silent like Canary.

Nash sighs heavily, "I know it hurts, but it really is for the good of *everyone,* it ends this way. The Mother was hoping you could sway the Prince to reason." He plops down next to me and glances over, the low torch light from the hall shining on his angular handsome face. He's probably hoping I'll respond to his intuitive knowledge of all the things that have transpired since we last saw each other.

I don't.

The Mother is a deity who is fickle and mercurial. I believe in her, but I will not pander to her pleas to save the Azure Warriors from their impending war. I hope they all burn.

He adjusts his shimmering orange Shirwani that is bright against his dark honey colored skin and black hair. He smells of the sea and levity.

His dark eyes take in my sand covered white lace and silk dress, bare feet, and unkempt hair. "Our friend the Black Fox has retired her mask, giving her men over into my care with a special task."

I grunt, not believing him. I pieced together her animosity toward Vasilius had to be more personal, and the only person who could've hurt Vasilius, Calix informed me, was his runaway bride, Svetlana Brozna, the Slate Princess.

Nash must see the disbelief on my face because he says, "No, she really did. We were both enjoying dinner with the royal family and the High Monk of Luminum, when the discussion of your death sentence came up."

My stomach clenches, but Nash continues in his lyrical voice. "You don't know this because you were too busy trying to die on me upstairs at the time, but she was the witness to the sale of your indenture, and read through the contract thoroughly... noting every clause, which was fortunate, because what she testified over our meal, kept the imperial family from being removed from power. Did you know the High Monk of Goldill has the authority to do so? And breaking an indenture contract is grounds for removal... especially if it was never legally dissolved."

My breathing stops. He shakes his head and chuckles, "Of course the Emperor accused her of selling her word for a traitor, which led to the removal of her mask. Took it off in front of everyone. You should've seen the Emperor's face." He mimes bulging eyes before he peers at me, yet I remain quiet. "Can't exactly kill a neighboring Princess without consequences. The Slate Knights are funny that way. No one can kill you but them. The only one not surprised was Prince Vasilius."

He brushes the dust off of his pants. "I thought that would have earned a comment, no?"

I give him a stare, promising death, and he brightens, "See! You're learning to communicate much more effectively than Canary." He shifts his long legs in the sand, crossing his fingers together. "I'm sorry about the Warlord. I really am, but I have good news for you... I'm taking you back to Faurst for the Pilgrimage."

I feel nothing. It isn't a surprise really, not when the Black Fox—Svetlana had been so concerned with her people being caught in this war. Then it hits me like a stone to the head. It's not my problem to worry about.

I don't care. It's *their* problem.

Now, I'll be fine watching Luminum turn to ash and rubble if only to have them feel what we felt four hundred years ago after the slaughter.

"Are you ready to leave these piss poor accommodations he gave you?"

With those words Nash earns my respect.

I nod. The captain hides his relief well, but I can practically smell it on him. He stands and reaches out. I study him before taking his hand. He yanks me up and gags. "First stop is Svetlana's home to make you decent. This dress color is atrocious. Love? Feeble. Red is for passion. A stronger and more *persevering* color, don't you agree, Ruby?"

When I don't answer, he makes a scoffing noise and leads me out through the tunnels until we arrive under the night sky. The silent guards glare, and their malice buzzes like wasps threatening to sting me to death.

The streets are quiet, only occasionally broken up by shouts of celebration. It must be in the early hours of the morning when those who stay up late go to bed and those who rise early haven't stirred from their beds.

The hour of ambush. I check my surroundings, but Nash is moving quickly, and I feel no stabbing of warning along my skin.

Outside is warmer than the cool dungeon, and I know I won't miss it.

Or Calix.

Or this cursed Empire.

One of Svetlana's massive men throws a black cloak over me, lifts my exhausted form onto a horse before riding next to me. He seems to be my guard—or companion, however you want to look at it. We travel down the hill, our path lit by candles, votives, and lamps lining the streets, arriving in a quiet neighborhood with modest homes behind black metal gates. Many of their yards are filled with fountains, flowers, and mature palm trees.

If I didn't hate it here so much, I might find it beautiful.

We enter the gates of the largest home in the neighborhood and after we stable our horses, the captain leads us inside, nodding to the short, bald, beady-eyed man who opens the door for him—Philpot.

I never thought I'd miss the small, prim man, but I find the emotion swell inside me. Perhaps it is only because he's familiar. The little man winces when he catches my smell and practically drags me down the hall into a master bedroom, where piles of boxes are stacked nearly to my waist. I raise my brow, waving a hand to the stacks as he hauls me around to a bathroom, resembling the one back in the Red City. "Gifts from Nash," he answers with an eye roll as if I'm an imbecile.

He leaves me, locking the door behind him as he goes. I never imagined I'd be back where I started when I first came to this country; being dragged to a bedroom and ensuite bathroom to be cleaned up as I hold grief in my heart.

I undress and sink into the tub, scrubbing as vigorously as I can, trying to get the feeling of betrayal and anger off my skin from where it seeps thoroughly like the odor from a skunk.

I finish my bath and dig through the boxes until I find a red tunic and black pants. I'm a Ranger. I'll do my duty to my family, and I'll protect them from any threat. I have a purpose, and it gives me renewed strength—passion, like Nash said all those weeks ago and tonight.

Once I'm dressed, I walk into the living area of the home where the captain is waiting. He stands, a grin stealing over his handsome face. "Let's leave as quickly as we can. My ship is waiting. It will be a four-day ride to Heviin."

"Before we do. I have a Battle of Justice to win and Deysik to save from themselves."

Nash's smile falls flat, "No."

"I'm doing it."

"There's no need to go back. Your indenture is obsolete due to a clause in the contract."

"Of course. You purposely placed it there, along with the Black Fox as witness."

Nash blinks those dark eyes of his.

I raise a brow. "I'm not an idiot, Nash. Tell me why you did it? Why would you put that stipulation in there?"

"Because he paid one hundred thousand gold marks and wouldn't stop staring at you. When they want you for your body, they try to pay as little as possible. When it's for love, price is inconsequential... " He taps his nose, "It was only a matter of time before your soft heart would have revealed your true nature. The Prince may have forgiven you for being a Deysik with time but not his father."

It's my turn to blink at Nash's observation of Calix and even the Emperor. Nash moves to a tray and begins making himself a cup of *chaze* tea. "When I brought the Warlord to the townhouse, we waited a long while for Svetlana to show up."

He knew it was her the whole time. He stirs cream into his tea, before taking it with him to sit on a leather couch. "Once she arrived, we began going over the contract, but he was so distracted by what was taking you so long to come down, he wasn't paying attention. You should've seen how fast he flew up those stairs when we heard a body-sized thump above us. Thirty seconds later he barreled down the stairs with you, signed the contract without reading it completely, and off he went."

Puzzle pieces click into place in my mind, and I sink into the chair across from him. "That's why Philpot didn't come up and care for my wound. Did you give the men poison to lace their weapons?"

His dark eyes glitter with indignation. "Of course not... but it's common knowledge the fighter's practice such underhanded tactics. When you've been around as long as I have, you know how to orchestrate outcomes the way you desire, yes?"

"It's why Canary suggested I bleed a little."

Nash crosses his legs and extends a long arm across the back of the couch, a smile slowly gracing his sharp handsome face. "Still think the Traitor is worth fighting for?"

"I do."

Nash bobbles his head and finishes his tea. "My Ruby, you have a gift for seeing things in others, but are blind to yourself, no?"

I roll my eyes. Always in riddles with this one. "Do you think you'll ever tell me exactly what you think I should do? Or maybe tell me what you are? You did promise you'd answer if I saw you again."

"Never." He drums his fingers against the back of the couch and says, "Once we're out on the water, I'll *show* you what I am."

I don't miss Philpott's raised eyebrow from where he stands, awaiting his Master's commands.

"So I won't be able to run away."

Nash's eyes flash with a hint of lime green. "What do you think?"

I think he's baiting me. I would normally smile, enjoying the exchange, but I feel nothing but yawning emptiness. We stare at each other, both of us weighing our decisions. Finally Nash sighs. "Tell me what you need to save him."

I smile. "Just my braids."

Chapter 33

Nash murmurs something to the guards for a moment, who eventually shrug and allow Nash to escort me through the pits to the cell where Canary is waiting, sharpening a sword with quick sure movements, his lips firm together.

"Hello you, old bird," Nash calls. Canary pauses, looking at the returned captain and then to me, his face giving nothing away. The guard opens the doors from the hall, and I slip inside the narrow cell. The large, open door on the far wall reveals a sunny, green pitch beyond iron bars. Canary stands, eyes-wide, as he realizes what I'm doing before flashing furiously as the door locks behind me.

"You need to leave now, Alana. Once this door opens there's no escape," Canary hisses.

Nash glances at the guard's retreating form. "I realize you enjoy doing things the hard way, old friend, but you knew this would happen as soon as you smiled at our Ruby after she beat you for the first time.

I glare at the captain who crosses his arms smugly. "See. I can always peg them, no?" Nash says, laughing as he strolls away. "Make sure my investment pays off, Ruby, yes?"

The guards call out a five-minute warning.

I turn to Canary, feeling the need to hurry. By his frown, he's wondering why I'm here. My heart's pounding. "I need you to follow every *single* instruction I give you, understand?"

He nods, focusing on me as I go over how to survive the Battle of Justice. I remove the hidden pins, shoving them in my pocket, while Canary listens intently and doesn't ask questions.

A one-minute warning is called.

"I know myself enough to know I won't be able to do it Alana. I'm not practiced enough in maintaining complete control of my emotions when Deysik are present."

I think rapidly. "Can you come out on the pitch at any time during the fight?"

He frowns, nodding. "Alright then. I'll clear the field and relinquish my place at the end. You and Diedra will be together, Canary. I promise."

I close my eyes and take deep, slow breaths, channeling all the buried energy inside of me to slowly release it into my body so I'm not bottling it up. Canary leans his sword against the wall, staring at it for a moment as if questioning my instruction.

He straightens and nods, and relief sidles through me at his trust.

The doors open, and I reach out, squeezing his arm. "We will survive this."

I walk into the sunlight and onto the cushiony grass. All of the poles, rings, and flags have been removed from the arena, making it appear bigger than it is from the imperial veranda's vantage point.

It takes everything in me not to look up at Calix and his family, but I can *feel* him zeroing in on me. Pain tries to resurface, but I clear it from my mind. There is no place for any emotion on this pitch.

The crowd murmurs over my lack of weapons, but I don't pay them any attention, keeping my focus ahead of me.

Besides me, six Deysik enter the field in their human form. Most are malnourished, bruised, and angry. They're the ones who come ready to fight. The crowd boos and hurls insults as I take them in.

Only one isn't beaten down.

One isn't malnourished.

One isn't gazing at the rest of the competitors, but rather flicks his amethyst-eyes over me in a searing blaze.

He knows who I am. Or rather the title I briefly held. *Moskazi*. I inhale a deep breath in and exhale, steadying my focus on how I'm to survive for Canary to win.

The bell rings, and the Deysiks shift into their animal form. Two large wolves, one hyena, one bear, two lions, and the largest one, a tiger. The five smaller Deysik immediately take off like a shot for each other, testing each other's limits, but no one's really going for blood.

The tiger, however, zeros in on me, launching into a full lope and then sprint. I slowly lower myself to the grass, crossing my legs and close my eyes.

The vibrations from the pounding of his large paws, tearing into the earth, coming towards me, rattle up my spine. I breathe in and out in a slow rhythm. *Tap, tap, tap, tap.*

The cluster of thumps grow into a stronger vibration. He's close. A deep, male voice rings out in a guttural cry before a commotion echoes in the suites above.

Tap, tap, tap, tap, tap. I calm my heartbeat.

The tiger isn't going to stop. I knew he wouldn't. He plows over me, knocking my body back into the grass, and I hear him coming back around, snorting and huffing. He moves over me, his hot breath against my leg, hip, stomach, up to my shoulders, pausing at the scar on my collarbone. He takes in small sniffs, and I know he's taking in the history behind it.

The age I was when it was given.

He moves to my face, pausing at those scars. This is my truest test.

Will my enemy accept my intentions when I killed them? Will he know my intent was self-defense and to save the lives of those I served.

He puffs a breath, before he pulls away and chuffs. I crack open my eyes and find he's right above me, glowing eyes burning like purple flame. His orange, black, and white coat is no longer bloody but beautiful, shiny, and glossy, with muscles defined under his fur. He opens his wide jaw, revealing fangs longer than my finger, and his hot breath lowers over my exposed neck.

Tap, tap, tap, tap.

I will my body to relax as the tiger's fangs meet my skin, and I focus on breathing to the beat of my heart. *Tap, tap, tap.* From behind the unlocked barred door, Canary can see my signal that I'm okay.

The tiger contracts his teeth a bit, making it hard for me to breathe. Although it looks terrifying, the only way to soften a violent Deysik is to acquiesce to their dominance completely. Violence begets violence.

This is a show of trust.

This is the true way of the Deysik—one that shows I'm on his side, and I'm not here to fight him.

The lions on the plains in the ambush were caught off guard by this act, but they did not understand the true nature behind it. Did not understand *why* this works.

That Ertune gifted his Generals and armies with a failsafe. A backstop so they may move past their bloodlust.

In the distance, the sounds of the other Deysik cease fighting and small vibrations trembling through the ground tell me they draw near.

The tiger squeezes a little more, and my airway is completely closed off. The crowd is quiet—stunned. I'm sure they don't know what to make of this display because it isn't the violent and horrific battle they were expecting.

The tiger releases me, and I suck in a much-needed lungful of air. I feel him shift back to his human skin, with a familiar warmth in the air. He's quickly followed by the others.

Triumph flutters in my heart, giving way to hope.

A deep voice rumbles, "What does a *Moskazi* want with us?"

I open my eyes and sit up, flicking my hand twice, giving Canary the signal to remain where he is. The five lower themselves to sit on the grass, and the human tiger squats on powerful thighs directly in front of me.

The crowd is quietly murmuring about the turn of events. The large male is imposing and curious as he observes me, taking in every line of my body and face while I do the same.

His hair is dark brown, and his strong jaw is covered with a weeks-worth of stubble. His clothes are clean compared to the others, and I wonder briefly why he's so different before I push the curious thoughts aside.

I straighten my spine and speak softly, my voice barely above a whisper in Deysik. "I'll give you a way to escape from here and passage to a place where you won't be hunted. Somewhere where your kind openly live and are taught how to become disciplined in your gifts. I only request you leave peacefully back to your cells with your free ticket out of here and promise not to hurt, maim, or kill anyone while doing it. Take a moment to think it over."

My use of our native tongue confuses him, and the others glance to each other, their bodies relaxing further. I watch keenly as the Deysik soldier breathes in my scent. My honesty.

He rolls his shoulders back and an arrogant tilt of his head contours his face. He moves away. "I could just kill you—"

"I've never known a stupid Deysik, and we don't have time to argue," I say slowly, with a softness that contrasts against my sharp words, reaching into my pocket. The man follows my movements with suspicion until I extend my hand as if to shake his in an agreement.

He stares, his amethyst gaze going from my hand to me as if rereading all of the signs before trusting his instincts. His warm calloused palm glides into mine and covertly maneuvers my pins into his possession.

"Pass them to the others. You have exactly two minutes to get back to your cells and make your escape while the focus is on me."

The large male looks from me to Canary by his cell entrance, his jaw clenching. "Where do I meet you?"

"At the port city of Heviin in four days," I say, giving him the name of the ship Nash gave me. He nods, stands, and signals to the five Deysik to leave. Without question, without thought, they roll to their feet and run at a full sprint back to their cells.

Before he leaves, the Tiger Deysik meets my gaze, and I feel his power swell around him, extending towards me the same a sniffing dog would. I cock my head to the side. "You're an Alpha?"

A blink and a nod from the male.

"So are my brothers and father."

He frowns, shaking his head as he reels his power back. "No, they're not. Your mother was."

A punch would have had less of an impact than his words. Not that women can't be Alpha's but that it was my mother he spoke of.

Stunned, I blink, but before I can ask him what he means, the squeal of multiple doors opening and metal clanging rings out. The Deysik and I turn to find the field flooded with ten Azure Warriors.

My stomach drops and searing anger slaps along my skin like a thundering stampede. The Deysik soldier pauses and looks out at them and back at me. I can see he thinks I've betrayed him and a sudden weariness falls over me.

"What's your name? I'd like to know who I'm fighting beside."

I scan the doors and find a single figure watching as his grandson walks onto the pitch.

Toriey.

It seems the Emperor doesn't want to be embarrassed by my display of peacemaking with Deysik when he wants a war between the two.

The Deysik soldier's chest is rising and falling rapidly, and I know his protective instincts have spiked. He turns to me, and I raise a brow, waiting. The question is more to focus his energy and distract him. His eyes begin to glow, and I hold up a hand and offer a suggestion. "Why don't we show them what we're made of without weapons or claws. I think it would be fun."

"But they're going to kill us."

I smile, and when the Deysik flares his nostrils, I know he's picking up my controlled rage. His broad shoulders rise and fall with his chest, and he shifts his weight. He seems to swell with his power, and I reply, "First blood. Remember? That is how we win. If you show them what animals they think you are then they will continue to treat you as such."

He pauses and scans his opponents who wait for Raine in full battle armor to approach. The gold and silver shining in the sunlight like a fallen star meant to destroy any and all darkness from its path.

"My name is Zenok."

"Your rank in your country... is it important?"

He nods. I walk around to stand directly in front of him, intrigued with his size and intelligence compared to the others I've met in this country. Facing him, I speak in my native tongue, "Stand here and breathe. If they attack you, defend yourself *only*. Are you capable of controlling your Shift?"

His face twists into a snarl, and I feel the vibration of his growl pass through my body, rattling my ribcage. I smirk. "Good. Because I'm going to get us some weapons."

I turn and leave him behind, heading straight for Raine.

If Toriey wants his Champion to be my killer, then he'll be sorely disappointed. Raine trained with Canary for two weeks. He's been tutored by his grandfather—the same man who taught Calix and Vasilius all his life.

But he doesn't have my combined experience. I'm a little disappointed in the Commander.

I break into a run and sprint towards Raine. While I have the focus of two additional Bluey's, seven make for Zenok.

There goes our plan. I also can't help but feel insulted. After I showed off on the training pitch, he gave me three opponents? Child's play.

Speed and lack of armor are on my side, but I must maintain that advantage, or I'll really be in trouble.

Raine pulls his sword, and like any other wise warrior, he charges and swings in a downward diagonal arc. I twist and avoid the swipe, grabbing the inside of his elbow using his momentum to flip over his body, kicking an approaching Bluey in the chest, knocking him to the ground. My body weight yanks Raine off balance, and I jerk his sword free from his loosened grip, bringing the heavy weapon up to meet the incoming blow from the remaining Azure Warriors.

"End them quickly. Show no mercy or you will die," Drake's voice says, piercing through my focus.

I lunge sideways to move away from the fallen Bluey's to avoid any surprise attacks. I only have a moment to maneuver with the attack taught me by Canary. My arms are straining under the blows of the Bluey's blade slamming into mine as if to crush me into the field. Raine and the second Azure Warrior are rising to their feet when there's enough space between my opponent's sword and chest.

Inserting my body, I twist my back to his chest, striking my elbow into the side of his jaw, right below his ear where his mask ends, knocking him unconscious. He drops like a sack of flour while I take in a roar and the sound of battle reverberating across the pit from behind me. I don't wait to snatch my opponent's sword from his lax hand, as a sick sort of violent glee fills my chest, swelling out through my nerves, heightening my five senses.

The crowds are in a frenzy under the heat of the sun beating down on us as I draw up the scents of fresh grass, sour sweat, and coppery blood. The supine leather of the sword's grips are a balm to my tortured soul and where love once stood as a pique of bliss, violence swells in a fiery condition ready to devour all in my path.

With two swords, I roar and begin my attack. I sweep my blades in a cross arc and twist before stabbing forward, sending the Azure Warrior backwards into an unarmed Raine. With the two temporarily distracted, I turn and haul back to Zenok. The Deysik soldier has four on the ground, blood leaking from underneath their armor on their arms and legs, and I huff a snort.

The man knows his enemy and their weaknesses.

With his bloody sword, he bellows a war cry, and with the same power and speed of Calix and Vasilius he attacks the remaining three. His brute strength is unmatched.

He's a flash of black shadow amongst the brightness of the Bluey's, dancing in and out, cutting and gouging through the armor. Injuring and wounding but not slaughtering. His prowess tangles with the sweltering rage pouring through me. By the time I join the fray, they are all down on the ground, moaning in agony.

Glowing purple eyes meet mine, and the thrill of combat edges my senses. Only years of learned control allow me to risk assessing the downed men and their ability to move. It's quickly apparent that they're permanently maimed. I don't take time to wonder if their healing ability will be a detriment or asset in this instance.

The black, dark abyss that's a part of me wants them to be crippled.

I look up to Zenok finding his entire focus behind me.

Mother's braids. Raine. Toriey's grandson.

Zenok pushes past me before taking off at a sprint, and I curse, running after him, snarling in Deysik, "Don't touch him; he's mine."

The only way to get through to a Deysik is to lay territorial claim. A guttural growl fills the air, snapping towards me, and I realize, too late, that it won't work on an Alpha.

Mother, take me.

The crowd surges with renewed cries of excitement as I vaguely notice from behind, men entering the field to carry off the wounded. Just ahead, the two standing Champions attack Zenok, and the Deysik slams into them with such force it knocks them backward.

The three battle for all their worth; Zenok in cold fury, Raine in frustrated strikes, using his armor to his advantage, and the single Azure Warrior Champion with skills more finely tuned to the caliber of opponents I'm used to.

The Tiger Deysik could defeat the Champion if he gave him any attention, but his sole unwavering focus is on Raine. It's a blood lust. A conquest nearly met.

It's a mark of death.

I pause out of the way from their battle and can practically detect the glimmering hatred wrap around Raine as Zenok slams his sword against his armored forearm. The metal rings so loudly the vibrations buzz along my skin. The two Azure Warriors' breaths begin to come out in heavy pants, and Zenok's growls leech into the air.

The Bluey I had knocked unconscious, rolls to his knees, and I groan. He should have stayed down. Zenok must realize his odds are about to shift and decides he's finally had enough of the games. He brutally kicks Raine backward to get him out of the way before herding the armed Champion away for one on one combat.

And then I feel it.

The ripple of power building like the static of a thunderstorm draws my attention back to where I find glowing sapphire eyes behind a golden mask searing into Zenok fighting with the Champion.

Raine stands weaponless, looking back from where his grandfather awaits to the formerly unconscious Azure Warrior who is now pushing to his feet. The recovered male stares at Zenok with a fiery lethal gaze while Raine's face twists into an expression of regrettable determination

No.

No. Not the killing blow.

The Tiger Deysik is lost to bloodlust and hate, indifferent to all else, and he has no chance to save himself.

I don't think but react on instinct, dropping one of my swords, I lift the remaining one over my head and heave it toward Raine, striking him in the shoulder joint. It throws him off enough he falls with a cry of pain as blood pours from his wounds.

Raine snarls a command in Luminum that goes unheeded as I sprint for my fellow Deysik battling with a frenzy, intending on victory.

But Zenok is so lost to his intent, he doesn't anticipate his opponent dropping his weapon, giving the Champion an opportunity to shove the Deysik backwards for a breather.

But it's all a ruse. Behind Zenok, anonymous blazing sapphire eyes are directed onto my ally.

My heart seizes in my ribcage before I lunge towards my ally in a desperate run.

No.

Sick, twisted resolve funnels down into my belly, and I hiss as the energy inside of my core surges in righteous fury, flinging through my body as I slam into Zenok's side, right as the Bluey unleashes his killing blow...

And strikes me in the chest.

Chapter 34

Clear, blue sky veiled with thick, pillowy clouds floats above me as I cough up blood gushing into my esophagus. I convulse, hacking away as my body tries to clear the debris from my lungs. Droplets of red, rain down on my face, and spill out of my mouth and onto my neck.

The grass is thick underneath me, and I move my limbs, desperate to feel something other than pain.

How could I be so stupid as to die here in Luminum's fighting pit?

I wiggle my fingers and toes, in desperate terror, hoping to find everything intact. I heave to my side and cough, as consuming pain racks my ribs while Drake's voice cuts through my stupor, *"USE YOUR HEALING GIFT!"*

I listen on instinct and training, grabbing for that inner power and pushing it out towards every line of sinew and nerve ending of my body. I shove it through the tracks of my veins and the air sacs in my lungs.

"*Moskazi*!" Raine calls, and runs towards me, kneeling down, but fear punches through me as my survival mechanisms kick in. I scramble backward, uncaring if I'm still injured or healing, but with every force of energy shoving to my body and chest, I have more mechanics than comprehensible.

I should be dead. Split apart into nothing but organs and bones.

I skitter away, looking all around for Zenok, finding him on the ground, unmoving from where I shoved him.

I look back to Raine, knowing he has the advantage and can kill me at any time. Only he stares in shock, his young, fresh face holding sweat beading along his forehead. He stands, eyes narrowed in disbelief and confusion, while his jaw falls slack. He barks two commands in Luminum to the other Champions who collect themselves before stumbling off the pitch. Raine gives me one last look before disappearing with his grandfather into Eregonus while the crowd howls in outrage.

I'm perplexed and disoriented. Why didn't he kill me? I push to my feet and blink rapidly, as all the blood rushes from my head. I wipe my face and go to check on Zenok while warning bells toll along where my spine meets my skull. I don't like that their ambush came without warning, but them leaving is of more concern.

I remember what Nash said about shoring up his bets. I need to get the Deysik out of here if he wants to escape.

I crawl on my knees and shake him, but he doesn't move. I check his pulse and find it strong and steady. Someone screams an obscenity and sound flickers in and out. I shake my head trying to clear the disruption. I press a bloodied hand through my hair, pushing back the loose strands back into my braid, trying to orient myself with the new situation.

Being the center of tens of thousands' displeasure is disorienting. A dull prickle of warning strikes the back of my neck, and I close my eyes, taking a calming and focused breath.

The sensation doesn't go away, but rather intensifies.

I need to leave.

"Zenok, you need to wake up."

Nothing. He's dead to the world. A tightness bands around my ribcage and I turn to find Canary entering the field. The temptation to gaze at the imperial box on my right hovers over me, but I tell myself it would only be to sneer and show them my disgust.

The pain in my neck increases.

"Zenok!" I hiss, smacking his cheek. Again, nothing.

My internal warning helps the rational side of my brain win out, and I move to stand and take a moment to look at the scarred face of the person who helped me perfect my fighting. I wouldn't have survived this far without it..

"Please, help me get him up," I say to Canary.

Canary remains silent, boots sinking into the grass. He holds his sword against his shoulder, head bowed, and hand rubbing his eyes. I swallow at his show of emotion and say, "You earned your freedom, Canary. Help me get him out of here and go be with Diedra."

The pain from my neck now radiates along my spine and jawline while I watch in bafflement as he shakes his head, drops his hands from his face, and levels his sword at my chest.

I find his stone gray, eyes watering and a look of agony wracking his features. My heart sinks with the realization and knowledge my body tried to warn me of this deception. The man I have come to enjoy and love like my own brother, the man I laughed with, cried with, and grieved with; the man who championed me against everyone else, has done something irrevocable.

He has betrayed me.

The voice I had worked so hard to hear and come to enjoy listening to, says, "I'll only earn her if I kill you." He gasps a breath, "I'm sorry, Alana. Forgive me."

Then he lunges forward, bringing his sword down in a great arc.

Never would I have thought that Canary would betray me this way. Never.

A lifetime of practice and indeed, muscle memory keep me from being cleaved in half by Canary's attack.

I know three things with stark clarity.

The first is, Canary will give no mercy.

The second is, if I am to survive, I will need to fight in the manner of all Rangers.

The third is, to knock him unconscious is the only option I'll choose because as horrible as his betrayal is, I can't destroy Diedra.

I move to the side and bend forward to duck the sword as it changes directions just as quickly as Canary fights.

The benefit of training and fighting with the best, not only my whole life, but for the past three months, is I've come to know their habits, their weaknesses, their strengths, and their blind-spots.

I did it with Drake, and I did it with Canary.

I roll my body away from his blade, skittering backward before he can whip the weapon back towards me. We back off enough to face one another, and I catch movement from Canary's cell, which shows Teegu smirking behind the bars in my periphery.

It seems the Emperor is determined not to let me live. Or Calix.

"You've been holding back all this time," Canary says, his voice clashing together like two rocks. "I told you I know how to read fighters, and you Ruby, have shown nothing but a shadow of your skill. Let's see if I'm bringing it to the surface for all to discover what a Ranger's truly capable of."

My heart sinks. He knows what I've been desperate to hide. For the past year, I've been learning the common style of battle, fashioned after the Azure Warriors' techniques. It was the only reason I struggled with fighting ever since I left Panthum. By law, we are not allowed to reveal our strengths in combat.

"And what do you think you found out?" I ask, attempting to put off the inevitable. I take in deep gulps of warm air, trying to pull in as much oxygen to my blood as possible to help me think more clearly.

"That you're skilled beyond comprehension. You left enough clues; Nash knew it. Even just now, you could have killed them within seconds, but you kept them alive."

I say nothing, just glare at the man who had become my best friend. Knowing the maneuvers I will be forced to disarm him, the problem won't be getting the weapon away from him but the hand-to-hand combat necessary to knock him unconscious so I can live.

My oldest brother always delighted in pushing me into the ground while barking at me to twist my body a certain way or move to get out of an impossible hold. He enjoyed giving me hours and hours and hours of training. Training I hated. The training I forced myself to practice until I moved like an eel in the water and became just as slippery.

And it will be the thing that saves my life. Connor said as much: Drake loved me, and that was why he pushed me so hard. I didn't believe him—not until today.

Canary's handsome, scarred face twists with regret, determination, and hopelessness. "I'll make it quick."

A jolt of anger and grief hit my nerves, causing my body to tense. Drake speaks to me, and I'm wrapped in a brief moment of familiarity, *"You died on the mountain in Rising Pass. You made your sacrifice. Fight for yourself now. Don't hold back!"*

Canary charges, stabbing and swinging, and I barely miss each sweep of his sword as I dance away, leading him near the door of my old cell before I get close enough to grab ahold of his wrist, pulling my body closer to his, to avoid the slice of his weapon. He throws his right fist towards my face, but I roll my grip, contorting my body to whip around the elbow of the arm holding his sword, striking his chest with my own, effectively taking some of the wind out of him.

It allows me enough time to keep his blade against my body while I grip his weapon's hilt guards with my hand. I leap up, walking my feet in kicks, striking him in the face as I pull away, using his unshakable hold on the sword as leverage.

Canary punches the inside of my knee, and we fly apart. But he must have expected it to some degree because he slices into my waist as he rolls over onto the grass. I snarl and bear down on the pain, using it to force my body to move faster.

He shoves to his feet and flicks the sword, causing drops of my blood to fling from the steel. I hone in on the pain and rage from the wound, wondering how Diedra will handle the news of what he's done.

"Don't fight this, Ruby."

"Don't call me that, you coward," I snarl. "You had a choice to say no, and you didn't take it. Do you think they won't betray you just as easily as they did me? Do you think they would ever allow a Traitor to marry the Royal Surgeon?"

His face twists into one of anger and hurt, his scars white against his face. He attacks, and I pull from the inner well of the energy ball that swirls inside of me. I shove a bundle of light into my wound, sealing it away before I smash it to my limbs, moving faster than ever.

Faster than even Canary.

I run forward, dodging his twisting blade meant to skewer me and twist his wrist to a painful angle, forcing him to drop the weapon before I kick it mid-drop, sending it spinning out of reach.

The crowd roars. I want to yell at the Royal family for their treachery, but it will do no good. I'm the villain in their story.

We strike with elbows and fists, knees and shines, blocking at each other with the fury and tenacity of enraged bulls fighting for dominance. Canary dives for my middle, and I leap backward and try to slam my elbow into his face, but he counters by knocking it away. I block his next punch, and we grapple for each other.

I need to end this now.

He attacks like a starved bear after Spring, devouring anything it first sees. He throws out a leg, tripping me, and rolls me to my back on the grass, digging me into the dirt. But this is where I practice cold logic.

Years of wrestling with the stronger Deysik partners my brother would pit me against serve me in this moment.

He shifts just enough to give me room, and I kick him in the balls and sit up, slamming my elbow into his jaw twice, sharply, discombobulating his senses. He coughs a raspy breath, snarling at me, while trying to recover, but in the next second, I grip both of his ears and slam my forehead into his, knocking him out and allowing him to fall face-first into the grass, unconscious.

I gasp for air and roll to my feet, feeling all the repressed emotions of the past few minutes shoot up inside of me, and I roar down at his prone body in rage.

Prick deserved it for betraying and trying to kill me.

His betrayal cuts deeper than Calix's.

I walk over to the arrowhead, where I had pushed it into the grass during my time out of my cell this whole week and pry it up. Walking back to Canary, with grim satisfaction, I lean down and slice his right cheek in a thick straight line where he has no scars.

He will forever remember the moment I defeated the undefeatable.

Technically, I lost, but it doesn't matter. Canary's the one unconscious, and I'm not.

Besides, I don't care what the rules are. I'm free and Nash is taking me home.

I stride to Kenzok who is stirring to life and jerk my chin, commanding him to follow me out. When I exit this pit of Champions and Traitors I make sure to exaggerate my movements, knowing I'll most likely never see him again—either of them.

The crowd has frothed into a fury, and people are screaming and arguing. From the sound, grows a smile of hurt and bitterness. I don't bother looking at the imperial box. Save Diedra and Vasilius, they don't deserve my acknowledgment.

I break into a jog to Canary's cell where I can find Nash and the High Monk waiting along with my freedom.

Chapter 35

Fifty of Svetlana's mercenaries ride with us from Goldill to Heviin. Most are indeed Slate Knights from her homeland—or so Nash says.

We leave the capital city unharmed or harassed by anyone. I was half expecting the Emperor to come after me himself. The urgency to return to Panthum beats inside of me like a war drum. I need to get home to prepare them for the irrational conflict Luminum will wage against them.

A small part of me misses having a wide chest to rest against, until I remind myself it's what led to the mess I'm steeped in. Nash's tale helps distract me from the city we approach. Heviin. Calix's stronghold.

I'm disguised under a black hooded cape that keeps me surprisingly cool from the summer sun baking the hard-packed dirt. A hot breeze brings the scent of wildflowers off the meadows below the Northern Ikpeazu Mountains.

For the first three days I'm silent as I brood and think. It's not until the fourth day, I ask Nash to tell me the story of the Slate Princess who revealed herself to keep me from death.

"How did you become friends with Svetlana... the Black Fox?"

Nash shifts the reins in his hands. "She was my younger sister's friend first. They met when Svetlana would summer with her mother's people in Nakka. The two became fast friends, nigh inseparable, and when my sister died, Svetlana wished to attend the funeral. Her brothers refused as she was contracted to be married at the time, but nothing would stop her from going. Her brothers beat her within an inch of her life."

The seajacking captain's jaw flickers before glancing to the defective Slate Knights around us. "She fled her wedding with her most trusted knights and never looked back."

The rolling hills are covered with fields of alfalfa, freshly cut, piled in neat parallel lines. I shift my weight in the saddle. "Why?"

Nash watches a flock of dark birds circle high above us, his body shifting gracefully with the movements of his horse. "She never met Vasilius. The two corresponded with each other for years and fell in love. When they were to be married against her wishes, she believed it was because Vasilius didn't care about her desires. In truth, he had no idea there was a conflict, as her brothers never relayed that particular information, thinking it was cold feet on her part. It wasn't until she became the Black Fox she understood the depth of Vasilius's devotion, even if he's been soured by the jilt."

Don't I know it.

I pull the leather-encased flask off my hip and take a swig of water before wiping sweat from my brow. Nash threatened me to fill it at every stop—mother hen disguised as a prick.

"The fortress is just up ahead, where I'll purchase supplies and smuggle the stowaways onboard," Nash explains. I nod, our horses plodding along the busy road. "We will need to plan how you will enter Faurst. Henry will not be pleased you've returned sooner than your five-year sabbatical."

He's trying to keep me talking, and we discuss options of how to get past the Mother's Monks and enter the shadow of towering walls as we near the city gates.

The Bluey guards ahead mostly wave travelers along through. They merely nod to our group as we pass, not bothering to check us. With Currell at an end, people flood back to their home territories. We enter a large, colorful market that is full of vendors and stalls, selling marinated meats, roasted vegetables, rare fabrics, trinkets, and jewels, all teaming with people still on the high of matchmaking celebrations.

I find no joy in observing the city here like I did while on my journey to Goldill.

Twenty minutes later, Nash finds rooms for us at a shabby inn. Most likely, he didn't want to spend more of his retirement on our group.

"The men will be out for the evening. You're welcome to join them if you wish, but I think you would rather hide in your room and sulk, no?" Nash smirks, handing me my room key and tossing me a small pouch of gold. Surprise cuts through the haze lurking over my thoughts, but Nash is already walking out the door, sunshine gleaming over his dark hair. "Buy something with the Bluey's gold to extract a different sort of revenge, yes?"

"Like what?" I ask, cradling the velvet pouch that causes my heart to stutter. No one has ever given me so much, not even Calix.

"Rubies." He laughs while descending the stairwell behind me.

I shove open the door and freeze, overcome with a bout of dizziness. The tiny space is too tight, reminding me of my dusty, empty cell in the pit. My chest rapidly rises, and I slam the door closed, pocketing my key, while the memory of being locked away and forgotten, stabs through my center.

My stomach turns, and I want to get as far away from this room as I can. It's only when I'm back at the stables, breathing in the calming scent of horse and leather, I decide to go for a ride. Everything here reminds me of Calix.

I crave the open air of the alfalfa fields outside the city, and this is the first time I have truly been by myself in nearly a year and four months. A boon, Nash, the mother hen, most likely knew I needed.

I saddle my horse, making sure to grab a canteen of water, avoiding the packed markets and packs of Bluey's that seem to be growing in number. Towering palm trees are planted every twenty feet, and it rankles me that this beautiful place could belong to someone who spurned me in the worst way. I studiously ignore the large white stone building to my left—the fortress and Calix's home.

I make my way to the eastern gate, passing the guards stationed there, speaking to a tall, fit gray-haired man. The Blueys here are stiffer, with their chests puffed out. I pull my hood lower over my face and tell myself to look ahead, not turn to make eye contact, even if I want to stab him in the gut. Toriey.

Fury and heartache run as rampant as a disease, and I tell myself not to give into the stupid aching hole in my chest where my heart used to be. It can't hurt if it doesn't exist. I shove that pain into a bottomless pit where it will never see the light of day.

As the Commander turns, my bay horse trots past. The sun is on a lazy descent, six hours from sunset, the hottest part of the day. I remember

Calix saying something about a hidden grotto in a wooded area near the mountains, too dangerous for anyone to venture because of the proximity to the Ikpeazu Mountains.

It sounds like the perfect place to be alone.

I ride that direction for nearly an hour, through grassy plains and over a few hills before I spy an area where I suspect it would be.

I cross a long stretch of open field and up a gentle sloping hill before I reach the tree line where I can hear the sound of crashing water. The woods spread wide with large trunks and thick reaching limbs, heavy with leaves, creating the perfect canopy of shade and with enough room to allow for a breeze to relieve the heat of day. The leaves underfoot crackle as I ride into the cool dark, following the roar of water.

Then I hear a cry that sours my gut. It's the laughter of delight originating from children.

Children should not be here.

My skin pulls tight as I climb down from my horse, throwing a single rein over a low tree branch, and walk, my canteen swaying from its strap with my steps until I find a large high cavern with pockets of light streaming through the different holes in it's roof with moss and foliage dangling down. The cascading waterfall inside, pours into the bowl of a deep-glacier blue pond.

Three girls shriek and jump into the water from different levels of overhang, splashing each other, their laughter echoing from the grotto walls arching above.

All the blood drains from my face as Vivian turns from where she swims in a simple shift and finds me staring.

"Alana? What are you doing here?" she calls uneasily, more to signal to her sisters who whip from where they are on the banks of grass and ferns. I find the light pink scab on Pippa's cheek and hairline where she cut herself and accused me of inflicting it. I see the terror on their young faces.

Fear from retaliation. They truly think I am a monster—a murderous, violent Deysik.

My gut knots painfully. I don't find Calix anywhere protecting his precious nieces. I don't see any sign of adults, tutors, servants, or Azure Warriors.

It seems Pippa chose to keep her promise of running away from her new guards because I don't see a single Bluey anywhere. I take a deep breath, and turn to leave when a sharp, stabbing sensation grips at my neck. I suck in a breath.

I grab the dagger from my waist as my skin burns and my vision sharpens. "Well, look who it is," a deep voice calls out.

I turn into a blast of wind as the Ariportia from outside the Red City lands in front of me, tossing a hungry look to the water-logged Princesses. His hand moves to his belt in a relaxed gesture, sticking a thumb in it. Four more Ariportia land all around the grotto's entrance.

"The girl with the Blueys." He turns his head, exaggeratedly searching around. "Only I don't see any." He grins, sending a skimming chill down my spine. "How fortuitous."

The girls swim to the raised bank of the pond near the waterfall.

"So, did you decide if you're going to join us? I've been looking for a new slag since the last one gave out on me. Humans just can't keep up."

The girls look at me, despair and silent tears soaking into their already wet cheeks. Vivian whimpers, and Olga whispers for her younger sister to shush. These cowering girls only now realize the consequences of their actions. Stupid, stupid girls.

I was left to squander in a dry cell for a week because of two of them.

I stare at a pale, shaking Pippa, who moves in front of her sisters as if to shield them from me and answer with all my impotent rage, rising to the surface. My skin tingles and my vision sharpens upon the three trembling girls as deadly as a scalpel. I draw up energy from within to destroy. It's filled with rage and vengeance.

"I did."

Pippa's face breaks. The Ariportia leader turns with a vicious grin to stare at Pippa, and I move. Releasing all my vicious anger and turmoil, I throw my dagger at the next closest male, striking him in the heart, killing him instantly before swinging my metal canteen with all of my explosive rage. I hit the leader in the temple, knocking him to the ground like the sack of bovine manure he is.

The other three Ariportia launch themselves at me as they begin to draw their swords. I leap at the one closest to the girls, the dry dirt and leaves crumbling under my boots. His sword isn't out of his scabbard yet when the force of my body brings us splashing down into the cold pond.

Water swallows us, pushing down my nose as I can feel his blade slice across my stomach in a searing line. I rip his dagger from his belt and slit his throat as quickly as possible before he can stab me. I pry the sword from his hand and swim for the girls, my stomach burning. Under the thick, blue water, I hear their shrieks and screams as they move to hide under the roaring waterfall. My lungs sting when I pop my head out of the water, sucking in a much-needed breath of air only to be slammed back into the depths.

I twist and roll, cutting at anything that grabs me, but the Ariportia is doing the same. He slashes my arm and cheek. The sharp pain causes the inner beast inside me to roar. I jerk back, blocking his next attack, and stab him in the eye, twisting the dagger. My grip on the sword slackens while I push away from the wings and feathers in my face. Red smears across the water as I swim for the surface.

The muddy soil smushes between my fingers, jeopardizing the hold I have on my weapon, and I haul myself out of the water, searching for the last Ariportia.

My neck prickles sharply once more, and I roll as a sword comes down where my head once was. I growl, dropping my dagger, and the Ariportia pulls back to stab me in the center of my chest. I knock it aside before it grazes my skin, and kick the Ariportia's elbow, hearing a satisfying crack and his roar of pain. I sneer at the grimace on his face as he curls his body over his broken arm.

"Run to my horse!" I yell to the girls who are still huddling behind the falls. I roll to my feet, snatch up my dagger, and throw it before he can reel back. It lands perfectly, hitting him in the neck. He stands, eyes wide with surprise, and I yank the sword from his hand as he falls back into the pool where the other two-winged bodies float.

Where is the last one? The Leader?

I clamber up the banks, searching the woods and canopy above, but I can't find him.

The girls scramble up the bank, crying hysterically.

"Cry later. Breathe and think," I demand sharply as I tuck the sword through my belt, and run, picking up Vivian. Her little arms wrap around my neck so tightly I can't breathe. I ignore the blood I'm covering her with as I rush to my horse, who still stands at the tree.

"I thought you were going to murder us," Olga says through sobs, grabbing Pippa's arm and helping her over the bank. Vivian's little body trembles against mine while I frantically glance around, looking for the wounded Ariportia. I pry Vivian's hands loose and set her just behind the pommel of the saddle.

"What did I tell you about Rangers and honor? We do our duty no matter what, and I don't remember a single person relinquishing my duty to protect you three," I say roughly, taking a knee so Olga can climb into the saddle. My arm burns, and I don't trust being able to help her up. I touch Vivian's dangling leg, speaking softly to the girl. "Wrap your arms around Olga's as she holds the saddle horn, understand? Squeeze with your thighs as hard as you can and hold onto Cloud. Don't let go for anything. Even if you're in pain. Don't. Let. Go."

My breaths are ragged coming out of me, and I ignore the pain in my middle as Olga uses my knee to reach the stirrup and settles herself in the seat of the saddle, Vivian in her lap, arms wrapped around each other, together holding on to the saddle horn as I've instructed.

"His name is Cloud?" Vivian asks, and I know it's to keep her mind from what she just witnessed. "Yes. He's as swift as a summer storm and will carry you to safety."

I gesture for Pippa. Her face is pale, lips bloodless, and she shakes her head, taking a terrified step back. I rise, grab her arm and haul her forward, but she begins hyperventilating. "I can't do it. I'll fall. I can't do it. I can't."

I grab her by the face, squeezing her cheeks painfully, forcing her to look at me and snarl, "Pippa, do you want your sisters to *die*?"

She shakes her head, and her whole body starts to tremble. "You love your family more than anything. I know you do because you wouldn't have gone to the lengths you did to get rid of me, unless you believed you were protecting them. *Right*?"

She pauses, looking at me with guilt and shame in her azure eyes and nods, tears falling to meet my hand on her face. My heart breaks for her with what she's going through. What I would've become if my father hadn't sent me away. What I still am. "Then get on the hor— Cloud and get them to safety," I say softly but with a firm bite, releasing her cheeks.

"You need to come with us," she cries, grabbing my shoulders.

I shake my head and pull my bloody hand away from my stomach. "You won't make it with me. I'm too heavy."

A growing urgency prickles on my neck. I grab her waist and with strength I didn't know I had, I throw her behind Olga, my arm and stomach sizzling with fire from my wounds. I slap the horse's rump, running next to it while drawing my sword, scraping up the last of the energy in my reserve inside of me. There's not enough to heal me and keep going.

I've made my choice.

The Ariportia leader drops from the trees, attempting to halt the horse. I advance and push the horse's head away, roar and swing, causing him to leap back, his wings kicking up leaves and hot air. The horse and girls skitter sideways.

"Go! Kick his ribs, Pippa. *Kick*!" I bellow, hoping the volume would help scare the horse.

The horse steadies his feet before breaking into a trot.

Not fast enough.

"KICK!" I bellow. Pippa's heels connect hard, and the horse canters. I shove all the energy into my legs, and I fly through the trees next to them. They're almost there. Almost to the valley.

My gut tells me the Ariportia is too much of a coward to risk being out in the open. Sunlight warms my skin as we reach the edge of the trees. The male's snarls advance from behind. He's too fast.

I slap the horse's rump with the blade as needles stab the back of the right side of my neck in dire warning.

I pivot on my left foot, kicking out with my right. My foot connects with his abdomen, pushing him back as our blades sweep forward, flashing in lethal silver.

My reach is too short.

His isn't.

I jerk back my leg too late. His blade slices deeply across my inner thigh, and I scream. The blow spins me to my knees, and I catch myself on the golden green grass as blood pumps freely from my mortal wound. I sob, agony ripping through my thigh with the realization, I'm going to die.

My sword is on the grass next to me, just out of reach. My chest heaves and my arms burn from their wounds. I have less than a minute. The Ariportia curses somewhere behind me, but he must know he's won against me, and I'm no longer a threat. I'm spent.

I sag, breathing heavily, feeling my life drain away. There is nothing left in me to fight. No more energy, no more glittering light.

I'm going to die. I've already suffered enough. I should just let go and give in.

I lift my head and swallow a sob, watching the girls as they ride out into the sun and the open valley beyond where I see in the distance, what earned the Ariportia's ire.

Two groups of riders approach in a thundering gallop. One blue and the other black. Toriey and Nash.

"In your final moments, you're going to watch as I pick those Princesses off one by one," The Ariportia says with a twisted smile, walking over to a bow and quiver of arrows lying on the ground in a heap as if tossed there, before he comes to stand feet from me.

Horror and burning heat scorch my body like a wildfire in a dry field. My wounds pause from aching as fury fills me, and my skin flashes hotter.

I scream in utter rage against my potential failure. I've never failed at a task or duty. Not one.

He will *not* kill those girls—*my girls*. He will not!

With trembling hands, I untie a sash from my tunic wrap and maneuver it around my wound, twisting it tightly, slowing the gush before tying it with a vicious yank, my movements clumsy.

He pulls back an arrow and releases it into the sky.

"NO!" I cry out and gasp as Olga bends sideways in the saddle before Pippa yanks her back in place, a shaft striking the ground where they were moments before. *Good girl.*

Tears stream down my face. The Ariportia snorts over his miss.

As he bends to pick another arrow, a section of Azure Warriors breaks off, heading for the girls, but the rest do not stop. Two black mercenaries charge ahead of the pack, reminding me of how two approached me after the Ariportia battle. I beg the Mother to stop their deaths.

I've done everything I can to save them. They can't die now. No!

My entire body burns with impotent rage, and I attempt to extract from my well of energy, clawing at its base, searching desperately in every corner for something, only to find it empty. He notches the arrow and aims it high, pulling back. *No.*

I'm a Ranger. Beast of the Riband. I am my father's daughter. I am my mother's daughter. I have their strength running through my veins.

I'll not fail my girls.

The girls I read to, told stories to, taught how to defend themselves. Girls who hurt, like I did. Girls who lash out, like I did.

Girls I'll not fail.

Mother help me, please. One last time.

I lunge for the sword's pommel and shove upward with all of my might, snarling out a battle cry, swinging my weapon with everything I have.

He releases his arrow with a *thwang* before my sword meets his bow.

Chapter 36

The sword cuts through the weapon, rendering the Princesses safe as resolve so hot and frantic steals through me like lightning, holding me steady on my wasted thigh, but I do not feel it now, as I stand against the Ariportia, my sword in front of me gleaming, ready for combat.

The Mother would not keep me alive to fail.

In the distance, a snapping of broken arrows and a startled cry echo in the tree rimmed valley, but the consistent horse's hoof beats continue undisturbed. They made it.

"You, filthy slag!" The Ariportia bellows, enraged.

A tear slips out as I inhale a joyful breath.

And then I hear it. My name carrying over the ripples of heat and shadows across the plain.

"ALANA!"

It's a call I'm intimately familiar with. One that sets my heart racing with disbelief. He can't be here. He hates me.

"ALANA." The cry echoes deep into my soul, and a tear falls as I hear it again, closer this time. How is he here? How is he here!

A gust of wind sweeps from the plain, cooling my sweat-soaked skin, leaving me strangely frozen. The Ariportia turns to face the approaching warriors, his face falling slack in disbelief.

"It can't be—"

An arrow slices through his chest, leaving him stunned for a moment before he opens his mouth in a silent cry and falls backwards, dead.

I drop my sword and with only a whisper of hope do I turn to find two of the Black Fox's mercenaries less than a hundred yards away, their black garb flying in the wind behind them, black masks nowhere to be seen.

They came for me.

Master Baylor.

And Drake.

Love so great and desperate slams into me, and I smile with blinding joy.

I know they won't make it before I bleed out. My body begins to tremble, and cold sweeps over me making it difficult to speak in my native tongue, the language my dead mother taught us, and the language all Rangers speak.

"You came for me."

Drake's face breaks, and I know he understands.

"I love you, Drake. I've never stopped. You carried me through life. Bury me anywhere but here. I love you."

Black sweeps in, and all I hear is his roar filled with animalistic agony.

PART III

THE FURY

Chapter 37

DRAKE

I am about to witness my sister's death, and all I can think about are the last words she ever said to me.

When I leave here, I never hope to see you again for as long as I live.

I wounded her, over and over and over and yet she never backed down, not until the day I used her aspiration against her and to my everlasting shame, broke my little sister's heart.

My own seizes in my chest, gaze narrowing on her bandaged thigh, smelling the blood from here. I saw, heard, and felt her pain when the blade cut through her. And now she stands against her enemy in a perfect defensive stance. *Just like Connor taught her.*

Shame rips into me for not being the one to perfect her techniques.

"You, filthy slag!" I hear the Ariportia snarl across the infuriating expanse. I'll relish tearing him apart. The curling beast inside of me aches to be released, pushing against my skin.

Do not Shift, a soft feminine voice whispers in my head.

The wind changes direction blowing our scent towards her, but she can't smell us, because she is not a Deysik. She can't know the last person she expected is coming to rescue her, and the thought nearly breaks me. She should have always known I'd come for her.

"ALANA!" I bellow, desperate for her to hold on. Desperate to distract her opponent. Silently begging for her not to engage before we get there. Rage sears underneath my flesh.

With my Deysik ears I hear Master Baylor exhale as he shoots his arrow, hoping to buy her time, but we both know we will arrive too late; her artery has been cut.

"ALANA!" I roar, fear like I've never known stabbing my belly.

Because what Alana cannot see from her vantage is a cluster of Ariportia are nearly upon her, flying low over the canopy of trees. Her opponent whips his head towards us, catching our scent. "It can't be—"

Master Baylor's arrow pierces him through the heart, and he falls, and I'm filled with lethal satisfaction. The Shift burns under my skin, and I bear down on control of my second skin. The beast snarls against my restraint, clawing desperately to save Alana.

My sister turns her head, and I witness the realization cross her beautifully scarred features when she finds us. Her big, wide smile that I hated for so long breaks across her face, not a hint of anger or malice in it but instead one of pure joy and love.

She drops her sword; tears streaming down her face and extends her arms out in a desperate reach for safety. I can smell the blood leaching from her body and her coloring with it, leaving her tan skin pale. *No. No. No. No.*

Through my heavy panicked breaths, thundering hooves of horses, the crying of Princesses as Azure Warriors surround them, and the beating wings of the approaching Ariportia, I hear her speak four words in Deysik. Ones that crush my heart.

"You came for me."

My face crumples, and tears are wind-ripped from my eyes.

"I love you, Drake. I've never stopped. You carried me through life. Bury me anywhere but here. I love you."

I can hear her heartbeat weaken. Her damn heart that's too big for her body. The heart that loved and protected and comforted anyone near her. The same heart that loved her bastard brother against all his abuse.

My inner beast battles against me in a frenzy begging to Shift.

She's so focused on me, she doesn't see the Ariportia descend before black wings swallow her whole, and I bellow in rage, shame, hopelessness, and grief.

I nearly Shift, but Baylor snarls a warning, keeping me in check.

A woman drops to kneel next to Alana, her hand slamming against her arterial wound. In a second, her features are seared into my brain. She's stark and beautiful with cruel eyes as dark as her braided hair and the feathered wings rising from her back. Pale pink lips against olive skin, whisper, "It seems the Dread dynasty will live another day thanks to you." Alana screams, and my beast rises to the surface in a killing rage.

Do not shift, son, my mother's voice warns in my head.

I kick my horse harder, willing him faster as more Ariportia land further back in the forest, and I hear them gathering their fallen soldiers and weapons. She rises, gesturing for her men to leave. "Your mother was a fool to run from her fate," she says tsking. "It seems you'll have to do."

We are almost there. Hold on Alana. But it's a lie I tell myself.

The woman stands and gestures for her men to take Alana's unconscious form, turning to me with a vicious smile, and with a great beat of wings they shoot into the sky, just before we arrive with the Azure Warriors and Nash moments behind us.

I failed her.

Burning hatred for the Prince of Luminum consumes me.

"We'll get her back," Master Baylor promises, and it's the only thing I can cling to as I turn to Nash and snarl one word.

"*Rost!*"

EPILOGUE

FIDIR

Epilogue

The sound of machines, whirling and humming, fills the electric air as I stride along the factory lines with a single person.

"What is your production quota," I ask the tall, broad-shouldered man beside me.

His voice is deep and calm when he replies, "We'll have ten thousand hotswords ready in a month."

"Why is it so slow? Do I need to motivate your people with threats?" I ask, gaining pleasure in the pause Alana's father allows to show his displeasure. The man looks just like her two brothers, tall, black hair, eyes of cobalt blue, and powerfully built.

"No, my Prince. We are merely waiting for more materials from the mines to be manufactured and shipped here. We will meet any quota you demand."

I like this, Jaferov. I can respect a man who puts his people ahead of himself. My own parents are selfish creatures, holding to long traditions and never questioning the way things are done. We use our technology, our advancements, for our own gain and are leagues ahead of everyone else on this continent, but are we allowed to show it? No.

All because of a text from the Old Gods, warning Panthum's mortal royals that disrupting the magic here would set off a chain reaction that would unleash an army of Beasts that would rival the Deysik in difficulty to kill and burn the country to ash before it falls on the rest of the world.

The Old Gods, who created the Mother and Ertune, saw what mischief their children caused. They fought and killed one another until only two were left. With the Mother's help, they created their own beast warriors before she left their home to make her final stand against Ertune.

If she failed—which she did—Panthum would hold their ground, but the magic here is tenuous. The monsters here are somehow fed from its power, and my people have been finding ways to harness their skins for mortal use.

The Deysik, fleeing their war-torn country four hundred years ago, were key in controlling the monster population that was at that time outnumbering our people. The Queen back then, decided to use them as a solution with the agreement: Keep the monsters at bay and we will give you refuge.

The problem was, Deysik were just as monstrous as the ones that roam our borders. Their strength and ability to shapeshift is a power that I don't like. Somehow my beautiful Alana was spared from the blight.

Without her, I wouldn't be where I am today. She was instrumental in figuring out that the Deysik language was the key to translating their scribblings before they abandoned the mortals here.

Ertune didn't create the Deysik, like Panthum's old Gods didn't create the Monsters here. These creatures are gatekeepers or conduits for the magic in the earth. The shifting of powers, stirred by Ertune and the Mother's war, created a spike in another part of the world, awakening someone or something in a place unknown.

A thousand years is a long time to gestate.

All powers come in three.

The three God Galaxies mirror that power on this world, and the stars never lie.

War is coming, and it is time for my parents to take their responsibilities seriously and protect their people. I thought I was the Mother's Heir and with my foolish arrogance and lust for discovery, I sacrificed my greatest asset and best friend.

I will do everything in my power to return her back home by my side where she belongs. She has always understood my thirst for knowledge and progress for Panthum. She is the only one that truly understands.

I grit my teeth, annoyed with myself. I turn to her father.

"Send out your Rangers to search for more sheds, we need as many as we can find."

The older Jaferov, bows his head respectfully, his face clear of all expression. I'm impressed with that skill most of all.

"May I ask why the hurry to stock up on these supplies?" he asks in a low subservient tone of voice. I smirk.

"Panthum is ripe for its debut, and I plan to hold all the power. I just need my Mother's Heir to return home."

The man's sapphire gaze shoots to mine, flaring wide, and I grin.

As Alana would say, *Mother's Braids*, I hit the target.

I can see why she gets a rush out of outsmarting her opponents.

We make a perfect match.

Acknowledgements

To say this writing journey has been bumpy is an understatement, and I could not have succeeded were it not for my husband. His words of encouragement, his proofreading, and his ability to make me laugh like no one else have been the boon I needed to survive. I love him with all my heart, and I'm glad we're choosing to always work on ourselves for each other.

My children, you have been my biggest cheerleaders, always curious about my writing and proudly sharing with everyone that their mom is a published author. I adore you all. You bring immense joy to my life. Remember, with persistence, learning, and laughter, you can conquer anything.

I extend my heartfelt thanks to my readers, friends, and family who have purchased and read my book and taken the time to leave reviews, spread the word, and embark on this thrilling storytelling journey with me. Your patience and support mean the world to me.

To my ARC and Street Teams who have liked, shared, commented and tagged me, promoting me and my work in the Bookstagram community, I couldn't have had the reach I do without your endless support.

To my lovely, beautiful, dark, hilarious Instagram friends for being the first to support me in whatever new venture I take with this book. The support system is the sisterhood I never had. Love you until the Mother takes me.

An artist can recognize another and I'm so grateful for the infallible works of my darling Cover Artist MeLisa Stone, who has the gift to create and bring to life my vision and every time I've given her free artistic reign she blows me out of the water. I sure love you!

Lastly to my editor and champion, Lauri Schoenfeld. Thank you for all of your hard work and promotion of Veiled Voyage and Veiled War. Love you!

About the author

Photo by Raquel Acevedo

Jennifer Maughan lives in Northern Utah with her husband and three kids. When she's not writing, she's constantly envisioning more scenarios to play out in her next book. She is often found by the pool, at the gym, in the mountains, or in her cut-flower garden. Veiled War is the second novel in her Veiled Gods Series.

www.ingramcontent.com/pod-product-compliance
Lightning Source LLC
Chambersburg PA
CBHW070558300726
48975CB00006B/1633